The Bride Wore Starlight

Also by Lizbeth Selvig

Seven Brides for Seven Cowboys
The Bride Wore Red Boots
The Bride Wore Denim

Good Guys Wear Black
Beauty and the Brit
Rescued by a Stranger
The Rancher and the Rock Star

The Bride Wore Starlight

A SEVEN BRIDES FOR SEVEN COWBOYS NOVEL

LIZBETH SELVIG

AVONIMPULSE

An Imprint of HarperCollinsPublishers

Excerpt from *The Bride Wore Red Boots* copyright © 2015 by Lizbeth Selvig.
Excerpt from *Everything She Wanted* copyright © 2016 by Jennifer Ryan.
Excerpt from *When We Kiss* copyright © 2016 by Darcy Burke.

EPub Edition FEBRUARY 2016 ISBN: 9780062413963

Print Edition ISBN: 9780062413970

Avon, Avon Impulse, and the Avon Impulse logo are trademarks of HarperCollins Publishers.

AM 10 9 8 7 6 5 4 3 2 1

For my mother, Grace Feuk,
who taught me all about the stars when I was young,
and for my husband, Jan, the love of my life,
who has been watching those stars with me for forty years.

Acknowledgments

FIRST AND FOREMOST, a huge thank you goes to my dear friend and writing partner Ellen Lindseth for coming up with the inspirational and perfect title "The Bride Wore Starlight." I loved it the moment she said it.

Thank you to my family, who all had to work as hard on this book as I did since it got written in the midst of two weddings, a long vacation, and many travels. I know if they'd had to hear "I'm so stressed, I'll never get this book done," one more time, they were planning to lock me away and take away my chocolate. I really can't thank them enough or come close to telling them how much I love them all. Special thanks to my amazing sister-in-law Robin who follows me everywhere and supports me with her whole heart.

My critique partners get the biggest thank-you in all my books and deservedly so. Naomi Stone, Nancy Holland,

and Ellen Lindseth are full partners in my writing journey—I wouldn't have any books published without them (at least not good ones!).

To my beta reader extraordinaire, Jennifer Bernard: You are honest, inspiring, and amazing. Thank you for taking time out of your precious writing time to read my drafts.

Tessa Woodward, my phenomenal editor, gets the Most Epic "Talking Selvig off the Ledge" award for not firing (or even laughing at) me when she got an e-mail on the day this book was due, saying, "I am in a panic. This book isn't done and it doesn't work. Help." To which she replied, "We've got this," followed with an edit letter that began, "Wow. I know you were worried, but I beg to differ." Thank you, Tessa, from the bottom of my heart.

Elle Keck, my "second" Avon editor, is always taking care of the details and making sure I know I can do this crazy job. She kind of rocks.

Hugs to my agent, Elizabeth Winick Rubinstein, who cares for my career as if it's her own. I know we have great things coming together in the future. XO!

Thank you to the men and women who serve in our military, and who have inspired several of my characters, especially Alec in this story. I hope I paid respectful tribute to those who come back from service with wounds and sorrows that they must struggle with daily because they chose to protect what we love and cherish. For more information on helping our wounded vets, please visit The Wounded Warrior Project: www.woundedwarrior-project.org

And, really, most importantly of all, thank you to my readers. Every time I hear from you telling me how one of my books made you happy, or helped you, or touched a special nerve, it makes those nights of pushing deadlines way worth it!

Chapter One

THE MIRROR WAS her enemy. Once upon a time that hadn't been the case, but now Joely Crockett Foster turned away from her reflection wishing memories were as easy to ignore.

They weren't. After two months in the hospital and six in the assisted care apartment that was both home and rehab facility, living in the past was now her stock in trade.

"You look gorgeous!" Her favorite nurse, Mary, a pretty, rosy-skinned woman of Mexican heritage, voiced the compliment warily in her perpetually beautiful and happy accent. "I tol' you we would make your hair and makeup turn out beautiful."

"Thanks." Joely sighed, accepting the praise with effort. This special day deserved her best behavior.

"Harper and Mia will be so excited," Mary added. "They have been trying to get you fancied up for weeks."

Her two older sisters.

Mirror, Mirror on the wall, who's the fairest Crockett of all? It's you, Joely!

She could hear Mia's and Harper's voices from across the years, from back when they would brush her thick hair, put it in ringlets and bows, and dress her like a honey-haired Snow White. She could remember smiling at her five-year-old image.

Now, unless forced—like today in order to prepare for her sisters' double wedding—she no longer looked in mirrors.

A double wedding.

She was thrilled for her sisters, of course, but still, if she'd been in the mood, she would have laughed. All through their teenage years and even into adulthood, Mia and Harper had rarely gotten along. That the two of them were sharing a wedding day constituted nearly miraculous cosmic humor. To Joely, however, the humor and the miracle were overshadowed by apprehension.

Mirror, Mirror… Her sisters had honored her by begging her to be matron of honor for both of them, but the facts that she was no longer the fairest Crockett, that she hated photos more than she hated mirrors, and that she was about to be a sitting duck for every camera-wielding guest at this wedding, left her dreading the celebration.

The only consolation was that she would get two bridesmaid ordeals over with in one excruciating wheelchair roll down the aisle. She'd survive.

Just as she had survived after the accident.

The drifting back started, and she fought against all-too-familiar memories. This day was not supposed to be about her.

"Hey, you." Harper's soft, cheerful voice, brightening the small room as she entered, finished the job of shutting down Joely's dark thoughts. "Ready for my wedding day?"

"No, but she's ready for mine!"

Mia followed, the eldest Crockett sister commanding the room as she always did. But today, a warm smile and an aura of happiness that hadn't come through her cool physician's demeanor before she'd met Gabe Harrison softened the effect.

Harper all but skipped across the floor and threw her arms around Joely. Unlike Mia, Harper hadn't always exuded confidence, much less the ability to command, but nowadays she did. After running the Crockett family's huge Paradise Ranch with her fiancé, Cole Wainwright, for the past seven months, she'd gotten a fast dose of reality and life lessons that had turned her into the de facto head of one of Wyoming's most prestigious ranching families. It seemed so weird to think of her sisters as moguls.

And they were both radiant moguls, even in jeans, T-shirts, and cowboy boots—blue for Harper and bright red for Mia. A rush of gratitude and love mitigated Joely's deep sadness and unwarranted twinges of jealousy. She might have been the first to marry, but Harper and Mia would be the first to marry for rainbows, white doves, happily-ever-afters, and all the rest of true love's platitudes.

The only cliché left to Joely was the one about a husband leaving his wife for another woman. Tim Foster, by far her worse half, was still legally married to her, yet she hadn't seen his handsome, cheating face since last August—nine months ago when she'd come back to Wyoming for her father's funeral. In September, when she and her mother had nearly died in a car accident, Tim hadn't bothered to send more than an e-mail telling her he was so sorry and to let him know when she was on her feet again.

Joely had three more sisters in addition to Harper and Mia—sweet, beautiful triplets. The kind of young women who wouldn't call cow dung shit if they were paid to do it. Their collective name for Tim Foster was DoucheWipe of the Year. Joely supposed that was accurate enough in the triplets' cute way. But her husband didn't deserve anything cute, even an epithet.

"Hey, Joellen Brigitta, come back here this instant."

She focused on Harper, whose cocoa-brown eyes searched for her attention from mere inches away. Even though she wasn't the sister with the medical degree, Harper had less tolerance for hiding away in depression than Mia the doctor did. With her artist's intuition and understanding of people, Harper had an uncanny way of knowing exactly when Joely was falling into pits of memory or troughs of despair.

"Sorry, Harpo." Joely forced lightness into a quick, covering lie. "I was imagining the whole wedding. You both look so beautiful, and I didn't expect to see either of you before I got to the house. I thought you'd send Mom or the triplets."

"No," said Mia. "They're herding the men, since we aren't allowed to see them."

"Besides," added Harper. "We wanted to spend time with you. It'll be crazy later, and we wanted time to thank you for doing this. We both know it's hard for you."

"This isn't hard." She lied again as a lump formed in her throat behind the words. "I'd do anything for you."

"We know." Mia took her turn giving a hug. "But you can't fool us about it not being tough."

Being in the public eye had once been Joely's forte. Junior and senior rodeo princesses, high school rodeo queen, homecoming queen, Miss Wyoming…she'd had a lifetime of practice. But comfort in the spotlight had gone the way of mirrors and cameras. Now the thought of being in a crowd of people tied her stomach in knots strong enough to hold a bucking bronc.

"Okay, I'm out of practice," she agreed. "I'm not ready to face all the pity and sympathy."

Harper knelt in front of her wheelchair. With her forefinger, she gently touched the start of a long, crooked scar that ran from Joely's right ear to her throat, traversing her cheek and angling across her jawbone. Joely flinched, caught Harper's hand, and shook her head.

"It doesn't show the way you think it does," Harper insisted. "You're beautiful, and I don't care how much you chew me out for saying so."

"Don't lecture me on your wedding day." Joely grumbled, but her melancholy lifted slightly.

Having her big sisters to herself, feeling them rally around her even though they were now in their early thirties and she only three years from joining them, made the world seem as it once had...safe and rife with possibilities. Life seemed less discouraging. In just minutes, however, life outside the confines of her contained world would pour in, threaten to drown her, and safety would flee.

"Time to go," Harper said. "We've got your dress at the house, and by the time we get there, the men will have been relegated to the Double Diamond."

The Double Diamond had once been a neighboring ranch belonging to Harper's fiancé Cole and his family. It was now part of Paradise, and Harper, because she was a successful artist in addition to a ranch owner, had turned the former homestead into a community arts center and retreat. Today it was bachelor central. For the first time, Joely's spirits lifted toward the joy of the day.

"So I won't get to sneak a peek at your two gorgeous grooms before you do, huh?"

"Not if Mom has her way." Mia laughed. "As much tradition as she can shoehorn in—that's the theme of this wedding."

"You two are far kinder than I'd be."

"Nah," Harper said. "You'd be fine with it, too. She's finally absorbed in something fun and all-encompassing for the first time since Dad's death. We stand up to her when it's really important. Otherwise, we're just glad to see her happy."

Another small pang of jealousy, wrapped in a solid dose of homesickness, lanced through Joely's heart. Since Harper had come back to Wyoming from Chicago and

Mia had returned from New York, everyone but the triplets, who worked in Denver, had a place in the huge log ranch home their mother had named Rosecroft. The heart of Paradise Ranch. Because she'd been so long in the hospital and rehab, Joely missed the day-to-day interactions the others shared there.

Not that she could blame anyone but herself. Harper had been trying to get her to move home for months, but even once she'd grown more mobile many long weeks after the accident, Joely had opted for this assisted living apartment in the VA's long-term care facility. Because of Tim's VA benefits, she got a hefty chunk of the cost covered. The bills that weren't covered still came out of his pocket, and she didn't have a single qualm about continuing to take advantage of her absentee husband. In this place she could at least pretend she was independent, and she didn't have to face the constant barrage of sympathy she'd get at home. To keep the status quo, she could most of the time ignore her jealousy.

Mary returned with a walker. "Take this with you," she said. "You might need to go somewhere the chair won't."

Joely set her lips in aversion. She was permanently injured but not ninety.

"I'm going to Rosecroft, the church, and back. No walker."

"C'mon, this is no time for vanity," Mia chided. "Bring it. Bring your crutches, too. We want you prepared for anything."

For a moment Joely had to fight back a surge of irritation. All along she'd done everything for this double party exactly the way she'd been asked. Couldn't they let her make one decision? She let the testiness dissipate without a fight. Once again she reminded herself that the day wasn't about her wishes.

"Fine. Put the walker in the trunk, but I'm not using it," she said.

"Fair enough." Harper kissed the top of her head and pointed to the overnight bag on the bed. "Is this your stuff?"

Joely nodded. Mia pushed her chair out into the hallway. Mary locked the door behind them.

"See you in two days. Make sure you have fun." Mary kissed Joely on the cheek—more like a mother or a loving aunt than a nurse.

"I'm sure I will."

She wished she believed it. She wished even more she was coming back to her safe cocoon tonight.

Her sisters chattered with each other all the way down the hall, and their voices blurred into white noise. Joely looked at her good right leg and foot that rested easily on the chair's footrest. If only people could stand for hours on one leg like a flamingo. She rubbed the thigh of her shattered left leg, crushed when the payload chains on a flatbed had snapped and sent half a dozen eight-foot diameter logs plunging onto the highway in front of her truck and horse trailer.

After four surgeries and eight months of healing and therapy, she had mobility in her hips, could flex the left knee, careen around with crutches, and limp along slightly faster with a walker. Her left leg was an inch shorter than the right, however, and that foot turned outward about ten or fifteen degrees. Some of the nerves that controlled minor movements were crushed beyond repair. Even though there was no need to amputate the leg, she sometimes wondered if losing it wouldn't have been less traumatic.

Give it time, they all told her—the doctors, nurses, and physical therapists. In time she could retrain the muscles to work differently. And there were braces. There were sleek new wheelchairs. There was always hope.

Hope for everything but the life she'd once known or the life she'd wanted to build.

"All right, Queen Joellen, your coach awaits." Mia set a hand on her shoulder.

Joely blinked and saw the open car door. Leaving the building hadn't even registered with her.

Easily she moved her good leg from its rest and flipped up the footrest. With two hands, she helped her left leg onto the ground where Mia took over, flipping the leg rest out of the way, setting the chair's brake, and reaching for her hands.

"Up you come," she said and pulled Joely to a stand.

In a move perfected over the months of occupational therapy, Joely braced a hand on Mia's shoulder and hopped in a circle until she could back into the seat of Harper's new hybrid Highlander. Moments later she was fully in and ready to go.

She had to smile at Harper's choice of vehicle. Her second sister was determined to turn Paradise Ranch as green as she could, and she was perfectly happy to take all the jeers and teasing that came with implementing her convictions in a fairly conservative state like Wyoming.

Joely agreed whole-heartedly, and before her accident she had been primed to take over running the ranch herself. She would have run Paradise exactly the way Harper and Cole were doing. Now, however, she no longer had the fortitude to stand up to taunting from ranchers who thought windmills in Wyoming were ridiculous and ugly, or to oil company executives who badgered her to let them drill on the ranch. Then there were lesser fights, like ranch hands who thought a once-a-year, uneconomical, old-fashioned round-up using horses and cowboys instead of gas-slurping four-wheelers and helicopters was an inefficient and unnecessary way to show appreciation of their heritage.

As the third child behind two such strong and successful sisters—the artist and the surgeon—Joely had learned to use her assets to create success by following and people pleasing. She didn't make waves.

The scenery on the way to her childhood home never failed to stun with its stark beauty. Paradise Ranch's fifty-thousand acres lay forty miles south of Jackson and stretched west below the Teton mountain range. Even in her darkest moments, the land brought Joely tranquility—however fleeting. During the half-hour ride from the VA complex, neither Harper, who drove, nor Mia, who sat in the back leaning forward between the seats, seemed to notice that Joely's minimal comments were only aimed at keeping them talking so she didn't need to.

They reached the quarter-mile-long main driveway to Paradise, which wound through thick grassland dotted with stands of juniper, spruce, and cottonwoods. At the end stood Rosecroft, a sprawling, two-story log home with a front porch the full length of the bottom floor that could hold a small country's population or a large wedding reception—which it would in several hours. Small gardens thick with colorful, welcoming flowers surrounded it.

Rosecroft was a slightly silly name for a main ranch house in the middle of cattle country. A croft, as Joely understood it, was a small English cottage. This, her mother's pride and joy of a house, was anything but small. And her mother's favorite flowers weren't even roses, although they were a close second as evidenced by the number of them adding liberally to the rainbow of colors in the flowers. Morning glories. Those were Bella Crockett's most beloved blossoms, and even as Harper pulled the truck up to the garage, Joely could see the mass of vines climbing delicately up the eastern side of the house with their sea of powder blue and lavender blooms open to the morning sun—the colors her sisters had chosen for their wedding.

But Joely's father, Sam, so the story went, had promised to take his bride anywhere in the world for their honeymoon, and she'd chosen Scotland. Her favorite place had been a charming bed and breakfast called Rosecroft. She'd brought the name home and, when the time came, given it to her own dream house.

"Okey doke." Harper called over her memories. "First stop."

Joely didn't have time to open the door before her mother had it open from the outside and nearly crawled into the seat to give a huge welcoming hug.

"Hello, sweet girl. Welcome home!"

Joely accepted the hug, thrilled to see her mother looking so healthy—her cheeks full of warm color, her stance strong and healed. She'd been injured badly, too, a fact that still haunted Joely with guilt. If only she hadn't—

"Come on now, let us help you out and up the steps," her mother said. "Look who's waiting. She's almost more excited than I am."

Up on the porch, her hand raised in greeting, stood their grandmother, Sadie. Slim and snowy-haired, leaning easily on a signature black cane adorned with bright red poppies, she looked like a spry eighty-year-old. But Sam Crockett's mother would be celebrating her ninety-fifth birthday in a month. Joely smiled in genuine pleasure. The woman was a force of nature. But it was getting harder for her to leave home, and Joely hadn't seen her in over a month.

In fact, Joely had been home only a few times since the accident. Whenever the family got together, they usually came to her.

"Hi, Grandma," she called when she stood on one leg beside the car.

"Hello, darling," Sadie called back.

It took a sister on each side and a few awkward moments of maneuvering to get up the four porch steps. Once she'd accomplished the task, her grandmother wrapped her in yet another embrace.

"Welcome home, beautiful child," she said, the love in the words sincere and almost tangible.

"So!" Her mother joined them. "Isn't it exciting? What a beautiful day."

It was—a gorgeous, blue-skied May 20, headed for a perfect seventy-five degrees.

"Everything looks gorgeous, Mom," Joely said. "This is a perfect place for the reception. I saw the tent canopies out back when we drove in. Even the Henhouse Hilton is decked out."

The Hilton was their father's outrageously ornate chicken coop. Today its picket fencing was adorned with denim blue and lavender bows—Harper's blue and Mia's pale purple.

"How are the guys doing?" she asked, as Mia and Harper rolled the wheelchair behind her and helped her sit.

"According to Alec, they're having a fine old time," her mother said.

"Alec?" Joely asked.

"Gabe's groomsman who couldn't be at the rehearsal yesterday."

She'd paid little attention to anything but learning her own job the night before. In all honesty, she didn't realize a groomsman had been missing.

"Alec and Gabe served in Iraq together. He's a very nice boy—handsome, polite. He's inside now, in fact, picking up some forgotten items. The guys might be having fun, but they're as scatterbrained as pregnant women today. Someone's cufflinks, someone's shoes, someone else's cummerbund." Her mother laughed.

"Did someone say Cummerbund?"

"Benedict Cummerbund?"

"He's coming to the wedding? Awesome! I wonder if he likes triplets."

With those words, the porch was invaded by three of the cutest young women on the face of the planet; they dropped the Benedict Cumberbatch jokes in favor of squeals when they surrounded Joely.

The trailer babies, the triplets, the movie stars. Joely hugged them all at once the best she could—Grace, Raquel, and Kelly.

"You three get more gorgeous every time I see you," she said. "And you never ever dress the same—what's with lookalike time?"

All three wore jeans and a solid red T-shirt. They exchanged a look of mischievous fun, more like high school sophomores than the twenty-four-year-old businesswomen they were.

"It's been such a hoot to confuse the men," said Kelly, who could charm heat from an Eskimo with her playfulness and bright personality. "They have no idea who's who."

"We haven't done this since high school," added Raquel.

"It's mean but it's also awesome fun," finished Grace, the sister Joely always thought of as the spiritual soul of them all because she never failed to live effortlessly up to her name. It was fun to see impishness in her eyes—the tiniest of imperfections in her perfect self.

The triplets had always been eerily identical. Joely knew who was who—most of the time—but the girls had done their share of purposely trying to confuse parents and siblings when they'd been small.

"But that's all beside the point. You look wonderful, Jo-Jo. You're getting better; I can see it in your eyes."

"Aw, Gracie, if you say it, it must be so. It's good to be home," Joely said truthfully.

"It is," Mia agreed. "Come on, let's go in and eat lunch—it's not a big spread, but Kelly's here, so it's delicious."

The triplets ran two successful restaurants in Denver, and Kelly was the master chef—which was clear every single time she took to the kitchen.

"I'm starving," said Harper.

"How can you eat?" Joely asked, her own stomach already a fluttering mass of nerves.

"It's going to be a long night." Harper grinned. "I'm planning to have energy to spare. After lunch we'll have plenty of time to get dressed and over to the church. We've assigned Grandma Sadie to be your personal assistant, Jo-Jo. We fought over her, and you won."

The thought of spending time alone with her grandmother eased Joely's nerves. Grandma Sadie had always been the best storyteller and imparter of wisdom in Wyoming.

"Sometimes a girl just gets lucky," she said.

They moved inside and the earthy comfort of the big house enveloped her. Their mother had exquisite taste, but she'd also been a practical rancher's wife, and the decorating was decidedly western, in maroons and reds and oranges with pools of blues and indigos to cool the space like a sunset. Rosecroft, with its sitting room to the right, then the two-story living room and the dining room with its table big enough to seat twenty people straight ahead, greeted her like another person.

She hadn't lied—for a little while, at least, it was good to be home.

"We've got a chair set up with an ottoman for your leg," Harper said. "Or would you rather just stay in the wheelchair?"

She would rather get the day over with and go back home, she thought, but she was already being annoying and ungrateful. Everyone was being so overly helpful that she couldn't bear to let them see a lack of effort on her part. "The chair," she said.

Once again they ensconced her like a queen, chattering with each other, including her as if she'd never been gone. But then, without warning, all five of her sisters, her mother, and her grandmother disappeared. One minute she was talking to Mia, the next everyone had left her and migrated to help in the kitchen.

Not that this was unusual. Or deliberate. Unless she was the center of attention—as she'd been at pageants or even this morning—she was always Child Three, the one people assumed would just be there following the crowd. Her sisters would return *en masse* from the kitchen and pick up where they'd left off—clueless that she'd been abandoned, but innocent of intentional neglect. It had never used to bother her, and she shouldn't be irritated now, but she was.

Lately she seemed to live in a state of irritation.

The dining room was cavernous with nobody in it but her. This was the space her mother had dedicated to the country that had inspired the house. It boasted a stunning photo panorama of the Scottish Highlands, a picture of Rosecroft's namesake in Scotland, and chair cushions, curtains, and a beautiful runner on the sideboard against one wall in the muted blue, green, and subtle red tartan of the clan MacKinlay whose ancestors owned the B&B where her mother had stayed and fallen in love with all things Scottish.

It was also as un-western Wyoming a room as would be found anywhere in the house. Joely had always loved the classy incongruity of their Scottish dining room, just as her mother did.

"You look lost."

She started at an unexpected, masculine voice and swung her gaze to the dining room doorway. Her mouth went dry as a summer drought, and her pulse hiccupped before it began to race. The man who stood there with a hot smile and a confident demeanor owned a pair of the sharpest hazel eyes she'd ever seen, sandy-gold hair the color of a palomino stallion, and a jaw and cheekbones strong enough to have been chiseled out of Wyoming granite. Most unsettling of all was a smile that likely could have charmed Sunday school teachers out of their knickers—in any era past or present.

After she'd stared for an impolite number of seconds, Joely lowered her eyes and cupped her chin so her thumb rode up the left side of her in order to hide the scar. She'd convinced herself it made her look thoughtful and masked the self-consciousness she'd never suffered before the accident.

"I might be lost," she said. "But I'm probably not."

"You're Joellen."

"Not unless you're angry at me."

He raised one amused brow. "I'm not."

"Then it's Joely."

"I admit it; I knew that. What I don't know is how a pretty little thing like you could possibly be sitting all alone like this in a house full of women."

She stared, not sure whether she was annoyed at the "pretty little thing" epithet or surprised at his mind-reading ability, since she'd been wondering the same thing.

"My whole family is in the kitchen through that door. I could ask you the same thing. What's a patronizing cowboy like you doing in my mother's dining room knowing my name when I don't know yours?"

The grin widened, and he strode into the room, dark denim jeans fitted nicely on his hips, a subtle plaid shirt tucked at the waist, and a casual brown sport coat giving him a touch of western class. He reached her in three strides, his cowboy boot heels beating a soft, pleasant cadence on the oak floor. "Alec Morrissey," he said, holding out his hand. "Alexander if you're mad at me."

The name left her stunned again. She knew it. Anyone who followed rodeo knew it. But he couldn't be *the* Alec Morrissey—the one who'd won three PRCA titles and then dropped out of sight half a dozen years ago…She shook her head to clear it before she could blurt a question that would sound stupid. She kept her hand over her scar by pretending to scratch her temple and took his hand to shake it. His firm, dry masculine grip sent a small warning shiver through her stomach.

"I'm not," she said.

"Not what?"

"Not mad at you."

"Ah. Even if I'm patronizing? Or if I admit I'm not a real cowboy? Which I'm not, by the way. I wear the boots because they're comfortable."

She wanted to tell him she'd only forgive him if he promised never to call her a pretty little thing again. Her father had called her that, but not in a proud papa kind of way. It had been more a "you're my delicate little flower, don't worry your pretty little head over such things" kind of way. But based on the confidence this man exuded, Joely doubted she could tell him to do or not do anything.

"Well, I can't lie. I'm disappointed about the cowboy part. But if you swear to quit being patronizing, I won't be mad."

He pulled out a chair beside her and sat backward on it, comfortable and easy, looking as if he'd lied about not being a cowboy and straddled seats and saddles every day.

"Ma'am, if calling you pretty is patronizing, I can't swear because any promise I made I would break every time I saw you."

The arrogant amber-eyed devil. She let her hand drop from her face without thinking, smiling in spite of herself. "So, really, who are you?"

"One of Gabe's groomsmen. I'm up from Texas, and I'm supposed to be staying away from the girls, but I'm the designated errand boy, so I'm here collecting forgotten items."

Alec. Of course. Her mother had far undersold the good-looking quality. But a boy? Lord, no. Whatever he was that wasn't a cowboy—or a famous rodeo star—he was a man's man, and dangerous if you were a female.

"Texas. That explains a lot."

"I said I was from Texas. I didn't say I was a Texan."

"Semantics?"

"No, the truth. I worked in Houston for the last two years. I'm a born-and-bred Minnesota boy, although I grew up in central Wisconsin."

"The land of dairy cattle."

"It is. And you grew up in the land of beef cattle. Sometime I'll tell you about all the things we have in common, pretty Joely."

"Really. Please don't bother ever to do that."

"Why?" He looked her straight in the eye. "What's wrong, Joely? Did you shut me down because you had a serious accident and now a little scar makes you too self-conscious to get close to anyone?"

Her shock was complete and paralyzing. How dare he?

"That was inappropriately rude." She managed to croak out the admonishment while her cheeks flushed with embarrassed fury. "And it's completely untrue."

That was a lie.

"I've gotten to spend some time with your mother and sisters the past few days. They told me about your injuries and your unusually long stint in rehab. But I personally know a little something about long stints. I can promise you'll come back from this. You shouldn't hide."

He leaned forward, gently placed a long forefinger beneath her chin, and tilted her head up, bringing their eyes to within mere inches apart. She hadn't thought shock could drill any deeper into her heart, but he dumbfounded her. After staring at him too long one more time, she managed to jerk her head free.

"Who do you think you are?"

To his credit, he looked momentarily contrite. "I'm sorry," he replied. "That was out of line." His confidence bounced back almost immediately after his apology, and he flashed the knicker-removing smile once more. "In truth I'm only here because you're part of my current mission." He reached into the sport coat pocket and pulled out a thick envelope. "This was hand-delivered this morning. Gabe asked me to sign for it, so I did. Now it's fallen to me to make sure you get it." He handed her the letter and stood, pushing back his chair. "I'll stop bothering you now. It was nice to meet you, Joely Crockett. I'll see you in a couple of hours at the wedding."

She didn't correct his mistake with her last name and barely noticed him start back across the room. She'd read the return address on the envelope, and none of Alec Morrissey's forwardness or his apology mattered any longer. After eight months, her husband had finally surfaced, and from the thickness of the envelope, she knew he hadn't sent her anything good.

Alec turned to glance back at her. "Everything all right?" he asked.

"None of your business," she said quietly.

"Fair enough. Hey?" His question from across the room forced her to look up even though doing so made her light-headed. "Save me a dance."

Her jaw went slack. "Is that some kind of joke?"

"Not at all. Sounds like it's time you got back out on the floor. I'd like to be one of your first partners." He turned but hesitated. "You know. If you don't want to sit here all alone—just get up and go find your family."

Tears beaded in her eyes at the thoughtless ease with which he managed to insult and humiliate her at the same time.

"You're awfully quick to judge me, Mr. Morrissey. What, you listen to a few things my mother has to say and now you think you know all about me? Don't you dare presume to tell me what I can and cannot do. Or what, in your high-and-mighty opinion, I *should* do."

"Joely. I'm sorry. I know I'm being a jerk. I'm just a guy not known for my tact, trying to toss out tough love. I shouldn't have."

"What makes you think I need tough love? That's pretty arrogant."

"You're right. Let me make it up with that dance tonight."

"I. Can't. Dance." She nearly spit the words.

He smiled and shook his head no. "Sure you can. I'll see you later and prove it. And, I am sorry I pissed you off."

He left. Finally.

She fumed at his retreat.

Pissed her off? There hadn't been a bigger understatement since "Houston, we have a problem." Of all the superior, condescending buttholes. She wouldn't dance with Alec Morrissey if she had two working legs.

She cooled her irritation with a long, slow breath and dropped her gaze to the envelope on the table. She knew she should wait until after the weddings to open it, but aggravation had her ripping open the flap, pulling out the sheaf of papers, and attempting to slog through the legalese that swam before her eyes. Moments into the task her anger turned quickly to shock, and her stomach dropped even further from where Alec the Ass had left it. Tim the DoucheWipe had just pulled the plug on her life.

She covered her face with both hands, but this time it wasn't to hide the scar.

Chapter Two

PLEASE BE INFORMED *that benefits will be terminated as of June 1—*

Five minutes after daring to read them for the second time, Joely tore her eyes from the words staring at her from the page and gave in to disbelief and anguish.

She didn't care about the divorce Tim was finally willing to discuss "amicably," according to his lawyer's typed personal note—she'd demanded a separation and then divorce before he had. It was the dictated instructions, the lack of empathy or concern of any kind, and the straits she was now in, thanks to Tim's actions, that left everything from her stomach to her heart feeling like it was curling up and dying.

She didn't doubt for half an aching heartbeat that he knew exactly what day today was and that this was where his legal edict would arrive.

She heard the laughing, excited voices from the kitchen, heralding her family's return. With the panic and swiftness of a thief about to be caught, Joely slapped the letter, divorce terms, and insurance notations into a rough pile and shoved them back in the envelope, ripping it in the process. She barely got it tucked beneath her butt before Mia, Harper, and Kelly entered.

"I'm so sorry," Harper said. "We didn't realize we'd all trooped into the kitchen at the same time."

"It happens," Joely said. "No matter. I met Alec."

Her mother entered behind the three girls and let her gaze dart around the room. "Alec? He was here?"

Joely nodded.

"Isn't he adorable?" Kelly asked. "Gabe is so happy Alec took him up on his invitation to come live here. He got a job with Breswell Trucking in Jackson, and he's doing great."

"He lives here?" Joely let her surprise show. "He said he'd come from Texas."

Her mother nodded. "He did, about two months ago. We'd only met him once before all the wedding festivities. He's such an inspiration."

"Alec Morrissey…" Joely tried out his name again, slowly.

"I know. It was like meeting a rock star at first," Kelly said. "Didn't you think?"

"So it *is* him? Alec 'Mayhem' Morrissey?"

As she recalled, he'd been the national junior champion saddle bronc rider and later PRCA champion several years in a row.

"Sure is," Kelly agreed. "Since his time overseas, he hasn't participated on any rodeo circuits. Even so, he's still the hottest cowboy I've ever seen. With the exception of my new brothers-in-law." She grinned at Mia and Harper.

"Nice save." Mia raised her brows.

And yet, Alec Morrissey had made a point of saying he wasn't a real cowboy. Why would a man whose profession was the quintessential definition of cowboy say such a thing? She'd answer that when she figured out why her husband had ignored her for the past eight months. Stupid men with their secrets and game-playing.

Alec Morrissey's nickname, Mayhem, hadn't had much to do with the rodeo itself but with the destruction of hearts and reputations he'd left in his handsome wake. Buckle Bunnies, those rodeo-crazy girls who had their cowboy hats set for the Mayhem Morrisseys of the world, might have been impressed with his prowess, his smooth tongue, and his penchant for his extreme sport—but she was finished with pretty, shallow men who thought their handsome faces and their laurels gave them license to say anything they wanted.

Or, in the case of Timothy Foster, *take* everything he wanted.

Joely inhaled again, slowly and deeply. "You do have two very sexy cowboys walking down that aisle today," she said and shifted to make sure none of her special delivery papers showed. "A washed-up rodeo rider can't hold a candle to them."

"That's my girl!" Harper set a bowl of sliced strawberries on the table and hugged Joely tightly. "Knows where her loyalties lie."

That was her—always loyal as a rescued pup. Joely set a smile on her face and started the job of faking her way through lunch. It would be good practice for the rest of the day.

Kelly spoiled them with homemade potato leek soup and loaves of crispy-crusted rosemary bread. The salad was cool and fresh, and they sprinkled strawberries on the greens like candy, groaning in happy ecstasy over having their talented chef home to feed them. Everything was light and fun and girlie.

Joely smiled and laughed along with them, and she knew they'd all tell each other later how good the outing had been for their wounded, cloistered sister. They should try to get her out like this more often. And while she didn't begrudge them their happy day or even their concern for her, Joely detested being the object of pity. Once more she wished she could go back to Mary where nobody worried and mostly left her alone.

"That was fantastic," Harper said when they'd finished the dessert of individual fruit tarts Kelly had created. "What a perfect lunch. I might even still fit into my dress."

"Me, too." Mia rubbed her stomach. "I had visions of Raquel having to put her foot in my back and tug on the laces when I heard Kel was cooking for us. You found something perfect."

Kelly beamed. "Thanks. I love tiny fussy lunches like this—and for this occasion it's even better. What do you think, Jo-Jo? You've been awfully quiet."

She smiled and waved to dismiss the accurate observation. "I'm overwhelmed by what you magically do in the kitchen," she replied. "This was so good, and it's fun to listen to all your voices and just be here with you."

And it was, really, in an emotional whiplash kind of way.

"How's the physical therapy going?" Grace asked. "I hear you've got your little apartment set up so pretty now. We all want to come and visit before we go back to Colorado next week."

Those were two completely unrelated statements, and Joely didn't know which would be the more immediately painful to address. However pretty the apartment had "gotten," it wasn't going to be hers much longer, and PT was nothing more than a necessary drudge.

"Therapy is...what it is." She shrugged. "Not much more progress to be made. It's like a maintenance session at the gym."

"Haven't they found you a good-looking therapist to spice things up yet?" Raquel asked.

Everyone asked the same question. Her sisters had been teasing her about it for six months. Wink wink, nudge nudge, everyone bet she was hiding a hunky PT somewhere—and that's why she was still at the VA apartment. In truth a hunky PT in her world was as mythological as a unicorn. She rotated between three therapists—a fifty-five-year-old father of four, a very nice woman quite overweight, and a fresh-out-of-school girl who was so gung-ho she was more depressing than helpful.

"We're still searching," she said with a practiced grin. "Send any and all applicants my way."

Her sisters were in heaven as the teasing continued, but she was just glad to be off the hook for answering any more questions about Alec Morrissey.

"I swear you girls are going to talk your way right into missing your own weddings."

Grandma Sadie made her way into the room, her steps spry, her cane more of a security measure than a complete necessity. It didn't make a sound on the oak floor, but it was still as much a part of their grandmother as her beautiful, white hair.

"We know you'd never let that happen!" Harper rose from the table and met Grandma Sadie with a kiss to her cheek. "We do tend to forget the time when we're together, don't we?"

"There were many years when you all weren't together, so I understand your excitement," Grandma said. "It's a blessing that you're together now. But come now, time to get a move on. Less than two hours until the ceremony."

"Let's clear the dishes," Mia said. "Then head up to dress."

"Melanie will get the dishes. She's here now. Time for you six to forget anything but the party."

In Joely's opinion, Melanie Thorson, the wife of the ranch's foreman, Bjorn, was Paradise's resident superwoman. She homeschooled her three kids, kept track of all the ranch hands and their families, ran her household like a master contractor, and still had time to pitch in and help with anything anytime.

"Come on, Jo-Jo, we'll get you back in your chair." Grace and Raquel moved to her side.

The envelope beneath her leg burned. She couldn't let them see it, not yet, but clearly she hadn't thought through her plan to hide it.

"It's all right," she said quickly. "Let me talk to Grandma for a minute. Didn't you say she's my personal assistant?" She smiled as sweetly as she could and waved her sisters and mother out of the room. "You all get going and we'll manage. We'll just be slow."

On any other day the sisters might have thought the request suspicious. On a double wedding day, however, they let her have her way with no questions. Only her mother hesitated.

"Is everything all right, sweetheart?"

"I'm fine, Mama, promise." She accepted a kiss. "I have some questions for Grandma that's all, and I haven't had a chance to talk to her much yet. You go ahead and help the others."

Her mother laughed. "Actually, Gracie is my minion today. You and I are in the ranks of elite for this party, I guess."

"Then we'll enjoy it while we can," Joely said. "I can't wait to see you in your dress. I remember when you brought it up to show me."

"All right. I'll go get started then. There's a lot to do when you're my age."

"Listen to that girl." Grandma Sadie spoke for the first time. "You don't know anything about age, missy."

It was true. Bella Crockett was far from an aged woman. At fifty-eight, she had lustrous chestnut hair she wore past her shoulders, flashing blue eyes, and she could still rock a pair of jeans and a T-shirt as well as her daughters. She'd worked hard on Paradise Ranch, but the life hadn't bowed her. Now that she'd recovered from her accident injuries, she seemed prettier than ever to Joely.

"Some days, Sadie, I think you feel younger than I do." Her mother smiled. "But not today. Today we bring a lot of life back to Paradise."

She kissed Joely one more time, did the same to Grandma Sadie, and left the room with a smile and an elegance Joely knew she and her sisters had never noticed when they'd been kids. She wondered if her father had ever really known what a classy woman he'd been married to for thirty-four years.

A wave of sadness washed over her. They were closing in on a year since a heart attack, which even his doctors hadn't seen coming, had taken the robust, active Sam Crockett. What would her tough, hard, focused father have thought of this day?

On the other hand, the chances they'd all be here celebrating two weddings together if he were still alive weren't high. All six of his daughters had left home once they'd hit college age. They hadn't returned to stay until his death. It was likely Harper would never have fallen in love with Cole and probably a sure thing Mia wouldn't have met Gabe. The only one whose life might possibly have been better was her own. Chances were she'd have come back as she'd been planning before his death—but the trip with her mother to California wouldn't have happened as it had. And she wouldn't have been hurrying to get back to the ranch, pulling a loaded trailer too quickly to stop when the chains on that logging truck had snapped. She wouldn't have killed—

"Joely, honey, time to tell me what's wrong." Her grandmother's voice was strong with only a hint of elderly quaver.

Joely looked up, surprised. Unconsciously, she'd buried her face in her hands and was pressing away the start of a headache behind her eyes. Grandma Sadie had taken a seat beside her and waited for a reply. Joely admired her beyond words, the serene matriarch with sadness but no regrets in her life, and she still had a little time to go before it was finished. With determination, Joely pushed the past away and shifted in her chair to pull out the envelope.

"This came. I don't want to tell the others yet. I'm always the bearer of bad news."

Grandma Sadie took the envelope with its now-unruly sheaf of papers sticking haphazardly from the opening. "Tell me about this," she said, as she pulled them out and unfolded them on the table.

"Tim is agreeing to the divorce but only to half of what I asked for. He says it's time for me to stop being unreasonable because I more than used up any share I had coming of the household income on my horse and all she cost over the years." Joely's throat closed over the words, and tears welled in her eyes. Grandma put one mottled hand over hers.

"It's all right to grieve. It was a terrible thing to lose Penny in the accident."

Bless her grandmother. She never used unhelpful platitudes.

"I'm sorry," she said. "It should be a happy day."

"It will be. I promise, honey. What else is in the letter? I can see in your eyes there's more."

"He doesn't want me submitting for benefits any longer. Once he can cut me loose, he's planning to marry his girlfriend, so he's ready to put her on his insurance. As of three weeks from today, I will no longer have coverage."

Grandma Sadie sat thoughtfully, her strong hand still covering Joely's. She patted softly with her fingers, and each tap sent a tiny dart of warmth through the skin. "Fortunately you will get new coverage," she said. "But this will affect keeping your little apartment, I suppose. Oh dear, I'm sorry. That's what's upsetting, not Timothy. You know I think you're well rid of him, even though it's not pleasant."

"You don't think I'm terrible? God isn't going to frown down on me for not trying harder with him?"

Her grandmother had the strongest belief system of anyone Joely had ever or would ever know. But for as staunch and forthright an old woman as she was, she had a gentle outlook on her faith. Joely craved the gentleness now.

"He doesn't like it when his children hurt, Joellen. This was not your choice. I never told you this, but I took it upon myself to write that boy a letter when you were first injured. I didn't mince any words with him."

A mixture of pride, embarrassment, and utter gratitude bubbled into a giggle that helped effervesce a little of the dark hurt away. "I wish I could have read it. You're a little fearsome when you're on a tear, Gram."

She looked positively affronted and then added a huge grin. "I don't go on 'tears.'"

"Not unintentional ones." Joely grinned, too. "The politically correct term is 'speak your mind.'"

"I'll give you that one, child. I'm far too old to do anything less. But my point is that Timothy Foster didn't even do me the courtesy of sending a rude reply much less come and care for you. I don't know many humans who have that little charity in them."

Joely had never thought of it in terms of Tim lacking a human quality. He'd simply been the man who'd hurt her and she the woman with so little to offer a husband that he'd walked away from her.

"Is it all right if I hate him?"

The words felt guiltily good to say.

Grandma Sadie patted her hands again. "If you can manage not to, after a time, you will feel the better for it. Right now? I'm afraid I'm struggling with a little hatred myself. He hurt one of my babes, and that's difficult to forgive."

For once the tears in Joely's eyes were tears of relief, and for a few moments the anger and even hatred in her heart were pure, instead of jumbled and guilt-ridden.

"I honestly don't know what I'm going to do," she said. "If I lose access to my care…to my home I—"

"That apartment is not your home." Grandma Sadie interrupted her without apology. "It's your cave. You've been hiding there to do whatever healing you've had to do, and I'm not saying you didn't need it. But you don't need it any longer."

The idea terrified her, as it always did. "I promised myself a year," she said quietly. "That's what the doctors always said. 'Give your body a full year to repair and recuperate.' Not that it's made so very much difference."

She lowered her eyes as the truth crashed around her in a familiar tidal wave. She would never walk normally again. She would never tear around the barrels on the back of a gazelle-like horse. She would never...

"You are alive." Grandma Sadie's admonishment cut through the roiling emotions. "Don't look for sympathy about losing your home. It's been waiting for you a long time."

Speaking her mind. Here was proof her grandmother would speak it to anyone—even one of her "babes." Joely stared at the table, chastised but not changed. She'd thought so often about returning to Paradise that she could play out the act of moving back in her head like a movie. It never had a satisfying ending.

"I'm not interested in coming back and being a burden to everyone here."

"Why would you think such a thing?"

"I can't run my own errands. I can't get to my own doctor appointments. I can't go up and down stairs, so everyone would have to move to accommodate me. Harper and Cole will be newlyweds. They don't want a child to care for in their new life."

A long, patient sigh floated through the air, and Grandma Sadie shook her head. "I could spend from now until the wedding ceremony begins listing the reasons all those complaints are wrong-headed," she said.

"But you're going to have to figure some of them out for yourself. Until then, I will talk with you about your worries any time you'd like, but no more right now. You get yourself into that chair, and we'll go to my room and get each other ready. I want only one promise from you—one sacrifice today."

"What's that?"

"You put yourself, Timothy Foster, and all your fears away for the day, and you don't let them out again until we can concentrate on them. You were right and kind to keep this news from your sisters for the moment."

"I'm not totally self-centered. I know it's their day."

Joely found another smile and her grandmother returned it. Sadie stood. She still held herself with pride and determination, the soft roundness of age only emphasizing the fact that once she must have been a curvy stunner.

"Oh, sweet Joely. You are self-centered. You always have been. But one thing you are not is vainglorious. You have possessed a heart of gold from the day you were born, and you want people to honestly like you. It's time to turn a little of that inner kindness on yourself. Come now. Let's get dressed for the big party."

SHE DID, OR tried to do, what Grandma Sadie ordered. In her grandmother's spacious bedroom suite on Rosecroft's first floor, they spoke no more about Tim, or the foreboding papers he'd sent, or about the injuries that made it so much more of a challenge to do anything she'd once taken for granted.

Grandma Sadie regaled her with stories from her own wedding seventy-five years before. No fancy, frilly white dress for her—just her best blue-and-pink flowered Sunday frock with a single rose pinned to her shoulder. Joely's grandfather, Sebastian, had been "handsome as Gary Cooper and Errol Flynn together" and had splurged on a new tie and a new pair of shoes for the occasion.

There'd been a small ceremony at the same little church the girls were getting married in today and, also the same as this wedding, a huge party here at Paradise with every kind of homemade treat conceivable and a fiddle band that played until all hours.

By the time Joely stopped giggling over the stories of cousins and neighbors plying the main fiddle player with whiskey so he'd play faster, she was dressed and ready to face the mirror.

"Now." Grandma Sadie stood behind her, gripping her waist as Joely held the foot of the old sleigh bed frame and took a deep breath. "You look at yourself and tell me you don't forget all your troubles."

The dress was a confection. A floating, swirling combination of blue with lilac streaked through the chiffon layers, the gown flowed from a wide gathered ribbon of purple at her waist into a shimmery full-length skirt that covered her twisted leg. She couldn't help but feel better wearing it. She'd been working hard enough on her upper-body physical therapy that her arms and shoulders didn't even look too bad in the strapless bodice.

"It is pretty, isn't it?"

"The girl in it is pretty. The dress just emphasizes it."

There was the platitude. Joely turned in place and hugged her grandmother, who looked elegant in a peacock-blue suit worthy of Queen Elizabeth. She even wore a jaunty little fascinator, adorned with a peacock feather and a lavender bow. She was the pretty one.

"We both look good," Joely agreed.

"Oh, much better than good. We'll catch all the boys' eyes."

The twinkle in her eye proved Sadie Crockett wasn't just talking to exercise her jaw. She'd lost a husband and both her sons, but she revered life. Two new grandsons were about to walk down the aisle into her world, and she'd already caught their eyes, all right—as the undisputed head and heart of Paradise. And because they were two amazing, good men, Joely knew they'd helped heal a little of the loss in her grandmother's wounded heart. She would definitely dance with them, and other men, at the reception tonight.

Save me a dance.

Joely's heart fluttered at the memory of those words from the arrogant Mr. Morrissey Rodeo Star, and she shut down the annoying sensation with a firm press of her lips one to the other. She still couldn't quite fathom his nerve. The few men she had come in contact with since her accident had been kind, solicitous, understanding.

Cowboys were such…cowboys.

I'm not a real cowboy. I wear the boots because they're comfortable.

Jerk.

A quick, snappy knock on the bedroom door preceded it being thrown open. In tumbled the start of the party—five women and a teenager dressed like the blue-to-indigo spectrum of a rainbow. The triplets; Mia's best friend, Brooke, from New York; and Skylar Thorson, Bjorn and Melanie's daughter who'd developed a friendship with Harper because they both shared a talent for art wore dresses in varying shades of blue and lavender in lengths from knee to ankle. Joely's dress looked like a purposeful mix of all of them.

"Oh my," Grandma Sadie said with a hand to her chest. "You all take my breath away."

"And you two are gorgeous!" Kelly grabbed Joely in a tight embrace, and they both wobbled. "Sorry! Sorry!" She laughed. "I forgot. You okay?"

"Of course." She tamped down resentment. This was precisely what coming back here would always entail—people being careful, apologizing, watching out for her.

Kelly backed up. "Harpo and Mia have gone ahead with Mom. Alec is here with the van for us."

Alec?

Her heart sank. Great. Fantastic. She'd not only have to face him in close quarters again, but she'd have to hear him schmooze them the entire twenty minutes to the church. She pressed her lips together in frustrated compression to keep any hint of a snarky retort behind them.

But suddenly he appeared in the doorway, as if someone had rubbed a rusty horseshoe and summoned him. He looked past all the bridesmaids, who made eyes at his long, muscular body like he was Christmas and dessert all rolled into one package, and caught Joely's gaze with laser-focused hazel eyes, the brown-green color of an autumn forest.

She shook her head, annoyed with the bad poetry invading her brain.

"Why, hello, pretty lady." He tipped a tan cowboy hat—not part of the official wedding attire, so was that another fake cowboy item that was simply "comfortable"?—and winked. "Looks like you're ready for that dance."

A spark of annoyance at herself morphed into full-fledged anger at him. "Mr. Morrissey. Even if I could, I wouldn't dance with you if we were the last two people on Earth."

Her sisters gasped as one, but to her astonishment, Alec burst out laughing.

"Pretty Miss Joely, that's the best challenge I've been issued in a long time. I accept."

Chapter Three

THE TWO BRIDES were already at the small church when the van full of bridesmaids arrived. Joely wheeled herself into the small anteroom where the women would wait for the ceremony to start, and her eyes misted at the sight of her stunning sisters in their gowns. The dresses perfectly reflected the two women Joely loved with all her heart—the reason she was willing to go through this for them.

Mia's dress was traditional: frothed with white ruffles on the bottom and a sweetheart neckline showing off the elegant length of her neck and the graceful sweep of her shoulders. The skirt parted slightly in the front—a subtle slit to her knees—allowing her to show off a pair of beautiful, red cowboy boots, something she'd worn for good luck since she'd been a child. With purple and blue flowers and one red rose in the center of her bouquet, she made a truly exquisite bride.

Harper's dress was a simpler, strapless A-line with a pretty shirred bust. Below the gathers she'd laced a wide, denim belt that showed off her small waist and curvy hips, and the front of her skirt was embroidered with shades of exquisite, denim- and indigo-colored flowers. She looked like a beautiful explosion of fairy asters and bluebells. Her cowboy boots were gorgeous blue leather embossed with white flowers.

Joely momentarily forgot any self-consciousness. "You two could model in magazines. I knew you'd both be gorgeous, but this is way beyond what I'd imagined."

Mia stooped and wrapped her in a hug. "Thank you, sis. It's still a little surreal."

"It won't feel that way when the music starts." Joely touched Mia's cheek. "I'm so happy for both of you."

Mia looked over her shoulder, smiled at Harper, and reached back to take her hand.

"Who'd have thought only a few months ago that I'd get to know my older sister better than I ever did when we were kids?" Harper asked. "It took two guys to knock some sense into our heads. It would be embarrassing if they weren't so amazing. They brought a whole family together."

Joely shook her head. "Maybe they were part of it, but this wouldn't have happened if you hadn't made steps toward each other. It's true. I know for the most part I've been out of family dynamics for the past eight months, but I've still been watching. The family is healing."

As soon as the words were out she regretted them. It was true the Crockett family had changed and even improved in some ways since the death of their father, but healing was something she herself would never fully experience. She might not have to spend her life in a bed, but the person she had been would never return. Still, she held her head firmly up and suffered through the smothering hug Harper added to Mia's.

"I'm so glad to hear you say that," she said. "I was hoping this celebration today would cheer you up and push you to keep moving forward. You're healing, too, Jo-Jo."

Joely didn't correct her despite the sting of the words. In truth the better term for her status was "stabilizing." It was where she'd stabilized that had killed her hope.

WHEN A KNOCK came on the door and Melanie Thorson poked her head into the room to tell them it was time, everything was ready. A double wedding ceremony could have been chaotic, but this one had an air of perfectly choreographed calm.

Joely felt like the only exception. Once out of the anteroom, after she got her first glimpse of the little church sanctuary, her stomach roiled and she gripped her bouquet of blue asters, white roses, and purple thistle with sweaty palms. The church held a hundred and fifty people, and every pew overflowed with relatives and friends who'd known the Crockett family for decades. In fact, some of their ancestors had known the first-generation Crocketts, Eli and Brigitta, the great-great-grandmother whose name Joellen Brigitta shared, when they'd homesteaded Paradise Ranch in 1916.

She couldn't understand why, even seated, her head suddenly swam as though she'd been slamming back whiskey shots—which normally she and her sisters could do with a fair amount of expertise. Not until a pair of strong hands rested on her knees and a quiet masculine voice pulled her out of her thoughts did she realize how high she'd let her heart rate skyrocket in nervousness.

"Joely? Are you doing all right?" She looked into the eyes of Russ Wainwright, who smiled his encouragement even as his brows knotted in concern. A former ranch neighbor, Cole's father, and now moments from being Harper's new father-in-law, Russ was someone Joely had known her whole life. He was of her parents' generation, and the corners of his deep brown eyes crinkled with crows' feet etched there by years in the sun, rain, and snow.

"I'm okay, Russ."

"You're looking a little glassy-eyed, sweetheart," he said. "Can I get you some water?"

"No, I'm good, honestly." She caught her breath and halted the escalation of her breathing. "I got a little dizzy from anticipation, that's all."

Russ was paired with her since he was Cole's best man, so he'd be the one pushing her chair down the aisle. When she looked past him and saw that the rest of the groomsmen had joined them in front of the doorway to the sanctuary, embarrassment flared in her chest and rose in the form of heat into her face.

"It's pretty warm in here," Russ said, as if he could see her flushing. "You'll be fine once we get moving,"

"I will. Thank you."

She wasn't about to tell him it was the thought of her first public appearance since the acquisition of her chair, a useless leg, and the scar that shone like a hideous banner on her face that made her ill. His features were filled with the exact sympathy she saw and dreaded wherever she went, but he was too kind for her to stomp on with self-pitying words.

"Everyone is right here if you need anything. Don't you hesitate to ask."

She nodded, her face still warm but her head clearer. She took a long, steadying breath and lifted her eyes. Her gaze slammed straight into Alec Morrissey's hot hazel irises. As if she'd been struck in the back with a sledgehammer, her deep breath was arrested half finished. All the effects of her deep breathing techniques were wiped out in one wildly uneven heartbeat.

Decked out in his full wedding attire—dark denim jeans, a western-styled tux jacket in navy blue with a matching vest, and a black dress Stetson that replaced the battered tan hat he'd worn earlier—he looked like a model for Cowboy Gods R Us. She stared at the snowy-white shirt collar that rested against the tanned skin of his throat, its pointed tabs forming a V beneath his Adam's apple.

Not a hint of sympathy shone in his eyes. He winked and chased it with a bedazzling smile before she could say a word or turn away.

"See you at the altar," he said and took Raquel's arm.

An instant of jealousy flashed through her belly—not of Raquel but of her perfect, functioning legs. What she'd give to be gliding down the aisle on a handsome man's arm. Not for her own wedding—she'd done that once under the influence of infatuation and naiveté and never would again. But for today, for this wedding, she'd take Russ Wainwright's arm in a half a heartbeat and call herself blessed if she could walk beside him rather than ride helplessly in front of him.

Skylar started down the aisle first with her dad, Bjorn, at her side. Mia's friend Brooke went next with Harper's long-time friend and manager, Tristan Carmichael. Grace was paired with another veteran friend of Gabe's, Damien Finney, and then Alec led Raquel to the doorway.

The music swelled in Joely's brain, and for an instant dizziness threatened again. Angrily she pulled herself together. It was stupid to be such a weakling. Nobody was here to look at her—how many times had she told herself that? She lifted her chin in preparation when Gabe's brother, George, took Kelly's arm. She let herself smile. George Harrison. Everyone, even those her age, who had the slightest love of music, smiled when George introduced himself. His mother had definitely possessed a sense of humor.

Before Joely's nerves could attack again, her turn arrived. Russ placed a warm hand on her shoulder and pushed her to the sanctuary door, then onto the white aisle runner. She forced a smile, felt the scar on her jaw tighten and pull, and then she heard it: the murmur, faint but growing slightly as she progressed until they were whispers and small gasps. The guests stared with a full array of emotions: surprise, admiration, sympathy, and worst of all, pity.

With her eyes fixed ahead, she watched each couple separate and take up traditional spots on either side of the altar. Finally, in the middle, she saw her sisters' grooms—Cole, tall and muscular, a classic, ruggedly handsome cowboy through and through; and Gabe, movie star gorgeous with a long, lean build and a heart of pure gold. At last the murmuring of the crowd disappeared and Joely's heart finally expanded in a moment of unselfish excitement for Harper and Mia. They would both have amazing husbands. If only she'd been so wise in her choice.

The last person in the wedding party stood proudly in front of Gabe—ten-year-old Rory soon-to-be Harrison. He'd been orphaned when his mother, a friend of Mia's, had passed away the past November. But Mia had been named his guardian in the will, and today Rory was in the middle of his own love affair—with his new mom and dad. And they adored him right back. Joely knew the boy held four rings in his tuxedo jacket and jeans pockets—no frilly little pillow for him, thanks all the same—a caretaking duty he'd accepted with the obsessive focus a ten-year-old mustered when he wanted something and wouldn't let it go. Rory wanted this wedding as much as anyone. He knew each ring and to whom it belonged. He had each in a designated pocket and knew right when he needed to produce it.

He grinned at Joely when she passed, and she managed a wink and smile in return.

Russ angled her chair so she could see down the aisle, and once she was settled, the music paused before the old, traditional Wagner Bridal Chorus filled the small space.

Joely had to smile again—their mother truly had put her fingers into the planning pie. But the old-fashioned cliché lifted her spirits as almost nothing had done so far. Some things were good when they didn't change.

First Harper, with their mother and grandmother on her arms, got her walk down the aisle. Cole met her with the perfect amount of wonder in his eyes. Joely caught her grandmother's eye as she turned to head back out of the sanctuary and return with Mia. When her red boots took the one little step up to the altar, Mia squatted in front of Rory and gave him a giant squeeze. When she stood to meet Gabe, his eyes shone with unshed tears. Joely's heart melted further.

Two perfect men.

The ceremony passed in a lovely blur. All the men removed their Stetsons and held them reverently, Rory performed his duties as ring bearer flawlessly, Harper snuffled through her vows, and Mia didn't shed a tear—both in perfect character. And when the pastor pronounced the two sets of husbands and wives, the synchronized dips of their brides garnered Cole and Gabe almost as much applause as the two long, long, long kisses that followed.

When the four newlyweds finally came up for air, their groomsmen let out a simultaneous "yee-haw!" and eight black cowboy hats went sailing toward the church ceiling.

Joely cheered with the rest of the party, her self-indulgent melancholy forgotten, and waited for the strains of Mendelssohn's wedding recessional to play out, fully expecting a matching bookend to the traditional entrance—but she was surprised. Not even a cowboy-themed song got air time. Instead, Bruno Mars's "Marry You" twinkled out over the congregation, it's bright, happy, chime-filled tune inviting everyone to stand and dance the brides and grooms out of the church.

Joely even survived the raucous trip back down the aisle. Russ showed his still-youthful side as he jigged behind her and turned her chair in a small, celebratory circle, surprising her but making her laugh. By the time she reached the foyer, she could look back and see the rest of the party totally getting their boogies on. Kelly and George bumped hips all the way down. Alec twirled Raquel under his arm. By the time the entire party was out of the sanctuary, Rory, too, was hopping up and down like a dwarf on speed.

"What did you think of that, pretty Miss Joely?"

She whipped her head around to find Alec looking down at her. He placed a hand on each handle of her chair and leaned forward. The exquisite scent of spice and musk muddled her head, and all she could fashion for thoughts was that her face flamed hot and he looked like a very tall, cold drink of danger-laced water. She couldn't even muster up anger at "pretty."

"It was a lovely wedding," she said.

"Lovely?" He grinned. "That sounds a little understated. I saw you hip-hopping your way out here. Thought you said you couldn't dance."

That did it. The man was nothing but a one-annoying-trick pony. Same lines over and over. Her fog cleared and she leaned forward herself, bringing their faces just inches apart.

"Knock it off," she said. "I don't like the dancing jokes. I don't like the pretty Joely jokes. Stop ruining the wedding for me."

Once again he seemed anything but taken aback. He straightened and smiled. "It won't seem like a joke once you've danced with me."

The smallest hint of something more than teasing glinted in his eye, but she couldn't read it. It had to be the wedding buzz—everything about it, people included, was affecting her brain.

"I'm not dancing with anybody," she said.

He stood and shocked her again by holding out his hand. "Fine. Then at least walk with me down the outside stairs. It'll be faster than going all the way around back to use the ramp."

"I'm perfectly happy to use the ramp."

"No you aren't. You don't want to stand out, right? Just stick with me and you won't."

The man was unbelievable. What was his obsession with torturing her?

"I can grab three strong guys to help me haul you and the chair down together, like a queen on her litter. Would you rather that?"

"What is wrong with you?"

"Not a thing." He laughed. "What's wrong with you?"

She couldn't believe this conversation was taking place moments after a beautiful wedding ceremony, with

Bruno Mars still singing the guests out of the church. Alec Morrissey was a lunatic. A borderline mean one.

"Would you like a run-down?" Petulance and anger mixed to form a sort of hissing retort, like she was a cat being forced to swim.

"Of what's wrong with you?" he asked. "Other than being the most defensive maid of honor I've ever met, you mean? No. I already know you have a leg that doesn't function properly, and I totally understand that. I've also heard you can stand on your own, so I assumed you could hop down the steps if forced. I'm willing to act as a helper, that's all. Other than that, the list of what's wrong can't be all that long."

Cramps and muscle spasms when she did try to hop, a crooked spine that loved to cause her pain, scars on more than her cheek...She thought about throwing all the proof of how wrong he was in his face, but a stab of pride kept her from letting them fly. How did he know so much about her anyway?

"Why?" she asked.

"Why what?"

"Why have you chosen me to pick on? Because I'm the poor girl in the wheelchair? Do you have a bet with one of the other guys that you can get me to dance and make a fool of myself? Are you fascinated with disfigurement?"

"Hey." He stopped her with the firm word and the first flash of anger in his eyes. "I don't do things like that. I don't know anyone who would. And you need to stop doing them to yourself. I saw a beautiful woman who intrigued me, so I asked about her. That's the whole of it. So stop making yourself more important than you are, stand up, and take my arm."

She covered her mouth with one hand, thinking it would hold in a stream of furious retorts. What flowed around her palm instead was laughter—first a snort, then helpless giggling, and finally a full-fledged laugh.

"Unbelievable," she said, when she could. "You have to be the most arrogant man I've ever met."

"Why, thank you, ma'am."

"As well as a liar. Alec Morrissey. No cowboy my broken ass."

He leaned down again and whispered this time. "Your ass ain't what's broke. I asked. If it were, we'd have come up with a different plan."

Once more her mouth opened in surprise, and then she caught an unmistakable glint in his eyes. She snapped her jaw closed and released a resigned sigh. "I can't deal with you. Go away." But the corners of her mouth twitched mutinously.

"C'mon, Joely." He took a step back and held out his hand. "I'm not proposing a lifelong commitment. Just let me take you on a short walk, and then you can be done with me."

"That's all it will take?"

"For now." He raised and lowered his brows in an abbreviated waggle.

"Heck," she said. "That's no kind of promise."

He smiled. For the first time, she noticed he had two shallow, handsome dimples.

Dang.

Harper, Cole, Mia, and Gabe had the church doors open and were leading the way outside. Half the wedding party followed, but Russ Wainwright and Raquel appeared next to Alec.

"Can we help you down the stairs, Joely, sweetheart?" Russ asked.

She glanced at Alec, who merely shrugged to tell her it was her choice.

She shook her head and reached for Alec's grasp. "I think I've got it. Would you just grab the chair?"

"Sure thing."

The contact with Alec's strong, long-fingered hand didn't do anything to quell the annoyance dancing in her stomach. Or was it attraction? Or just a very long time since a man had taken her hand?

The reminder that she was a married woman flashed through her like lightning, but it was too late to do anything about it; Alec held her hand fast. And as soon as her way was cleared, he tugged gently and braced his feet so she could stand and get her solid leg beneath her.

"There you go," he said.

Her eyes came level with the button of his simple, flat cross tie. That put him at roughly six feet, she thought inanely, although, in truth, no thoughts *but* inane ones filled her head. Up close his eyes shone a dark, rich amber, and his full, upturned lips made him appear prone to smiling. His hat looked so natural on him he might well have been born with it on.

Yeah. Not a cowboy her butt...

"I'm going to let you go, and you take this arm." He held out his right elbow. "Just think of me as a human hiking stick."

He hadn't said "cane." He hadn't said "crutch." She offered a tentative, grateful smile, took a deep breath, and nodded. Raquel shot her two thumbs-up and took Russ's arm, pleased as a kid who'd gotten her way.

What could have been horribly awkward turned out to be an easy experiment in forming a partnership. Alec seemed to know instinctively how to step where she needed him for support, and his arm offered a perfect grip that she could lean into as firmly as she wanted. It took a dozen or so strides to get the coordination right, but slowly she figured out how to step firmly with her right leg and use Alec's weight to help swing and step quickly with her left. She'd walked like this with two crutches, but this felt so quasi normal—she almost enjoyed it.

Almost.

They came to the stairs, and she froze. A flat path was easy. Going up stairs was awkward but doable. But going down threw her weight forward, and she didn't have the strength or balance to keep from pitching headfirst down the flight.

"We're doing great," he said. "There are only six."

Again she noticed the difference in how he spoke to her. "*We're* doing fine," he'd said. She didn't know this man from any random person, and yet he knew how to speak as if they'd been doing this forever. Most impressively, he didn't sound like a physical therapist.

"I really should have a body on the other side, too," she admitted reluctantly. "I suck at stairs."

"Here's the deal." He removed her hand from his elbow and took it with his left, then wrapped his right arm loosely around her waist. "It's your balance that's got you spooked. You haven't practiced with it, but your left leg is strong enough. Trust yourself. You know the drill: bad leg—"

"First," she finished. "Yes. But it doesn't hold my weight."

"Eventually it will, but for now we'll step together, and you lean into me when you're using that leg."

How did he know so effortlessly to tell her what to do? It dawned on her that he'd probably had plenty of bangs and bruises when he'd been on the circuit—this was likely second nature for him. And now lucky for her.

They navigated the stairs like they'd been doing it for years. She'd never have made it on her own, and such an exercise had been clunky at best with a physical therapist. When she stood at the bottom of the steps without aid of a crutch or two side walkers, her satisfaction had to rival that of any successful mountain climber's.

"Wow," she said, unable to keep the pleasure from her voice.

"Why are you surprised? You're a ranch girl; you're tough."

The compliment—because it was one the way he'd said it—took her aback. She hadn't been anything more than a suburban California trophy wife for four years. And she was the furthest thing there was from tough.

Her body had proven to her in a hundred ways over the past eight months just how fragile she was. Already her lower back was tightening and her good leg aching as she stood there contemplating Alec's words.

"I'm not really a ranch girl." She leveled her gaze at him with a sardonic smile. "I only wear the boots because they're comfortable."

To her satisfaction, the slightest deepening of his skin tone proved he caught her jab. Still, he grinned. "Touché."

"Do you need this, or shall we put it in the car?" Raquel pushed her chair up beside her and Joely shook her head.

"It'll be a while until we leave for the reception. There are pictures to take. I'll sit."

Alec released her waist and held her hands while she maneuvered into the chair seat.

"Thanks for escorting me out of the church," he said and flashed his dimples.

She couldn't help but laugh at him. He really had said everything perfectly. "My pleasure. Glad I thought of it."

He raised her hand and placed a kiss on the back of it. The antiquated practice was so unexpected she couldn't speak. He spoke for her. "Next we dance."

"I..."

He left before she could say another word, and she stared after him, watched him greet Harper and Mia, giving each a huge hug and kiss on her cheek, and marveled at his easy greeting of their grooms—slapping each on the back and shaking hands. He moved like a beautiful, confident athlete, a runner or a...well, a bronc rider—with perfect grace and balance. No wonder she'd felt so secure beside him. He walked with a half-swagger, half-rolling stroll that it looked like nothing could topple. She'd spent a brief five minutes in his care, and now she missed it—missed the few seconds of illusory independence his support had given her. It was the first of even that little bit of confidence since the accident.

With effort she tore her gaze from him and tried to remember how annoying he'd been all morning. And how bossy he was. And how she would plan her escape from his insistence she dance. But as she rolled herself into position for a reception line before pictures, all she could really remember was the feel of his arm around her waist and how effortless it had seemed for him to walk her down those impossible stairs.

She steeled herself for the rush of guests and their words of greeting and sympathy. After a time, however, she numbed her emotions to cries such as, "Oh, Joely, you're looking wonderful," or "We're so grateful to God that you're all right."

Smiling and nodding grew easier, and eventually she even greeted old friends, whom she was honestly glad to see, with genuine warmth. Her shoulders had relaxed, and her self-consciousness was easing when the last of the guests came through the line. One more duty performed and one step closer to the end, she thought.

She heard the familiar voice before she saw its owner. For an instant she went perfectly still, knowing her imagination had to be playing tricks on her. Leaning forward in her chair, she glanced down the line, and her stomach made a queasy flip.

She nudged Harper. "Really? You invited her?"

Harper looked, and a frown blossomed on her face. "Of course I didn't. Mia wouldn't have either. She has to have finagled a date. Wait. Look, who she's with—Brett Johnson. He's a friend of Cole's, and he *was* on the list. She must be his plus-one."

"I thought he was smarter than that," Harper mumbled.

"A lot of time has passed," Harper said gently. "Maybe she's mellowed."

They both knew she hadn't. Her reputation hadn't changed since she'd been a teenager.

Heidi Maria Bisset—emphasis on the second syllable and don't forget it.

Joely had built her high school and college reputation on being the girl who got along with everyone. She'd been very good at it, too, with everybody except one person.

"Hi, Joely. Remember me?" Heidi Bisset stepped in front of her and squatted, her face pained and kindly, as if she were talking to an old woman with dementia.

"It's only been five years, Heidi. Oddly enough my brain wasn't wiped clean in the accident."

"The accident!" Heidi gasped, and her hand with its long, exquisitely manicured nails floated down to rest on Joely's thigh. "I'm so sorry about your face and your leg. What a devastating outcome for you. I'm just glad you're okay."

"I am. Thank you." Joely held her tongue.

"I think you're so brave," Heidi continued. "Out and about in public and not being self-conscious of your handicaps. You're an inspiration."

They were twenty-seven-year-old women, but listening to the obsequious whine in Heidi's false compliments sent Joely all the way back to school again. Heidi was a stunning woman, the way she'd been a stunning girl, with legs to make a thoroughbred racehorse envious and skin still as flawless as fresh cream. Yet she'd been envious of Joely their whole lives. The old rivalry was ridiculous. Especially now when Joely was no longer any kind of competition for Heidi to worry about.

"You look good, Heidi." Joely managed not to grit her teeth.

"Why, thank you!" Heidi's cloying smile showed she still loved a compliment. "You'll always look good no matter what's happened." Her fingers skimmed down her own cheek. "It's hardly noticeable."

Before Joely could process the woman's sheer, ballsy rudeness, Harper reached for Heidi's hands and pulled her into a hug. "It's such a surprise to see you," she said.

Joely owed her sister something huge in repayment for that. She turned to Heidi's date, the hapless Brett Johnson, who wished her well. The last four guests filtered past and once again Joely was startled to find Alec beside her.

"So," he asked, watching Heidi and Brett head off toward their car. "Who's the beauty queen?"

Joely stared at him. Did he know how far into his mouth that comfortable cowboy boot of his was, or was he truly clueless?

"Wanna meet her?" The words came out with a little more piss and vinegar than they should have.

"Oh, I met her. Heidi Bis*set*. Her poor date had to stand there while she promised in no uncertain terms to get better acquainted at the reception. Just wondering if she's anyone I should beware of."

"Maybe," Joely said, fighting a sudden spark of uncalled-for jealousy. "She's the only person who's ever threatened to kill me."

Chapter Four

JOELY CROCKETT FOSTER was funny, which was not what Alec had been led to expect.

He found himself shaking his head and laughing more than once during the next hour's photo session. As he coaxed Joely more and more often into leaving the confines of her chair for pictures, she loosened up, and he got a tiny taste of her natural humor and ability to perfectly time a great snarky comment. After a little while she seemed to lose the little black cloud she'd dragged with her to the wedding.

"Talk to Joely. Maybe compliment her a little. She needs someone besides her family to cheer her up." Gabe had come to him that morning, and along with the request he'd told Alec about her horrendous car accident, the interminable rehab she was still undergoing, and its limited success.

Alec had agreed equitably, with no ulterior motives. Talking with a woman would be easy enough. Bringing her a drink and complimenting her dress were tricks any decent pickup man had learned in high school. All were acts that would be as easy for him as falling off a bronc and just as quick to perform. He'd looked on Gabe's request as a chance to rack up a good deed for the weekend.

But from Gabe's simple request, Alec had formed a mental picture of a sad, shy, somewhat frightened young girl with a broken body. The permanent images in his brain of all the frightened-faced, broken men he'd seen in Afghanistan had only fed the preconception. When he heard "injured limbs," that's simply where his mind went.

He couldn't have been more mistaken. Joely Crockett was not only crazy beautiful, she was strong and stubborn if a little self-pitying. It didn't matter that she couldn't walk a step without help, she had the sculpted, attractive arms of a gym rat, which told him she wasn't weak. So she had a six-inch scar that zigged from mid-ear to her throat. It took nothing away from her heart-shaped face, flawless complexion, and piercing blue eyes. It was those eyes that had told him how wrong he'd been. They did show sadness, but not in a scared, shy way. Her sorrow went far deeper than the loss of mobility or the insult to her face. It was the kind of sadness that spoke of failure, and he recognized it. He just didn't know her well enough to understand why she believed she'd failed.

Once the photographer was finished and Alec had secured all the bridesmaids into a borrowed van with Joely secure in the passenger seat, he climbed behind the wheel and twisted to look at the full load of gorgeous females ready for the trip back to Paradise Ranch.

"All aboard and settled?" he asked.

"Drive on, Jeeves," one of the triplets replied.

He couldn't tell them apart, even though they all wore slightly different dresses in slightly different shades of blue or purple—or peri-friggin'-winkle as someone had corrected him earlier. The three were as alike as cookies from a mold, and they'd been dressing the same and confusing the hell out of everyone for two days now. Good thing they were sweet as chocolate and cute as baby lambs. Though they were hardly babies, he admitted.

"Yes, ma'am," he said. "Joely, you feeling safe enough with us?" A chuckle escaped. "Now that I have you out of the open I aim to get you to tell us about this would-be assassin from your childhood. You can't get out of telling me anymore now that I'm within her sights."

"For crying out loud." She rolled her eyes but then smiled. "I should never have brought it up."

"Are you talking about the Heidi story?" Another triplet giggled. "You have to tell him. It's the stupidest funny story he'll ever hear."

"Darn right," the first triplet said. "One thirteen-year-old attempting to kill another using a skunk? It never gets old."

"I suppose," Joely said. "It is the story of one of the world's true masterminds. And in fairness you did ask if you needed to beware of her."

Skylar Thorson leaned forward between the front seats. "What's the Heidi story?"

"It's ridiculous is what it is," Joely said.

"It's entirely book-worthy." Laughter spilled from the third triplet, who sat in the far rear of the van. "I might just try my hand at a murder mystery where that's the killer's signature. When I start my next career as an author."

Skylar tapped Joely's shoulder, grinning already. "Tell me!"

"It was fourteen years ago."

"It was her first beauty pageant."

"It was *not* a beauty pageant, Kel," Joely said adamantly.

Kelly—in the light blue dress. Alec made a mental note.

"It was a made-up competition to see who could be princess attendant of the high school rodeo team. Something extra between being junior and senior princess. Practically every junior high girl entered, so it wasn't anything that cool. All you had to do was sell the most Rodeo Booster buttons. If you did, you got to ride your horse around the arena during the fall high school rodeo and then be the official helper to the senior princess and the high school rodeo queen."

"Was it a big deal?" Skylar asked.

"I thought it was kind of ridiculous to tell you the truth. Sell buttons, be a sort-of-a-queen. It was so lame, as we used to say, but it was something to do for the heck of it. Heidi, on the other hand, wanted this more than anything and worked her butt off. She even semicheated by offering sales on the buttons and free gifts if people bought them—like mini candy bars and things. She'd been a junior princess in grade school and had been trying for three years to get this title, too. She had a step-by-step plan for her life: junior princess, attendant, senior princess, high school rodeo queen, Miss Rodeo America. As far as she was concerned, there was no other career track back then."

"But you beat her, right?" Skylar clasped her hands beneath her chin as if praying for the happy ending.

"By thirteen buttons."

"Thirteen was her unlucky number!" Skylar sat back in her seat. In the rearview mirror Alec watched her grin as if all of this was just unfolding. "I'll bet you didn't cheat."

"It's embarrassing to admit now, but I didn't even really try all that hard. My dad just knew a lot of people, and we went into town a lot. I asked anyone I met, but I honestly didn't expect to win. I don't remember the details anymore, but when I did end up winning and Heidi had lost her last chance? I was shocked, and she was steaming mad."

"So Heidi threatened to kill her," Kelly said. "Nobody would have paid any attention, except she said it, screamed it really, right in front of the whole gymnasium full of kids and families. We were all, what, ten or so?" She looked from Grace to Raquel, who nodded as one.

"Seriously?" Skylar nearly choked on laughter. "If we said anything like that today, we'd get hauled out of school in handcuffs."

"I don't think it came out like 'I'm going to kill you,'" Joely said. "It was something on the order of 'You stink so bad Joely Crockett. You deserve to die like a stinky skunk, and I know where there's a family of them. I should put them all in a room with you and kill you with their smell.'"

"The really ridiculous thing is, she actually did try," Raquel-or-was-it-Grace said. "She had three brothers. The oldest one was a pretty creepy guy who's long gone from Jackson, thank goodness. He was the one who helped her catch two juvenile skunks and sneak them in Joely's open window."

Alec turned his head and stared at Joely in disbelief. "That must have been ugly."

"It was, although I only lost a fake bearskin rug, a pair of boots, and the dust ruffle on my bed. It didn't kill me because even though they put a towel under my bedroom door, they forgot to close the window all the way." Joely laughed. "It could have done a lot more damage. Fortunately, the animals were young and only had tiny stinks. Dad and Skylar's grandpa, Leif, live trapped them and sealed the trap in an airtight container long enough to release the little guys."

"I hope that Heidi person got into a lot of trouble," Skylar said.

"She did. She never forgave me for that either."

"And there was karma," Kelly said. "Joely went on to win both the senior princess title and the high school rodeo queen competition. The year after that, she was homecoming queen. Every time, Heidi was first runner-up."

"All right!" Skylar pumped her fist in the air.

"What about Miss Rodeo America?" Alec asked.

Joely shook her head. "I never competed for it. Someone talked me into participating in the Miss Wyoming pageant and then I won so—"

"I remember when you won!" Skylar said. "My whole family was there!"

"I remember that, too." Joely looked back at the girl. "That was really special."

"So did you become Miss America, too?" Alec asked. "Did I miss that?"

"It would have been Miss USA, but no. Thank heavens. Way, way too much pressure."

"She was in the top ten, though," Kelly said. "And she got to have a really big stage for her platform, which was preventing animal abuse. She shut down a half dozen abusive facilities throughout Wyoming that year."

"I didn't personally do it. I just told people about them. It's true, that was a great vehicle for promoting something I felt strongly about."

"Two small poultry operations, three super-awful puppy mills, a man who had fifteen or so starved and neglected horses, and one fox farm where they were electrocuting the foxes by—"

"Stop!" Joely cut Kelly off with a sharp order. "I don't need to relive it—I saw it in person."

"I'm impressed," Alec said. "An animal rights advocate. Brave indeed."

"I wasn't affiliated with any organization," she said. "I was generically for the rights of animals not to be abused. My platform was that we humans are supposed to be the smart mammals—but instead we can be downright cruel sometimes."

"Is this a soapbox?" he teased.

She bristled visibly, and her ruffled feathers pleased him. She did have fight beneath the passive, slightly depressed face she presented in her wheelchair.

"And what if it is?"

"I say stand on it," he replied. "Sounds like you know how."

He could tell she was going to snap at him again— he already recognized the quick set of her lovely mouth and the storm settling in her eye. She apparently hated even oblique references to her standing or moving like a normal person, no matter that they were inadvertent and intended as compliments. Somebody, or several somebodies, had allowed her from the start to assimilate with her wheelchair like a Star Trek Borg. She now considered using crutches an unpleasant way to move and barely considered standing as feasible, despite being able to manage both with help.

He didn't see Joely as a diva, but clearly she'd gotten used to things being easy for her throughout her life, with her gorgeous face, beauty pageants she couldn't lose, and her family's overprotectiveness. She was stuck and wallowing in her circumstances now with no tools that would allow her to dig out of the defeatism. He wouldn't pull rank on her yet, but he could see that others seemed blind to the fact she hadn't accepted hard work as her only way forward. Maybe he'd be the one to give her an object lesson in fighting for herself. Maybe not. But somebody had to tell her that no crown was going to appear on her head and make this reality show all better. Unfortunately, it didn't look like it would be her family. They clearly adored her too much.

"Didn't you want to be a veterinarian?" Skylar asked, interrupting any words Joely had been going to let fly. "I remember that from your Miss Wyoming interview."

"Do you have, like, an eidetic memory or something?" Joely asked. "That was five years ago."

"No." Skylar scoffed at her. "I remember because I used to want to be a vet, too, but I can't do math, so I'd never get into vet school. Say, can you learn *how* to have an eidetic memory? Then I wouldn't suck at math, and I *could* be a vet."

Laughter broke the last of the tension that had started to form. Out of the mouths of babes, Alec thought, often came logic so warped it made sense.

"I wanted to be strictly an equine vet," Joely said. "But my dad made me see that horse and small animal veterinarians didn't have much use around here. When you live in cattle country on a cattle ranch, you need to concentrate on cattle—even take a public health or food production specialty. That wasn't my thing at all, so I gave that idea up and went for saving all animals with a soapbox instead of with medicine." She sent Alec a sideways micro-glare. "It's all for the best. I suck a little at math, too."

"You do not!" Kelly said.

"Okay. Maybe it was organic chemistry." Joely scowled and turned back to stare out the window.

"You're hilarious." Kelly snorted. "Harper was the artsy fartsy one, you and Mia were the scientists. You even studied animal science. I figured you just changed your mind about vet school."

"Let's go with that."

There was something in Joely's tone—a weak undercurrent of anger, a note of resignation—that told him she was done with the whole subject of vet school, even though her answer was clearly sarcastic. The woman was growing more intriguing with every passing mile.

ALEC STOOD ON the expansive, multi-tiered back deck at Rosecroft and couldn't help the sense of amazement that hit every time he visited. All a person had to do was walk into the little foothills town of Wolf Paw Pass adjacent to Paradise Ranch lands, and the reputation of the Crockett's legacy crashed into him. Whether it was the picture of Eli Crockett in the general store he'd started, the map of the area with Paradise boundaries outlined in red hanging in the post office, or talk of the new, successful windmill farm on the enormous spread's southeastern border, Alec had heard enough about the fifty-thousand-acre spread by the first time he'd visited to be awed.

It was impossible to truly get the scope of the place, Gabe had told him, until you went on a fence-checking mission that required days in a pickup or on a four-wheeler, or got a view of the endlessly varied landscape from the seat of a plane or helicopter. Seventy-eight square miles of grassland, wooded foothills, mountainscapes, and beautiful creek bottoms were deserving of all the reverence they received.

Alec had neither ridden the fence lines nor seen Paradise from a plane, but he partially disagreed with his old army buddy. Just looking toward the Grand Teton massif sixty-five miles distant, his jaw dropped knowing the space in between had been privately owned for almost a hundred years by the family surrounding him. He couldn't fathom the freedom or the responsibility such ownership offered and required. His childhood on the streets of Minneapolis had been the exact opposite of free until he'd gone to live with an uncle and cousin in Wisconsin at age fourteen.

He'd learned the value of hard work on his uncle's small dairy farm and had gotten his only freedom when his cousin had introduced him to local rodeos. He'd been as shocked as anyone to learn a skinny kid from a big city had a natural talent for roping and riding bucking horses. The rest, as the cliché went, was history. He'd run away to the professional rodeo right after high school and loved it. From Wyoming to Texas he'd lived in wide-open spaces just by moving around.

Just until 9/11 had changed the world for everyone.

He stood now on an impressive multiple-level deck at the back of Rosecroft, the name of Paradise's main house, two glasses of wine in hand, and stared at Grand Teton. For all his travels, he'd never been to the national park. He'd always intended to take his favorite horse and spend several weeks exploring the countryside in each of several parks—he'd had a list. But the list was long lost—along with his favorite horse. He hadn't dared bring up the lost horse subject with Joely. From what he'd heard that was a taboo subject, but it was something they had in common.

"Hi there, cowboy."

He turned at the sound of the sweetly pitched voice and came face-to-face with Skunk Girl. With a swift mental kick and a quick bite to the inside of his cheeks to stop a laugh, he managed a friendly smile.

"Hi back. It's Heidi, if I recall."

"Ooh, very good!"

She was a stunner, he had to admit—the kind of platinum bombshell he'd practiced all those pickup lines on years ago. Taller than Joely by a solid four inches and leggy even in her red strapless dress that came, sort of modestly for her personality he thought, to her knees, she looked like she would still knock the socks off a pageant judge in a swimsuit competition.

"You came through the receiving line at the end—made it easier to remember."

A slightly crestfallen shadow flit through her eyes, as if it bothered her he hadn't simply remembered her for being fabulous.

"Is one of those for me?" She leaned a hip provocatively against the deck rail and lifted the corner of her full, red-as-her-dress lips in a flirty tease as she eyed the wine glasses in his hands.

Alec kept a sardonic smile from his face with effort.

"I'm sorry, ma'am, these are spoken for. Another has caught my bartending affections, I'm afraid."

"So sad." She sighed. "Well, perhaps your drink card will have an opening a bit later in the evening? I'm a big fan of yours. It would be a treat to get to know you better."

"I'm honored to have you say so, but I believe the evening is pretty full. If things change you'll be the first to know."

A good pickup man also learned how to fib smoothly.

"Who's the lucky girl? Your wedding partner I presume?"

As if it was any of her business, he thought. On the other hand, nothing could really be hidden at a wedding reception, so no point in making a scene over her forwardness.

"No." He leaned closer and whispered as if imparting a huge secret. "As a matter of fact I scored the matron of honor. I understand she's an old friend of yours."

Heidi's features went through a complicated set of emotional contortions, and she ended up, somehow, with sympathy.

"Isn't it just so, so sad about Joely? The poor girl. She used to be so attractive."

"You don't think she is any longer?" The hairs on the back of his neck stood up in defensive annoyance.

"Goodness no, I didn't mean it like that." Heidi backpedaled with easy composure. "I just know she's had a difficult time coming out in public, and I can understand. She looks so different."

"Oh?"

"She *was* cute as a bug's ear, let me tell you." Heidi shook her head. "But I'm glad she's doing better. It's so good of you to try and make her feel comfortable. The perfect wedding date. I'd say she is a lucky girl."

"Or I'm the lucky man. Heidi, it was nice to see you again. Enjoy the rest of the wedding."

"And you be sure to come and find me if you have a free moment. I'd love to hear about your rodeo days, Mr. Morrissey."

A sure-fire way to make certain he never shared that drink with her, he thought, as he faked a friendly wink and headed away from the scenery, mountain, and woman to find Joely.

She was seated not in her wheelchair but at one of the tables set in the spacious yard, close to the rented dance floor and DJ table. She watched him approach, mild amusement in her eyes.

"I see you had a chance to formally meet Miss Heidi," she said, when he set the glass of Chardonnay in front of her. "I have to say, you two would make beautiful babies."

He nearly knocked the glasses over as he stumbled into a chair. "Excuse me? What the hell?"

She laughed. "Okay, that was a test. If you had agreed with me, I was planning to slug you."

"I don't think we know each other well enough for that."

She shrugged. "True that. I think I would have enjoyed it, though."

"Sorry I couldn't be more accommodating."

Her smile warmed him. He liked seeing her relaxed and comfortable rather than defensive and reclusive.

"I'll get over it," she said.

"Whose seat am I taking?" He looked around the table at four purses scattered on the denim-colored table cloth, and a few shawls on chair backs.

"Nobody who'll care. Mom, Grandma Sadie, Russ Wainwright."

"Which purse is his?" Alec grinned.

She didn't acknowledge the ridiculous line with more than a long-suffering glance. "Everyone is off getting drinks. Thanks for the wine."

"My pleasure."

"Look." She straightened in the chair. "I know you've been asked to act as my personal guardian angel and slave tonight, but I don't need you to babysit me. I'm just fine. You're free to go hang out with your friends."

"First of all, I don't do what I don't want, so I'm not here under duress. Second, I can't help but wonder why *you* aren't off with your friends."

"Somebody has to keep Mom and Grandma busy."

"Look around," he said. "Do you see any lack of people here for them to talk to?"

"I don't want to cramp anyone's style," she said, switching from one excuse to another as smoothly as lawyer on redirect. He'd hoped she was over that.

"You need to stop with the excuses. If you don't like your siblings just say so, but quit hiding behind your injury."

Her cheeks puffed outward as if they were filling with the angry the words he knew she was about to spew. He braced but didn't apologize. Let her keep getting angry. Anger was better than self-pity. This probably wasn't in his job description as a guardian angel, but so be it. When her face had finished flushing to a nice hue of pink, she could no longer contain her fury.

"How dare you? You play the funny, all-round Boy Scout, but you're no more honest than you're accusing me of being. I know who you are. Everyone does. And yet you mention nothing about your real life."

"You know what used to be my life," he said mildly. "I don't mention it because it's not relevant. I'll tell you anything you want to know about my real life now."

"Why did you lie about being a cowboy?"

"I didn't. I work as a dispatcher at a trucking company."

"That's crap. You don't just stop being the best at what you do."

His curiosity was piqued. Did she not know his life story? The thought was shocking and slightly exhilarating.

"Sometimes you do. Do you know why I quit?"

"You lost your partner. I'm sorry. And if you wanted to quit, it's none of my business what went into the decision. Just like it's none of your business why I make the choices I do. You have no right to tell me what I should and shouldn't do."

She *didn't* know. How bizarre and rare. He grinned at her.

"All right. We'll make a pact. For tonight, there'll be no talk about our pasts, whether that's yesterday or ten years ago or the days we were born. Clean slate and truce." He stuck out his hand. "Deal?"

She eyed his proffered handshake and blew out a breath. Finally she slipped her cool, soft hand into his. "Deal."

"So it follows that we only talk about the present or the future."

"The future?" she asked.

"Like what happens when the DJ starts and I have no desire to come up against Heidi of the Skunk."

She sputtered a little but didn't call him on the nickname that was more than a little unfair all these years after the episode that inspired it.

"I have five sisters who'll all be willing to run interference."

"The trouble with that, you see, is that I told Heidi Bisset I was here with you."

Joely dropped her head into her hands and shook it slowly back and forth.

SHE MANAGED TO hold Alec off for forty-five minutes. As she'd promised, each of her sisters danced with him, and he made every partner look good. And after every dance he returned to his seat beside her and cheerfully told her their dance was next. She couldn't deny how much she wished it could be. She'd once loved dancing. But watching the easy, graceful sway of bodies during slow songs, and the jumping up and down fist pumping that the upbeat tunes required, she knew beyond any doubt that her crushed calf, twisted knee, and crooked spine wouldn't handle the moves.

Her mother danced with Alec and even Grandma Sadie took her spin with him. Afterward, he returned exhilarated.

"Your grandmother is an amazing woman. I swear she's more flexible than I am."

"I guarantee she's more flexible than I am," Joely added.

"I think you can't make a statement like that unless you have empirical data to back it up."

"Give it up, Morrissey," she replied.

"How about you give it up with me, Morrissey? Or should I add Mister and be polite?" Heidi stood before them, her slinky red dress setting off her perfect, seemingly ageless body. Joely aged fifteen years in her own mind. "Could I interest you in a dance?" Heidi asked.

Alec stood and Joely stared at him. "Really?" she mouthed when he caught her eye.

"I'm sorry, Heidi," he said. "But I just agreed to dance with Joely."

He gave her no warning, just grabbed her hand, hauled her out of her chair, and wrapped his arm around her waist, automatically supporting her weak leg as she shifted into his embrace. Breathless, she looked into his eyes with no idea of what to do next.

"Ready?" he asked.

The shock on Heidi's face was enough to force Joely into an immediate bid for Oscar consideration.

"Of course!"

He led her to the dance floor casually, with the same unhurried steadiness he'd offered at the church. The level floor and easy pace made this trip even easier, and Joely had no time to fret over her shuffling limp. With his hip bracing hers at each step, she didn't feel like the awkward center of attention.

He found a relatively empty corner of the floor and took her fully into his arms. Michael Bublé sang out "Save the Last Dance for Me," and she had just enough presence of mind to understand the irony. Her heart pounded with exertion and excitement, but try as she might to breathe deeply, her pulse refused to calm. The scent of his familiar aftershave, the firmness of his arms around her, and the brush of their torsos as he started to sway only heightened her rush of exhilaration.

"Okay," he said. "This is above and beyond. Thank you for playing along; I owe you."

"Maybe you planned this." She managed to put a tease in her voice, breathe, and start concentrating on her leaden feet all at the same time.

"I wish I'd thought of it. It's kind of brilliant."

She stumbled slightly over one of his feet, but he held her fast.

"I can't talk and concentrate on this at the same time," she said. "I can barely handle smelling you and concentrating—"

She stopped, mortified. She hadn't said that. She couldn't have. She'd only had two glasses of wine. He started to laugh.

"Do I need to apologize? I didn't think I'd forgotten to shower."

"No." She wanted to melt into the floor—but then again, falling to the floor was actually her nightmare, so she made herself look directly into his eyes. In the early evening sunlight they were almost sea green, with flecks of golden brown in a starburst around the irises. "You smell good. Whatever you have on is highly distracting."

Heaven help her, she was making it worse. She stepped on his foot again with her good leg.

"Hey." He stopped them and held her still, letting other couples swing around them. "Thank you. Now don't fumble for words anymore—you don't need to. Let's start over and you try shifting your weight foot to foot. Get used to the new gait you have now."

With all her heart she didn't want the dancing to be fun. She was right about herself, damn it. She couldn't do these things; she knew her own body. But she hadn't figured Alec Morrissey into the equation. He turned out to be a masterful teacher and more understanding than she had a right to expect.

Before she knew it, they'd been on the floor for three songs and the fourth started—Queen's "Crazy Little Thing Called Love."

"Do we need to take a break?" he asked.

"One more? I love this song."

His grin more than answered her question. "You command. I obey."

"As it should be!"

Her bad hip ached. Her knees trembled slightly. Her "gait" hadn't really smoothed out in fifteen minutes. But she also hadn't enjoyed music this much in months. The songs brought genuine pleasure, and the freedom from her chair and walker was intoxicating.

"Ready to try it on your own?" Alec asked.

She frowned. "How do you mean?"

"You've tried it just holding my hands, now let go. Simple. I'll be right here."

"Oh, I don't know."

"Only if you want to."

It was the first time he hadn't pushed. She relaxed back into his embrace and let him lead in the stripped down side-side-rock back step of swing dancing. There was no swinging, but she'd learned to rock back on her good leg and lean into his hold when the weight was on the bad one. She executed her longest string of steps for the night and accepted his cheer when he caught her to his chest.

"You're a wonderful teacher!" She giggled. "I have to admit I was wrong."

"So then try the last move I'll teach you tonight. You don't even have to let go. Just move back, hang onto my hand and spin under my arm on your uninjured leg. Plant your less solid foot when you're facing me again and I'll grab your shoulders."

"Easy peasy," she said jokingly.

He counted down the steps, then pushed her gently away. Everything went perfectly until she'd completed three-fourths of the circle. Her good knee buckled slightly, and her bad leg touched down before it was supposed to. Like a shoelace coming undone, her legs tangled and then splayed. Joely lost any hope of balance and crashed through Alec's arms to the floor in a painful, messy heap of lavender and blue. For one moment sheer panic engulfed her as faces appeared above her and multiple voices collided with one another.

"Don't move, Joely."

"Does it hurt, Joely?"

"Can you hear me? Did you hit your head?"

The questions reached her through a fog the way they had eight months ago on a highway while she lay in a twisted knot of steel and broken glass. And then, in one quick second everything cleared. Her brain told her this was just another panic attack and reminded her she had them all the time. She pushed at the wedding guests bending too close and struggled to sit. Her tailbone stung and her elbow smarted, but she hadn't hit her head.

"Hang on, now. Just wait for us to check you out and make sure you're okay." Alec pushed her firmly down.

She grasped his fingers and flung his hand off her shoulder. "Don't. I'm fine."

"You might have—"

"Believe me, after what I've been through, I know what I might have, and I don't."

She rested her uninjured knee on the floor only to find she couldn't put enough weight on the other leg to hoist herself up. And she couldn't kneel on the bad leg. Tears of frustration and intense embarrassment threatened to make everything even worse. And then her sisters appeared.

"Oh my gosh, Joely, honey." Harper squatted in her gown and put her hands on Joely's cheeks. "What happened? I'm so sorry."

"I was being stupid," she managed to say. "I just tripped myself."

"Are you all right? Mia's on her way. Let her check you out."

"No!" Joely hadn't thought her face could burn any hotter, but the idea of her sister the doctor having to examine her in the middle of her own wedding…

"Help me up." She held a hand out to Harper, ignoring Alec, who extended his arm as well.

Her sister braced and pulled Joely to her feet. The guests on the dance floor cheered and clapped while she prayed for a fissure to open in the earth and swallow her. Making a spectacle like this had turned her nightmare into reality.

"I just need to hang onto your arm and get back to my seat," she said quietly to Harper. "Everyone needs to stop hovering."

"When they know you're all right."

"I *am* all right."

"Okay, c'mon. I'll get you back and get you some wine."

"I don't think I need any more of that, thanks."

She took one wobbling step with Harper and immediately missed Alec's rock-steady hold. All she'd have to do was turn to him and he'd take over, but that wasn't happening. He'd gotten her into enough trouble—talking her into stupid tricks she no longer had any business attempting. He was hot, he was sweet, but more than either of those, he was dangerous.

And he took the last shred of dignity directly out of her hands by swooping in, scooping her into his arms, and striding across the floor.

"Put me down, what are you thinking?" She kicked at his hold but connected with nothing but air.

He had the audacity to laugh. "It'll be over in three seconds."

"Make it be over in one. Now."

He set her in her chair and stared her down. "Calm down."

"Don't you dare tell me that—"

Her tirade ended when Mia appeared. "I'm fine!" Joely snapped at her. Mia only smiled.

"I believe you. Just let me ask you questions so I can ignore you for the rest of the night."

"Anything to get everyone away from me and you back to having fun."

"I was having a wonderful time watching you," Mia replied. "You did great. And the slip was totally graceful."

"How comforting."

Once Mia was satisfied all truly was well, she kissed Joely on the cheek and went back to dancing. The crowd of worried relatives dispersed, and she was left alone with Alec.

"What can I get you to drink?" he asked, way too cheerfully.

She shook her head furiously. "I don't want a thing from you. You're bad for me, Alec Morrissey. You bully and trick me into things I don't want to do, but no more. Go dance with the triplets—they all have a crush on you."

She didn't know that was the case, but he was exactly their type so it could be true.

"C'mon, Joely. We were having a great time."

She sighed and tamped down her anger and then turned her tired gaze to him. "Please, Alec. Go hang out with the others. I just want to be alone for a little while."

"Fine. I'll come back and check on you."

"Don't."

"You know what?" He shook his head. "You need to work through this injured diva act you have going. It'll backfire on you one of these days."

And just like that he was back to being a jerk.

Chapter Five

IT ONLY TOOK him two days to show up at her apartment door, a bouquet of daisies and yellow roses in his arms along with a six-pack of hard cider, a bag of fried chicken, and an apology on his lips that didn't quite match the infuriating twinkle in his eyes.

She hadn't talked to him since sending him away after her fall at the wedding. The rest of the party had gone without further humiliation—although the incidences of people clucking with concern over her well-being had never ended, which had robbed the special night of some of its glitter.

Harper and Cole had left on their honeymoon first. When they returned, Mia and Gabe would take theirs. The triplets had gone back to Denver where their restaurants flourished. Joely had returned gratefully to the cocoon of her apartment.

She'd survived the weddings.

She might even have succeeded in putting the difficult moments of it into perspective if she hadn't had to worry about her immediate future. A future with problems she had no idea how to solve. Grandma Sadie had agreed to keep their secret until Joely could make some calls and come up with a few options. The trouble was, she'd never had to take care of such things before—she'd always had people who knew more than she did: her father, coordinators of pageants, and professors at school. Her husband. Her stomach knotted every time she thought about Tim and how little he'd ever told her about the workings of his business, of their life—of his life. Now she had no idea how to begin unraveling her predicament.

So when Alec appeared on her threshold, he represented just one more tightening tug on the knot inside of her, especially because he brought along the most beautiful flowers. She was a sucker for flowers.

"What are you doing here?" She kept her eyes on the roses rather than his face, her annoyance real but her will to fan the spark into anger weak.

"I don't like bad blood between me and anyone."

"Bad blood." She scoffed. "That's a little over dramatic."

"You started looking at me the moment you fell at the wedding as if I could and would pass on the plague in a heartbeat. The look is still there. That's bad blood in my book."

"I'm not looking at you any way."

"You did when you opened the door. Thank goodness I brought the flowers or I'd have a laser hole through my forehead." He put one hand to the skin above the bridge of his nose and rubbed. "It's still a little warm."

She couldn't help but snort laughter and shake her head while she took the flowers from him. "I was not that angry. I'd only have used the laser had I actually flashed people on the dance floor. But nobody saw above my knees so…"

He laughed appreciatively. "See? You do have a sense of humor about it."

"I have a sense of humor about yellow roses and daisies. You got lucky."

"I'll take it. Could I maybe come in and apologize again? I did bring dinner."

She could smell the chicken and her mouth watered.

"What would you be apologizing for?" She raised her brows.

"Whatever you need me to."

"You don't have any idea why I got upset, do you?"

She rolled her chair back and allowed him to enter. He stepped in, and for one moment he contemplated his answer. She waited for what was sure to be a glossy spout of slick-tongued rhetoric. To her surprise, he shook his head.

"I admit, I don't. I understand you were embarrassed, but not why it lasted more than a minute."

She wanted to be angry that he didn't get it, but she could only think that it suddenly seemed a fair enough question. How could anybody understand what it felt like to need help but not want to be pushed? That it was frightening to lose part of who she had been and even more frightening to think about letting that loss show in front of the people who made up her world?

"Come on," she said. "I'll give you points for an honest answer."

He stepped in and the small room got smaller. He was hardly an enormous man, but his aura, his spicy musk aftershave, and his wind-blown handsomeness all combined to overpower her senses.

"My mama's lessons pull me through again." He stood over her and smiled. "'Alec, don't try and hide the truth. When it comes out, and it always will, it won't be nice and simple anymore, it'll be a wildcat that'll sink its teeth into your butt and hurt like heck.'"

"She sounds like quite the homespun woman. A little like my grandmother."

"She probably would have been a lot like Sadie," he agreed. "She and my dad died in a car accident when I was twelve. But she got off plenty of good advice before then."

"Oh, I'm so sorry!"

"It was a very long time ago." His voice soothed. "Sad but not painful anymore. I grew up with my aunt and uncle, and they were great."

Matter-of-fact cheerfulness covered a darker emotion she couldn't quit put her finger on.

She frowned at his story and his matter-of-fact cheerfulness. She'd had her issues with her father, but she wondered even now if she'd ever get over losing him so early. She covered her discomfiture by teasing Alec as she ushered him farther into the apartment.

"So you never tell a lie, then, Pinocchio?"

He chuckled. "I won't swear that was the case early on. There may have been youthful indiscretions."

"I'll just bet."

He moved without replying through her living room area, such as it was with its one love seat, one armchair, a lamp, and a tiny end table. He set the sack of food on the table in front of a ground-floor window that served as her eating area and then turned back toward her.

"So I'm sorry, Joely. I didn't mean to embarrass you in front of the wedding guests."

Genuine surprise washed over her. "You do know."

"I know what I needed to say, and I mean every word. But as I told you, I don't understand."

"I was upset because I got talked into doing something I didn't want to do."

"And you did a fantastic job at that thing, which you didn't believe you could do at all. So you fell." He held up a hand to ward off her indignant protest. "I don't mean that wasn't a big deal. I get that it was. It's not a lot different than getting tossed from a bronc after only one or two seconds. You feel like an idiot."

"The difference is, you got on that bronc of your own free will."

"I didn't force you to dance."

The words were so calm, so nondefensive. She didn't even mind arguing with him.

"I beg to differ. I recall being hauled out of my chair and then thanked for being a good sport."

He shrugged and dipped his head slightly. "Touché. You're right. But to my credit, I did ask if you wanted to quit and sit down and you refused." He smiled. "Not to say I wasn't happy about it. I was having a great time."

She could feel the flush blossoming off her shoulders and rising up her neck. How could she admit after all her complaining and blaming that she'd been having a great time, too?

"Okay. I'll concede I got a little carried away. But that's exactly what I don't want to do."

"Where are your plates?" he asked. "I'll grab them for us."

Bossy and presumptuous, she thought. How did he know she hadn't eaten already? And yet, he was so pleasant about everything, so big and present, she couldn't help but enjoy the moment.

She pointed. "That cupboard, bottom shelf. There's some fruit in the refrigerator—early strawberries. I'll grab those."

He didn't say more until the table was set, and he'd found a bottle opener for the hard cider. Although he filled her apartment, he moved with effortlessness around her, never bumping into her chair, never waiting for her or getting in her path, never too big for the space. As if this were just another dance.

"It's not a feast," he said. "But it's my peace offering."

A surprising dart of guilt pricked her conscience. "You didn't have to do this."

"No. But like I said—"

"No bad blood. I know. I'm sorry I made you feel there was any."

She picked a drumstick out of the bag of chicken and bit into it before she could think too hard about the greasy calories. She tried to be so good about her eating.

Now that she was chair bound, she wasn't in the kind of shape she'd always maintained before the accident, but she loved fried chicken. She took a big, crispy bite and sighed. It had been a long time.

"Really good," she said over her mouthful.

He bit into his thick piece of white meat and nodded. "I'm a sucker for this stuff. I'm a sucker for junk food. There, now you know."

He didn't look like any junk food junkie to her—no puffiness or extra poundage anywhere. Just a tall, lean, sandy-haired cowboy.

"So here's my big question," he said. "Why do you want so badly to avoid getting carried away?"

The question took her aback. Wasn't it evident?

"I don't want to do something stupid and reverse the little progress I've made. I fell once shortly after my recovery started, and I ended up having three more surgeries."

"Okay," he said. "What are your restrictions?"

"Restrictions?"

"What have they told you not to do because it would be dangerous and cause more injury?"

She stared at him. Seriously? What was his problem?

"My restrictions are sort of obvious don't you think? I could have reinjured something falling like I did."

"I could have gotten hurt coming over here to see you."

She blew out a frustrated breath and set her piece of chicken on her plate. "That's not the point."

"It is, though. Your body might be out of shape and out of practice doing what it used to do, but it's basically healed."

"It's *not*!" She banged a fist onto the tabletop. "People keep saying that, but I have a spine that's crooked, a leg that's crushed, and a face that's scarred. None of that will heal."

She couldn't read the expression on his face—as if he had something to yell back but couldn't quite make himself do it. She wished he would. She didn't want to be the only one here with high emotions.

"None of those things will go back to being exactly what they were," he said. "But that doesn't mean they aren't healed. Or healing. You proved on Saturday you can do things you said you couldn't. You danced. Why are you remembering the two minutes of embarrassment and not the twenty minutes of amazing fun?"

"I…" She couldn't answer.

"Because you're not used to being embarrassed. You're not used to being less than perfect."

Her anger bubbled over again and words rushed back to her in a torrent. "How dare you? That was cruel. When did I ever say I thought I was perfect? I wasn't. I'm definitely not now. You don't know me, so quit judging everything I do."

"Did you know a person can Google you and get your whole life story?" he asked. "Did you know there's a Wikipedia entry on you? I've learned a lot."

His sudden changes in topic were starting to throw her. She felt purposely ignored and slightly ridiculed. Her amazement at his rude audacity kept growing.

"I did know. It's because of Miss Wyoming that's all. And you don't listen to me, but you're stalking me?"

He laughed. "For the record, I'm listening to everything you say. I'm not stalking you, and I'm not trying to be mean. I looked you up to fill in the gaps, find out what you used to do—learn the things we didn't get a chance to talk about on Saturday before you kicked me out of your life."

"Yeah? I kind of wish you'd stayed gone," she mumbled.

"No you don't. You're having fun. Second time in a week. When's the last time you argued with someone? Does anyone even dare start an argument with you?"

Once again she had no comeback. Of course she argued with people—her nurses, her physical therapists, the Miss Wyoming pageant coordinators who desperately wanted her to do a story about bravery and overcoming adversity.

"I...argue plenty."

"Then this is no big deal. I enjoyed reading about you online." He grinned. "You are an amazing person. Plus, I loved the pictures of you in the bathing suit competition five years ago. The judges picked the right winner."

"Oh my gosh, what a sexist thing to say!"

"See, now here's what I mean. Why are you angry? You entered the pageant, you were proud to do it, and I think it's a great thing, too. Why is it sexist for me to say something about it?"

"Because...that something is not the point of the competition."

"Of course it is! The question being asked was who models the swimsuit best? It was a beauty competition. I didn't say you were showing off because you're fast, easy, or bad."

The whole conversation was going nowhere, she thought. And she was losing her appetite for the chicken. Why was he here to pick on her? Why was she allowing it?

"Maybe this isn't such a good idea," she said. "I'm not sure all this is good for anyone's digestion."

Once again his laughter rang out. "Good for digestion? You sound like someone from your grandmother's era. C'mon. Eat your free chicken dinner and duke it out with me. I'm trying to get that pretty little girl who danced at her sisters' wedding to come up out of her hidey hole, because I kind of liked *her*."

"Sure. Everyone loves a girl who can stand up and dance."

She knew her bitterness was unfair—he'd been nothing but kind.

"You're a tough case aren't you, Joely Foster?"

She ignored the "tough case."

"Don't call me that. I'm not keeping his name."

"Ahh. Sorry. When will that be final?"

She averted her gaze. "As soon as I sign the papers."

And once she did, she'd be entitled to a quarter of what she and Tim had owned together, if she was lucky. She'd effectively give up the home she'd created, all her possessions except the ones she could prove were her own and hadn't been lost in the accident, and any benefits she'd received from Tim's insurance. Nine months ago, when she'd gone to California with her mother to pack up her things, leave her husband, and come back to Paradise Ranch, she'd had a plan. She'd take over the management of Paradise Ranch and help her mother save the family legacy—which her father had left in financial straits.

All her plans had died in a split second of devastation and agony.

"You don't sound very happy about this." Alec's voice was suddenly gentle. "Is the divorce something you want?"

She straightened and squared her shoulders. "You bet I want it. It was my idea. My husband is not a good man—he's cheated in more ways than one."

"Is there a reason you haven't signed the divorce papers?"

She shrugged. "Pride. Despite being the one who broke up the marriage, he's winning everything and making me look like the bad guy. I'd like very much not to roll over and play dead, but I have no leverage. We were only married three and a half years, and he made most of the money."

"Doesn't mean you can't fight him."

"And drag it out forever? No. I want him gone. I just have to think a few days, and I'll have someone look over the papers to make sure I'm not missing something. Then it'll be done."

"And you can move on."

"I won't have much choice."

"Hey." He leaned forward over the table so he could get closer to her. She waited for him to touch her as he had the other day at Paradise, but he drew her eyes to his with no more than his voice. "It sounds like he's baggage you don't need. You've got a nice little place here and you'll do fine."

Without warning, a dam on her emotions gave way and tears beaded in her eyes. From the moment Alec had arrived she'd been off balance, teetering between the reality that was her life and some unspoken fantasy he evoked about being swept away by a strong, handsome man who'd make everything bad disappear. But he wasn't a prince, and there was no white horse tied to a parking meter outside. She'd failed. Again. The real reason she hadn't signed the papers was that once she did, her marriage would be just another thing she'd killed.

"Hey, hey," he said again. "What did I do this time?"

"Nothing."

She swiped at her eyes and pushed her chair away from the table. Hanging onto her composure by a very short, thin thread, she reached her living room without sobbing. Such emotions were ridiculous—she wanted this. Wanted her independence. Wanted freedom from Tim's arrogant, dictatorial ways, and from the constant knowledge that she'd failed him. He wanted her so little that he'd gone to someone else and barely attempted to cover his tracks.

Alec was in front of her in seconds. Squatting at her knees, he placed a hand on each of her chair arms and held firmly so she couldn't push away.

"You aren't fooling me. This is about more than signing papers if they're something you want to sign in the first place."

"It isn't about anything else, though." She swallowed more tears. "Because of the papers, I...I have to find a new apartment. Tim has cut off the benefits as of June first, and that gives me barely three weeks to find someplace I can afford. I don't know why that got to me right here, right now. I've known about it since the morning of the weddings."

"Oh. I'm sorry."

He didn't say more for several seconds, but she could see the thoughts whirling through his brain. She braced for the inevitable platitudes, solution suggestions, and words of comfort, and promised herself she wouldn't deck him for telling her she could go live with her sisters because they had plenty of room, and she'd be okay.

"This is great!" he said.

She nearly fell out of her chair.

"Wha—?"

"It's a whole new world opening up for you, Joely *Crockett*. You can make any decisions you want. Go anywhere you like. Who's going to tell you what to do?"

The tiniest flutter of excitement fought through her panic. It flittered away as quickly as it had come.

"You know, you have this really annoying way of forgetting the special things I need to consider. It isn't exactly easy to find a place with wheelchair-friendly space, nursing assistants, and easy access to physical therapy—not to mention someone to get me around and pay for it all since I have no job."

He stood and ran a hand through his hair. For the first time he looked slightly disgusted.

"Why do you do that?"

"Do what?"

"Throw up a constant series of road blocks? What do you need a nurse for? Right this minute you're handling an unexpected guest perfectly well without anyone's help. Are you required to go to physical therapy at a certain place or time? Why not get back behind the wheel of a car and take yourself places? Get outside and take walks, strengthen that leg and get rid of the stupid chair. Find a damn job. You're smart, beautiful, and strong. Why are you letting this ass of a husband, since that's how you're describing him to me, keep you down even though he's not around? Or maybe he's not the reason you've given up so soon."

"Given up?" She nearly rose out of the chair just to smack his smug, handsome face. He'd gone too far. "I don't know you. Every time I think I'm simply imagining how forward and arrogant you are, you come back with something more insulting than ever."

"Has anything ever been truly hard for you, Joely Crockett?" He ignored her tirade as usual. "I think you've had it pretty easy up until now, and you don't know how to work hard. Or push past the pain."

"I take it back." Tears of pure anger clogged her throat. "You're beyond arrogant. What on this or any other planet gave you the idea you have any moral authority to lecture me on working hard or dealing with pain?"

He moved toward her again, slowly, his face twisted in painful apology. She waited expectantly for the words, pulling her crossed arms tightly to her chest in righteous indignation. But there was no "I'm sorry." He took a seat on her sofa and extended his right leg. She pressed her lips together.

"I can show you my moral authority," he said very quietly. "An IED in Iraq is what gave it to me."

Without any other explanation or warning he pulled up his pant leg. Rising from the top of his right cowboy boot was a cold, gray, titanium post. Joely's head spun, her stomach lurched, and she dropped her head into her palms, folding in half in her chair as she began to sob.

Chapter Six

HE HADN'T MEANT to spring it on her. He hadn't intended to tell her tonight at all; people who didn't know about his leg sometimes never found out. He let the leg of his jeans fall back down over his boot. This visit had never been meant as a chance for him to teach a lesson, as one-upmanship, or to shock Joely into feeling sorry for him. The only thing he'd wanted was to make up for the abrupt end to their evening the past Saturday.

But he'd found her to be so far into self-pity she didn't even know she had a problem. So far into it that a normal conversation hadn't even been possible. Everything they talked about somehow came back to how hard things were for her. And he completely understood. Three years before, he'd been right where she was. Now, however, he had sympathy but no patience for watching people give up. Joely was on the edge of a clifftop saying no to everything and trying to push away any semblance of her old life. The ground underneath her was giving way, and if it crumbled before she figured out how to step back and look around, she was going to fall.

What was going to save her was the spark she still held inside. He saw it clearly every time she got angry at him or when she forgot herself and laughed. It had burned the brightest when she'd asked to stay on the floor for one final dance song. That's when he'd known she wasn't really stuck in the chair. And why, when she'd done nothing tonight but throw up excuses, he'd lost his cool.

He let her shock from seeing the prosthetic so unexpectedly wear off, saying nothing but watching her face turn from white to green. He'd seen every reaction possible to his leg, from abhorrence to sympathy to interest, and everyone started out somewhere on the sliding scale of surprise. Joely also had guilt to deal with, since she'd been berating him for his unwanted advice. She didn't need to feel guilty, but her sickly looking skin wasn't from revulsion. He'd seen plenty of that, too.

Finally her cheeks soaked up a little normal color from the oxygen in her calming breaths, and Alec put a hand on Joely's thigh. He leaned forward until he could nearly touch his forehead to hers.

"You okay? You looked a little green for a couple seconds."

"I can't believe you kept that a secret. I…" She rubbed her eyes and dragged her palms down her cheeks as if to try and wipe away the emotional exhaustion from the past few moments.

"Nearly everybody who followed my rodeo career knows why it came to an end. A few don't, though, and neither do most people I meet for the first time. Depending on how long I think I'm going to be with the person, I'll let them know about it or not."

"So I'm on the 'doesn't need to know' list."

"On the contrary. It was just a matter of timing. I didn't come here tonight to show it to you."

"Why not? Wouldn't that have made our conversation a little less—"

"Snarky?"

"Maybe. I'd have had more sympathy. I'd have given you more leeway."

"Leeway to harass you?" He smiled.

She wasn't ready to smile yet. She stared at his right thigh. "I'm sorry."

"I'm not looking for sympathy. I'm not looking for anything."

"And yet, here you are, with a bionic leg and me who feels two inches tall."

"I don't like to see people give up on doing what they want to do. You had a problem for every solution tonight, and I didn't like seeing that in you."

"Oh, what do you care?" She looked down at her lap. "God, Alec, you lost your leg?"

He winked. "I guess I did. And I do care, or I'd have just kept letting you act like a little wounded bird."

"Isn't that what I am?"

"You were. Now you're just a woman with a challenge. Or two."

She ignored his micro-lecture this time. "But I couldn't tell you have a challenge. I mean you just can't tell! Even dancing."

"It wasn't easy to get to the place where anybody said that. And that's my point. You still *have* your leg. Quit whining that it doesn't work right and *make* it work."

"I don't think it's—"

"There you go again. Don't say don't. Don't say nobody understands. Don't say you need a nurse or a bus or a driver or anything else. Just say 'I want to do it myself.'"

"Look. I will never live up to what you're asking me to do. So you have your life together. Score for you. We don't even *know* each other—why are we having this mortifying conversation?"

His voice lost a little of its strident punch, and his words softened when he spoke again. What didn't change was his forthright delivery.

"Because you need a friend who won't bullshit you. You can't win this one on your looks and talent, but you can win. I only know that whoever's been helping you isn't helping you anymore."

"You don't mince words do you?"

He laughed and waggled his brows, letting a little of his swagger back in. "I only pull punches with hopeless cases. Pretty lady, you ain't one of those. And you certainly aren't an ass."

Her face went blank then, and her blue eyes dulled as if she'd shuttered them to ignore the world while she processed it. He stood up, walked to the eating area, grabbed the two bottles of cider, and returned to her. She didn't look up, but he put one bottle in her hand.

"I'd give you whiskey, but I haven't got any."

"I do."

His brows shot up again. "Seriously?"

"Our dad taught us all to drink whiskey. He might have had six girls, but by gosh they weren't going to be any sissy girlies drinking little red fruity drinks all the time." Her voice remained flat, but at least the words were about what she could do rather than what she couldn't.

"So here I bring you a wimpy drink."

"No. This is an acceptable alternative to beer. Even though we all like Scotch, we don't all like beer."

"And you?"

"In the 'like' group."

"I brew my own. My dog likes it."

"You have a dog?"

"Do you like dogs?"

"Kids born on ranches are required by law to like dogs. And horses."

"Good. Then, yes, I have an enormous dog who likes beer. And pretzels. And vegetables. It evens out."

The first glimmer of light returned to her eyes. It wasn't a spark, but the shutters were cracking open.

"What's his name?"

"Her. Rowan. An Irish wolfhound mixed with, I don't know, elephant I think."

"Sounds, uh, interesting."

"She's adorable."

Joely eyed him skeptically. "Really? You said 'adorable'?"

"Even one-legged soldiers can be sappy about some things."

She still wasn't ready for the joking, which she proved by letting her features close down again.

"How much of your leg?" The question came out in a near whisper.

"Did I lose?"

She nodded and swallowed, her hands folded in her lap, her gaze not quite steady on him.

"From seven inches below my knee."

"I'm sorry."

"Don't be. It's been three and a half years. I'm used to it."

"So tell me. What am I supposed to do with this knowledge—that you're the better man? Am I supposed to magically change my attitude and be a new person? Suddenly everything is amazing and golly gosh I can do this after all?"

One of her hands clutched the neck of her cider bottle, the other the plastic arm of her wheelchair. Both sets of knuckles shone white through the skin as if she held onto what was familiar for dear life.

"First thing is down that drink. Give yourself a nice little relaxing buzz this once, and then swear to me you'll never drown your sorrows in alcohol again. That's another thing I have the moral authority to lecture on—it doesn't work."

She took a swig and he followed suit, letting the tart-sweet fizz of the fermented apples slip easily down his throat.

"What if I want you to leave so I can process all this?"

"Then I'm out of here. No questions. No hard feelings." He started to stand.

"I didn't say that's what I wanted for sure."

He relaxed back into the cushions. "Okay. Then what you do next is nothing. Or you ask me questions. Or you make a list of the ten things you have to do first to get ready to move. And you talk to Gabe. Helping people through this kind of thing is what he does."

Her new brother-in-law was a patient advocate at the hospital here on the VA complex. In fact, being her advocate was what had led him to Mia. He definitely knew his way around the system.

"He'll know soon enough," she said. "He's a gem, and I wouldn't have gotten through this without him, but he's so busy right now. He and Mia are building their house, and while Harper and Cole are gone, they're running the ranch, too. Plus he has the veterans and the wild horses."

Gabe ran a special program for veterans suffering from PTSD and traumatic brain injuries. He and Mia had discovered that working with wild mustangs held almost magical healing powers with the vets, but administrating the program took up hours of time.

"You probably don't know my connection to Gabe yet, either," Alec said.

"Just that you were army buddies."

"He was my CO during my first tour in Iraq. He was already home here when I went back to the Middle East for the second time as a civilian contractor in 2012, but he searched me out when I came back wounded. They transferred me here from Minneapolis, and he was a godsend. I was where you are now only twice as deep into my hole. He set me and one other guy up in housing and got us looking for jobs. He got the idea for the intensive small group program he runs from those first six months with us."

"You inspired him."

"Nah, he inspired us. And created success out of nothing with guys like me. That's all I want to pass on—a little of what I learned. And the first lesson is—ask for help but don't expect it—ask for exactly what you need, not a genie to generally fix everything."

"After knowing me for the equivalent of hours you've decided that? You must think I'm a stunningly horrible person."

"I think you're stunning, period. And confused. And scared. You don't even know what to ask for."

She didn't reply. For a long time neither of them said another word. He had no way of knowing what was going through her head, but he had time to study her. He could see the former beauty queen in her thin frame. Based on the pictures he'd seen, she'd lost weight after her accident and hadn't recovered yet. Not that he judged anyone on body score—he'd evolved that far since his youth. Still, he hadn't lied to her when he'd told her she was stunning. Slight and bordering on waiflike though she was, Joely still had the curves to spark a man's libido and an underlying strength that she hid but made her intriguing as a mystery.

It had been a long time since he'd allowed a woman to capture his interest. He had no appetite anymore for his "Mayhem" days or the parade of women who'd loved cowboys and stroked his ego. He also had no interest in the closeness of a one-woman relationship. You had to put your heart on the line in a relationship, and you had to protect it. He was done being in the position of protecting someone he loved. When he loved someone, they always ended up lost to him. His interest in Joely stemmed from nothing more than their similar injuries and his desire to help her get her life back the way Gabe and so many others had helped him. The quivers of pleasure that seemed to grow stronger each time he looked at her were just a bonus. He could appreciate satiny, dark blonde hair, long-lashed blue eyes, and a laugh that rang like an angel's as much as any man.

"You're right." Her voice barely crossed the short distance between them. "I *don't* know what to ask for. I need to tell my family what's going on, but they'll just fuss and hover, and I hate that."

"That's a good start, not wanting your family to fuss. So—decide exactly what you do want. Right now you say you don't want to put anyone out and you don't want hovering, but you're waiting for them to come to you anyway and suggest solutions. Ask them for the things you want and nothing else."

"I don't know what I want."

"Sure you do. You want to be able to do what you did before. So, make a list."

Another very long silence descended, and Alec said nothing to make her hurry. He'd lectured her enough for one night, and if he ever wanted to see her again he would be leaving soon.

"I think I might want to be alone."

Even though her words mirrored his thoughts, they still stung coming from her first. This was different from him having the foresight and courtesy to leave on his own. He nodded and worked to keep his features easy and pleasant.

"I can understand."

"I'm sorry. It's rude. I just…I don't know."

His disappointment vanished. Misery and confusion filled her face, and he'd put it there. He remembered well the feeling of despair when he'd first confronted the need to quit feeling sorry for himself and make his life work again. He stood, took the bottle of cider from her hand, and set it on a little end table beside the couch. As gently as if he were scooping up two baby birds, he took her hands. They disappeared into his grasp, and he rubbed his thumbs over her knuckles, amazed at the soft skin and dismayed by their limp fragility. She'd been so sure and alive at the wedding. For all too short a time she'd been strong and free. He prayed she'd find the strength again soon.

"You have so much to think about. Don't worry. I can promise you things will work out."

"You would know."

"Joely." He made her look at him. Her eyes revealed only exhaustion. "I didn't reveal my leg to lord it over you or make a statement about moral authority. You have to do things because you want to, not because I said there's only one way to do them."

"Okay."

He squeezed her hands and set them back in her lap. "I don't suppose I cleared up the bad blood. But I did learn that I admire you. You're strong."

For the first time in long minutes her eyes flashed to life.

"You know what I hate more than anything? Platitudes and patronizing. So stop it."

He held up his hands in surrender. "You're right. I am sounding like a kindergarten teacher. Fine. Buck up, Joely Crockett. Get out of your wheelchair seat and get a life."

He grinned at her wide eyes. She didn't look happy, but she didn't look like a lost kitten either.

"I hate you a little bit," she said.

"Good. Passion."

A small sound, a little like a snort, made its way from her throat. Alec started toward the door. "Want me to put the chicken away?"

"No."

"Okay." He turned. "One thing before I go. Tell me the top three things on that list you're going to make."

"What?"

"What do you want to do next?"

"Want or have to?"

"Sometimes they're the same."

"Get you out the door." She hid the tiniest of smiles. "Sign the papers."

"Excellent."

"And find the impossible new place to live."

"Easy one." He continued to the door. "Come and live with me."

"Aren't you hilarious?" Her cheeks flushed with full color again, and the blue in her eyes had blossomed back into a deep sapphire. She was watching his gait as he moved away. Good. She wasn't shying from the idea of his missing leg—she was curious. "Not in this galaxy or the next, Cowboy."

He wiggled his brows. "Okay. See you in the one beyond that."

ALEC PULLED INTO the garage of the L-shaped, ranch-style house he'd closed on less than a month before. Knowing he owned the place still awed him, although some days he wondered what had possessed him to leap so quickly into a more or less permanent spot, in a town that would only remind him every day of what he didn't want to do anymore.

The only answer was Gabe Harrison. Now that they were no longer CO and soldier, or mentor and mentee, Gabe was a good friend. When he'd turned Alec on to a perfect, decent-paying but mindless job that could lead to other opportunities but held no pressure, Alec had been hard pressed to say no. Pressure was no longer his thing. And then he'd seen this place and he'd been sold. No apartment building would have allowed his freakishly large dog, and the house had been finished and upgraded to perfection before the owners had defaulted on their mortgage. So, it had been affordable and, most important of all, the half-acre yard was fenced. Rowan the moose-dog was thrilled.

The instant he touched the garage-to-house door-knob, Rowan's thumping-bass woof resounded and her big nails clacked along the hardwood floor as she trotted to meet him. He braced himself and wondered randomly if Joely's required-by-genetics love of dogs would extend to a lummox like the one he lived with. She was friendly, loyal, and wouldn't hurt a rabbit. She was also six five when she stood on her back legs. Something the dog did too often.

A lot of people who claimed to be dog lovers cowered when they met shaggy, massive Rowan.

He pushed open the door and spread his arms, priming himself as he did every day to catch the hair-covered cannon ball that launched itself at his chest. Her front paws landed on his shoulders, and her cool, wet nose nudged his neck, cheek, ear, and eyes, looking for hello kisses. Alec scratched the sides of her head and nuzzled her, finally pushing her to the ground once she'd had a plenty good greeting.

"Hullo, Dum-ro, I was just talking about you."

Rowan backed away once she'd assured herself he was home to stay. She trotted toward his back deck door and waited.

"The girl I was with said you sounded 'interesting.' I don't think she imagines you as very cute, so she's going to have to meet you and get straightened out. What do you say?"

The visit with Joely hadn't gone as he'd planned. He didn't regret a single thing he'd said to her, and he was relieved to have the prosthetic reveal out of the way. He hadn't planned on the night being such a thorough onslaught, though. Getting her to see him again was going to take some fancy talking. Fortunately he was pretty good at bullshit.

There was one problem. He wasn't bullshitting when it came to Joely. From the start he hadn't been able to think of her with the same casual insouciance he did most women. There'd been no meaningless flirting on his part—at least, not after the first five minutes of talking to her. And she definitely hadn't flirted with him, so he hadn't had to feign interest the way he'd had to do with, say, that woman Heidi.

He let Rowan out the back door and stepped out after her.

No. From those first moments, when he'd found Joely alone in her family's dining room, his interest had been genuine. It wasn't like him. He hadn't let himself analyze why.

"C'mon, Rowan. C'mon, girl. Bring it here!"

The giant dog was snuffling around her favorite ball and knew full well what "bring it here" meant. For the moment, however, she ignored him. Alec rubbed his thigh above the prosthetic and imagined removing the socket and sleeve sooner rather than later. He could almost always go an entire day and be fine, but once in a while he had a day where it took nothing to get the leg and its stump aching and burning with pain. It had taken all his grit to walk normally out of Joely's little apartment.

Pride. Sometimes it was stupid, but most of the time it served him well.

Joely Crockett needed a little more pride and a little less self-pity.

It was funny, though. Her self-pity didn't extend to purposefully making other people wait on her. She seemed able to embrace her solitude until she could hitch a ride on other peoples' plans. He'd decided she was no diva. She'd simply lost who she'd been before the accident.

A soggy, stained softball hit his right foot, and Rowan wiggled her body in front of him like a hairy exotic dancer. Alec laughed again. She'd give him five or six good retrieves before her interest was exhausted. They had these ten minutes of undisciplined exuberance each time he returned home, and then his beast turned into the world's most talented couch potato. For as big and fast as she could be, she was quite a medium-energy dog.

After the fifth ball toss, Rowan let the ball lie where it landed and started her routine mosey around the yard. Five minutes later Alec let her in the house and handed her a giant bone biscuit, which she accepted with enthusiasm and took to the middle of the living room floor to crunch with surprisingly ladylike dignity.

It was only seven thirty, and since he hadn't ended up eating much with Joely, he searched his cupboard, found a can of disgustingly wonderful Beefaroni, and popped the easy-open lid. While it nuked, he grabbed two pieces of bread—whole wheat, his only concession to nutrition— and smeared them both with peanut butter. When the microwave dinged he grabbed a beer, the local craft brew he'd decided beat Budweiser all to hell, took his bowl, sandwich, and brew to the den off the living room and sat.

Beefaroni and beer with his dog. Not as pleasurable as fried chicken with a beautiful woman but still satisfying in a knuckle-dragging bachelor kind of way. He'd long ago accepted that social refinement wasn't his strong suit. Proof: he should have picked up steak and strawberries and champagne for Joely. Maybe that would have been more impressive.

He settled into the couch and put his leg up. Resting it gave him enough relief that he decided he could scarf down the food before changing clothes and taking off the prosthetic.

Tough. Yeah, he was such a tough guy. Too damn lazy to move any more, at least at the moment, was closer to the truth. He was tired.

And, after half the Beefaroni and half the bottle of beer were gone, he knew he was also mildly depressed. Maybe he did regret a little bit the way he'd gone after Joely.

No. You know you needed the same kind of tough love three years ago. Somebody had to do it for her.

But still. You got more flies with honey. She was a girl—you had to be more gentle than with a stubborn, angry cowboy.

She's tough. I can tell by...

By how? He frowned to himself. What made him think he knew her so well?

Call her.

Oh no. He wasn't going to be one of those panty-waist guys. He wasn't needy. He did what had to be done.

Tell her you're sorry you got tough with her. That you know she'll be just fine. That—

His cell phone ringing halted the argument with himself. For one second his heart gave a hopeful skip. Maybe thinking of her had conjured a call from Joely. It took only one second more to realize that was ridiculous on its face and another second to answer without checking the caller ID.

"Alec Morrissey," he said.

"Well, slap my ass with a junk yard saddle. It is you, you one-legged freak. Where the hell have you been?"

The voice stunned him nearly into silence.

"Vince?" he asked. "Damn, is that you?"

"Me and about ten more pounds since I saw you last. Holy shit, man, it's good to hear your voice. Do you know how long I've been looking for you?"

A little guilt and a great deal of regret sliced quickly through Alec's gut. Aside from his cousin, Buzz, Vince Newton had been his best friend within the rodeo community since high school. A bull rider to Alec's bronc rider, Vince had always complemented Alec's talents and vice versa. For a season, after Buzz had decided to re-up for a second tour in Iraq and Alec couldn't get his butt out of the Middle East fast enough, he and Vince had tried to start something new—a partnership in team roping that would lead them into other events and competition for all-round honors. But Vince wasn't a roper, and the stress of trying to be what they weren't had strained their friendship. They'd both dropped the idea like nuclear waste and so rescued their relationship.

They'd stayed close until Alec had made his own insane trip back into the belly of the Iraqi beast and come home one limb lighter with a chip on his shoulder the size of a bomb blast. He'd let a lot of things slip away while creating his new life.

"Oh man, so long. It's been three years at least. My fault, totally, I admit it. How'd you find me now?"

"I live in the area, too, bro'. Came back about a year ago. I happened to hear your name in town the other day, and someone said you'd moved just outside of Jackson. I just dug until someone was willing to give up your number."

"Aw, hell, Vince, that's great. I'm glad you did. So where are you?"

"East, about fifteen miles out of Jackson. Got me a little spread—forty acres. I'm raising some bucking bulls and breeding some broncs. Got me some chickens, some dogs, and a kid."

"A what? What the devil are you talkin' about, boy?"

"Remember that cute little bunny used to hang around us—Wendy?"

"'Course I do."

"I married her. Then I knocked her up—in the right order and with her permission, I might add."

"No way! You son of a gun."

Alec grinned to himself. Vince had never been the best-looking cowboy on the circuit, but he'd certainly had more than enough charisma to make up for it. If their circle of friends had been a high school class, Vincent Newton would have been voted "Most Likely to Date Every Girl on the Planet and Never Marry."

"Yeah. Nobody believed it when it happened."

"How the mighty have fallen."

"Nah. You'll never get me to admit that. I've got me a little girl name of Olivia Beatrice who thinks I'm a hundred feet tall." Pride, so thick Alec could have grabbed it from the line and spread it on bread, oozed from Vince's voice.

"A little girl," Alec said. "That's fantastic. I hope she looks like Wendy."

"Jerk. She does."

His old friend's chuckle warmed him. Alec rubbed the inside of his left knee. "It's great to hear you so happy. You still riding at all?"

There was a slight pause. "Some. Mostly low-level stuff. A little individual calf roping."

"What? You suck at that."

"Yeah, but I gotta tell you. It's damn hard climbing on the back of a bull when you've got a sixteen-month-old whose mama is teaching her to pray Daddy comes home safely. Shakes your sense of immortality."

"Huh." Alec snorted in appreciation. "I never took you for a smart man, Newton. Did a bull finally throw you hard enough to knock some sense into your head?"

"Nope. Roped and hog-tied by the love of two good women."

"Okay—enough. I don't want hear anymore girlie-novel shit come out of that mouth. Let's leave it at I'm happy for you."

"And that leads me into one reason I called. I'm hoping you've had time to get back into the scene again. You figure out that gimp leg of yours enough to get back on a horse?"

Alec's throat squeezed shut and a pain in his chest he hadn't felt in a year throbbed like a fresh wound. He'd known rodeo would catch back up with him sooner or later. He'd known this was a dangerous place to settle. In his deepest heart, however, he'd believed he'd had time to brace for impact.

"I've been on a horse." He managed to push the words past the fist squeezing his larynx. "Just no bucking ones."

"So...you're trying to tell me I won the bet."

"There was no bet, butthead. I told you—"

"You told me you'd ride that horse one day or die trying."

"That horse" was a blue roan appaloosa gelding, sweeter than a day at your grandma's unless a person even thought about putting weight on its back. A saddle blanket on that animal's back would flip the switch that turned him into the embodiment of his name: Ghost Pepper.

"I wimped out of that bet. I admitted it. I accept it."

"And I told you, a bet's a bet."

Alec could hear the laughter behind Vince's words. The man was on his way to making some point, but Alec had no clue what it was. After three years all contracts were null and void as far as he was concerned. Besides, it was far too late to collect on the bet. Ghost Pepper had to be in his late twenties now and retired to some beautiful pasture with other equine greats. Or he could be dead. That was a real possibility.

"What was the wager anyway?" Alec tried to make light of the wager he knew perfectly well. "A case of Bud? Hell, let's settle up. It's on me."

"You can buy me a case of beer anytime you want, bro'."

Alec sighed. Was his oaf of a friend seriously still going to make a stink about the hat? His stomach dropped at the thought. The hat was sacred. It rested in a plain white box on his closet shelf, and he wasn't about to give it up for the sake of a bar bet made ten years before under the influence of too many tequila shots.

A flash of annoyance surprised but galvanized him. It was Buzz's hat. He was Buzz's cousin. Damn it all, the hat wasn't going anywhere.

"Hey, Vince, look," he said, "you know it's great to talk to you, but what's this really about? I don't ride broncs anymore, it's not physically possible. Ghost Pepper is long gone and—"

"Oh ho, buddy, that's where you're wrong."

"Oh?" Alec asked warily.

"Ghost Pepper is very much alive and, literally, kicking. Wanna know how I know?"

"I'm on the edge of my seat."

"I'm lookin' at him."

Alec sat back in his chair, stunned. He hadn't expected that. "'Scuse me?"

"He's eating like a horse right outside my barn. Gorgeous, sweet-tempered, and talented as ever. And I want you to come over here and learn how to ride him."

Chapter Seven

"ALMOST HOME, SWEETHEART. How are you feeling?"

Joely smiled at her mother, who sat in the passenger seat of her pickup truck clearly happy to be on Crockett land again. They were still nearly fifty driving miles from Rosecroft, but her mother's face had finally lost the drawn, devastated shadows of grief that had lined it for the past three weeks. They'd flown the 960 miles to Los Angeles from Jackson twenty days ago, to take care of packing and sorting Joely's belongings, fighting twice with an angry Tim, quitting her part-time job and her volunteer positions, and packing up her beloved Penny along with the mountains of tack and equipment that went with owning a champion barrel racing horse.

Now they were on the final few miles of a marathon drive back to the ranch—the empty ranch since her father was no longer there. Still, both she and her mom couldn't wait to be home. Joely was determined to make this move *the most positive thing she'd ever done. Taking over management of Paradise Ranch would be good for her. She could do it with Cole's help. With Leif and Bjorn's help. With her mother's help. It wouldn't matter that Paradise was in financial trouble—they would turn things around. Her life was about to turn around—she could feel it. She pressed the accelerator down a fraction of an inch. The big Ford pulled the three horse trailer so easily—especially with only one horse in it. The speedometer in the truck crept toward eighty—far too fast, but this part of the highway, cutting through the southeast corner of Paradise, was always deserted. They were almost home.*

A voice from somewhere outside her head, as if she were dreaming, screamed at her to let up on the gas. She laughed. Just this once she was going to live free, not be rule-bound.

"I'm doing fine, Mom," she replied. "How about you? You don't seem to mind coming back."

"It's hard, but it's where I want to be. My goodness, that's quite the load he's carrying up ahead."

Finally Joely eased on the brakes slightly. The semi and flatbed was still a ways ahead, but the pile of logs it hauled extended above the semi's cab. Joely checked the stretch of board-straight road ahead and saw nothing. She could pass the log truck—they were catching up quickly to the slow-moving vehicle.

She turned on her blinker and saw the first chain snap just as the bloink-bloink of the turn signal sounded. Someone outside her head screamed again. The chain flailed in the air like a drug-crazed rattlesnake.

"Brakes, Joely," her mother said. "I don't like the look of that."

"Let's just get past him. I don't like it either."

She had no time for either choice. A second chain snapped. She could hear the angry explosion of the two metal snakes biting into one another. And then the world turned into a series of flashes that made no sense. Flying bark, a horrendous grinding crash, a spine-snapping dead stop, smashing glass, the rings of a tree's cross section so close she could almost count them.

The voice screamed again. Her mother.

"Mom? Mom?"

Nothing

Voices and snips of words. Excruciating pain as strong hands rolled her onto something very stiff and hard. She couldn't move her head. Blackness.

"The horse won't live."

The screaming from outside her head again. Crying.

"Don't let her die."

Had she said that out loud? Who? Her mother or her horse? Wait. The horse won't live? What did that mean? Blackness.

Chopping air, loud, percussive. Blue sky moving above her until, suddenly, blades of metal spun into her vision, making her dizzy. Helicopter rotors. Then a lift and a jolt. Pain sliced through her, slashing every atom in her body. A ceiling with little strips of green neon lights.

This had to be what an alien abduction looked like.

"Joely, can you hear me?"

Slowly the green lights and the gentle voice she didn't recognize faded into a gray fog. She struggled. And once again came the screaming from somewhere beyond herself.

"Joely? Joely, honey, wake up. You're okay, you're safe."

She sat straight up and grabbed… "Mia?" Joely gasped in relief. This was reality. Mia hadn't been in the accident.

"You're okay," Mia said again.

In a miraculous rush, Joely's brain cleared and the memories faded; the dream became a dream. She was not in a medivac helicopter. She was in her room. In her apartment. Mia was staying overnight. Yes. Helping her pack. She breathed more easily.

And then the embarrassment slammed her. That, too, was familiar after waking many an orderly or night care nurse over the past months.

Sobbing racked her head to toe. "I'm sorry, Mia. So sorry."

"For what? There's nothing to be sorry for."

"For being so stupid. These dreams are ridiculous."

"They aren't. They're helping you cope, believe it or not. Your mind is letting the images out so you can eventually let them go. Don't try to hold them back. This is why you need to come home and not go off on your own. It's time to be there with us and forget moving into town."

"No! This is exactly the reason I'm not coming back. I can't stand putting this burden on others. I need to stay in my own space where my dreams and my body won't be in anyone's way."

"For crying out loud." Mia took Joely's face in her palms. "Listen to me. That's asinine, honey. You can't bother us. One for all and all for one. It's truer now than ever."

"Not according to Alec Morrissey."

"Alec? What does he have to do with this?"

"He has a prosthetic leg."

"Uh. Yeah?" Mia knotted her brows, clearly needing an explanation for the non sequitur.

"I didn't know about it. Not until a week ago when he told me I needed to quit whining and stop waiting for everyone to help me, and then he yanked up his pant leg with no warning."

"My goodness, how dramatic." She didn't sound like she thought it was the least bit out of line. "And he told you to quit whining? In those words?"

"Pretty much."

"Of all the arrogance." Mia grinned.

"Oh, nice. Some sisterly support. What are you smiling about?"

"Believe me, I think Alec Morrissey *is* maybe a little arrogant. But in this case, he's right. Or partially so. It's true you can't just wait for people to help you. You do have to buck up and make your own decisions."

Mia's words stung even more than Alec's had. A single, embarrassed tear burned at the corner of Joely's eye. Mia ran one thumb beneath it.

"Why do you think I'm moving to my own place?"

"I didn't mean you've been whining, Jo-Jo. Alec was not right about that. You never whine, but you don't tell us honestly what you need either. We *want* you to ask for help. We want you to come home and start learning to be independent around people who love you."

"And take up even more of everyone's time and energy? Confirm that I'm a demanding person who has evidently been driving everyone insane the past eight months."

"Stop it, you know better than that." Mia drew her into a hug even as she chastised. "If you haven't learned by now that none of your sisters is going to feel sorry for you, then you're an imposter Crockett who didn't grow up in our family. If you were driving us insane, we'd let you know it. Am I right?"

Joely had to concede. With the possible exception of their oldest triplet, Grace, not one of the Crockett sisters knew how to mince words. "Yes," she said, her voice small in the dark bedroom.

"Then believe that I, that *we*, adore you, and all we want is to help you take the next step in healing. If it takes arrogant Alec Morrissey to aggravate you out of your shell, then I'm a fan."

Alec Morrissey.

Every time she heard the name the most confusing mix of feelings assailed her: shivers, annoyance, happiness, despair, a deep desire to punch him…a deeper, hotter desire to try kissing him. She wondered if she had some variation of Stockholm Syndrome—finding her tormentor attractive.

With a deep breath and a long exhale that released the last of the dream's hold on her, she also released her sister.

"Do these dreams happen often?" Mia asked.

"Not dreams plural. It's always the same dream—reliving the accident." Joely wiped her eyes with steadier hands. "I guess they happen a couple of times a week."

"Have you told your therapist?"

Joely said nothing for a long moment. She'd dreaded telling Mia or Gabe what she'd been keeping secret since moving into this apartment.

"I'm not going to a therapist—not that kind. He wasn't helping."

"Oh, Joely."

"I know. I know what you're going to say—that I could have looked for someone new. That it was helping in ways I couldn't see. That I can't keep all this bottled up inside."

"That's exactly right." Mia's eyes were stern in the dim light. "And so, if you know all that, then why have you quit?"

"We were rehashing the accident. Rehashing my marriage. Rehashing my relationship with my father. I can rehash things on my own. If I know all of this is, quote, normal behavior, then I don't need a counselor to keep telling me so."

"He's there to help with problems that crop up as you go. Like dreams that won't go away. Or maybe like Alec Morrissey?"

"Oh no. I'm not talking to any therapist about a cowboy who's the model amputee to my pathetic accident victim. I was with him when he danced—he's got it all figured out. I'm still working on it."

Mia smoothed her hair. "Yes. And you're doing fine. But it's four in the morning and you're exhausted, and things seem worse than in daylight. Do you want me to stay in here with you?"

"No." Joely buried the further embarrassment Mia's question raised. She appreciated her sister's unhesitating support, but when she thought sleeping together was necessary, Joely knew she'd let her fears go too far. "I really am used to this. The dream wakes me up but it doesn't keep me awake."

"Good." Mia stood. "But I'm right in the living room if you need me."

"I know. Thanks."

The night closed around her again once Mia left the small bedroom. Small—that was the secret. She loved the compactness of her space. The fact that she never had to navigate more than a few feet and never had to make room for another person was comforting and kept her safe. Rosecroft was enormous by comparison, and it was lousy with people and sound and constant interaction. The thought of living there filled her with apprehension.

Despite her assurances to the contrary, Joely didn't find sleep in the early morning darkness, although it was true the dream wasn't the cause of her racing brain. Like Hitchcock's birds, the tasks awaiting her come morning swarmed her thoughts: wrap up her pictures, pack the last of her few dishes, clean out the refrigerator, strip the bed. Sign the stupid divorce papers.

Her heartbeat accelerated in familiar anger. She wanted nothing more than to be rid of her husband. Throughout all the trials of the past nearly four years, he'd been nothing but unsupportive, unemotional, and demeaning. He'd changed almost the day they'd returned from a dream honeymoon in Alaska. From suave, charming, and solicitous, he'd become critical and demanding.

Now he wanted to keep everything in the house she'd worked so hard to make a home. Granted, she'd been gone for nearly three-quarters of a year, and if the new love of her husband's life had been living in the house, then Joely didn't want much. She wished there were some way to make him pay a little and prove he, not she, had been the wrong-doer. But there was nothing. She had no power over him.

It took a full hour to calm the whirling inside her brain and finally drift off into a dreamless sleep. Dreamless until pictures of Alec Morrissey floated through her mind in montages of male beauty—wide cheekbones, thick sandy brows, tousled hair with the barest touch of wave to it. And a smile that could probably have solved the Middle East crisis. A beautiful, impish, sincere, forthright smile that was as confusing as her feelings for his sudden presence in her life.

When she swung her legs to the side of her bed in the morning and reached for her walker, she stopped and looked down at her pajama-clad thighs. Beneath the cotton fabric, her left thigh had a scar to match the one on her face. The shattered patella had been repaired, but the two main calf muscles—the larger gastrocnemius and the inner soleus—were crushed and had atrophied to the point where the injury's aftereffects were visible and always would be. But she couldn't see it through her pajamas.

Alec Morrissey's face was fresh in her mind, and his words echoed in her memory. "Of course you know what you want. You want to be able to do what you did before."

She did. More than anything. But she'd never race around a barrel cloverleaf or ride a reining pattern on Penny's back again. Chances were she'd never really ride at all. Still, if she was going to live on her own, she'd have to relearn a few skills. Like getting to the bathroom without a ridiculous walker.

Picturing the long, successful moments of her dance with Alec, Joely pushed the walker to the side and stood, putting ninety-eight percent of her weight on the good leg. Once she stood solidly, she increased the weight on her left leg and balanced as evenly as she could. The injured leg swung forward easily and she placed it on the floor. For several seconds she panicked, longing for the safety of the walker or crutches—or a pair of arms. Gritting her teeth, she stepped fully onto the leg and rushed the other forward, keeping herself from stumbling with sheer willpower.

The second step was just as difficult, but the third and then the fourth were more coordinated. She counted the halting, shuffling steps as if they were advances up a cliff side. Six. Seven. Eight did her in.

Her left calf gave out when she took too long a step. With a grunt and a failed grab at the door jamb, she ended on the floor in a heap after a fall as graceless as the one she'd performed at the wedding dance.

"Joely?" Mia appeared within seconds. "Oh, God, what happened?"

"Seems fairly obvious to me."

"Are you all right?"

"No." Aggravation and embarrassment poured into her voice. "I'm an idiot. I need everyone to stop putting ideas into my head about what I should do and what I need and let me do things my own way."

"C'mon." Mia held out her hand and stooped to put her other arm around Joely's body. "Let's get you up."

Joely slapped her hands away. "No! I can do this. Just let me get to the doorway."

"Joellen." Mia's voice sliced, sharp and firm, through Joely's angry fog.

"What do you want?" Joely snapped.

"Ask for the help you need, damn it. Why are you blaming me for this? I do not think you're brave for scrabbling around on the floor by yourself."

She was so sick of weeping. Of feeling weak. Of trying to convince herself she didn't need help. Despite that, the tears fell once more. She held out her hand and let Mia pull her up. At least her sister didn't try scooping her into her arms.

"I'm sorry. I didn't mean to blame you. I was avoiding blaming myself." Half sobs made her hiccup.

"What happened?"

"I tried walking on my own." She swiped the tears angrily from her cheeks. "Seven whole steps. Wow. I had no business being so foolish."

"Really? You got seven steps on your own? Have you walked alone before?"

"No. That's the foolish part."

Mia threw her arms around her. "I think that's fantastic! Good for you."

Mia had lost her mind. "Excuse me?"

"I'm serious. *That* was brave. Now you know if something is seven steps away you can get it. But why haven't they been making you walk in PT?"

"I wouldn't let them," Joely said. "I knew this would happen."

"Then this was even more of a breakthrough. One step at a time!"

"If you utter another cliché, I might just hit you."

"Sorry." Her cheerfulness said she wasn't.

Breakfast was already on the table when Joely finally wheeled her way, dressed and subdued, into the kitchen. Eggs, bacon, English muffins with melted butter pooling deliciously in the crevices. She had no idea where her sister had come up with any of the food. The refrigerator had been stocked with little more than yogurt and juice and some milk for cereal.

"Death by cholesterol, I see. Yum," Joely said.

"Dietary rules are changing all the time. Plus you need some meat on that frame. Trust me, I'm a doctor."

"Hah. You're not. You're a bully sister."

"Thank you! I'm quite proud of that, too. It's been hard raising you five."

Joely couldn't help but laugh. Mia knew as well as each sister did how little time they'd all spent together in the past ten years. The sad but true fact was that they'd grown apart once each had left for college, and only their father's death the past August had brought them back together. Amelia was the oldest and the bossiest, and possibly the smartest, but she'd been the first to leave home. She'd seen them through teenagerhood but not much more. It was good to have her back.

"There shouldn't be that much to do today." Joely transferred deftly to the kitchen chair.

Mia nodded agreement. "We'll get the packing done and clean tomorrow."

The simple fried eggs were wonderful, and the crispy bacon crunched and melted into smoky, salt-fat deliciousness against her tongue. After her short night and inelegant start to the morning, Joely couldn't figure out why a clichéd, death-by-bacon breakfast tasted so amazing and lifted her mood. Maybe it was no more complicated than she'd survived the night and might get through the day.

The knock on her door at eight forty-five took her completely aback. Mia, on the other hand, tried to subdue a pleased smile. "Now who could that be?" she asked.

Joely started to rise and reach for her wheelchair. "Are you plotting something?"

Mia held up her hand. "I'll get it. I know you can do it, but I'm faster."

"Way to be sensitive."

"Just my famous bedside manner." Mia grinned, but when she opened the door she gasped.

All the smug expectation fled her face. Joely looked at the visitor and, with a jolt like the one that had slammed her when the log hit her car, she met the eyes of her husband. Shock fired down her spine and gripped her vocal cords, so she could neither move nor speak. It had been nine months since she'd seen him. She'd looked the afterlife in the eye at least twice, but Tim had barely troubled himself to check on her. Now he showed up? Mere days before the move that was supposed to mark her independence?

"Hello, Douchebag-in-law," Mia said, her calm back in place, her face passively pleasant.

Tim had the momentary courtesy—it certainly wouldn't be conscience in his case—to show his discomfort. He was, however, consummately suave, oozing confidence and wealth even in jeans and a polo shirt. Of course, the polo was no bargain basement rag but a dark blue luxurious knit with a hunter green collar turned up in proper preppie style and Gucci splashed liberally, if mostly tastefully, across the front between his gym-toned shoulders.

"Amelia." His jaw tensed. "Nice to see you, too."

"Oh, did I say nice?" she asked, and held the door wider. "Look, Joely. We have a surprise guest."

"Joely?" Tim's face, fairly youthful for a man nearing forty, creased in concern. "My God, honey, you're skin and bones. And your face—I had no idea how prominent that scar was. I'm so sorry."

Hot resentment burned through her chest. It didn't matter whether he was truly sorry for her injuries or sorry because she'd lost the look he'd once so cherished. She had the reckless and irrationally violent wish to bloody his nose and fancy collar with a right hook.

Sadly, she'd never honed a right hook.

"First of all, don't you ever call me honey again." She finally found her voice and rejoiced at its strength.

"Second, don't say you're sorry because I don't look the same—this didn't have to be a surprise to you. Third, what gives you the right to be standing at my door unannounced?"

He stepped past Mia, his eyes gentle but not contrite—a look Joely now recognized as patronizing and controlling. He was not tall and not beautiful, just average in height and passingly handsome. As he approached, Joely caught the salting of gray at his temples. That was new.

"Jo, I am still your husband."

He was the only person who'd ever insisted on calling her Jo. Once she'd thought it personal and intimate. Now it only fed that weird, violent desire to slug him.

"You're not my husband. Not in any way except on paper. That's bad enough."

His eyes smoked over, and the line of his mouth tightened. She'd never spoken to him like this, and a lightbulb moment sent her stomach recoiling in disgust with her old self. She'd known before her accident that she was divorcing this man—he'd cheated on her after all. But had she really once been so obsequious? Sweetly refraining from angering him so maybe he'd keep loving her? Until this moment she'd never seen what a pathetic stepping stone for his ego she'd become—and he'd expected.

"Fine," Tim said. "I can play this angry, too. If still being my wife legally only is so abhorrent, why haven't you signed the divorce papers?"

"You came from LA to Jackson to ask me that?" She allowed a sarcastic snort. "I could have answered you over the phone."

"I don't want just an answer. I want the signed papers in my hand."

"I see. Well, I'm sorry, but that's not going to happen. Not here this minute anyway. I'm not finished looking at them."

"Looking at them?" It was his turn to scoff. "Bullshit, Jo. You've had them for nearly a month. Get them, hand them over, and let's be done with this."

"Nothing would make me happier." She glared at him standing over her like an angry parent. "But you'll get them when I'm sure exactly how badly I'm getting treated in this deal, and when I've decided if I'm going to do anything about it."

"You aren't getting treated badly. You took half the household goods. You aren't entitled to another thing."

Most of the furniture Joely had removed from her Los Angeles house nine months ago had been damaged in the car accident, but she didn't go there. The accident hadn't been Tim's fault.

Then again, if he hadn't ruined the marriage she wouldn't have been driving with her living room sectional and antique china cabinet, plus the rest of her things stuffed into the front half of a horse trailer in the first place.

"I put equity into that home, too. I got some furniture, but I should get a portion of the value of that house."

"You got that in spades with the amount I put into your personal training, your riding, and that goddamn horse."

He was losing his cool as much as he ever lost it, but his eyes and his words took on a mean cast. Tears filled her own eyes in a rush as his words socked into her broken heart.

"Get out now, Tim," she said quietly. "You'll get the divorce papers when I'm ready to sign them."

She didn't know where she'd come by the ability to stand up to him without caving, but it kept her from losing her composure completely. To her surprise, he didn't get angrier. Instead, his mood flipped. He pulled out a chair and sat beside her at the table, reaching for her hands.

"Hey," Mia called. "She said 'leave,' not 'sit,' Gucci boy."

Man, she loved Mia. Joely held her hand away from him. Tim tried to take it anyway, and she pulled away, almost violently.

"No you don't," she said.

"Please. Joely. I need the papers signed." He'd gone from badgering to begging. "I didn't come to get or make you angry. I came to appeal to the beautiful, understanding side of you I always loved."

"You've got to be kidding. Gag me with a collar covered in someone else's lipstick, Tim. You don't get to mention love." She stared at him a long minute. "What's the rush after nine months of not caring whether I lived or died?"

"I cared."

"Oh, don't even."

Sadness morphed into full-fledged fury. She leaned forward, catching a glimpse of Mia's amazed, almost proud, expression. Her sister still stood by the open apartment door as if waiting for someone. Or maybe just for the chance to toss Tim Foster out on his designer logo.

"Sandra is pregnant."

The surprises he'd lobbed to that point had been annoying little grenades compared to his announcement. It fell like a ballistic missile into the heavy silence of the room. Bile rose in Joely's throat, pushed upward by a mewling choke of pain she couldn't halt.

"I'm sorry," he said and grabbed her hands, which she tried to free with frantic yanks against the fast hold. "I truly am."

"Pregnant?" She barely felt the word push past the sickness and pain in her throat.

"We want to get married. That's why I came to give you a little push."

Pregnant. Married.

She remembered with awful clarity the harsh lighting in the LA County hospital room. The fear, the grief. The aching loneliness until Tim had arrived. Fifteen weeks—a little girl, too early to be called a stillborn, but too late and large to be a simple mass of tissue cells. She'd been recognizable as a baby but hadn't really been considered one.

Then, instead of gathering her up for comfort or even saying he was sorry and sad, Tim had simply kissed her on the head. "It's for the best," he'd said. "We weren't ready."

Dear God she had been.

But it had taken *Sandra* to make him ready.

Her head went light as a helium balloon, and she bent double, resting her forehead on her knees to keep from having to hold it up. Tim tried to wrap his arms around her, but she flailed at him.

"Don't. You. Touch. Me."

Where were the stupid papers? She'd sign them now. Or as soon as she could breathe.

"Jo, come on. This is silly. We're moving forward. You and I just didn't work from the beginning. We know that. We can part friends."

From the beginning?

So her entire marriage had been a gigantic mistake? Every minute of it? She struggled again to loosen herself from Tim's hold.

"Hey, buddy, the lady asked you not to touch her."

A familiar voice cut through her pain and arrested the tears threatening to make her lose her last shred of dignity. She lifted her head and got an entirely different kind of shock than the ones she'd been experiencing the past fifteen minutes.

"Alec?"

What on earth was he doing here? She remembered Mia's earlier anticipation.

"Good morning, darlin'," he said. "Ready to drive me to breakfast?"

Chapter Eight

DRIVE YOU TO *breakfast?*

She stared so long without speaking that Alec stepped forward, laughing, and came in close enough to her side that Tim had no choice but to release her and move out of the way. Alec kissed her on the forehead and pointed at her plate.

"You forgot, didn't you?"

He played the part—which he'd clearly made up on the spot—perfectly.

She got it. He was making an extemporaneous rescue. And although his lightning-quick adlibbing was impressive, she wanted to punch him almost as much as she did Tim. How arrogant were these two? One figured all he had to do was rant and posture and she'd cave; the other assumed she needed his machismo to save her.

"Don't worry," Alec continued, soothing but not, at least, patronizing. "It's understandable. We planned it last minute—just a working breakfast. Remember now?"

She shoved away the old grief and the new pain Tim had caused, and leveled stern eyes at Alec. "That's right. *Very* last minute. So we could work on your papers for commitment to the asylum, as I recall."

"Exactly. Because I agreed to let you drive my truck. Automatic incarceration if anyone finds out."

The man was dang quick. And her pulse nearly choked her when she processed his words. Drive his truck? He was joking, but still...

She literally opened her mouth to protest, but Tim stared at them with such confusion that she closed it. The idea of letting him think she *could* drive was too enticing. Her creep of a husband didn't need to know she had no intention of climbing behind anybody's wheel.

"What do you mean?" She pierced each man with a defiant glare. "I'm an excellent driver."

"Okay, Rain Man." Alec grinned.

"Huh?" Joely frowned.

"Dustin Hoffman? The movie *Rain Man?* He always said he was an excellent...Oh, never mind."

"Ah. Well, I missed the reference because Tom Cruise was Rain Man," she said.

"Nope. Tom Cruise called his brother Raymond 'Rain Man.' You need to study up on your movie references."

"For God's sake!" Tim stepped forward again, his face flushed in frustration. "Who is this mentally unstable person, Jo? Is he even safe to be around? I don't have time to fool around here listening to college dormitory trivia. Please just get those papers for me and sign them."

His veiled insult of Alec irritated Joely. She'd found the ridiculous movie exchange funny, but maybe that was only because Tim looked so completely put out. Alec, on the other hand, seemed unfazed by Timothy Foster.

"Hi," he said and extended his arm. "Alec Morrissey. I'm your wife's driving instructor."

Joely covered her mouth with one hand. Not many people turned Tim speechless, but he stood silently a moment, thoroughly nonplussed. Joely caught sight of Mia, who'd closed the front door, followed Alec into the living room, and watched with an almost tangible air of delight.

"What the hell? Joellen can't drive," Tim said at last. "She's in a wheelchair, for Pete's sake."

"Oh? I don't know where you got your medical degree, but a wheelchair does not necessarily correlate with an inability to drive." Alec looked toward Mia. "I think Dr. Crockett there will back me up."

"I will," she said. "Many people with physical challenges are able to drive."

Tim looked as if he'd been besieged by a troop of *mentally* challenged monkeys. He shook his head. "The papers, Joellen."

"Look." All at once, her mind was clear. Seconds ago she'd been so hurt she'd determined to hand him whatever he wanted. Now he was simply making her angry. She'd been putting off going to a lawyer, but she had to make at least one visit even though she was certain she wasn't legally entitled to anything more than he'd offered. Which was nothing. "I wish you'd called ahead. I have one more thing to do before I give you the papers. I promise I'll have them in your hands before..." She swallowed the pain for a second time. "Before your son or daughter is born."

"That's not funny," Tim said.

"Fine," she replied, her unmitigated anger at the man she'd once believed she loved making her as calm as she'd ever been around him. "I'll have them to you by the end of the week. Unless there's something I find to fight."

"There's *nothing* to fight." His partially clenched jaw made his words tight and cold.

"That's not for you to decide."

"Hear, hear." Mia spoke quietly from her perch on the arm of the living room chair, where she smiled over her words.

"I thought you were more mature than this," Tim said. "What do I have to do? Sit here and wait for you to decide you'll be an adult about it?"

"Don't you mean adult-erer?" Mia asked.

Joely nearly laughed out loud. She didn't remember Mia being so quick to sarcasm, but she loved it. Her sister had been an uptight, all-business surgeon until she'd met Gabe. This new Mia was definitely someone you wanted on your team—she was besting Tim at his own controlling game.

"Please don't stay," Joely said. "Go home to Sandra and wait for the mail."

"I didn't come here to turn around empty-handed."

"Well, you might just have to, my friend," Alec said. "Joely has an appointment with me, and I don't think either of us wants to wait while you keep arguing with her. If she said she'll have what you want on Friday, she'll have it. I know that about her." He held out his hand to her and smiled. An easy, fool-anyone smile that made her knees weak. She could have kicked herself for putting her hand in his, and yet it felt so good—on more than one level. "Ready?" Alec asked. "Let's grab your things and go. We can show Mr. Foster out on our way."

She hesitated. Why was Alec really here? Joely couldn't make her brain function at a level higher than stupefaction. What did she do now? She wasn't going with Alec to make good on some seat-of-the-pants ruse, but if she called him on his playacting, she'd look like an idiot in front of Tim. He'd already made a fool of her and her marriage.

"Sure," she said, before she could stop herself. "My purse and sweatshirt are in the bedroom."

"I'll get them." Mia stood and beamed at her and Alec as she passed.

Joely narrowed her eyes. There was going to be a little "Come to the Lord" meeting later. Her life wasn't one people could just manipulate.

And yet she let Alec pull her smoothly to a stand.

"Chair, crutches, or arm?" He crooked his elbow and spoke as if he knew every nuance of her normal routine.

She eyed her bedroom, the bathroom, and the front door.

Seven steps. She could probably get to the bathroom.

You're going to regret this.

"Let me run and brush my teeth," she said. "Then I'll use the crutches."

Run? Five minutes ago she would have bitten someone's head off for using that word in reference to her. Was showing off to Tim really worth this? Even Alec looked surprised when she extracted her hand from his and steadied herself.

"Sure," he said.

It took more effort to try to keep the concentration from showing on her face than it did to cross the tiny room to the bathroom door. One step, three steps, five steps. Her muscles quivered. Her breath came in quiet, heavy puffs, but she held it when she passed Tim so he wouldn't hear.

She grabbed the doorknob as if it were a life preserver, shuffled her last steps into the bathroom and closed the door. With a barely stifled groan she sank onto the toilet seat and rested her arms on her thighs, embarrassed for the first time by how little she'd allowed her physical therapy to really help her the past few months. She was in worse cardio shape than Grandma Sadie.

For two long minutes she sat and calmed her racing heart, got back her breath, and tried to decide if she could possibly make it back to her wheelchair. Forget the crutches. She also tossed out a prayer that Tim would be gone when she reopened the door, and she wouldn't have to continue with this ridiculous theater at all.

Finally she stood and picked up her toothbrush. Then she forced herself to look in the mirror. Her scar jumped out as it always did, and Tim's words jumped through her heart right with it. "And your face...I had no idea..."

Of course not. He hadn't cared enough to come. Tears beaded in her eyes as she jabbed her toothbrush into her mouth. She detested Tim Foster; why should she be crying?

She took a few extra minutes for the tears to stop. She splashed them away before smoothing a touch of makeup along her damaged jawline. With a fortifying breath she opened the door.

The tableau had changed only slightly. Mia had Joely's purse and sweatshirt on the table. Tim stood closer to the front door. Alec, God bless him, stood outside the bathroom with her crutches. He caught her eyes, and his smile held no more teasing, only empathy. Another epiphany thundered into her head. He really did understand her awkwardness and pain.

She settled the crutches beneath her arms. "Thanks," she said so only he could hear.

"No problem. Ready?"

The whole farce was ludicrous—an unnecessary exercise she wouldn't have to go through if she would simply give Tim his stupid divorce papers and send both men packing. Instead she answered him.

"Ready."

"She'll be back shortly," Alec said to Mia. "We'll run those couple of errands."

Mia nodded, playing right along. "No hurry. I'll pack up the last of the kitchen stuff and start on the bedroom."

"Sorry," Joely began.

"Nonsense. You kids have fun." She turned to Tim. "Brother-in-law, I'm guessing that's the last time I'll call you by that name, you have a fun flight back to the land of people who don't deserve my sister."

He ignored her as he had for most of the visit. "I'm staying in Wolf Paw Pass until I have the papers."

"I'm sorry to hear that."

Alec opened the apartment door and inclined his head to Tim. "After you."

Joely hung back while Tim left and watched him stride arrogantly down the hall. When he was out of earshot she turned to Alec.

"Just let him go. We don't have to follow him. This is ridiculous."

"It is," he said, "but he'll be waiting because he's a blowhard. He knows he's a dickhead. He's just not about to admit it."

"Don't be crude," Joely said. "I prefer Douchebag. It's slightly more refined."

He laughed. "Why it should matter I don't know. He's both."

"Let's go. But I'm not driving any truck. I seriously can't drive."

"You can. It's your left leg that's injured. This is an automatic so you can do what needs to be done with your right."

"I'm not driving."

"Okay."

Alec was right, Tim waited for them outside. When Joely lurched her way to Alec's truck on the crutches she had never let herself get used to, Tim watched her with focused, fox-like eyes. He seemed to take her all in when she stopped a few feet from where he stood.

"Interesting," he said.

"What do you want?" she asked. "Besides the papers. Which you'll get."

"You led me to believe you were completely incapacitated, and that's why you were so desperate to stay under my benefits as long as you could. I'm not seeing the immobile invalid I expected to find. Have you been freeloading off of me, Jo?"

To her surprise, Alec tensed beside her even before she could clench her own fists. He took a step toward Tim and lowered his head like a bull warning of a charge.

"I've been pretty civil with you," he said. "But you're stepping over the line, buster."

Tim laughed in his face. "Me over the line? I've been nothing but generous with a woman who seems to be taking advantage."

"Look here, assh—"

"Stop!" Joely grasped Alec's arm and tugged. "Don't stoop to that, Alec. Tim, it's time for you to leave. I'm not even going to enlighten you with the truth. You never made a single attempt to find it out for yourself. So think what you want. We're done except for the partying."

With that she whipped open her purse and pulled out the thick, folded sheaf of papers. Tim's eyes widened like he was seeing the Holy Grail.

"You want them? Will it get rid of you so I can tell myself this is the last I'll see of you?" She dug for a pen, and while she did, Alec took the papers from her hand. "Hey!" she said.

"You're not handing them over under these circumstances. You haven't let him bully you yet. Don't let him start."

"This is none of your business." She reached for the papers, and he let her grasp them but held one end as well.

"It's not. And I'm not saying what you should do with them other than hang on until you decide what to do. He shouldn't get to say."

"Now who's being the ass?" Tim said, derision dripping from his words.

"It's still you," Alec replied. "But even so, if fifteen minutes from now Joely still wants to sign these and give them to you, I'll drive her to your hotel myself."

"I thought *she* could drive."

"Yeah, but it'll get rid of you faster if I do it."

Tim finally gave up. With a snort and an angry mutter he shook his head and turned for his car. "I need those in my hand within twenty-four hours," he said without looking back.

"Or what, Tim? You'll take me for all I've got? You've pretty much done that."

He left the parking lot in his rented Lexus and Joely sagged with relief.

"*Hasta la vista*, baby," Alec said with a curl of his lip.

"Thank you, Lord," Joely added. "Now I don't need to pretend to drive anything."

"No, I think you should anyway," he said.

"Excuse me?"

"Truck's right here. Climb in."

He pointed to a gorgeous, royal blue, Ram pickup. With an extended cab, polished aluminum hubcaps, and a luxury trim package, it was enough to make any cowgirl who'd ever pulled a horse trailer catch her breath. Joely's caught and stuck as she imagined this beauty smashed to oblivion on the highway.

"No way," she said.

"Just sit in it."

"No. Because I know what would come next. One little push after another until you make me try and drive. I'm not ready."

"Stop your whining and just get in."

"Arrogant, egotistical—"

"Stubborn, mean, rude. Yeah, I've heard them all. Look, you stood up to Gucci Tim. It's time to stand up to yourself and stop getting in your own way. You've gotten this far. I'm not about to let you give up."

She stood still, confused. "What exactly are you doing here this morning?"

"Mia called me last night. She said you needed something distracting and annoying to get your mind off moving, and she thought of me."

Joely bit her lip to keep back a grin. "She actually said that?"

"She absolutely did. So how could I resist? I clearly love being somebody's most annoying person. Then I walked in, and you were wrestling with Mr. Wonderful. The rest just happened."

"I was not wrestling!"

He shrugged. "He had his hands where you didn't want them."

"True." A pang of sadness for what she'd believed had once been lanced through her heart, and the failure of it all struck her again.

"Hey." He surprised her by touching her on the cheek. "Don't mourn him."

"I'm not." She brightened with effort.

"Good. C'mon, let me help you into the truck. Give it a try."

Her pulse zigzagged anxiously through her body. "Alec, I don't think I should. I haven't been behind a wheel since…" She bit her lip again.

"Since the accident," he said for her. "And you're scared. That's normal."

"And my legs don't move fast."

"We aren't going anywhere but mostly empty roads. Come on, Joely. Be brave. For ten minutes face your fear."

"I'm not brave."

"You're wrong."

She closed her eyes and tried hard to conjure up her annoyance at him, but it had driven off with Tim. Now it was Alec she wanted to convince she wasn't a wimp. When had she transferred that need to him? With a deep breath, she nodded.

"Do you want me to help you in, give you pointers on climbing up, or just figure it out yourself?" he asked at the door of the pickup's cab. "No wrong answer.

"You're asking? I thought you just jumped in and took over."

"Normally." He laughed. "But I remember how I hated being treated like a mindless two-year-old when I was learning to walk again. I wanted constructive help, not coddling."

Her gratitude notched upward. The man was two-sided—an arrogant guy who had a true underlying layer of nice. She didn't know what to do with that. He could bowl her over and then cheer when she got angry and picked herself back up.

"Good leg on the running board," she said. "Then bad leg. Good leg in. Then bad leg."

He nodded. "Give it a go."

The hardest part was holding all her weight on the injured leg for the first step up. After that her body didn't move elegantly, but she managed to stuff herself into the driver's seat. She looked to Alec for approval, and he gave her a modest, cheerful thumbs-up. To her surprise, she found the simple acknowledgment more satisfying than the enthusiastic praise she was used to getting from her physical therapists. She hadn't climbed Denali after all; she'd gotten into a truck.

A moment later Alec slid into the passenger seat.

"Take me for breakfast dessert," he said and dangled the keys.

She almost protested again. Instead she met his gaze, and something inside gave a little twist. Unexpected courage flowed directly into her veins—maybe because he sat beside her so nonchalantly, as if she'd never crashed a car and now hadn't driven in close to a year. She took yet another deep breath, accepted the key slowly, and put it in the ignition. Before she turned it, she moved her right leg several times between the accelerator and the brake.

"You'll be fine," he said.

Her racing heart slowed a tick.

After the mirrors had been adjusted, the seat put perfectly in the right place, and her surroundings thoroughly checked, she couldn't procrastinate any longer. She put the truck in reverse, looked in the mirror, and shot backward like a bullet. With a squeal and a hard stomp on the brake, she came to a jolting halt.

"Oh, jeez," she cried.

He didn't twitch a muscle. "Nice start."

"Alec, I don't want to do this."

"Too late, you've already done it. You're fine."

"How can you be so frickin' calm? What if I smash up your truck? What if I smash you up?"

"I've ridden horses *trying* to smash me up with a lot less protection than I have in this truck. I'm not worried. And I have insurance."

He could not be this calm. It wasn't natural. Still, she remembered what a master performance he'd given this morning in front of Tim. The man must have nerves of steel.

She got out of the parking lot with only a few more jarring stops. The accelerator pedal took the lightest touch of any vehicle she'd ever driven, and combined with her unease, their forward progress would have made the rawest of student drivers look accomplished. Through it all Alec remained unperturbed.

She turned out of the VA center complex and relaxed slightly on the paved county road. A few moments of driving brought her away from the medical center's traffic, and she let out a breath she hadn't realized she'd been holding. It was seven miles to the small town of Wolf Paw Pass. She could do this. Suddenly, she was flying. In a truck, on the ground, at forty-five miles per hour, she was free as a falcon let loose to hunt.

"You're smiling."

"I'm driving," she replied.

"You are. Pretty amazing right?"

"You've been here, too, haven't you? Feeling this."

"Took me six months after the accident. I had a six-speed Mazda, and I had to give it up because of the clutch. That was a big hurdle for me. I still miss driving a manual transmission. I could, but it's just not as slick or quite as quick and safe with no feeling in the foot. I finally chose to compromise. And that made the difference. I found out that being able to drive is a big step in recovery."

She could definitely see that. If she could drive, she could—

She cut off her thoughts. She had no vehicle. She had no way to pay for insurance even if a car magically appeared in front of her. And just because she might be able to drive somewhere didn't mean she could do anything once she arrived. This was jumping far ahead of herself.

Nonetheless, the feeling of having wings made her just a little bit high.

The semi appeared in front of her after she rounded a gentle curve in the mountain road. With a screech she slammed the brake and banged forward into her seatbelt. Beside her, Alec's torso took a similar jolt.

"Whoa!" He gave the first sound of surprise since they'd started.

There was more than plenty of room between her and the big truck, and she managed to keep from stopping fully, but the calm joy she'd begun to feel vanished, replaced by a white-knuckle grip caused as much by embarrassment as fear.

"I'm so sorry," she said, barely loud enough for him to hear.

"You know why that happened, right?" he asked.

"Yes," she said, her voice sharp. "Because I'm not ready for this."

"No." He returned to calm. "This would have happened even six more months from now. Your brain has to remember that bad things don't happen every time there's traffic. It's trying to protect you—just tell it you're fine. You'll remember now that semis and trailers appear."

"You're making this pop psychology crap up," she said.

He grinned. "But it makes perfect sense, right?"

She blew a huge breath slowly through her lips. "Yeah. I admit it. I saw logs rolling at me."

"Don't bury the fear—recognize it and move on."

"What fear did you have to move on from?"

"Same things. Vehicles appearing from nowhere. People jumping out from places I didn't expect. Loud noises."

"That's awful."

"It's what professional help is for. War sucks, but soldiers don't have to stay damaged."

"I will try to be more like you." She fixed her eyes on the road, humbled and slightly overwhelmed by his attitude. How did you get through trauma like his with such a perfect attitude?

"Oh, honey, don't do that. Be more like you."

That was good advice, too, she supposed, but too easy to say. She didn't bother telling him that her very few marketable skills had been taken away in the accident. What did a barrel racing former Miss Wyoming turn to when she'd turned to rodeo and beauty pageants in the first place because her childhood dreams were unrealistic?

Whatever it was, she had to find it soon—or live off her sisters' good will for the rest of her life.

Melodrama. She'd always been told she was good at it.

They reached Wolf Paw Pass five minutes later, and Joely let the self-pity go in favor of concentrating on small-town driving. She progressed to comfort more quickly than she had in the parking lot as she cruised down familiar Mountain Street, the town's main drag. Wolf Paw Pass had changed over the decades and grown from a tiny town of six hundred to double that thanks to the veterans' center complex nearby and a combined forces training grounds for military, police, and fire professionals.

Despite the influx of people and the transient nature of a military population, the town retained its secluded, rustic feel. The town council took great pride in maintaining original buildings and keeping the charm of the friendly little community intact. Many shop fronts had been there since long before Joely's time.

"Which will it be for breakfast dessert?" Alec asked. "Ina's or Dottie's?"

"Dottie's has amazing coffee cake. But Ina's has those scones she serves with one little scoop of ice cream."

"Your choice. We're celebrating your wheels."

"Hmmm." She wrinkled her nose, contemplating two good choices. "Scones. Ice cream in the morning is too decadent to pass up. Plus, I can show you my digs."

"Your what?"

"Two blocks over from Ina's—the little place I found that didn't require a huge deposit or the first and second months' rent."

"That sounds minorly iffy."

"Or serendipitous."

He nodded his approval. "So Ina's is two blocks ahead. Can you parallel park?"

"Sheesh, Alec. I'd kind of like to shoot you all of a sudden. Haven't you tortured me enough and had enough excitement?"

He shrugged. "In for a penny, in for a pound."

"That's very quaint."

"I had a sainted grandmother a lot like yours once. She used to say that. But she was kind of a troublemaker."

"Swell. That's where you got it."

"Proudly. There." He pointed at an empty spot half a block from the little shop that was their destination—Ina's with the pretty lilac-colored awning and red-and-pink curlicue lettering.

She stopped the big truck beside the car in front of the space and put it into reverse. With a jerk she backed up too far. She shifted and shot forward three feet. Alec began to laugh. With a rocking, jerky inefficiency, Joely worked to figure out the accelerator's true touch, and by the time she'd shimmied and jolted her way into the spot, she was choking on her own laughter. Alec sat back in his seat and rubbed his forehead.

He snorted. "That was like parking in a spinning washing machine. Did you learn to do that all by yourself?"

She wiped her eyes. "Crap. I'm sorry. I used to be able to back a four-horse trailer into a tight spot on a diagonal. Guess some things aren't like riding a bike. My leg didn't want to move back and forth the way it should."

"We'll just make sure all your parking spots are straight from now on. You never have to do this again as far as I'm concerned."

"Yeah? Well, whether I passed the test or not, I'm done parking anywhere for the day. You're driving home, Cowboy."

"Okay."

She frowned. "That was too easy."

"Nah, I proved my point."

"Yeah. With me, the poster child for unsafe driving."

"You'll get better. You've got legs now. You can get where you need to go. A big first step."

"Not a step at all. I have no car and no way to get one until all the insurance mess is settled. That could take another year I'm told. I'll be sticking around town pretty closely."

"But wasn't the original plan for you to go to the ranch?"

"It was." She pointed down the street to one of the oldest business buildings in town, the last on the block that could use a solid renovation. "But I decided that if I want any chance at earning my own money, I have to live where I can get to a place of work by myself. Believe me, it's not ideal, I know. Still…" She trailed off with a shrug. "Nothing's ideal anymore."

"Let's go see this new apartment."

She swung slowly alongside him on the crutches, and although she tired quickly, the sense of satisfaction growing in her as they neared the place she'd rented kept her going. Her sudden buoyed spirits surprised her. The decision to move here had been another act of sheer stubbornness, and she'd spent the days since signing the one-month lease second-guessing the choice. But taking Alec to see it, on her own with no explanation or justification necessary, gave her a sense of independence she hadn't felt since the accident. If she was honest, she hadn't felt it in four years.

"It's in the basement of the building and was renovated probably five years ago. It's not bad—some cosmetic stuff needs doing, but it's livable. Above me is the thrift store and Cyril Grimes' Jackson Hole Properties."

"Okay," he said.

They reached the old building front, its brick façade stained with age.

"Around the side," she said.

They followed a cracked sidewalk lined with struggling hosta plants and day lilies, and turned the building corner. Joely's optimism died in an explosion of shock. Beneath the small overhang over the stoop of her new door, seated on the concrete, stiff and unmoving with its head slumped awkwardly to the front and side, was a body.

Chapter Nine

ALEC PULLED UP short at the sight of the figure on the cement stoop and reached for Joely's hand at her cry of shock. He didn't blame her. The man clothed in a thin wool overcoat and brown, cuffed dress trousers was certainly still enough to be a corpse.

"Oh, Alec, is he…?"

"It's unlikely." He stopped her from voicing the word and stroked her thumb with his in a gesture of comfort. Despite his words, he guessed it wasn't completely out of the question that the man was dead. The nights were still dipping into the thirties here in the higher elevations. If the person was old or infirm, he might have succumbed to cold. Or natural causes.

"We should call someone," she said.

"I'll check on him."

"Oh, don't. What if—"

He squeezed her hand this time, and she clung to him. He liked the feeling of her body huddling into his side like a nervous pup. He'd seen enough bodies in his life that the idea of checking on this one didn't frighten him, but she clearly didn't want to find out the worst.

"It'll be fine," he said. "You can just stay right here."

She nodded and released her grip on his hand and arm.

Alec approached the man and studied him. He thought he saw the coat front rise and fall, so he leaned over him and put a hopeful hand on his shoulder. To his relief the body was supple, not stiff.

"Sir? Sir, is everything all right?"

It took several gentle shakes and a few more called "hellos" before the man opened one rheumy eye and blinked. A second later he started violently with a throaty cry of surprise.

"Don't!" he said. "You can't do this."

"Whoa, hey, it's all right." Alec stepped back. "We're not here to hurt you or do anything. Just making sure you're okay."

He jumped up, as agile and quick as if he'd found himself on fire. The action was all the more impressive when it was clear the man had to be in his late seventies or perhaps older. His coat flew open, revealing a fairly neat, green print, button-down shirt.

"You aren't Alastair," he said in a strangely proper accent, faintly British.

"I am not," Alec agreed. "Are you waiting for him?"

The man's features calmed, and his eyes cleared. "I am searching for him."

"Here on this front stoop?"

He clamped his coat together with one fist. "Of course not," he said. "I apologize for falling asleep. I am here looking for Joellen Crockett."

Alec frowned slightly and looked back at Joely. She shook her head, indicating she had no idea who he was. The man was very slightly shabby and wore a multiple days' growth of gray, hedgehog-bristly beard. His clothing, however, was clean, and he had on a thick, blue stocking cap with about five inches of a gray ponytail hanging beneath the back edge.

His eyes shone, bright and astute, and his words were definitely accented—softly European and educated. No smell of alcohol or anything to indicate he hadn't bathed recently or was homeless clung to him, although a large, tightly stuffed cloth bag stood beside the wall on the stoop.

"I'm Joellen Crockett." Joely arrived beside Alec and leaned forward on her crutches. "Who are you?"

"Since I arrived in town, people are calling me Mayberry," he said, amusement lighting his eyes. "I have been staying in various places around the area, including one night in the local jail for a complete misunderstanding."

"Mayberry?" Joely asked, her voice intrigued.

"An old television show." The old man puckered his brows sympathetically as Joely adjusted her stance. "You're quite a bit too young to remember it, my dear. Broken leg, 'eh?"

"Something like that," she replied. "What show?"

"It was called *The Andy Griffith Show*. They say I'm like the character Otis the town drunk in Mayberry where the show took place. However, as most people are finding, I am not an alcoholic."

He was confusing is what he was. He looked like a homeless man, although the tidiest one Alec had ever seen, yet he spoke as if he'd come from a youth spent in England and seemed to know Joely.

"I'm Alec Morrissey." He held out his hand.

Joely leaned on her crutches and extended her hand as well. "I'm Joely. This is my apartment."

He took each of their hands in turn with a firm, sure grasp. "I know it is. Joely. Such a lovely name. I found out you were moving here when I asked about your family at the café. Small towns are quite amazing when it comes to knowing everything about their local citizens."

Alec made a mental note to talk to Joely about the over-willingness of her new neighbors to impart information about her. The man seemed harmless, but telling strangers where people lived went again every safety-conscious rule Alec could think of.

"How do you know my family?"

"I don't really, my dear. I knew your grandmother. I was hoping you would do me a great favor and deliver a note to her whenever you see her."

He reached into one deep pocket and pulled out a sealed blue envelope with "Mrs. Sadie Crockett" penned on the front in neat handwriting.

"What is this?"

"Just a greeting," he replied. "Nothing nefarious. I am here looking for my nephew. My great-nephew, to be precise. I discovered Sadie is miraculously still alive, and I thought I would make contact."

"Who is your great-nephew?" Joely asked.

"Not a local. I've followed his trail, so to speak. The fact that he's come here is just a happy coincidence."

"I'd be glad to give this to my grandmother. Is there a way for her to find you again? Where are you staying?"

"Mayberry" picked up his stuffed bag and slung it over his shoulder.

"I stay wherever the spirit moves me to each night. Sometimes the local campground. Sometimes with others who rove as I do. Once in a while at a hotel. If Sadie wishes to find me, she can." He moved from beneath the porch overhang and smiled. "I'm sorry to have startled you this morning, and I thank you most kindly for your help. I'll let you get to your plans for the day."

"Hang on, can we take you…home?" Alec exchanged a quick glance with Joely, who shrugged and nodded.

"No, no. Thank you. I prefer walking."

"Your nephew. Is that Alastair?" Alec asked.

"I'm afraid so." Resignation filled his eyes as if he'd just about given up on this person. "Fills my sleep with worried dreams. A good boy with some poor ideas. However, he's the closest thing I have to a grandson, or a son for that matter. And we get on well enough."

"And you have to find him, why?"

"He's been away from home. I'd like to find him while I'm on my travels."

On his travels? A lost great-nephew. Secretive notes.

Who was this man?

Mayberry started down the walk. Joely looked at Alec, his own confusion and slight amusement mirrored in her eyes.

"Do you have a real name?" she asked.

"Mayberry actually does fine," he replied, and continued down the walk.

"But…" Joely shrugged in bewilderment. "How do you know my grandmother?"

"She used to babysit me."

With that bombshell he continued moving smartly away on his scuffed, white running shoes. If they hadn't just spoken to him and seen the character lines etching his face, Alec wouldn't have known he was an elderly man.

Joely turned to him. "What on earth was that?"

Alec waggled his head, equally mystified. "Talk about a character. You have no idea who he is?"

"Not a clue. Seems like someone with an official town nickname would be known to everyone. Then again—I was away for years and incarcerated for the past three-fourths of one. What would I know?"

"Thought maybe you'd remember him from when you were a kid."

"He wasn't here when I was growing up."

"Well, let's hope he is truly who he says he is—not that it helps overly much. I don't honestly know a thing about him. Which leads me to the next point. Why are people so careless as to tell a stranger where you'll be living?"

"He could have found me a hundred ways. This is Wolf Paw Pass—by this time next week everyone will know what I have for breakfast."

"It's not safe."

"It's safe."

He liked that she thought so. And he hated that she thought so. Arguing would be pointless. He'd just have to keep an eye out on her behalf for a while. Joely was a puzzle, too. In their short time together he'd seen her as both a lost woman who seemed determined to wallow in self-pity and a stubborn little spitfire who forged ahead without thinking. This was definitely the latter.

She let the topic of the mysterious Mayberry go and made her way to the porch stoop. She took it alone, placing her crutch tips deliberately, her concentration obvious. She went to the front door of the apartment and peered through a sidelight before taking the key out of her pocket. "Want to come in?"

She unlocked the door and he followed her inside. Tan carpeting had been freshly cleaned in the living room they entered. Straight ahead lay the kitchen with appliances and a small eating area. To the right of the living room was a hallway leading to a decent bathroom and two small bedrooms.

"Seems nice," he said.

"I think it'll be fine."

He leaned against a wall near the front door and crossed his arms casually over his chest. "Can I ask a question? I don't want you to think I'm criticizing, because I think this is great."

"Okay. What?"

"Why *not* just go back to the ranch? You're jumping from despair over having to move because your support staff will be gone, to living completely alone. Wouldn't there have been a happy medium?"

She hung on the padded arm rests of the crutches and lifted her chin slightly. "Honestly?"

"Yeah."

"You."

"What?" His heart dropped a little. Encouragement was all he'd intended—not dictating a life change. He didn't want to be responsible for this. "I didn't mean—"

"I know what you meant. This is because of one simple thing you asked me: why did I think I needed a nurse at my beck and call? Then you proceeded to show me the answer is that I don't. And just so you're clear, that's me hating to admit you were right. Unfortunately after that I had two choices, neither of which I wanted. I could live alone or live with my hovering sisters."

"You don't like people hovering?"

"The truth is I don't know what I like. That's why I finally decided to try this. It might be a complete disaster, but I can't stay where I am. So I signed a month's lease. I can survive that long."

"I knew I spotted a little spark of bravery in there." He pointed at her heart and smiled, hoping to see the spark shine in her eyes.

"It's not bravery." There wasn't a spark, but the glowing ember of latent excitement he did see satisfied him. "It's confusion mixed with stubbornness. I want to be where people don't know me. I still figure people will feel sorry for me and want to help but not because they think they know what I feel. I know. It doesn't make sense."

"You'll figure it out. For the record, though? I don't know you, but I don't feel sorry for you either."

"I knew that within three seconds of meeting you." She almost smirked.

"So where does that leave me?"

"Locking up and taking me to Ina's, I guess."

"Good enough."

Ina's mini scones and ice cream were phenomenal—awful nutritionally but a great breakfast dessert if all a person cared about was contented indulgence.

They talked about nothing—the most relaxed nothing Alec had ever experienced. He told her about buying his house. She told him about the house in California. She liked chocolate. He preferred salt. They both liked animals. They both liked movies, but she hated death and violence, and he liked the *Kill Bill* duo. Still, she admitted, she couldn't help watching *Die Hard* for Bruce Willis, and he admitted to having a soft spot for Disney. He'd never tried so hard not to impress someone only to end up being impressed himself. Joely was no diva ditz. She was reasoned and funny and smart. They didn't talk about their injuries or their accidents. She didn't bring up the impending divorce, and he didn't talk about the rodeo. There was plenty of other nothing to discuss.

After the scones were long gone, Alec sat back in his red-and-white-striped booth seat and absently rubbed his knee just above the socket of his prosthetic. He normally paid little attention to it during the day, unless something particularly stressful made it chafe, but today it sobered him. He was fine, but what was he really doing playing the all-knowing expert for Joely Crockett? She was lovely. She was fun. She might need a mentor. But he was really the blind leading the blind. In a support group or system, like the one Gabe had set up, two injured people wouldn't be a cliché. But he and Joely kind of were. One limping body attracted to another.

"Oh my gosh, how did we spend ninety minutes here?" Joely straightened in her seat and stared at him like a shocked rabbit. "I need to get back to Mia—she's doing all my work for me."

"Easy conversation," he said, condensing his musings into one simplified observation. "That old time flies thing."

"It was good," she said. "And I'm no longer fuming about Tim. Thanks."

"Have you decided what to do about his papers? Are you going to take them to a lawyer?"

"Yeah, about that." She lowered her eyes. "Admission time. I already have. I just didn't want to tell him. I can fight for spousal maintenance, but I wouldn't get much if anything after just four years of marriage. The house was his before we got married. And, the other thing is—if insurance money comes through from the accident, I don't want him to have any future claim on it. I have every intention of handing him the papers. I just didn't want to do it because he stood there and demanded them."

"I wish there was something I could do."

"That's nice of you. There's nothing to be done. I'm not sad about the divorce. I'm mad because he's getting off like the wounded player. It's the sense of injustice. I'll be glad when it's done."

"So, don't tell him all this. Make him go home and wait for the papers like a good little boy—it'll be something novel for him. That's the impression I got."

She laughed humorlessly. "He's not evil. He's just rich. Some rich people make their lives about getting what they want. I got used to being rich, too. But it was totally fake."

Alec's cell phone vibrated in his pocket and he frowned. He'd taken the morning off after Mia had called him to ask for his help with Joely. It was only ten thirty, so nobody from the company would be checking on him.

"You can get it," she said. "It's fine."

He pulled out the phone and checked the number. His heart sank. Vince again. He hadn't had long enough yet to think up excuses for ignoring his harebrained rodeo ideas.

"I'll wait," he said, his voice tight.

"Ooh. Sounds like someone *you* should talk to and get the conversation over with."

"An old buddy. The same way Heidi What's-her-name is your old buddy."

"Oh dear. Well, fine then. You have my permission to ignore him." Her smile blossomed, and he laughed.

He was stuffing the phone back into his pocket when the text message notification sounded. He frowned again and pushed the button to view the message.

I know you're ignoring me, but check this out. Just caught him doing this right in the pasture. Tell me it doesn't give you chills of longing.

Alec couldn't resist torturing himself. He scrolled to the attached picture and caught his breath—shocked at the effect seeing the animal had on him. Beads of micro-sweat broke out on his forehead.

"Day-umn." The curse whistled almost silently through his teeth.

"Something wrong?" Joely asked.

"A ghost from the past," he replied. "Albeit a beautiful one."

"Oh? Well now, I think since you've met my past and we found a not-dead-body together, I should get to see this ghost." She held out her hand and wiggled her fingers for the phone.

"That's failed logic," he replied. "Those two things aren't related to each other, so they don't follow into me handing over anything."

"They're both traumas. C'mon, let me look at her." She grinned so impishly he had to give in.

"Well, it's a him," he said. "Sorry to disappoint you."

He gave her the phone and the picture of Ghost Pepper caught mid-buck. The horse looked as good as ever. Alec hated the adrenaline pumping through his body. Had it been the adrenaline of excitement, he'd have embraced it. This, however, was nothing but dread.

Joely turned immediately into the equivalent of a little girl who'd been handed a panda baby or a bunny and squealed in delight. "Oh my gosh. What a gorgeous horse!"

"He is that."

"Is he yours?"

"Hardly. He's the prettiest, sweetest-tempered horse you'll ever meet, until you put anything heavier than a packet of sugar on his back. Then he'll start with this—twist and rage like he's trying to kick out the gates of Hades."

"This gorgeous thing is a bronc?"

"Yes, ma'am, he sure is."

"But you clearly know him. Did you ever ride him?"

There it was—the question that was going to drag him for the second time that week into territory he never visited.

"A very long time ago I tried."

"Tell me about him!"

"How about when we have more time? You said you needed to get back."

Her gaze went straight through to the most hidden parts of his brain. He could feel her reading the secrets there.

"I know a brush-off when I hear one," she said. "But I say, it's a ten minute drive home. There's time."

"There's no story." The surprise of seeing the old horse had sent him into a spin as effective as the ones that had spun him to the ground years before. "I never did get eight seconds on this crazy bastard. He had most of our numbers. There were a very few over the years who figured him out, but not many. He remains the top bronc even after fifteen years. It was just a surprise to learn he was still around."

For a moment she appeared ready to question his story. Instead she sank back and handed him his phone. "What breed is he? Appy?"

"Appy mustang. Bred to buck. He came from great bucking stock himself, but unfortunately, his babies haven't lived up to his reputation—they all get his gentle side."

Focusing on the horse made the conversation slightly easier. It took the spotlight off his former career.

"Who sent the picture?"

"That old friend whose call I ignored. He's keeping him at his place west of Teton Village and wants me to come for some sort of sick reunion. In fact, he talked me into giving him a couple old pictures he remembered of spectacular falls for promo at the rodeo this summer. 'Ghost Pepper is back.' I said he could have them if he kept my name off the bills."

"Oh, but how cool would that be to have you be his spokesperson? Think of the crowds."

"Nope." He didn't know how to shut her down without being rude. "That's not going to happen, so stop right there. I'm no poster boy for retired cowboys. They'll just turn it into a sideshow. I don't do sideshows."

He didn't know whether it was it was his tone or some note of warning in his voice, but Joely backed off.

"Fair enough. Are you going to go visit the horse?"

"I have to bring Vince the pictures, but I had no plans to see the horse. Why?"

She shrugged. "I thought maybe I could come along."

The thought stopped his negative thoughts cold. "Really?"

"Sorry, that was presumptuous. I just like pretty horses." Her words slowed and she shrugged. "It's probably not such a good idea."

"No." His mind raced in a new direction. "No, I think maybe it's a very good idea."

The words tumbled out before he could censor them. He didn't mind seeing the horse. It was Vince who concerned him. The guy should have been a traveling snake oil salesman. He could, it seemed, sell rodeo to a one-legged cowboy.

"I don't know."

"Vince wants the pictures by Saturday. You could be my buffer between him and his screwball ideas. In exchange I'll help you move on Friday."

"Sure," she said. "But don't you have, like, a job?"

Her bright mood made Alec's unwilling step into the world he'd left behind slightly more palatable. On the other hand, he was letting her pretty face influence him, and he needed to start watching out for that. All he'd wanted to do when he met her was get her to think about taking a few baby steps away from her wallowing. Today she'd taken a couple of kangaroo leaps and was dragging him along.

"I do have a job. But they like me. They won't mind if I take a personal day."

"A husband, a homeless body, a saddle bronc, a lot of empty calories, and a handsome guy to help move my worldly possessions. It's not even noon and I'm exhausted." Her laugh was the most carefree sound he'd ever heard from her.

It buoyed him, which was a good thing because, suddenly, the realization she was about to get involved with Vince and that saddle bronc, made him the one who wanted to go home and have a big old wallow.

Chapter Ten

TRUE TO HIS promise, Alec came along with half the
population of Paradise Ranch—her mother, Mia and
Gabe, Skylar Thorson, and even Grandma Sadie—to help
carry in boxes and unpack them in the tiny new apartment. With so many bodies, they made fairly short work
of the job. The men muscled in the large furniture—bed,
kitchen table, the sofas and chairs—Skylar unpacked
bathroom boxes, Mia and their mother worked in the
kitchen, and Grandma Sadie made it her job to get the
bedroom set up.

Joely found her grandmother starting to shake out
sheets onto the bed, her movements still coordinated
and efficient even at her age. Grandma was a wonder. She
could be elegant as Madison Avenue or the consummate
ranch wife, as she was today with soft, worn jeans and a
plaid shirt rolled at the sleeves. Her hands were slightly
gnarled with arthritis, but they weren't crippled. Her

shoulders stooped a little more each year, but she could still stand almost to her full five-foot-five-inch height when she tried. She rested more and drank a little less alcohol than she once had, but she still took a one-mile walk every day and could knit and crochet blue ribbon-winning sweaters, doilies, and blankets in the wink of an eye. Joely fully intended for her to live another twenty years and become the oldest woman in the world.

"Hi, Grandma." Joely swung into the room on her crutches and made her way to the opposite side of the bed. "You shouldn't have to do this alone."

"Nonsense." Her grandmother smoothed the surface wrinkles from the bottom sheet she'd just fitted to the mattress. "I'm not much good with heavy things anymore, but I always could make a mean bed."

"I know. You taught every one of us." Joely smiled. "To this day I'm the pickiest bed-maker I know."

"Then my life had been a success." Grandma Sadie chuckled and set the folded top sheet on the mattress to start opening it. "How are you doing, child?"

"Other than feeling hounded by my mother and sister to still consider coming back to the ranch? I'm fine."

"They mean well."

"I know. And it's not fair to say they're hounding me. Mom just keeps finding disgusting—her words—corners in the kitchen and is taking boiling water to the shelving, all the while telling me I wouldn't have to live in someone else's dirt if I just came back to my old room. Mia is obsessed with me being close enough so she can help me."

"But you're happy with this choice?"

"Do you want to know the truth? I'm doing it because I dug my heels in, and now I'm too stubborn to change my mind. I only signed a month's lease. I can leave if I want to. But don't tell them that."

Grandma nodded as if she approved. "I think it's good for you. I do."

"Thanks, Gram. You and Alec."

"He's a nice boy."

"He is. He's also annoying and pushy though."

"A little like your grandfather. More like your great-grandfather."

"Grandpa Sebastian and Great-Grandpa Eli. I've always loved the stories about Eli. He was a strong, smart man."

"Hmmm." Grandma Sadie adjusted the sheet and Joely propped her crutches against a wall behind her, then balanced on one leg to help. "He was smart. Cagey with a head for business deals."

"You knew him when you were a little girl, right?"

"We moved to the area when I was twelve," she said. "Wolf Paw Pass was nothing more than a stopover watering hole for cattle drives through Jackson Hole. Jackson town was not a whole lot bigger."

"And you went to school with Grandpa Sebastian."

"I did. Love at first sight. For him."

Joely laughed. She'd heard the story many times, but everybody loved the tale of how fourteen-year-old Sebastian Crockett had told everyone who'd listen he was going to marry Sadie Howard and then pursued her for the next seven years until she'd said yes at age nineteen.

And how they'd been married for sixty-eight years. And how she'd never looked at another man despite threatening that stubborn old cowboy many times he'd better mind his p's and q's or he'd find her keeping time in the house of one of Wolf Paw's wealthy and powerful.

"But, since Sebastian was one of the richest and most influential landowners in Wyoming, he wasn't worried. Much. He minded his p's and q's most of the time." She smiled in wistful memory.

"You two were the love story of the century around here," Joely said. "Even I remember that from when I was a little girl."

"Don't know as we were the greatest. We certainly did stay married a good long time."

Joely sighed. "I hope my sisters have as much luck as you. I wish Mom could have had longer."

"They were a great love story, too."

"Nobody really knows why." Joely frowned. "Dad was so demanding and opinionated."

"Not like anyone else in his family." Grandma Sadie smiled again.

"Touché."

"I'm glad you have a little of his stubbornness. You'll need it. But I know you're going to be fine."

"Well, I'm glad you have faith."

"You always have to have faith, child."

Joely didn't tell her how shaky her faith was most days. It had started crumbling the first time Tim had cheated on her. What was left had turned to shifting sand the day she'd learned her horse died in the car accident.

But she grinned. "Faith. Always. Got it."

They finished the sheets and blanket. Grandma Sadie put cases on the pillows and then went to the closet where she retrieved a large box Joely had never seen before.

"What's in there?"

"Something all the women on Paradise Ranch started together the day after your accident. It was for your bed the day you came home. You're not in your room at Rosecroft where you were headed that day, but you are in your own place. And this is definitely a homecoming."

Joely lifted the cover off the box and stared at the richly colored, quilted fabrics that greeted her. Hesitantly she stroked the textures and then delved beneath the folded quilt to lift it out. "Oh, Gram, what's all this?"

"A prayer quilt. Three sections, all made with fervent prayers that have now been answered."

Joely spread the quilt out on the bed and stared. Deep blues and blacks made up the top two-thirds of the design, dotted with bright whites and yellows that created a stunning starry sky. In one top corner, a handful of coppery bits of fabric formed a faint but discernible horsehead constellation. A horse the color of her shiny, chestnut Penny.

Tears filled her eyes. "Oh, Gram."

"And every person designed her own animal for you."

Across the bottom of the quilt, scattered on rolling fabric hills of deep greens, purples, and maroons, were a dozen animals looking up at the sky. In real life few of the creatures would have shared habitats, but it didn't matter, they all looked realistic and they all fit together like an eclectic family—a horse, a cat, a dog, a cow, an elephant, a kangaroo, a raccoon, a zebra, a penguin, a grizzly bear, an eagle, and a butterfly. Any animal Joely had ever said she loved.

"You love the night sky," Grandma Sadie said. "I remember finding you asleep on the back porch after you'd snuck out to watch a meteor shower or see the full moon."

"It's been a long time since I went stargazing." Joely stroked the exquisite design, each line of quilt stitching warm beneath her fingertips, as if the love and prayers came through at her touch.

"The animals need no explanation. You were always rescuing some poor bedraggled creature."

"I was," Joely said absently. "It's been a long time since I've even had pet. Tim didn't like animals in the house."

Grandma Sadie sighed and shook her head. "I'm not even going to comment," she said, her tone blunt.

"I don't know why I married him, Gram." Joely echoed her sigh. "I wasn't as strong as my sisters were when it came to following dreams. Mine was never firm or decisive enough, and I figured Dad was right. He always told me that being a veterinarian was a great idea, but it would be a waste of time to become an equine vet or an exotic animal vet on a cattle farm. So, I didn't buck Dad, I found a different dream. Or so I thought. Tim convinced me when we met we'd do such wonderful philanthropic things together."

"And, you got approval from him," Grandma said.

"At first. Then he got just as critical as Dad." She lowered her eyes. "I'm sorry. He was your son, and I know you loved him and miss him. I loved him, too; we all did. We just couldn't please him."

Grandma Sadie moved close and stood beside her. She wrapped the top of Joely's head in a warm embrace and kissed her hair. "I know my son's faults. I know my own. Your father was never cruel, honey. Iron-willed, yes. But you need to talk to your mama. She's got insights and strengths you couldn't see when you were growing up. Your father loved you beyond words. He was just terrible at showing it."

"I love the quilt. I more than love it. I can feel the love in it."

"There is a great deal of that. Welcome home. I have been praying it's a very good and safe place for you."

For the first time in months Joely didn't cringe at her grandmother's blatant spirituality. She turned in her embrace and wrapped her arms around Grandma Sadie's waist. "I love you."

"And I you. Start to follow your dreams now."

Joely nodded against Gram's soft middle but didn't say that first she had to find if there were any she could even find.

Joely looked at the beautiful quilt again and decided that if nothing else even went in the room it would be complete. But they found another box in the closet and opened it to find pictures from Joely's old room at the ranch. She smiled at the memories and planned where to hang them here. At the bottom of the box were a dozen four-by-six sepia-toned photos in vintage frames. She pulled them out one by one and ogled her ancestors from

Eli and Brigitte to Sebastian and Sadie to her mother and father.

"These are gorgeous. I haven't seen these before."

"I framed them for you. You need your heritage around you."

Joely set them on her dresser top. "That's cool."

"I'm glad you think so."

"Speaking of the past," Joely said, "I have something for you. What do you know about a man here in town that they call Mayberry?"

Grandma Sadie squinted a moment and then shook her head. "I don't know anybody with a name like that. Then again, I don't spend much time here anymore. All my old gossiping friends are long gone. The wages of living too long."

"Don't say that!"

"I'm not going anywhere soon," she said, patting Joely's arm. "But it's true there aren't any of my generation left to speak of."

"Well, this man was outside the door here two days ago. He's an odd person—like a super-well-spoken homeless man. He's older, has a gray ponytail, and said he knows you. I have a note from him."

"Knows me?"

"Yes. Because you used to babysit him."

Sadie's eyes clouded, and she sat on the edge of the bed crooking one finger across her lips in concentration.

"I can't imagine," she said. "The only children I watched regularly were the Manterville boys. Trampas and Oliver. Talk about your despicable fathers. Mr.

Manterville was loud, opinionated, and mean when he drank, which was most days. They said he liked to lock the boys in the hen house when they misbehaved. Mrs. Manterville was a scandalous woman, not because she was mean, but because she smoked."

Joely snickered. "Wow, how terrible."

"Oh, my dear, back then it was. Smoking was the province of the men, along with the consuming of liquor. Genteel women wouldn't be caught dead around whiskey or cigarettes."

Joely couldn't help but laugh. It seemed ridiculous today. Health issues aside, smoking and women had come of age long ago, and the thought of a woman being ostracized for having a cigarette was hard to imagine.

"What happened to them?" she asked.

Grandma Sadie hesitated. "They lost their place— almost ten thousand acres—in a notorious poker game that involved your great-grandfather in fact. Mr. Manterville went to prison a few years later; I don't know what for. Both boys were young teenagers, and they split up and nobody ever heard from them again."

"That's amazing," Joely said. "I've never heard any of this."

Grandma Sadie waved her hand in dismissal. "Interest in that old story died out years ago. Not a soul in Wolf Paw Pass minded one whit that the Manterville family was gone. Life went on better for them not being here." She laughed in the comforting, wise voice that always blew away fears and spoke of a long future. Joely hugged her.

"The note is in my purse. I'll go get it."

"Nonsense. We'll finish here first. There'll be plenty of time."

"I don't think I like the idea of my family being involved in a scandal around a poker game."

"Oh, now, every family has skeletons." Grandma kissed her forehead again and patted her cheek, ending the discussion. "Now. Let's get the rest of this room put in order. I'm not sure who this man is you met, but we'll find out."

Her grandmother was so practical. But, then, she hadn't lived to be ninety-four by fretting over trivial things. Joely always got the impression Sadie Crockett had been one tough bird.

"What would you ladies like to find out? I'll tell you anything you want to know."

Alec leaned forward into the room, his hands braced on either side of the door frame and his grin advertising every impractical thing Grandma Sadie's calm, wise presence did not. With dust smeared across one broad shoulder of his dark gray T-shirt and his wheat-gold hair half hanging in his eyes, he looked like devilish fun in the flesh. For the first time since he'd so unceremoniously showed her his prosthetic leg, Joely tried to tell he had it. The only possible indication was that he stood on his right leg and let the prosthetic foot rest behind him. But that could have been any person's relaxed stance. He really was amazing, carrying furniture, lifting and bending. He'd mastered his changed body in a way she couldn't fathom.

"Why do you always think someone's talking about you?" she asked.

"I'm a narcissist. I like attention."

"Narcissists don't know that's what they are," Joely said. "You're just arrogant."

"Okay. Be that as it may, do you ladies want some lunch? Your sister ordered sandwiches and cookies from Dottie's."

Joely's stomach rumbled, and she exchanged a happy look with her grandmother.

"That sounds wonderful."

Alec entered the bedroom and extended an elbow to her and to Sadie. "Lean on me, girls. I'll come back for your crutches, Joely."

Grandma Sadie smiled like a schoolgirl, and Joely shook her head, holding in laughter. The man was incorrigible when it came to forcing his charm on everyone—and she found she couldn't hold it against him.

The transformation in the rest of the apartment stunned her. Her little kitchen table had been set with brightly colored red and yellow placemats along with a bouquet of yellow, red, and purple tulips. Her living room held the sofa and armchair, a coffee table she recognized from her father's old study at the ranch, and a television set up in one corner with a noon newscast showing without sound to prove it worked. The bathroom's items were unpacked and stowed in the cabinet. A full roll of paper filled the holder beside the toilet.

"This is crazy, you guys," Joely said. "You've gone above and beyond."

"Just tell us if you want something changed around," Gabe said. "We'll do whatever you want until you kick us out."

"Kick you out?" Joely planted a kiss on his cheek. "You can all live here and wait on me. This is awesome."

Mia gave a snort of laughter. "That service disappeared when you skipped the coming-to-live-at-home stage. This is your deal, sweetie. Order us around now, because once we're gone…"

"As if I could get rid of you that easily." Joely hugged her sister and watched their mother climb down a stepstool from her perch on a countertop, where she'd been smoothing paper onto a kitchen cupboard shelf. "You guys will have spies everywhere around here."

"Maybe." Her mother nodded. "I admit I'd likely be the organizer of that ring. I've been told often enough I worry too much. On the other hand, this is a nice place, Joely. I give it my stamp of approval."

That made the move official and all but complete. They sat in one amassed troop on the floor, Dottie's phenomenal sandwiches in hand, joking and chatting. The topics, for once, were not about accidents, or nurses, or losing apartments, but about Skylar's boyfriend, Nate, about spring calving on the ranch, about riding the fences with four-wheelers and how it was so much easier than covering what felt like a million miles on horseback over three weeks. It was fun to watch Gabe, a rancher only by marriage, turn a little pale at the stories of searching through heat and cold and rain and even snow for downed wire and broken boards on horseback.

Alec fit right in, catching up with Gabe on their friend-ship and laughing over old stories like only good friends could do. Joely watched Alec surreptitiously, surprised at how easy it was to include him here with her family. She flushed with a strange combination of embarrassment and pleasure the one time he caught her watching, but he didn't say anything, he simply smiled. The apartment began to feel warm, cozy, and safe. Like home.

The move was a small one by any standards, and it was finished by three o'clock. Joely had a short list of things she needed to purchase, but she'd work on acquiring them over the coming days. Other than that, she had staples in the cupboards, milk, coffee, eggs, and yogurt in the refrigerator, and dinners frozen and ready for the next week thanks to her over-protective family. It was no problem to believe this move had been a brilliant choice, and getting used to living life on her own would be as easy as learning how the microwave worked.

"Can we do something about dinner now?" her mother asked when the last shelf was papered and the last of Joely's few dishes were put away. "We could order in. Cook for you here. Go out?"

"You know what? I think I'd just like to putter around and get used to the space," Joely said. "Would that be okay?"

"Of course, sweetheart. Sadie is tired anyway."

"She worked hard today."

"It was fun. You can bet she enjoyed it."

A strange sort of high took over her body as she said good-bye to everyone. It made no sense. Her body, too, dragged with a fatigue she hadn't felt since the early days of her accident when all she'd wanted to do was sleep. This, however, was the high of excitement. She'd made a decision, stuck to her guns in the face of everyone else's doubt, and now she had a new apartment. It didn't even bother her too much that she'd been so beholden to others. Even able-bodied people got their friends together to help them move.

"Are you really going to be okay, then, by your lonesome tonight?"

Alec came out of the bedroom where he'd been adjusting a bifold door that hadn't slid properly on its track. He had a small toolbox in one hand. The last to leave…

"I'll be fine."

"Okay. Great."

And as suddenly as her high had hit, doubts crowded around, peering in on her happiness, telling her that maybe she wasn't *quite* ready.

"Are you in a hurry?" She winced. Why had she asked that?

"Only to let my dog out in the next hour or so. Something I can help you with? I'm happy to."

She stopped herself from making a ditzy-sounding "ummmm" and waved her hand. "No, not at all. You've done so much. Just thinking that Mia left a bottle of Moscato in the refrigerator and somebody should christen this place."

"You want to break the bottle on the front door, or drink what's inside?" He grinned.

"Gee, uh, let me think." She smiled back.

"I would be happy to christen the apartment with you, but what you should really have to go along with wine is a good steak."

"Steak with a fizzy white wine?" She shook her head. *"No bueno, muchacho."*

"A wine snob talking about an Italian wine in Spanish. Very talented, Miss Crockett."

She almost corrected him out of habit. Foster. Mrs. Instead she shuddered. She had to get those papers signed.

"I'm kind of a wine snob. Along with being a whiskey snob."

"I know you said your dad taught you to drink, but you're a connoisseur?"

"I know my Scotch."

"Favorite?"

"Hmm. I'm not too into the super peaty blends. A single malt. The Macallan, maybe, or Speyburn."

"Jeez. You are a snob. I was going for Wild Turkey or Jim Beam. But I suppose I could match you a Glenlivet."

"Good choice. Same region of Scotland. But you know what? When it comes right down to it, I'll drink anything."

"How'd I get so lucky? Can you hold your liquor?"

She wrinkled her nose. "No. Not like Mia or Grace. Harper, either. I'm done after two or three shots. Or a couple of glasses of wine."

"I might like to see you a little tipsy."

"I remember a certain recent wedding…" She grimaced at the memory.

His mouth lifted in a one-sided grin. "You were pretty fun that night. I'd forgotten."

"Liar. I don't think you forget anything. Ever."

"Tell you what. I know we have a date to go visit my friend's ranch tomorrow. If I can rustle up some food and we can christen your new digs properly, will you skip that outing and change it to dinner tonight?"

"I think I'm insulted. You're actually trying to get out of taking me somewhere. I've never been stood-up in person before."

"Hey. Nobody in his right mind would stand you up. I'm just switching the date venue."

"Who said tomorrow was a date?"

"Stop nit-picking like a dang girl. It's a date, okay? I officially invite you to it here and now. And I'm adding tonight. Dinner. I'll offer you two choices—Moscato and steak or a nice bottle of a red blend and steak."

She laughed. "So, wait. We either have to buy steak. Or buy steak and wine."

"Neither. I have the steak at my house. Two thick ol' ribeyes I bought just yesterday and haven't put in the freezer yet. I also have a bottle of red wine I got as a lovely parting gift when I left Texas to come here. I don't drink a lot of red wine."

"I remember. Wild Turkey."

"Nah. Those days are mostly gone. Not a wild turkey in sight in my liquor cabinet, I'm afraid. A fair amount of beer in the fridge. I haven't totally reformed."

"Yeah. A cowboy who didn't drink beer? I'd take you to an emergency room myself. Okay, here's the deal. I'll go on this date with you tonight, but I maintain tomorrow never was a date, so I'm not willing to let you call it off. It's a business meeting and a research trip. Maybe I'm in the market for a horse."

"In that case, I can do your research for you. You cannot buy this horse. Sometimes a fly would land on his back, and he'd lose his brain. That's probably exactly how Vince got the picture you saw. He's not a fun little horsey."

A tiny flash of irritation heated her cheeks. "And I'm not a stupid little, horsey-loving city girl. I've probably ridden more horses than you have. The bottom line is I'm *not* looking for a horse. But if I were, it wouldn't matter if the thing bucked or not. I can't use a riding horse."

He sighed and let her irritation roll off his back. With yet another of his charming grins he took her hands. "There you go again, Joellen Crockett. What am I going to do with you?"

Chapter Eleven

"DO WITH ME? About what, exactly?" she asked.

Alec loved the fiery flash of irritation in her eyes. He knew he shouldn't egg her on, shouldn't tease her so mercilessly, but the true nature of the woman before the accident came out at its best and strongest when she sparred with him. That made it hard to resist picking on her.

"You said you can't use a riding horse. Why?"

"Tough to ride when one leg can't tell the horse what to do, wouldn't you say, Mr. Expert? Don't see you out there either."

"Don't see me out there on a saddle bronc. Doesn't mean I've never tried riding a horse."

As always when he dropped a little grenade, she stopped and stared like a guppy through its fishbowl—big eyes, open mouth.

"You've ridden."

"Joely, haven't you ever paid any attention to the things amputees can do? Watched *Dancing with the Stars*? Seen the Olympics? Do you want a list?"

"No, of course not." She looked away.

"I'm not offended," he said, catching her arm. "I just want you to stop limiting yourself."

"I moved into my own dang place," she said, subdued. "Doesn't that count?"

"You know it does. Now you have to learn to enjoy it." He took her gently by her upper arms and made her look at him. "I'm done lecturing. I promise. You don't have to ever buy a riding horse. That's not the point, okay? Don't buy one because you don't want one, not because you can't ride one."

"You said you were done lecturing."

"I am. What's it going to be for dinner?"

To his delight she started to laugh. "You and I have the most ridiculous conversations. I don't think they even are conversations. They're more like little mini visits to the principal's office."

"Well then, stop getting yourself into trouble." He released her and waited for the comeback. Instead she put a hand on his cheek and leaned toward him. He thought his heart might just stop with her touch.

"I am who I am now, Alec. You aren't going to change me. But I know why you're trying, and it's nice of you to care."

Who she was "now." Did she mean she'd defined herself as a new person since the accident? That's precisely what he didn't want her to do, and she was right. He did care. But he shouldn't. He didn't need to. She had practically warned him off. He also sensed that if he didn't stick to his promise to stop lecturing, she wouldn't be so nice about warning him next time.

"Hard not to care," he said as breezily as he could. "We're gimpy-legged mates. I'm drawn to you. So. What's it going to take to get you to order dinner?"

"Fine. I choose the red and the Moscato. Red for the snob. White sparkly for the other person here who doesn't really like red wine but maybe should."

"My kind of girl. Want to come with me to pick up the meat? Or are you dead on your feet?"

Even through her spunk she looked tired. She'd rested on and off throughout the day, but for the most part she'd been as busy as everyone else. Beautiful and strong as she was, he knew she wasn't in the best cardio shape. Still, he hoped she'd consider taking the short drive.

"If you're not dead on your fake foot, I'm certainly not dead on my live one." She gave a little teasing smirk.

It shocked him. Nobody teased him about his missing foot. Even when he joked about the leg himself, coworkers, his family, even his friends were too uncomfortable with it to make fun. It's why he kept the existence of his prosthetic quiet from all but those who already knew or who got close enough to need to know. He wasn't ashamed. He simply hated the ever-present awkwardness it caused, however miniscule the amount of discomfort was. Now here came Joely, not only mentioning it but doing it on purpose and being proud of it.

Wells of grateful emotion filled behind his eyes, and his smile blossomed unbidden.

"What?" she asked.

"Nothing. Come on. Let's go get dinner. I'll introduce you to my dog."

"I'm not so sure those two sentences should have gone together." She wrinkled her nose in distaste and Alec laughed again.

"THIS IS YOUR house?"

Joely leaned forward in the passenger seat of the truck and craned her neck. Alec smiled with pride as she took in the front yard with its mountain view and wide lawn.

"It's a nice place. I was lucky to find it," he said. "Good timing meant I didn't have to put a very large dog in a very small house in town and scare the neighbors to death."

"So she is a scary, large dog?"

"Only scary looking. It's mostly the large that does it. Have you ever met a wolfhound?"

"No. I've seen pictures."

"You have a little bit of an idea then. Even before she stands like the human she thinks she is, I'm guessing her head will come…" He assessed her quickly. "About here on you." He slashed his hand across his own breastbone.

Joely didn't flinch. "That's a big dog."

"Big." He nodded. "But a harmless goon. Be warned, she's still got some puppy left in her even after two years. She's, uh, exuberant when I first get home. But wolfies like being lazy, so it's not bad once she settles down."

"I consider myself warned."

He showed her around the yard although there wasn't a lot to admire up close other than the impressive trees.

He hadn't had time in the short time he'd lived here to landscape anything, so overgrown foundation plantings were all that passed for attractive botanical touches. Joely still complimented the house, the brickwork, the front porch with its hand-hewn log railings, and she was properly awed by the crescent of mature trees curving around the east side of the house. Especially Alec's favorite, a gnarly limbed tree with long, elegant branches that flowed sideways, like a woman with beautiful, windswept hair. Its small, white flower blossoms were just starting to open.

"What a gorgeous Hawthorne." She pointed.

"You know them?" he asked. "I love how it looks like a lady with her hair blowing in the wind."

"My, how poetic."

"Oh, but beware. The flowers hide long thorns—like a rosebush. That lady knows how to protect herself."

"Sounds like you've been bitten once or twice? Put your hands where they didn't belong, maybe?"

"Smart ass."

"Just trying to get a few insights from The Lady."

He accompanied her slowly to the porch and she placed her crutches carefully on the uneven ground.

"Want an arm or just your crutches?" he asked.

"I'm fine. Thanks. Although I do have to say I'll be glad to set these babies down when I get back home. I haven't used them in eight months as much as I have the past two weeks."

"I never thought they got easier to use."

"You had crutches?"

"Really?" He shot her a look.

She covered her mouth with her hand and stifled a giggle. "Duh. I don't suppose you woke up from surgery already fitted with a working wooden leg."

Again with the easy kidding. He could love a woman like this.

"Wish I could have. Might have skipped a few painful steps in the process. But, I couldn't find a good pirate surgeon. Arrrgh. So I settled for carbon fiber. On this leg anyhow. I have a couple."

"Ooh, like a running leg? And a *Dancing with the Stars* leg?"

"Ah, so she does pay attention."

"I can be taught, yes."

"No dancing leg or running blade, but I have two different ankle assemblies with different ranges of articulation. And I have one called a dynamic response foot that stores energy when I walk and acts more realistic. They aren't pretty but they're better than a peg leg."

"You're an impressive guy. It's so natural for you."

"I've had three years to get used to it. It's never natural."

He studied the contemplation in her face and had a sudden urge to touch her, to feel the emotion and the questions there with his own fingers and find out what she was really thinking. It was silly—as if emotion could transfer that way—but she had such expressive features. He wondered if she knew how often her personality showed for the world to see. She'd be an awful poker player. He kept his hands to himself.

"Ready to meet the moose?" he asked.

"Sure."

He entered first and Rowan didn't disappoint. She woofed in happy greeting and jumped to put her paws on his shoulders as usual. Then she caught sight of Joely, and her eyes lit from inside as if Alec had brought her home a new, personal playmate. She pushed off of Alec and the wagging speed of her tail doubled, sending the vibrating motion throughout her entire, ginormous body.

"Hey, Rowan. Hi, girl." Joely's enthusiasm nearly matched the dog's. "Your dad wasn't kidding about you being crossed with an elephant, was he?"

She stroked and scratched the head and ears that did come nearly to her neck, but it wasn't enough. Rowan pushed forward until the pressure of her forehead against Joely's chest forced her to bend at the waist and wrap her arms around the shaggy canine head.

"You are a big ol' love." She made kissing noises and babbled something in baby gibberish.

Alec shook his head and laughed. "Don't do that. She'll never look at me again."

"C'mon, you don't talk baby talk to your baby?"

"Uh, no."

"Silly boys, what do they know, right, sweetie?"

Rowan licked at Joely's cheek, covering the scar up the side with a wet swipe. She laughed again. "Okay, yuck."

"C'mon, Dum-ro," Alec said, tugging lightly on Rowan's collar. "You need to go outside."

"Aw, don't call her 'dumb.'"

"What? No! Dum-ro as in Dumbo and Rowan. Elephant, remember?"

"Ahh. Okay. You're forgiven."

"Gee, thanks." He turned for the patio doors and Rowan followed. "Wish I could get immediate bonding action like the dang dog."

"Stop being so bossy and you might."

He grunted. Secretly, though, he was thrilled Joely had taken so quickly to the dog. He was even more pleased, and surprised at his pleasure, that she was in his house, seeing where he spent his time. Maybe she'd see him as more than Gabe's annoying, bossy, one-legged cowboy friend.

Then again, he didn't know why he'd want her that close. He'd just as soon maintain the snarky little relationship they'd formed. He didn't want to do tangled anymore. The desire for that kind of close relationship had died along with his cousin.

"Oh my, this is prettier than the front!"

Joely swung her way out onto the back deck and lifted her eyes to scan the beautiful view. Rowan loped through the yard, stopping to squat and then heading for her ball.

"The previous owners did a nice job," he said. "The landscaping is a little overgrown and raggedy but otherwise it's awesome. Sometimes I feel bad that the owners lost this place. I don't know the story—I figure it's none of my business."

"You were meant to have it then," she said. "You don't have to feel bad. Just be grateful. God smiles down and hands things out for free once in a while."

He scoffed quietly but nodded. "Sure."

They moved slowly around the perimeter of the yard, and Joely surprised him with her knowledge of the plants and the trees. The Asian lilies, coneflowers, and salvia. The burr oaks and the mountain ashes.

"My mom is a master gardener," she said. "I don't have her touch, but I learned a lot working with her. You saw her gardens."

He had. To say the flowers and landscaping at Rosecroft were impressive was an understatement. Naming the component parts of her garden, however, would not be his strong suit.

"She can come and fix these plantings up anytime." He laughed.

"She probably would. Mom loves getting her hands in good clean dirt."

They reached the house again, and Joely spotted the big four-wheeler that had come with the place. Another little bonus Alec sometimes felt guilty about enjoying.

"Those are pretty much a riot to ride," she said. "I really didn't want to admit it when my father started using them around the ranch—more often than horses for some things—that they were more efficient. I hated that the animals were being replaced. But I have to say— we used to do stupid things with these that were a lot of fun. My mom, the progressive, made us wear helmets. Once or twice it was a good thing, I think."

"I have a hard time imagining you as a wild kid," he said.

"Hey, I was a barrel racer. What's really wild is that Mom didn't make me wear a helmet for that. I remember getting so competitive I didn't care how fast or how low I got on those turns. I could have gone off into a barrel or worse any number of times."

"I remember." Alec did. Fondly. "Rodeo girls are gutsy and nuts. As crazy as bull riders I used to say."

"We'd have ridden bulls," she said, her face shining with a touch of defiant pride. "We're more bouncy and resilient than people think."

"Well, you're curvier and prettier at any rate."

"What a sexist thing to say."

"Is not. It's the plain truth. Being curvy and pretty doesn't take a thing away from being tough. It's just more fun to watch."

"You sound like you might actually miss it."

"Lookin' at the cowgirls? Sure. Anything else? Nope. No desire to go back."

Even as he said it his heart rate thrummed into a higher gear. She needed to believe him before he took her to Vince's tomorrow, and he hadn't yet planted nearly enough "I had my fun with rodeo" seeds. He needed to start, but he really didn't want to talk about it. He didn't want to analyze the skeptical look on that beautiful, open book face of hers.

"Let's get the steaks and wine and go make dinner," he said, before she could speak. "I've been hungry since we first talked about meat."

"Okay." She looked around again and her shoulders rose and lowered as she drew in a deep breath and then let it slowly back out. "It does smell more like the ranch here. It's nice." Her gaze lit on the grill in the corner of the deck, and she pointed. "I don't have one of those," she said. "I didn't think of that. Can you do the steaks in my broiler?"

He could. He was not a great cook, but he did know his beef. Still, the thought of wasting two gorgeous steaks in a broiler made his stomach ache in disappointment.

"I can cook a steak anywhere. But, we could grill them here if you aren't in a big rush to get back home. We can drink the wine at your place. I have some baked beans we could add to the menu."

"Veggies?"

"That I don't know; there are probably some canned green beans or something in the freezer. If I bought any it was just out of duty put in my head by my aunt years ago."

"Canned green beans." She laughed. "Awful, but you know what? I love them. It's sad."

"The French style," he said. "Smear 'em with butter and a little pepper. Gourmet."

"Man, don't ever let my mom hear you say that. That was my father's idea of healthy eating, and Mom let him have them every once in a while, but she wouldn't touch a canned vegetable if it would save her life."

"Here's to our fathers, then. That's where I learned to eat the stuff. My aunt could never train that out of me either."

"Fine. Let's eat here. My only regret is that we didn't bring the Moscato so we could have a meal truly worthy of making a real gourmand faint in horror."

"We'll see what we can find."

They turned for the deck, and a tank-sized blur of hair leaped in front of them. With a loud grunt, Joely plummeted to the ground and lay flat on her back with Rowan standing over her, a front paw either side of her chest, planting kisses all over her face.

Alec's heart stopped for one horrible second. He'd seen her fall at the wedding dance but that had caused the kind of concern he'd have felt for anyone. Now the pure fear that she'd been injured overwhelmed him into rare inaction. The kind of frozen inaction he'd experienced in Iraq when faced with the fear he'd felt too often that he was about to lose someone he loved—

His heartbeat jolted him back with a start. What was wrong with him?

"Oh my God, Rowan, get off. Damn dog—what the hell is wrong with you?"

He yelled at himself through the dog and dragged on Rowan's collar, completely baffled by her behavior. Shoving her out of the way, he knelt beside Joely, who had her hands over her eyes. Gently, more controlled now, he took hold of her shoulders.

"Honey, are you okay? God, I'm so sorry."

A mewling little sound grew from behind her fingers, and Rowan nosed her way back in. When the dog got her tongue deep into the hollow between Joely's jaw and shoulder, the sound grew into a screech. Of laughter.

Seconds later Joely was laughing so hard she gasped for breath. She grabbed at the sides of Rowan's head and manipulated her kissing mouth away from the ticklish spot that was giving her so much mirth.

"Get away, you stupid hound." Alec tried again to chase the dog off.

Joely gasped. "No, it's okay. She's all right."

"Yeah, but are you? You went down like a shooting gallery target. We need to make sure you're not hurt. I have no idea what got into her. She's not normally a jumper once she's said hello."

She waved him off and pushed herself up onto both elbows. "I know why. I think. Maybe." She shifted one hip and dug beneath herself. A second later she produced Rowan's ball. A deep, excited woof sounded when the dog caught sight of the toy. Joely gave it an awkward toss, but Rowan couldn't have cared less for the quality of the throw. She lumbered after it, tongue lolling, eyes shining.

"I'm really sorry," Alec said again.

"She's a dog doing dog things. I'm fine."

"You seem to do a lot of falling around me," he said.

"I do. Only we won't count this one as a fall. It could have happened to anyone standing here."

He held out his hand, and she took it with only a moment's hesitation. Her palm slid against his and an unexpected shiver shimmied up his arm when her fingers clamped around his hand. He tugged her to her feet, but the surprising core strength she used to assist him gave his pull more power than he'd intended. She landed against his chest with a grunt and a shy little laugh. Simple shivers turned to hot electricity. No sign of the girl unsteady on her feet remained. Instead he held an unanticipated bundle of soft, tensile strength in his arms.

"Hello there," he said, laughing to cover the chain reaction of pleasure sluicing through his body. "That was easy."

"But I'm not," she said with a quiet, teasing smile. "You can let me go now."

He didn't want to let her go; nonetheless he released her at once. He knew better than to think this was a good time to press his advantage, even though new desire whined at him like a teenage schoolboy. He settled for watching Joely dust off the seat of her jeans, rub at a Rowan-made paw print on her shirt just over her left breast, and twist sexily back and forth through her torso to test her movements.

"All in one piece," she said.

He turned away to break her spell, suddenly annoyed at his mutinying libido. "Good. That scared the crap out of me, by the way. Obviously I need to work on my dog."

"I'll just pay attention from now on. And here she comes. Hullo, baby. You're pretty in love wif dis widdle ball, aren't you?"

Even the baby talk was weirdly attractive. "Jiminy Christmas, she nearly kills you, and now you're rewarding her," he said gruffly. "I'm going up to start the steaks. You two have a wonderful time continuing to bond."

"Are you jealous?" she asked as he walked away.

"Hell, yes."

Hell. She was definitely a girl worth getting jealous over.

Rowan let them eat in peace, mostly because Alec put up a baby gate between the eating area and the family room where the dog moped like a prisoner. She'd fallen for Joely as if she hadn't ever been loved or petted in her life. If Alec hadn't found the way the two females interacted so fascinating, he might actually have been jealous, but Joely was a different person around the dog—easygoing, comfortable, and sweet natured. Her baby talk juxtaposed with the quick, snarky wit she turned so quickly on him, and he sort of fell for it, too. Not that he'd ever been into baby talk, but it spilled naturally from Joely's tongue, and he could imagine her speaking to a human baby that way. It was attractive in a way he'd never considered before.

They talked through dinner like old friends, laughing over the eclectic menu, drinking the red wine, and then switching to a lighter IPA they both declared less stuffy. Time whipped by in a blur. They seemed to be masters of cheerful, inane conversation. He was pleased and satisfied with the evening. Until she found the pictures.

They were done eating, Rowan had been allowed back into polite company, and Joely held the thick black photo album on her lap.

He'd dug out the old album after talking to Vince and agreeing to let him use pictures from the past. He'd known Buzz had kept the old photographs, and there were some decent shots. Buzz had loved his camera.

"Tell me about these pictures. They're wonderful."

"My cousin took most of them. We competed together, and he was the biggest camera buff. He actually sold a few photos to magazines here and there. These were his personal favorites."

"So you do think about the rodeo."

"I do when people force me," he replied. "These are what I was talking about—Vince wants a couple for promotion."

"This is you!"

"A lot of them are me. And quite a few are that damn horse. Buzz was determined to catch my eight seconds on him, so every time I drew the sucker we had pictures of the failure. The eight seconds never happened."

"That sucks."

He stared at her in surprise—again. No one ever said that either. He'd gotten nothing but platitudes from his fellow competitors over the years. After the accident, therapists, doctors, coworkers, too, had all offered words that meant nothing. "Just be thankful you're still with us; we are." "There's a reason for everything—maybe that horse would have killed you." "Disappointment and adversity makes you stronger."

All bull.

"It did suck." He didn't explain further.

"And now you get to see your old nemesis again."

"Believe me. It isn't because I want to. He's better left to the past. But I owe Vince, and it's one quick trip out of my life to go to his place and hand over a few pictures."

"Are you sure?"

He frowned. "What do you mean? Sure about what?"

"Sure this is better left in the past. I remember you. I remember the chanting when you'd be up. It was not an insignificant part of your life."

"No," he said slowly. "It wasn't. But it's a past part of my life."

"That sucks, too."

He swallowed back the resentment this conversation awoke. It wasn't her fault. He'd left the damn album right out in the open. She didn't know that he explained his break with rodeo to nobody, but she did need to understand that he wasn't going to be lured back into anything cowboy by Vince tomorrow.

"Look," he said. "I had a great time riding broncs. I was extremely successful. Now I'm successful doing other things, and I like it that way. The pictures are from the past, so don't romanticize them, honey. There are a lot of things a guy with a missing leg can do. A lot. But nothing is perfect—not even the best prosthetic leg and foot. So, tomorrow? Don't let Vince Newton convince you otherwise."

As he spoke, her eyes turned a clear, searching shade of blue. She placed her hand on his thigh and squeezed. An unexpected thrill drove up between his legs and nestled there uncomfortably.

"Is he going to try?"

"Try what?" His throat was strangely dry.

"Is Vince going to try and tell me you can do something you can't?"

"Vince could sell powdered water in the desert."

"He sounds dangerous."

"He'll give you the shirt off his back with no strings attached. But when he's got a scheme? Yeah, he's dangerous all right. Like the devil offering you wishes for your soul."

"Does he have yours yet?"

"Why would you ask?"

"You said you owe him. Just making sure you're okay."

He wasn't sure what to do with that line. Pure caring—that's what she offered. For no reason. He wasn't sure he wanted anything like that without strings—it obligated a person. He put an arm around her shoulders and pulled her into his side, kissing the side of her head before he could think better of it and jostling her hand off his leg. The relief was immediate.

"I'm fine. He's a friend, and he's starting a new venture that's all. I can afford to help him out."

"Then there's nothing to be worried about." She winked and actually rested her head on his shoulder.

He didn't know about that. Suddenly he was more worried about her than about the past or any ghosts it held.

Chapter Twelve

"THIS IS GETTING to be a habit." Joely smiled as she climbed into Alec's truck and pleased herself by settling into the seat with much less awkwardness than she had the previous two times.

He waited for her behind the wheel just as she'd asked him to. She knew he'd have been more than willing to meet her at her door, accompany her down the cracked narrow sidewalk to the street, and help her into the truck, but she'd wanted to do it alone. Her sense of pride at what most people took for granted every day had sent her mood soaring. To get ready, get her own breakfast, clean up her own kitchen, and make her own way out the door without the safety net of a nurse to call or the strong arm of a handsome man to grab was as exhilarating as any barrel race she'd ever run.

"How are you?" she asked.

"Fine." He cut the curt word short, his voice oddly cool.

She peered at him and he turned. "What?"

"You're not fine," she said gently.

"And you know this how?"

"I have ears?"

"So I haven't had my coffee. Buckle up."

"Alec, it's nearly noon."

"I overslept."

This was not the Alec Morrissey who just last night had grilled one of the best steaks she'd ever eaten and proceeded to make her laugh and chatter away like she hadn't done in months. Normally, surliness like this would have triggered an avalanche of ribbing, but she knew instinctively it wouldn't work this morning. This was clearly much more than a lack of caffeine.

Her mother had always told her that sometimes it was better to ignore an issue while the other person worked out his problems, so she made herself smile and settled back as Alec pulled into Saturday morning traffic on Mountain Street, his eyes straight ahead.

"Okay," she said. "Fair enough."

Her calm acceptance lasted only two blocks. When she spied Mayberry emerging from Kloster's Drug Store, his oversized cloth bag over one shoulder and a paper sack in one hand, her good intentions disappeared in a screech of surprise. "There he is!"

Alec tapped his brakes a little too hard and jerked to a slower speed. "There who is?" He followed the trajectory of her pointed finger.

"Mayberry. He's..." She hesitated, still surprised. "He's coming out of the drug store."

"He lives in town," Alec said. "Stands to reason you might see him."

"Yeah, I know." She watched the old, homeless man as long as she could. "He just surprised me. I figured he'd be scrounging in an alley somewhere not shopping."

"That's not too stereotyped."

"I know." She sank back in the seat. "Sorry. I feel this weird connection to the guy. He looks like he could be anybody's grandpa and yet—"

"Yet you found him sleeping on your front stoop."

"Exactly. And now I see him shopping like anyone else. Do homeless people shop? His clothes are mostly neat; his shoes are whole. There's nothing about him that's quite normal for a homeless man."

"So he's a classy bum."

"People don't say 'bum' anymore."

Alec hmmphed at her. She turned her gaze back out the window. Seconds later she gasped again.

"Now what?"

"I can't believe it. He's still here, too."

Her husband stepped out of Dottie's, smart as a billboard model, a cell phone pressed to his ear.

"Huh. Mr. Foster. What do you know?" Alec said. "I take it you haven't given him his papers yet."

"I haven't had time to go to the lawyer."

"And when you do? What do you want the lawyer to tell you?"

"I don't know." Her heart fell. She had no reason to be hanging onto the papers. How could she explain the deep fear that if she simply gave up on fighting Tim she would give up on any chance of restoring her self-esteem? "There's probably nothing he can say. I just want Tim to know I made him dangle a while."

For one instant Alec raised a brow in amusement. Then he shook his head. "In your opinion, what would be fair for him to give you?"

She'd actually thought about it. There was nothing concrete left to extract except time and money. It would be nice to be able to pay her bills. Maybe at some point there'd be a settlement from the logging company whose truck had malfunctioned and caused her accident, but that was being fought by the insurance companies at the moment, and she wasn't holding her breath. "What I want is for him to sell the house and give me a quarter of what he gets. But it's his property. He doesn't have to sell it. Besides, he won't. He loves it—with the pool and the tennis court. He'd never be able to replace it."

"Holy shit, you did come from the lap of luxury." The slight surliness was back in his tone, and this time it irritated her.

"Look, keep your judgments to yourself, buddy."

For a moment his mouth firmed into an angry line. Then all at once his entire face relaxed into contrition.

"Hell, Joely, I'm sorry. None of my crappy mood is your fault. I'm sorry about Tim. I don't know what the answer is."

"I don't expect you to." She stared gloomily out the window. Her good mood from the night before and from the anticipation of today's outing was gone.

The touch of his hand on hers surprised her. She looked down, watching and feeling at the same time as he wrapped her fingers with his. It was like a movie with sensation—real and unreal all at once. Tingles shot up her arm and relief flowed through her like salve on a wound. He squeezed.

"I admit it. I don't want to do this today. I'd much rather have my dog at a park and be enjoying a great spring day. I wish I'd told Vince to find someone else. There. That's the wimpy truth. I don't do wimpy very well."

"Well, let me do it for you. I'm an expert." She squeezed his hand back.

"You're tougher than you let on. Haven't you seen that this week? Why do you think I'm bringing you with me?"

"I do remember you saying this outing was a good idea."

"It's only a good idea to have you with me. I'm afraid you're a Band-Aid on a painful decision."

"Ahh. And when we're done are you going to rip me off slowly or get it over with quickly?"

"Maybe I'll just leave you on and let you fall off on your own when you're tired of sticking to me."

"I'm telling you again. I have the stupidest conversations with you."

"I like it. I'm starting to feel like I can say anything to you."

For that she had no smart-aleck reply. It was a little bit true. She liked saying any dumb thing that came into her mind to him. She liked laughing at what he said in return.

She especially liked that he didn't release her hand, even when they got out of town.

VINCE NEWTON CALLED his place The Bucking V and advertised it on a massive wooden sign at the start of his long, winding driveway.

Bucking V Ranch
Rodeo Roughstock—Bulls and Broncs
Breeding, Sales, and Rehabilitation
Vincent and Wendy Newton

"I'll be damned," Alec said. "He's serious."

"You weren't sure?"

"Vince is a smart guy with a lot of angles. I'm never sure what's going on in his head."

They rolled up the driveway and found themselves in a spacious yard between an older farmhouse and several weathered but sound buildings, including a large classic barn, an indoor arena, and several smaller sheds.

"Looks like a real place to me," Joely said.

"And it looks like Vince actually does live here." Alec pointed toward the barn. A tall, slender man who looked older than Alec by a dozen years hustled toward them with a rolling gait, his dark hair lightly salted with gray, and his slender face elongated by a dark, neatly trimmed goatee and mustache. He grinned from ear to ear like a happy spaniel, and Alec raised his brows in resignation. He opened his door and Joely followed suit.

"Alexander Morrissey, you son of a bulldog. I didn't think you'd actually come."

He reached Alec and enveloped him in a manly hug that included thumped backs and slaps to the cheek.

"You don't look any different, you ugly mug," Alec replied. "I had to come and see if you were lying through your teeth."

"No pie in the sky this time, boy. I'm serious about this. Business is already starting to grow. People nowadays want to know rodeo animals are treated well. We know they have been for a long time, but I'm doing my best to preach it to the masses."

"You go to some fanatical revival meeting and get religion?" Alec asked. "Since when are you a soft old bleeding heart?"

"How can you ask that?" Vince looked wounded, and then grinned. "I was always the animals' best friend."

"Uh-huh. Ain't saying you were mean, you weren't. But they were tools of the trade. Keep 'em healthy. Treat 'em fair. That was how you saw it back in the day. You laughed at those of us who carried apples in our pockets."

"Maybe that's why," Vince said. "Maybe I realized I wouldn't be where I am without the people who raised good stock. And without the stock itself. Some of us take longer to mature than others."

"Sounds like it had more to do with a woman than with comin' to Jesus on the back of a bull."

"Now there I'd have to agree. And speaking of women." Vince finally looked fully at Joely, and his wide grin got wider. "Who have we here? You're brave to be traveling with the likes of this one."

"I am," she agreed, leaning on her crutches and extending a hand. "Joely Fos—Crockett."

"Crockett?"

"As in Paradise Ranch, yes." Might as well get it right out there. "I don't live there, but my sisters and mother do."

"Can't live around here and not know about Paradise Ranch," Vince said. "And it's still a working operation, I hear."

"Very much so."

"Love to see it sometime," he said. "I hear it's a beautiful place—right on the river."

"I'm sure you could visit any time," Joely said.

"That's very nice of you. It's good to meet you, Miss Joely Crockett."

"Same here, Vince."

"All right. All right. Old home week is over," Alec said. "What exactly is it I'm doing here? I could have scanned and e-mailed you the pictures you want. You could have sent me a picture of the horse in return. But you insisted, so I'm here. Start pitching so I can blow you off."

Vince waggled his brows at Joely. "Such a mistrustful young man," he said. "Come on, I'll explain. But first I have an old friend for you to meet."

THE HORSE GRAZED in a large, grassy paddock outside the barn. Even though there were five other horses sharing his pasture space, Ghost Pepper stood out like diamond in a pile of iron ore. He popped his head up when the three humans approached the fence, and Joely caught her breath.

His roan hair coat glistened with a blue almost like fire in the sunlight. Even more striking, however, were the vivid gray spots dappling his rump, the charcoal stockings on his legs, and the dark cheeks and muzzle that left him a wide white blaze down his face.

"Hello, handsome." Her voice came out in breathy awe.

"He's a stunner, isn't he?" Vince said.

"His pictures don't do him justice."

"Hard to believe lookin' at him he's pretty much the Secretariat of bucking horses." Vince leaned on the fence. "You could put a baby under him out there and he'd darn near move around to keep the rain off of her. Put her on his back…" He trailed off.

The horse was built like a brick house. He wasn't a lot more than fifteen hands, but his muscled chest and forearms and powerful haunches put him less in the category of Secretariat and more in the horsy equivalent of a twenty-year-old Arnold Schwarzenegger. For the second time in as many days, Joely went gooey-hearted for a big animal. She thought briefly of the horse she'd lost in the accident, but Ghost Pepper was so different from Penny it almost wasn't like looking at the same animal species.

"Can I buy him, Dad?" She whispered to Alec and turned to him for the first time.

He stood five feet back from the fence, his hands at his sides, his eyes fixed on the horse. Whatever emotions roiled within him she couldn't read, but she could definitely see their intensity in his locked shoulders and curled fingers.

"Oh, I don't think so today, honey." His brows lifted knowingly. "Told you you'd ask."

"I'm not ashamed. Any horse lover would ask. You have to admit he's gorgeous."

Alec flexed his fingers. His eyes hardened into haunted steel. "He knows it's me."

"That's ridiculous," Joely said.

"Oh, I had enough conversations with this bad boy over the years. I don't doubt for one second he's laughing at how we've ended up."

"Then you need to turn it around and get the last laugh, my friend," Vince said. "I have the perfect proposition for you."

Alec unfroze and turned a flint-hard gaze on his friend. "Yeah, you told me about your pet publicity stunt, and I told you where you could put that idea."

Vince grinned. "But now you have to listen without that kind of language since we're standing in front of a beautiful woman."

"Language or no, I'm not saying yes."

"What's this great idea?" Joely asked.

"He needs to get back on this beast," Vince said. "Can you imagine the crowd at the show where that happened? They'd come all the way from Texas, Calgary, and Maine to see Morrissey and Ghost Pepper reunited. Especially given our man's handicap now."

"Wait." Joely frowned and sought Alec's eyes. They betrayed nothing but hard heat. "You'd capitalize on his service injury?"

"Dang right," Vince said, no apology to be seen anywhere in his face. "Rodeo needs a hero. What better than two old adversaries, one an ornery victor, one a newly hardened war veteran who doesn't let adversity stop him? It's pure gold."

"It's pure fantasy." Alec smiled, cocky in his answer, clearly certain his friend could talk all day and not move him.

"Wouldn't that be a little insensitive?" Joely insisted.

"No more than the guy on TV who danced," Vince said.

"Doesn't matter. Be as insensitive as you like." Alec shrugged. "It isn't going any further than right here."

"*Could* you ride him?" Joely asked.

"Nope. I told you. There are certain motions, gripping movements, and other things even the best prosthetic won't do. I've never had a death wish."

"You wouldn't die, you idiot," Vince said. "You'd fall on your ass and the whole place would cheer itself hoarse. No pun intended. It wouldn't matter if you stayed on half a second or all eight—you'd be a hero for just showing up."

"I don't want to be anybody's hero, Vince. Do you understand?" For the first time since arriving at the Bucking V, Alec allowed true anger to show. He jabbed his finger toward his old friend's face and glared.

Vince wasn't fazed. He spoke nonchalantly as Alec turned away from him.

"Okay, okay. I knew that would be a tough sell. Then how about simply showing up? A couple of times. No riding. Just tip your hat. Hell, tip Buzz's hat and let's do a tribute. Then introduce the younger generation taking your place and let old GP there do his thing."

Alec spun back so quickly on Vince that Joely gasped. He poked his finger physically into Vince's chest and balled the opposite hand's fist.

"Don't you bring Buzz into this. He rests in peace, got it? And I gave you permission to use an old picture of me—but I'd better not see Buzz's image anywhere. I'll cripple you, Vince. I swear."

"Hey." Joely put her hand on Alec's chest. "I don't know anything about this, but no need to get violent. I didn't come with you to watch two cowboys get into a fistfight."

"Not your business, Joely," Alec said.

"It is if you get your butt kicked and I have to hitch-hike home."

He turned to her and stared. She gave him a beatific smile, and he rolled his eyes. "You're insane," he said.

"You've got it backward. I'm the sane one."

Vince laughed. He grabbed Alec around the back of the neck and dragged his head forward until their fore-heads met. Then he slapped his cheek as he'd done before.

"I know you're not over Buzz, man. I'm not either. But this was his life, and all I'm saying is it doesn't hurt to remind people that he's a hero, too. You both are. Fine, we don't have to do anything. I'm just looking for a little rodeo love. When I found Ghost Pepper there was only one person who came to mind."

Oh, he was good, Joely thought. Very, very good. And yet his eyes shone enough to convince her he was also sincere.

"Snake oil salesman," Alec mumbled, and cuffed him on the cheek, too.

They pulled apart. To Joely's surprise, Alec smiled sheepishly at her and reached for her hand. He tugged carefully and she stepped with equal care into an embrace, moving her crutches out of the way. He wrapped an arm around her waist and kissed her forehead. "Thanks," he said.

She transferred her weight in to his hold and leaned against his long, muscular frame. Every nerve fiber in her body cheered with excitement at the contact, and she clung to him, not wanting to let go.

"Come on inside," Vince said. "I'll show you what I've been thinking about. You can say yes or no after you've looked at the mock up."

"It'll still be no," Alec said.

"Don't be a curmudgeon." Joely squeezed his middle as if she had an actual right to advise him. Touching him was heady, but the truth was she didn't even have the right to stay in his embrace. Still, he didn't let her go either. Instead, he followed Vince and let her hobble beside him the way he'd done on the church steps at the wedding two weeks before, and she couldn't help thinking how nice it was to have him take the crutches from her and carry them through the barn to the house.

Wendy Newton was a former buckle bunny, or so Joely had been told, and a tiny vestige of that personality remained. She had sunny, open facial features and a flirty friendliness that drew people in to her personal circle, even though she carried herself with the genuine naturalness of a woman who'd found her bliss. Alec and Joely were greeted like old friends and plied with lemonade and cookies while they looked through the photos Alec had brought.

"These are fantastic." Vince tapped on two pictures he'd chosen. I'd like to borrow them and bring them into Jackson, see if the resolution is high enough to use for posters. That okay?"

"Sure. Fine." Alec pushed the pictures to him, and Vince handed him a mocked-up show bill.

Jackson Hole Rodeo: Your summer rodeo nights are about to heat up, read the first.

We're cooking with Ghost Pepper, read the other.

"I've got endless terrible slogans," Vince said. "But this is the gist. No problem focusing on just the horse, if that's what you insist. I also have this dude." He flipped out a picture of a gargantuan Brahma bull. "Honkin' mean sucker named Ignition Wire. He's going to be famous—but he's not a draw yet. Ghost'll help advertise him, too."

"All right then." Alec said. "Looks like you've got all you need."

"I just need you to sign a release for the photos. Don't worry. It'll only give me the right to use them as promotion for the Jackson Hole rodeo."

"Yeah, it's no problem."

Alec seemed more relaxed now that he was inside and away from whatever memories Ghost Pepper evoked. His eyes hadn't lost their haunted shadow, but he no longer had his fists tightened into human brass knuckles.

"And so my work here is done." Vince sat back and closed the file folder that held his examples, prototypes, and now Alec's pictures.

Alec eyed him with suspicion. "That was too easy."

"Why?" Vince shrugged. "You told me how it was when we talked last week. I tried."

"So I can walk out of here and you won't harangue me about riding the horse?"

"Did I slap handcuffs on you?" He turned to Joely. "Do you see handcuffs?"

She chuckled. "No, of course not."

"So. Have some more lemonade and visit a while. Catch up. Hey, I know. Tell her about the hat."

Every bit of progress made toward relaxation disappeared from Alec's body, and once again he was a living ball of tension. "You really are a sonofabitch, Vince."

"Maybe. It's a good story, that's all."

"You are not setting a finger on that hat."

"I don't want the hat."

"What hat?" Joely asked.

"Come on." Alec stood. "We're leaving."

She wanted desperately to call him out for the ridiculous petulance and tell him to stop letting Vince get under his skin. But she remembered how angry he'd made her by telling her what to do about her feelings. There'd be time to question him later. Now she had to support him.

"Okay." She pushed herself from the chair as well, and met his eyes.

He closed his and pressed his fingers along the bridge of his nose. Under his breath he let out a rude expletive. "Hell, you're only going to ask me about it later," he said.

"Not if you don't want me to." When he scoffed at her, she shrugged. "Okay. Yeah, I probably will."

He sank back down into the chair and toyed with his mug. Finally he sighed.

"My cousin Buzz rode with us. We were four at the beginning: Vinnie here and Reece Hanson rode the bulls; Buzz and I rode the broncs. I don't know how it happened, but each pair had a good guy and a bad guy—personas kind of like professional wrestling. Dumb. Meaningless. Reece had the sweet, loveable reputation and Vince the tough guy persona—that was accurate enough. When it came to Buzz and me, though, he wore the white hat and I became the dark, mysterious, no-holds-barred bad boy. Damnedest thing is, I won the championships—enough so the tough cowboy image stuck, but Vince and Buzz were the true hell-raisers."

She looked to Vince and he grinned. "So far, he's got the story right."

"Fast-forward to 9/11," Alec continued. "The short version is, Buzz and I got all up in your face patriotic and went to fight the terrorists. I finished my tour, but Buzz had decided by then that military life was far more exciting than bronc riding. Over in the Middle East he was high all the time on adrenaline and righteous anger, and he stayed once I left. On his last leave home, he had no end of fun razzing me about my constant losses to the horse I couldn't ride. Drunk at a bar the night before he shipped out for his third tour, I told him…"

He shot Vince an evil-eyed glare to keep him quiet, and for the first time Vince complied. He simply nodded while Alec continued.

"I told him I'd bet my black hat against his favorite white one that before he got back for his next leave, I'd ride the damn horse or die trying. He was half a dozen tequila shots to the wind when he took the bet. He told me if I didn't stick to the back of the horse at least once he'd give the white hat to Vince, take my spurs, and I'd have to buy our beers for a year."

"It was a great bet," Vince said finally. "Funniest bet I ever made."

"It was a drunken bet that meant nothing. And it's null and void because the two principle participants no longer exist."

The story only left Joely with a dozen more questions, but the dull, haunted light in Alec's eyes had turned to a green-gold flash that warned her and everyone else to keep their distance.

"That's not true," Vince said with surprising gentleness. "You're here. And you know you never gave up on that bet."

The tension in the room swelled until Joely was sure the walls would burst from its thick, pressurized heat. Then, to her utter shock, Alec eradicated the strain with a near-maniacal laugh. He slapped his thigh and leaned across the table to clap Vince on the cheek twice before finishing with a friendly slap.

"You almost did it," he said. "You almost got me to lose it, but I'm older and wiser so it flopped. Here's the way it is, Vince. I have the hat. I'm keeping the hat because it was my cousin's, but we're the bad guys, Vince. We don't either one of us get to wear the white hat."

He wiped a few remaining tears of laughter from his eyes and looked at Joely. "See what I mean? He's smart as a beady-eyed Wall Street tycoon. He got me to tell a story I never tell anyone, but do you know? I'm glad. Now you've heard it, and we can put it to rest. Vince, go ahead and advertise Ghost Pepper. Usher him into a new era, and I can go on with my life. I'll buy the beer next time you come into town."

"How about we make that the day after GP's first appearance?" Vince nodded. "You have to admit, you want to come and see if the horse still has it."

"I do not." Alec shook his head.

"You haven't been back to the grounds at all, have you?" Vince seemed astonished, as if he hadn't actually put that piece of the puzzle together before.

"No need," Alec replied, a little too blithely. "And no desire."

"So, you won't come and have one picture taken with the horse?"

"Nope. Why ruin a good portrait?"

He grinned as if it were a joke, but for the first time since she'd met him, Joely saw a chink in Alec Morrissey's got-it-all-together armor.

Chapter Thirteen

Chapter Thirteen

HE FULLY EXPECTED to be pummeled by questions on the way home from the Bucking V. Alec stole glances at Joely, waiting for her barrage, prepared to be calmer than he'd been with Vince. He wouldn't blame her for anything she might say or ask, but he didn't have the energy to start the conversation himself. Weakness permeated every muscle, as if he'd run a marathon—or spent eight seconds on a bronc that was trying to shoot him fifty feet across an arena. He hadn't known talking about Buzz would affect him this way, although he'd suspected, which was why he never did it.

And after the way he'd acted? Yeah, Joely would rightfully have a lot of questions. He'd dragged her along "as a buffer," and she'd definitely earned a medal of valor for that job today. He'd kept himself from punching Vince at least twice because of Joely. And punch Vince for what? For telling the truth? For being himself?

He shifted his gaze to the woman beside him, unable to figure out why her presence didn't agitate him. She watched out the window as they traveled back to Wolf Paw Pass. Serene, comfortable, patient—her lovely face gave no indication that she wanted anything from him. There was no anger or tension in her. In fact, she filled the cab of the truck with a peaceful aura he couldn't explain.

After ten minutes his heart stopped hammering from anticipation of an interrogation. It thrummed, instead, in anticipation of a chance to hold her—any part of her: hand, shoulders, waist. He wondered what it would be like to have all of her against him, and a flash of erotic desire sluiced through his body, lodging low and hot in his groin. But sex, while an arousing fantasy, wasn't what he really wanted this minute. What he craved more than sex—as much as it maybe signaled the end of the world— was to make the healing serenity she exuded part of himself. If only he knew how.

He should never have gone to Vince's. Never should have set eyes on that horse. He definitely should have walked out before he'd told the story of the bet.

On the other hand, he'd faced the specter of having to attend the rodeo, and he'd beaten it back. Vince would try new angles of persuasion—but his biggest gun hadn't worked. Alec relaxed slightly and took one hand off the wheel to flex it. The motion relieved an unexpectedly high amount of tension. He repeated it with the other hand.

"There," she said. "You look better."

The words surprised him even though he felt their truth. "I do?"

"Yes. I'm sorry."

"You? For what?"

"For not realizing from what you told me before we went to Vince's how hard it was going to be for you. I should have said it was all right not to go."

She wasn't going to do it—ask a million questions and make him tell her the rest of the Iraq story or the leg story or even the hat story. Against all logic, she would not hound him.

"You had nothing to do with how hard this was or wasn't," he said. "I'm grateful you were there."

"It was interesting. Vince Newton is like someone out of a comic book. A fast-talking nice guy with no boundaries."

He laughed for the first time since his mentally unstable bout with laughter at Vince's. "He's not a bad guy. He's just a…" What was he?

"An annoying friend."

"Understatement. Look, Joely, I'm the one who needs to be sorry—"

She reached across the space in the cab and laid her hand softly on his bicep. "I told you. Don't be sorry."

He wanted to argue with her, because that's where he was most comfortable in their relationship, but he kept his sarcastic replies in check. In response, she stroked lightly down his arm. There was nothing sexual about the touch, and yet his body disagreed. His awareness of her scent—like fresh air and faint flowers—and of the energy in her warm, feminine-soft body, even with a slight distance between them, grew with each passing mile. She shifted in her seat and faced him more fully, her seatbelt pressing between her breasts, defining each as clearly as if she intentionally showed them off. He hardened like an undisciplined teenager. By the time he reached the front of the old stone store that housed her apartment, he wished with all his heart he had the cover of darkness for his walk to her door.

Or covers on a mattress.

That wasn't fair. This was so far from asking for sex. She was only being kind.

"You really don't have to get out you know," she said as he moved to unbuckle his seatbelt. "It's broad daylight. I can get to my apartment fine."

He shifted in his seat, tempted to let her go just so he wouldn't have to move. He couldn't make himself end the nondate that way. It may have been only a field trip, but he'd gotten her into it, he'd acted like an idiot, and he needed to at least end it like a gentleman.

"It's okay," he said. "It isn't because I think you can't do it or even that I'm worried about you. I'm starting to think you could even handle the homeless dude if he was there."

"I hope he's not. I don't want to handle him. But, yeah. I could."

Alec went for honesty. "I just want to end this not being a jerk."

"Who said you were a jerk?"

"Doesn't matter. Let me walk you to your door."

She laughed. "Okay."

He managed to get himself under control and follow her slow progression along the sidewalk. No Mayberry camped on her porch. No husband waited for her to produce papers. She turned the key in her lock, pushed open the door, and faced him with a satisfied smile.

"I have to say, that's always kind of a rush. No lobby, no night nurses, no check-in routine. Nobody but you knows I was even out. I guess I was living in a cocoon."

"Told you, you could do it."

"You did."

He truly didn't know what to do without the mocking banter between them. It left him lost for a course of action.

"Well, thanks..." he began.

"Would you like to come to Sunday dinner at the ranch tomorrow?"

Her request came out of nowhere. For one instant he almost said no, and then he comprehended that accepting meant he'd see her again.

"I wouldn't be intruding?"

"Hardly. The more the merrier at Paradise. Not even lying."

"Okay. Can I give you a lift?"

"Why do you think I invited you?'

She stood there so casually with the little bit of early June breeze lifting stray curls of her honeyed hair and flipping it across the impish smile on her lips. She brushed the strands away with a sexy little flip of her hand. Her eyes shone a pretty ocean blue in the sun, and she set her crutches inside the apartment so she could lean back against her door jamb, her hands behind her. The pose thrust her breasts forward again and tipped her pelvis in his direction, but she had no clue she was striking a provocative pose. Staring at her long legs encased in well-worn denim, and her slender, sexy torso in a heathery blue T-shirt that matched her eyes and hugged her like a whisper didn't help his imagination or his body any. His fingers suddenly itched to slip around her and pull her close so he could trace up her spine and burrow into her wind-blown hair.

Her smile softened as they stared at one another, turning as warm as her eyes, as kind as her thank you, and as sexy as the cowboy-booted foot she set flat-soled against the door frame. His body mutinied once again, and he fought for a long moment to come up with an appropriate good-bye. He failed.

Aw, hell, so much for gentlemanly behavior.

He reached without warning her, without any kind of finesse at all, and hauled her into his arms. He stole the kiss and thrilled when her lips gave way beneath his, soft but motionless. Too late guilt at the callousness tugged at him, and he drew back, but then her mouth firmed and molded to his, pulling him back into the kiss. Thrills sliced down his body and settled as hard flutters in his stomach. She tasted his mouth, opening and closing her lips on his once, twice, and a third time. He caught her bottom lip gently between his, then worried the soft, hot inside of it with a scrape of his top teeth.

She touched his lip with her tongue and licks of fire flew down the back of his neck.

Fast, unplanned, sweeter than hard cider and smoother than good whiskey, they kissed until sense finally returned and Alec pulled away.

"Okay," he said, breathing hard and licking his lips.

She mimicked him, and the sight of her tongue sealing in his kiss, dampening the spot his mouth had just conquered, took the strength out of his knees.

"Well, that was unexpected," she said.

"Unplanned." He tried to apologize, but he wasn't sorry for the moment of magic.

Taking a step back, he cocked his wrists and held his hand up in a gesture of surrender. "I didn't mean—"

"You could come in."

He shook his head. No way would he trust himself in that small space with her. The only place more dangerous would be back in his truck. "Thanks. I think I need to let that be good-bye."

"Yeah."

He turned, knowing he should say something but having nothing to say that wouldn't just aggravate the situation. She didn't look angry. She didn't even look confused. Her clear, blue eyes simply searched him as if looking for answers.

"Tomorrow?" he asked.

"Can you pick me up at one o'clock?"

He nodded and left her in the doorway, turning around one time just before he took the corner around the building. She had already gone into her apartment. Well, hadn't he just screwed that up royally?

The occasion for dinner, Alec discovered, was Harper and Cole's return from their honeymoon. They greeted him as warmly as if he were family, and he discovered the open friendliness he'd experienced at the wedding wasn't reserved for special occasions. He also discovered where Joely had acquired her talent for the quick comeback. Ribbing was a way of life at the Crockett dinner table. If you couldn't toss a verbal dart, you got left behind. And yet there was respect and deference to the two family matriarchs, Sadie and Bella. Alec knew for a fact both women were strong and needed no coddling. Nonetheless, they were treated like queens, especially by Cole and Gabe. The new sons-in-law missed no opportunities to step and fetch for their mother- and grandmother-in-law.

He compared the picture of the Crocketts' TV-family perfection with what he remembered of his early childhood and then life with his aunt, uncle, and cousin. His mother had been a high school math teacher and his father an over-the-road trucker. They'd seemed happy enough, but when his father was home, Alec remembered his mother scrambling to make his dad comfortable or happy or relaxed. She'd always lost the crisp efficiency and silly game playing they'd shared when Dad was gone.

Once he'd moved in with Buzz's family, life had been less of a roller coaster, but it had been all hard work and little play. His Aunt Christine had been a sturdy, nononsense farm wife who gardened, canned, cooked, butchered chickens, and kept house without complaint. Meals were served on time and without fail, and to this day she took great pride in her cooking. His Uncle Rick had been jovial enough, but he'd kept to his up-at-dawn, in-bed-by-dark schedule so that the days rarely varied in their routine, and Alec's junior high and high school years blended together in his memory. He had few memories of joyous, free-for-all Sunday dinners like this.

"We're getting our new house by my birthday in August!" Mia and Gabe's son Rory announced halfway through the meal.

"You are?" Harper stopped a forkful of thick, gooey lasagna halfway to her mouth and looked from Rory to Mia. "That's pretty cool."

"We finally got the loan secured the way we want it and the plans finalized. It took a lot of finagling, but they'll break ground as soon as we return from California."

"Where I get to ride Pirates of the Caribbean," Rory announced. "Pirates and a new house. Pretty cool honeymoon."

His audience seated around the massive dining room table burst into laughter. The boy was known for his precocious observations, but Joely had told him the kid could still crack up even the most staid adults.

"I'd better hear you behaved yourself on this amazing honeymoon," Sadie told him, waving her fork at him. "Most children don't go on those."

"I know. It's a fake honeymoon," he replied. "The real one will be in six months."

He garnered more laughter.

"And we know everyone thinks we're crazy," Mia added. "But we all three got married, so it's only right that Rory comes along."

"But I want to go to Disneyland, too." Harper adopted a high-pitched, whiny voice and held up her fork like a miniscule fencing blade. "No fair."

"Then you should have married my mom and dad." Rory crossed his spoon with her fork, and the two twisted the utensils, clashing like musketeers over the colorful placemats beneath their plates.

"I'm so glad you're home again to teach him manners," Mia said to Harper.

"I'm bucking for the best aunt award," Harper replied, the shaft of her fork clinking faster with Rory's spoon.

"Just wait until you have kids," Mia said under her breath.

Alec caught Harper's wink at Joely. "Want to join in, Jo-Jo?" Harper asked. "I could use a little help. This kid's pretty good."

"Hah!" said Rory.

"I'm afraid I'd hurt one of you," Joely replied. "I'll get the next duel."

"You looking forward to a passel of kids you can let fence at the table?" Alec leaned close and whispered in Joely's ear.

It was the closest he'd let himself get to her all afternoon. His impulsive actions from the day before had turned out to have consequences of severe awkwardness. Neither of them knew exactly what to do or say, and he hated the feeling. He was no Clint Eastwood, or his kid, or the dude who played Thor, or whoever else women swooned over these days, but he'd always had plenty of luck with women. He'd been Mayhem Morrissey after all. As of yesterday, however, this woman had him completely off-kilter and flummoxed.

"It'll be a long time until I do the kid thing," she said simply and stared at her plate.

"Aw, kids are great," he said, nodding to Rory. "You'd have pretty babies, that's for sure."

He knew the instant the words left his lips that what he'd meant as a compliment to her beauty had come off as clumsy at best and inappropriate at worst. But it was the quick pallor and biting of her lip that sent the words boomeranging back into his thick skull and made him groan. Her husband had just told her his cheater girlfriend was pregnant. He set his hand lightly on her forearm and, this time, leaned all the way to her ear.

"I'm so sorry," he said. "That was the worst thing I could have said. I didn't mean it to hurt you."

"I know," she said and an anemic smile followed the words. "Forget it, really. It's just a…thing with me at the moment."

"He's a di—"

"Douchebag," she whispered.

"Yeah." He smiled. "And so am I sometimes. I'm sorry."

"Oh brother." She shook her head and finally looked at him. "Foot in mouth syndrome doesn't make someone a jerk."

"All right, you two. Weapons down." Bella's voice halted both Alec's conversation and the dueling silverware. "I'd best not hear of any Crockett boys causing trouble in Disneyland. Dueling stays at home."

"I won't cause trouble," Rory said, scooping up meat sauce with his spoon. "Aunt Harpo's not coming, so I can't."

"Whoa!" Harper laughed. "Blaming it on me, huh? You little rat."

Rory grinned and then both his eyebrows shot toward his hairline. "Hey, Uncle Cole. Hang your spoon. Show Alec!"

Alec was surprised to be included in the child's table anarchy. He eyed the boy with exaggerated skepticism. "Don't get in more trouble because of me," he said.

"Nah. This is just funny."

"Grandma Sadie hates this trick," Cole said. "We should wait."

"But Grandma Sadie does it best of all!"

"I do hate this," Sadie said, her voice full of admonishment but her eyes twinkling.

"Do it. Do it, pleeeease!" Rory batted a pair of long, dark, very adorable-kid lashes. Alec wasn't quite sure if the child did it on purpose or unconsciously. He was still only ten, but he was a transplanted city kid with no lack of cagey skills.

"Rory, a little bit of fun at the table is great," Gabe said. "But it's not polite to interrupt the entire meal. Why don't you eat now?"

But Rory was giggling and pointing, and Alec turned to look. Side by side, Sadie and Cole sat stone-faced with the bowls of their spoons hanging from their noses.

"You're kidding me!" he said and failed at holding in a burst of laughter.

One by one the others followed. Harper, Mia, Bella. When Joely turned to him, her eyes and mouth deadpan but her spoon hanging securely from the tip of her cute nose, Alec lost it. Never, never, ever would he have seen this kind of lunacy at either of his childhood tables. He caught Gabe's eyes. His former CO was simply shaking his head.

"I give up. I married into a lunatic asylum," he said.

"Where's your spoon?" Alec nearly choked on the question.

"I have not got this particular talent," Gabe admitted. "The ball and chain has tried to teach me, but my nose is evidently not built for it. Go ahead. Try it."

"I think I need to study the technique a little more before I try something so difficult," he said.

He looked to Rory, who was placing and replacing his spoon on his nose, only to have it repeatedly slip off into his lap.

"Don't give up, kiddo," Harper said from behind her spoon. "You'll find the sweet spot eventually, I promise."

Alec had no idea how long the contest would have continued, but it ended abruptly with the clearing of a throat at the door between the kitchen and the dining room. A couple spoon hanger participants grabbed the utensil from its spot, and the other spoons clattered onto plates.

"*Kjære Gud,*" said the intruder.

"Hey, Bjorn!" Harper called.

"I'm, ah, sorry to interrupt." The ranch foreman scratched the side of his nose as if not daring to say more.

"Not at all," Cole said. "What's up? I know you wouldn't come all the way in if it wasn't important."

"Yeah, you just showed me why." He took them all in as if they were hopelessly certifiable. "Even though that image is now burned into my brain and I regret it, a lot, I need to tell you that the little mustang mare is in labor, but there might be a problem. We've called Doc Ackerman, but she's about an hour out."

"Damien Finney's horse? Panacea? What's going on?" Joely asked, setting her napkin atop her plate and standing. "When did you find her in trouble?"

"She started pushing about fifteen minutes ago, but nothing's happening. Baby should be out twenty minutes after they get to this point. Called the doc and she's with a colic out at the Johnson place. She'll get here soon as she can, but we don't have that kind of time."

Cole stood up next and Harper patted his leg. "You and Joely are the horse experts," she said. "Go. We'll finish up and be down in a few minutes."

"We can take my truck; it's right out front," Alec said.

"I've got the four-wheeler." Bjorn waved them off. "I'll meet you at the barn."

"CAN YOU DO anything for the horse?" Alec asked once Joely had let him boost her into the passenger seat and Cole had climbed into the back seat.

"I don't know," she said. "It depends on whether there's really a problem and if we can figure out what it is."

Alec had been around horses all his rodeo life, but he hadn't grown up with them like most cowboys had. He knew a lot about equine injuries and illnesses but precious little about mares and foaling. This mare, he knew, was part of a pilot program Gabe had started for former servicemen suffering from PTSD—a mustang adoption experiment that over the past six months had proven to be incredibly successful with four injured men. The men had bonded so well with the horses that Gabe and Mia were ready to add four more candidates to the program. It made keeping this mare safe all the more important.

"Could be a dystocia," Cole said.

"Where something's out of place with the foal, right?" Alec asked. At least he knew that much.

"Right. I helped with a few back in the day, when my dad was breeding reining horses. If all else fails we can call him. He's got more experience than I do."

"That's true. Russ is a wonderful horseman," Joely said. "But Bjorn's right. We don't have much time. If Pan's in trouble, somebody with expertise has to get here now."

"Yeah. Except, what I'm afraid of is that we're the experts, Jo-Jo," Cole said.

Alec pulled up to the barn and threw the pickup into park. He was out and around to Joely's door in seconds, and she didn't argue when he reached for her sides to lift her to the ground. He held her for a few seconds while she found her balance and took her crutches from Cole.

"Good luck," he said.

"Thanks. Hope we don't need it."

The laboring mare lay on her side in a thickly bedded stall. She was a pretty thing—a gray that reminded Alec slightly of a diminutive Ghost Pepper. When the new humans showed up at the stall door, she rolled to her belly like a dog and gave a long, wrenching grunt of pain. She swung her head toward her flanks and tried to swish her tail, which was wrapped from the dock to past the end of the tailbone in hot pink elastic bandaging.

"Poor baby. Hey, Pan." Joely handed Alec her crutches and hobbled her way into the stall first. She knelt at the horse's head and stroked her neck. "This isn't supposed to be so hard is it? Can we see if we can find out what's wrong, baby?"

Once again Alec heard the sweet, healing voice she'd used on Rowan that made him believe Joely could and would fix everything. The concentration in her face was not just compelling, it lit her up with more allure than a Hollywood camera crew could have done.

"Have you ever checked for a dystocia?" Cole asked.

"I felt a couple only after a vet told me they were present," Joely replied. "And then only because when I was young I got in the way of every vet appointment for the horses we ever had."

Cole smiled. "I remember that. Well, I can check her, but your arm is a lot smaller and might be better. There's not a lot of room in there. Are you willing to try it?"

"All right."

"There should be nitrile exam gloves by the first-aid kit in the tack room," Bjorn said. "Want me to look?"

She shrugged. "They won't be the long sleeves, so it hardly matters. Let's just do it."

Alec watched in fascinated amazement as Joely scooted around the mare's legs and found a spot where the restless back legs couldn't strike her. She lifted the wrapped tail and found the horse's poor, distended vulva. With no hesitation she worked her hand slowly into the birth canal until it disappeared nearly to the shoulder.

"I think you might be the bravest person I've ever seen," Alec said, joking.

"Or the dumbest," she replied with a tight smile. "Okay, I can feel the head. Hello, baby. But…" She squinted then gave a grunt as she felt around. "One foot…Dang. I can't find a second. It must be bent under."

"Crud," Cole said.

The phone in Bjorn's pocket rang and he grabbed it. "It's Dr. Ackerman," he said. "Hey, Doc. Joely's checking the foal now. Yeah, our Joely! Okay, we'll put her on." He handed his Samsung to Alec. "You're closer. Hold this to her ear."

He nodded, entered the stall, and knelt behind her, placing the phone against her ear.

"Hey, Dr. Ackerman," she said.

Alec lost track of the quick-flowing jargon and desperate scramble after that. With help from the vet, Joely located the foal's misplaced leg and gave it several tugs only to lose her grip each time in the slippery environment. Eventually, she procured a soft leather strap from the tack room and, with step-by-step instructions, secured it around the baby's hoof. In the midst of the rush, an agitated man who turned out to be Pan's owner arrived and planted himself at the horse's head, stroking and crooning as if he were comforting a human wife.

"Okay," Joely said to Cole. "I'll pull the leg straight, but you have to make room even though Pan will be pushing against us. It won't be easy."

"We don't have any choice." Cole took a deep breath as his hands took the place of Joely's inside the mare's body. With a red-faced effort he pushed the foal backward and Joely pulled on the strap. One minute later she let out a whoop.

"Yes! I think that's it."

"Yes, ma'am. There's the leg. And, there's the other. And there's its nose!"

Somehow they each got a hand on the foal and pulled together, encouraging the mare with gentle words.

"Come on, Pan, sweetheart, give us just a little help," Joely said a last time, and eight seconds later, the span of a perfect bronc ride, Alec thought, he added his own whoop as Pan gave birth to a wet, slippery-shiny bundle of baby horse.

Someone handed Alec two towels. Instinctively, he handed the phone back to Bjorn and passed the towels to Joely. With vigorous strokes she and Cole rubbed down the newborn until it snorted, jerked, and tried to lift its ungainly head. They both sat back in the bloodied bedding shavings grinning like idiots. Cole raised his hand, and Joely slapped a high five on his open palm.

"Congratulations, Mom," he said.

Their ages-old friendship shone through the mini-celebration, making the whole episode intimate and one Alec vaguely wished he could truly share. There was no jealousy, but he wished he were free to grab Joely the way he had when they'd been alone at her door and kiss her in his own version of congratulations. Instead, he watched the high five turn into a laughing hug.

"Yeah, Doc, it looks like the baby is fine," Bjorn said into the phone. "Okay, that's great. We'll see you when you get here."

A choked sob sounded from the other end of the mare, and everyone turned at the same time. Damien Finney, the mare's owner, had tears streaming down his face. Everyone burst out laughing.

"Finney, you big sap," Cole said. "Wait'll I tell Gabe his guy fell apart like Niagara Falls."

"Go ahead." Finney made no attempt to control his voice. "I have a baby, and Pan's okay. Best damn thing since I adopted her, man. Dang right I'm a mess. Hell, I don't even know what it is."

Joely lifted the foal's tail. "It's a colt," she said softly. "You have a boy, Damien."

The former veteran bawled all the harder. In response Panacea swung her head up, nudging him in the chest, and then hoisted herself to her feet.

"She's standing already?" Damien asked in wonder, reaching up to her muzzle.

"These mamas are tough," Joely said. "They have to be ready to protect their babies within minutes."

Damien scrambled up beside the horse, and Cole did the same, brushing at his jeans and scowling at the muck on his arms and shirt. "Nice," he said, but he reached for Alec's hand. "Thanks for your help, man."

"I did nothing except hold the phone."

"A totally indispensable job."

Joely shifted, too, got to her hands and knees and, with a grimace, reached up. Alec took her stained hand. She managed to get her good leg beneath herself but buckled back into the shavings when she brought up the left one. She let him reach beneath one armpit and lever her up, but then she brushed off his hold and made for the stall door. She was disheveled, covered pretty much head to toe in blood and fluids, and neither she nor Cole smelled like a spring rose.

"You did great," he said.

"We did," she agreed, but the light in her face and the celebration in her eyes from mere seconds before had vanished. "We got a little lucky being able to straighten that leg. It wasn't as complicated as it could have been."

"People are right," he said. "You're born to work with animals."

She held up her hand. "We're not going there, okay?" Her taut voice brooked no argument. "Cole and I have been around horses our whole lives. Cowboys learn stuff like this. You do what you have to do."

"That's not—"

"Alec." She wasn't smiling. She wasn't even understanding—he could see it in the opaque of her eyes. They were letting no emotion in or out. "I'm going to get cleaned up. You stay here. Watch the miracle of the new baby standing and of the mare's instinct taking over. The doctor will be here shortly, and she'll check everyone out. Come on up after that."

"Let me drive you back. You can't—"

"Oh, no, you don't." She pointed a finger at him. "You keep telling me not only that I *can* but that I *should*. Stay here, Alec."

She swung her body furiously between her crutches as she limped as fast as the metal legs would allow out of the barn.

Alec stared, dumbstruck at the inexplicable change in her personality. He turned slowly, and Bjorn set a hand on his shoulder.

"There's a lot going on in her head," he said. "I don't think anybody knows quite what's going to trigger what. She'll be okay."

Alec understood triggers.

"Thanks, Bjorn." He nodded and turned back to the stall, confused as the newborn colt in the shavings.

Chapter Fourteen

BLESSEDLY HOT WATER sluiced over Joely's body, carrying away the foal's birth muck, its smell, and a little of her physical pain. She ached after straining shoulder, back, and hip muscles in a way she hadn't since well before the accident. The water also washed away traces, she hoped, of an embarrassing flood of tears. She couldn't explain the overwhelming grief to herself, much less Alec—although she'd have to try after turning on him the way she had in the barn.

She and Cole had done a wonderful thing, but it hadn't been miraculous. The foal's birth could have been disastrous, but Bjorn had caught the trouble in time. With the vet on the phone, and experienced horse people surrounding them, she'd simply had to do the job without panic. She'd done exactly that. Rather than turn on Alec, she should have been rejoicing in his arms.

Instead all she'd seen in her memory's eye, during the whole wonder of a new birth, was the *loss* of life that had spun her world out of its recognizable orbit. Damien had a new baby, yes, but she'd lost two—one equine and one human. The horse, her sweet and talented Penny, had been her best friend, her only constant in three years of disastrous marriage and indescribable pain. The human baby? Joely halted the memory.

In that stall today everyone had cheered. A new, interesting, complicated man had stood beside her, pulled her up onto her ruined leg, and would have kissed her on the spot had she so much as smiled at him. He'd praised her. Told her she'd done something she was meant to do. In reality all she'd done was rip open her heart.

Maybe four years ago, had she done things differently, she could have followed the golden, ordained path to which Alec had referred. Back then the life plan in her head had looked much different, and she hadn't yet gone to her father and Tim—her new man at the time—excited about the plans she'd devised for her Miss Wyoming scholarship money.

Unfortunately she *had* gone to them. On the very weekend Tim had come to meet her parents and, unbeknownst to her, propose, she'd laid out her future for him and for her father. She was going to vet school. Finally. Now that she was done with planning every step of her future around the next pageant, the next beauty regimen, the next push-up bra or taping session to hold her safely in a gown with a plunging neckline, she was going to pursue her dream.

She could still see her father's absent smile as he listened to her from behind the big desk in his study filled with pictures of his male ancestors—three generations of them—like a hall of kings in a royal palace. "Joely, honey, that's a tough career. You shouldn't have to worry that gorgeous head of yours over cattle and public health debates and pregnancy testing cows. You've got talent most girls would kill for."

To this day she didn't know what he'd meant by that. That she had talent to be an actress or a school teacher or some other job "for girls"? Or had he simply implied she could trade on her looks forever?

"I'm not going to spend my life preg testing cattle," she'd told him. "You know I want to be an equine vet."

"Well, there would be a waste of four years of vet school." Again the words had been calm, non-confrontational, almost nonchalant and jokey. "A horse vet on a cattle ranch. What good would that do? You'd be much better off to learn the skills you'd actually need for working on a spread like Paradise and pick up the horse knowledge on the side. Besides, there's nothing that happens to horses around here that the hands can't deal with."

"Marry me," Tim had said then, right in front of her father. "Marry me and come do the animal charity work you talked about in your Miss Wyoming platform. With your scholarship money and my connections, honey, you can make a difference."

One man's criticism and another man's convincing charm had swayed her. As she looked back now all she could feel was disgust at her lack of self-worth and her willingness to do exactly as her father had suggested—trade on her looks to get what she needed. Sadly, it had worked. She'd become a former Miss Somebody married to a well-known LA businessman and had the world at her feet.

No wonder she couldn't fight for herself now. She was nothing but shallow beauty. And she didn't even have that any longer. She'd set her life on its current trajectory the moment she'd said "I do."

The only thing left for her to do was find a way to say she didn't. She could shake off at least one of her mistakes.

And not start another.

She turned off the water and wrapped herself in one of her mother's thick, oversized towels. She fought the urge to sneak into her old bedroom and curl up like a caterpillar in a soft, warm cocoon; she owed Alec more than the rude cold shoulder she'd given him.

Mia's jeans and lightweight sweater were slightly large on her. She stared at her image in the bathroom mirror, wiping away the condensation fog from her shower. Everyone told her constantly she needed to eat. Maybe they were right. She'd never not filled out a fitted top or the seat of a pair of Levi's. But now she saw for the first time that all her title-winning curves were starting to look flattened.

She studied the scar on her jaw as objectively as she could. It was ugly, no way around it. Winding and pink. She could work further with a plastic surgeon, and maybe sometime she would. She'd just been sick of surgeries after so many of them on her back and leg, and to get the scar even this far, that she'd put the brakes on any more dates with scalpels.

Ten minutes and one slightly camouflaged scar later, she finally left the bathroom. Coward that she was, she hoped most people would still be away at the barn. She would take as much time to process her thoughts and plan her speech as she could get.

He was there, and she tried to discipline her unruly heart when he rose from the couch in the living room, empty except for him, his concern, and his obvious hope that she was all right.

"Everything okay?" he asked. "You *look* much better."

"I was pretty gross." She hesitated. "Alec, I'm sorry I acted so weird. Guess it was my turn again."

To her horror, the pressure of more tears rose in her throat and pushed up behind her nose and eyes. She wanted to tell him about the grief, not sweep it away under the guise of being an overemotional girl. But no way was she opening that vein in front of him.

"And it's my turn to tell you there's nothing to be sorry for. You saved a horse. You need to pat yourself on the back."

The tears pressed harder to be let free. "I can pat myself on the back as much or as hard as any rancher can when he or she does what needs to be done." She managed to get out the words without falling apart. "This had to be done. Luckily it worked."

"That's a little jaded."

"It isn't. It's practical. That's ranch life."

"I know practical when I see it. And I know innate talent when I see it. You have the talent, sweetheart, with animals and with people."

For a few more long seconds she held back the emotion, unable to believe there could be more tears left after her pity party in the shower. The dam ruptured in one unstoppable burst.

"Don't…"

She waited for him to hand her a tissue and tell her everything was all right. She waited for him to fix everything like he always wanted to do, and she welcomed the thought. For once he could have at it and stop this ridiculous reaction to what should have been a wonderful day.

He gathered her to him and lowered them both into the soft cushions of the sofa. Without a word he held her, and she cried. She'd never cried for everything at once until today, and before this moment, she'd never let anyone see her cry for anything.

After five minutes the tears finally ebbed, and she stopped waiting for him to tell her what to do next. Her body curled into his exactly the way she'd longed to curl up in her bed earlier. She didn't want to move. She didn't want to look at him. All she desired was to stay locked in his arms where she was starting to believe nothing bad could happen.

At last he stroked her hair softly and kissed the top of her head. "It sucks," he said.

"I'm sorry." She broke the spell with her voice and pulled away from him. "That was childish."

"Sometimes it's the only thing that helps."

She couldn't imagine him breaking down this way, but she didn't say so. Straightening, she wiped her tears away with heavy strokes of her fingers and drew a deep breath for courage.

"I thought I'd come so far in the past few weeks. So much was because of you."

"You've done a lot of things you didn't realize you could do. All I did was irritate you enough to make you move." He smiled and caught a last tear from her cheek with his thumb.

She wanted to melt into the touch, but she wasn't ready for this closeness. He hadn't solved her problems—he'd only made her face them. The next steps she had to take on her own.

"I think I actually appreciate that now."

"I'd say we're making progress."

"No, Alec, wait. Before anything goes further between us, or I give you the wrong idea about getting involved with you, I think we need to slow this way down. In fact, I've come to the realization we need to part. As friends." Pain stabbed her chest at the words. She ignored it. "I haven't made all that much progress yet. I have a lot to figure out. I'm also still a married woman. If Tim sees—"

"You don't have to be a married woman," he said. "It can be over in five seconds."

"I'm going to the lawyer tomorrow. I'm drawing up a counter to Tim's offer that gives me spousal support until the insurance claim with the lumber company is settled.

That will at least send Tim a message, and I can survive on that and a part-time job."

"That's your way of getting back at him?"

"Money is the only thing he understands."

"No. He understands dickwad behavior. And he understands success. You being successful and overcoming his dickwaddedness will send a much stronger signal than tying yourself to him financially."

"There you go with unsolicited advice again. What I do about this is none of your business. We barely know each other."

"I don't know. I think we're more alike than different. I think we do know each other."

"I know you love to butt into my life."

"I want to know why you don't see your own potential. You just showed everyone what a fantastic veterinarian you could be. It's more than delivering a foal; it's about dealing with the pressure. Jumping in to solve a problem without fear or second-guessing. You have a gift, pursue that."

Anger surged through her calm. This was exactly what she'd listened to so many years before in her father's study.

"Don't talk to me about my gifts or what I can do with them. You talk a big story, but you have your demons, too, Alec. The difference is, I respect mine."

"What does that even mean?"

"You were there. I can't even get up off the barn floor on my own after sitting there for twenty minutes. So just like your excuse that there are things a prosthetic leg won't let you do, there are things a veterinarian in a wheelchair can't do."

"Then get out of the wheelchair."

"Then you get up on that horse." At the shock in his eyes, she nodded curtly and scrambled awkwardly to her feet. "That's right, Alec. You hide things, too. You haven't got it all so perfectly worked out after all, and you haven't conquered this injury as completely as you pretend. So from now on—no telling me what to do until you've got it all figured out yourself."

"You've got it wrong," he said as he also stood. "I don't get on a bucking horse because it's something specific I've chosen not to do. You? You're running away in general. You haven't made any big, philosophical decision about your life. You're reacting. To Tim, to your anger, to me. At least I ride horses. You say you can't ever ride again. How do you know?"

"Because I remember exactly what it requires and I can't do it."

"Aw, hell. You've never tried."

Her leg nearly buckled beneath her. She wished for her wheelchair. For its safety and its mobility and the extension of her body it had become in the past six months. She didn't even know where it was.

"I'm not competing in a 'who has the worst leg injury' contest with you. Our wounds are different. You have your reasons for not riding. I have mine. Nobody has the deeper hurt."

"I don't think this is about wounds," he said quietly. "I think it's about fear. I think this is because I kissed you yesterday and you kissed me back, and that means you did something crazy that you wanted to do. You don't know how to handle that, Joely. You need to learn how to be you and love it."

"I think maybe I'd like to go home now," she replied.

She didn't even want to respond to his ridiculous theory. Kissing him had nothing to do with her anger at his current arrogance—thinking he could comment incessantly on her life. She'd liked the dang kiss. She'd thought about little else for twenty-four hours. She just didn't want another. Alec Morrissey messed up her head.

"No," he said, throwing her further off balance. "You need to stay and put on a good show for your family. They want to pat you on the back even if you don't. I'll tell Gabe I have an unexpected emergency and need to leave. Someone will take you home later."

Really?

"Fine." She tried to sound flippant. It came out angry.

He nodded curtly. Halfway to the door he looked back. "Just so you know. The kiss was pretty amazing. You're a special woman in more ways than one. But it didn't mean I was looking for a sudden commitment. I don't want serious, heavy relationships. As you can see, they don't go well for me. So you didn't have to be nervous. I never intended to be more than a fling."

He left.

She didn't feel a shred of relief.

ALEC TOSSED HIS briefcase across the driver's seat of his truck to the passenger side and climbed behind the wheel, giving the door to the Breswell Trucking building a visual check. Locked and secured. He scanned the yard one last time for anything unusual, saw nothing but the small fleet of four trucks that weren't currently out on runs, and started the pickup. He'd stayed as long as he could justify. He had to go home.

He'd have blown it off and gone into Jackson for distraction if Rowan hadn't been waiting for him. Sitting in his stark, recently moved-into living room alone with his dog, the television, and a can of soup for company had lost its appeal over the past two days. Since the weekend's two disastrous days—dealing with Vince's grinding push to have him rejoin the rodeo topped off by effing it up with Joely—he didn't want to sit anywhere he'd have time and space to think.

He could take Rowan with him and go to that warehouse pet emporium in Jackson where dogs could accompany their owners into the store. It might be entertaining, or at least distracting, to watch people give wide berth to his monstrous pet. They could stop for fast food—Rowan liked a greasy burger as much as the next human.

By the time she was greeting him in her usual indecorous way, he'd decided to follow his plan. He was a big boy who'd survived happily without rodeo or Joely Crockett for the past three-plus years. He didn't need to sit on his sorry ass and contemplate navel lint just because he'd had a bad weekend.

"How about we go for a ride?" he said as he opened the door to the back. Rowan hesitated and looked up, backing away from the deck. She knew the word "ride." "No, you go out first. I'll check e-mail and then we'll leave."

She slipped out the door, and he closed it behind her. She eyed him balefully for a moment and then clumped down the steps like a sullen child. Alec made his way to the bedroom, unbuttoning his shirt as he went. He didn't have a fancy job where he needed ties or coats. In fact most of his coworkers were ex-truckers who preferred plaid cotton or logo-fronted hoodies. His wardrobe choice was generally casual dress slacks and button-down shirts with the occasional polo thrown in. He made it a point to avoid anything that hinted of western yokes, horse motifs, or cowboy culture. No boots, no ostentatious buckles. Definitely no cowboy hat. He still loved jeans and boots, but he wasn't going to advertise it at Breswell. The less often they remembered him as Alec Morrissey, the rodeo champion, the better.

He'd been there just shy of two months, and they were already taking him seriously. He'd moved from being a simple dispatcher for the medium-sized transport company to working with the schedulers. He was efficient and kept his mouth shut, and they all forgot, most of the time, he was anything but a nobody working his way up. The persona he was developing there helped him forget, too. He didn't honestly want to stay in the low-level job for long. There wasn't exactly potential for riches even if he rose to the top in a few years, but it was honest work. It paid a salary good enough to live on and kept him far away from the Jackson rodeo scene. Assuming he could keep Vince's annoying ideas from infiltrating his life, the job would serve him well until he decided what he wanted to do when he grew up. He wasn't in a hurry.

His shirt went into an old green laundry basket that served as a hamper. He'd worn the shirt twice, he could wash it. He unzipped his pants, pulled them down, and sat on the edge of the mattress in his boxers. With a sigh he eased his own leg out of the prosthetic socket and let the artificial limb slide to the floor. He pulled the pants all the way off and tossed them after the shirt. He rubbed the stump of his leg absently, glad for the relief from the pressure, and tried to decide if he wanted to go to town in shorts and play the wounded vet game, or just be normal as he usually was. It was warm today—he'd imagined the cooler shorts—but then the image of Joely standing beside him, seeing him bare-chested in his cotton boxers from Target sitting on the edge of his bed with half a leg sticking out like an appendage from his knee, gripped him.

For the first time in a very long while—years perhaps—his leg embarrassed him. He had no reason to think she'd react badly to seeing the empty space between the stump and the floor, but he suddenly didn't want to find out. Not that there was any chance of it happening; he just couldn't stand the thought of not being whole in front of her.

He stood and hopped the four feet to his walk-in closet, using a strategically placed dresser and chair as guides along the way. He grabbed his dynamic walking foot and jammed it on. Then he picked his most comfortable jeans off the floor where they lived when not on his body or in the wash. A few moments later, he was dressed, his work shoes had been swapped for running shoes, and his embarrassment had turned to anger.

Who was this girl that she made him change his routine mentally and physically just to get away from the memory of her slender curves, her bright smile, and her snappy comebacks? People met other people all the time. They went in and out of each other's lives, and nobody was the worse for the experience. Joely was changing something he didn't want her to change. She'd started out as a good deed, but she'd turned into a living, breathing, smart and insightful person. She'd dug beneath his façade. She'd exposed the little lies he'd told himself about being healed, even while she was healing herself. He didn't like that part. He wanted to be glad that he'd given her a taste of what was to come and let her go. Instead she was working her way into his life whether either of them wanted it or not.

Rowan stood by the patio door, her tail wagging her entire body. When Alec slid the door open, the dog jumped in and trotted straight to the garage door. He shook his head.

"You scare me," he said. "You aren't supposed to understand and process human speech. And I never even said anything about a hamburger."

Rowan yipped and looked pleadingly over her shoulder.

"Still have to make a quick check of e-mail," Alec said. "Come get your treat."

He settled Rowan temporarily with her bone and went to the computer. He went through the junk mail that showed up every day and scrolled down a screen before he saw the message from Vince. His finger froze over the name but only for a moment. He clicked and read.

"Here are mock-ups of two new flyers. If you approve the pictures I'll send them to the printer tomorrow. Ghost Pepper's first rodeo will be July fourth—that's just over three weeks. C'mon, man, put it on your calendar. Even if you're just sitting in the bleachers, you know you should be there. Your lady will be. I talked to one of her sisters about Paradise Ranch being a sponsor for the event that night. She was excited and agreed, and she promised to bring a big group from the ranch to watch. I asked her please to try and get the former Miss Wyoming to come. Yes, jackass, I did my homework on you and on her. Let me know about the flyers. P.S.—I lied. This is all about the bet and the hat."

Alec bolted to his feet, running his hand roughly through his hair. Damn. Damn. Damn it. The man was shameless. He dared to mention the hat after everything Alec had warned? And the scumbag had invited Joely to participate? That was below the belt.

After a minute the frustration abated. It didn't matter anymore, he reminded himself. Joely was not his lady. There'd never been anything between them, and she could certainly do as she liked. Still, he blew out a hard breath, trying to ignore the battalion of wings beating through his chest at the memories of the girl who didn't matter.

He sat back down and clicked on one of the attachments. He had to admit the flyer was eye-catching.

Colorful lettering at the top spelled out Jackson Hole Rodeo. The background picture showed the beautiful low mountains surrounding the rodeo grounds. In the middle was his picture—Ghost Pepper fully airborne, his back arched beneath his saddle and his body twisted in two directions—that insane move Alec had studied to no avail until his eyes had practically melted out of his head. Alec himself was stretched straight up, heels at the horse's neck, one arm raised in perfect position. The second flyer's picture showed Ghost Pepper head-on, and Alec was the airborne one, his legs and arms splayed on his way to eating dirt.

"Spice up your summer nights. Treat yourself to Ghost Pepper's return at the Jackson Hole Rodeo," read the first sign.

"Ghost Pepper—the hottest of the hot broncs: back for the summer at Jackson Hole Rodeo," said the other.

Alec studied them, distracting himself from his anger. After a few more minutes he hit reply and typed quickly.

"The pictures are fine. Make the headlines punchier—they're too windy like a girl wrote them. Use something like, 'He's back. And nobody can handle a Ghost Pepper.' Or 'Ghost Pepper returns…still so hot, cowboys eat dirt to cool down.' Not coming to the rodeo. Don't bring up the damn hat again."

He hit send before he could rethink his reply, and then he shut down the computer before crazy Vince could respond. The man was probably sitting there waiting for Alec's message.

"Let's go," he called to Rowan. "Ride in the car?"

She jumped to her feet and raced back to the garage door. "Let me grab my sweatshirt in case we stay out past dark," he said and went to the bedroom. He grabbed a zippered gray Wisconsin Badgers hoodie off the shelf in his closet, and his eyes drifted to the square, white box pushed as far back onto one top shelf as he'd been able to get it.

Anger swelled up against grief, and his throat closed with pain. He lifted his arms to reach for the box, but he stopped himself with effort.

No. He hadn't looked in the box in nearly four years. He wasn't going to do it now. Damn Vince for dragging all the memories and feelings back into play. The hat stayed where it was. If he were a stronger person he'd get rid of it, but the mere idea of such a thing was ludicrous. He wasn't a stronger person.

He pushed back the pictures of Buzz and his cocky, hell-raising grin taking everybody in and inviting each one to love him—which they inevitably had. "Keep this safe," he'd said of the hat. "It could be yours. You take that horse to eight seconds, and I'll take over the black hat when I get back."

Alec didn't want the hat. But it wasn't going back to being the object of a bar bet made over ill-advised tequila shots either. Vince could shove tequila bets up where the sun didn't shine until his ass got drunk. He wasn't getting possession of Buzz's ghost.

"It's your fault," Alec said aloud, his voice shaking. He hadn't talked to his cousin's ghost in years either. "You had to fall in love with the army life, you freak. If you'd come home with me, come back to the life you were supposed to love, I wouldn't give a flying shit about Vince Newton, I'd still have my leg, and I'd probably have won another championship on the back of the frickin' horse. So, yeah, I blame you."

He'd made the same speech to Buzz many times in the past. He knew his ghostly cousin was haunting the corner of some bar somewhere, laughing uproariously, and telling all his ghost drinking buddies that *his* cousin was hilarious.

"I'm serious this time," Alec said, still angry and feeling like an imbecile for talking to a half-empty closet.

He shut off the closet light, left the room, and grabbed Rowan's leash off the old table by the front door. All the way into the city, Rowan grinned out her opened window while the wind whipped her ears back and flapped her doggy lips so her teeth were bared to passing cars. By the time they reached the pet store, Alec's anger, if not every bit of fresh sadness, had dissipated and he knew he'd made the right decision to leave home.

Rowan did her job well, padding regally beside him down the aisles as he picked up a large bag of her dog food, two boxes of the bones she loved, and an expensive bag of meatier treats for special occasions. Two women oohed over her—true dog lovers. But two gave her obvious wide berths, their eyes reflecting the uncertainty that such an enormous animal could actually be safe. And when they turned down the toy aisle so Rowan could browse, a small girl of about ten actually let out a scream. It was all evilly satisfying.

It was after the child calmed down that a medium-sized beagle rounded the corner of the aisle, trailing a leash but no owner.

"Oscar! Oscar, you naughty boy, you come right back here."

The voice was vaguely familiar, but he couldn't place it until Oscar stopped stock still in front of Rowan and began to bay as if he'd found a moose or treed a mountain lion. His owner slipped in behind him and scooped him into her arms. "I'm so sorry," she said and looked up. Then she laughed, a smile of pure delight spreading across a wide, lush mouth. The girl who'd tried to murder Joely all those twenty years ago. He held in a smile of his own.

"Why, Alec Morrissey! I think I'm about to have a fan girl moment right here. Between you and that gorgeous dog, a couple of fantasies just came true."

"That's nice of you, Heidi wasn't it?"

He wouldn't have thought her mouth could stretch any wider, but it did. "You remembered! I'm honored. And, actually, this is serendipity. I've had a question for you for weeks and haven't known how to find you."

"I guess it's our lucky day." He smiled as he lied.

Chapter Fifteen

JOELY MET TIM in Wolf Paw Pass's small town park after a solitary dinner of Kraft Mac and Cheese and a ballpark-type hot dog. She was finding the brainless world of processed dinners to be all the gourmet cooking she could deal with since the weekend, even though her restaurant-owning sisters would have been horrified.

She'd swallowed her pride and rolled herself the four blocks from her apartment in her wheelchair. She'd worn raw, sore spots into her armpits by using her crutches exclusively for the past week. She could navigate the sidewalks more quickly in the chair, and she supposed it wouldn't hurt for Tim to imagine her as slightly helpless. She needed all the sympathy she could get from the man, and there wasn't an overabundance of it spilling from his Gucci-lovin' heart.

She could see he already waited for her when she propelled her chair along the walkway beside the gazebo in the very center of the park and made for the long, low open-sided pavilion that had stood along the park's west side for as long as Joely could remember. She wasn't late, but Tim was early as always. She tamped down her irritation. She'd asked him to meet here because it was anonymous and far more private than the close-set tables at Dottie's or the few booths at Ina's.

To her surprise, he smiled as she drew closer, stood up, and actually met her before she reached him. He scooted behind her and took the chair handles in order to push. Shock robbed her of any ability to protest, and she let him push her to the end of a heavy, wooden picnic table. A brown-and-white-striped bag from the bakery at the other end of town sat on the top.

"Thanks for finally meeting me," he said. "I do need to leave tomorrow despite what I said. I think we'd both like to finish this business."

Business. That's what their time together had been reduced to. She didn't feel any grief, just a slow, sad burn.

"I would," she said. "So I have a request, and then I'll sign." She pulled the thick envelope of papers out of an oversized purse wedged between her and the side of the chair.

He nodded and opened the bag on the table.

"Have dessert," he said. "A peace offering. And before you make your request, let me make you *my* offer."

"You have an offer?"

He drew a giant, chocolate-covered bismark from the bag along with a napkin and handed it to her. Despite her gourmet meal of orange-sauced macaroni, Joely's mouth watered, and her attitude toward the man beside her nearly softened.

"Oh my gosh," she said.

"Your favorite as I recall."

Suspicion crept into her charitable mood. "What do you want?"

He had the grace to laugh self-deprecatingly. "I haven't been very nice lately, have I?"

"What's the saying? I'm not even going to dignify that with a reply. Don't start being nice now. I don't like scary movies."

He shook his head, a smile still playing on his lips. "I'm nervous about the baby, a wedding, all of that. I haven't been myself. I'm sorry."

Oh, sweetheart, she thought. *You don't know yourself very well then. This week has been a crash course in classic Tim Foster.* She took a bite of the pastry, and a soft, sweet burst of vanilla cream danced across her tongue. She closed her eyes and almost groaned. Let him say whatever he wanted.

"I know you've tried every legal avenue in your power to get back at me," he said. "I suppose I understand that. And I know you're struggling right now with all the medical costs. I'm glad I could help you with those."

"That's big of you," she said, licking cream from her finger. "Since I did nothing to add value to the marriage or the home and wasn't really entitled to VA health care—which we all help pay for with our taxes. Rightfully so, I might add."

He sighed as if preparing to explain life to an argumentative child. "Don't make this so difficult, Jo. I'm trying to tell you that I know things are tough right now. It's not looking like the insurance companies are going to settle anytime soon."

She paused over another bite of the bismark. "How do you know that?"

"Honey, I'm your husband. All I had to do was ask."

She set the pastry down with deliberate care. "You are not my husband. Not in any way that counts. You're living with another woman, you got her pregnant while legally married to me, you've invited me off your insurance even though until the judge signs this decree I'm legally entitled, and it's my coverage, too. So, if I ever hear that you've looked into my personal affairs again, I'll—"

"Hold on now," he said and held up a hand. "I'm sorry. I hear what you're saying. I only went to find out the status of your claim, so I could make a reasonable offer. I didn't find out anything that personal."

"Just spit it out, Tim, so I can present my case, and we can be done."

"Fine. I'm not hard-hearted. I understand that I have money, and things are tight for you at the moment. I'd like to offer you a stipend for spousal support."

She stared in surprise. This was what she'd come for. "Oh?" she asked.

"Yes. Five hundred dollars a month for the next year. No strings attached except that you sign an agreement that it's a gift, it won't be used for anything but living expenses, and you won't ask for more at the end of the year. That's all just so it doesn't need to be put into legalese on the divorce papers, and I can use it on my taxes."

The evening light fogged to an angry red in front of her eyes, and with dizzying disbelief she tried to think of a response that wouldn't get her into trouble. Something Alec had said two days before roared through her brain. "Overcoming his dickwaddedness will send a much stronger signal than tying yourself to him financially."

She'd ignored him, but in a way Alec was right. If she agreed to this "stipend," Tim wouldn't see it as payment for wrongdoing. She'd be tied to an ex-husband for another year in a deal that made her nothing but his charity case. And he could brag about how charitable he was being—out of the goodness of his heart?

Without a word she picked up the envelope containing the divorce papers. She drew out the stack, flipped to the last page and dug briefly in her bag for a pen. With a quick, fluid hand she signed.

"What you just said to me was almost a bigger insult than having the affair." She flipped the sheaf of papers that now contained her declaration of independence back in order, folded them carefully, and placed them in the envelope. Before she slid it across the table she fixed him with a steady gaze he couldn't dodge. "You offered to pay me off so you wouldn't ever have to admit you did anything wrong. I'm not even sure what that would have made me—something not very admirable.

"Well, you can have what you want, and you don't have to pay me a cent. I want no ties to you or your new family, and good luck to you. But I want you to remember something. You and I know what really happened. You know exactly what you did to me, to us, and you know it was cowardly and, despite what you tried to claim, very hard-hearted. Tell people whatever you want now. That I was a terrible wife, that I made your life miserable, couldn't satisfy you, whatever. And you can tell them that in the end I lost my looks and could no longer remotely satisfy your need for arm candy."

"Joely, for crying out loud—"

She shushed him—something she usually considered the height of rudeness. There wasn't a lot of satisfaction in it, but his shock and slight confusion gave her enough for the moment.

"You don't get the last word this time. That's the only stipulation I'm putting on this signature." She finally placed the envelope in front of him.

"Jo, I'm—"

"No. There's absolutely nothing for you to say. Not sorry, not good-bye, not thank you. Nothing. Your chance to say anything ended when you left me lying in a hospital bed. Alone. You have two choices right now. Sit here until I'm gone and then get on a plane. Or get up and walk in that direction"—she pointed away from Mountain Street—"and take a slightly longer route to your plane."

She pushed away from the table and oriented her chair to leave. "Oh, and I expect those papers to be filed tomorrow."

She pushed away, looking inside herself for emotion—sadness, relief, anger, lightness, anything would have been fine. She was only numb. Fully expecting Tim to ignore her order and speak, she prepared her verbal shutdowns, but the final insult was his absolute silence. When she'd nearly reached the edge of the park, she took a quick glance over her shoulder. He was gone.

THE MAIN STREET was surprisingly busy for a Tuesday evening at eight o'clock. Most businesses were closed with the exception of the eating establishments and the main souvenir shop, Wanda's Wolf Paw Gifts. Wolf Paw Pass was a minor tourist destination. People came for the tiny Museum of Ranching at the edge of town, the good food at Dottie's, and now the Basecamp Grill, with its local craft beer, Wolfheart, that was gaining astounding regional popularity. But even for a pretty evening, with the sun starting to bathe the mountains in purple, the town seemed unusually bustling.

She stopped beside one lodgepole pine leg of the hand-hewn sign welcoming people to Founder's Park. Maneuvering to the outside of the pole where she was half-obscured by ornamental shrubbery, she let herself wilt into the chair seat and watch the glut of people. Slowly she surfaced from her detachment and let the shock of what she'd just done start to fill her. Should she be crying? Laughing? How was a person supposed to feel after a divorce? Why would she feel anything different from what she'd been feeling for a year? What stupidity had she shown turning down five hundred dollars a month? And then, without warning, the euphoria started to bubble up inside her. She'd done it. She'd freed herself—her signature had sealed the future. She'd given the man everything he wanted and let him off scot-free, and yet? Everything inside her felt like she'd won. The better person had rolled away with the last word and all the dignity. Even if she was the only one who knew that—it was enough.

She lifted her eyes, and the bottom dropped out of her newfound optimism, draining the joy as quickly as it had filled her. Directly across the street, beneath Ina's pretty, striped awning, Alec stood six inches from Heidi Bisset, his bicep bulging nicely beneath the tips of her moving fingers, their long elegance clear even from Joely's distance.

Pain rose from behind her heart, and her throat filled with suffocating down fluff, as if someone had stuffed socks or pillows—or a pair of buns-high Daisy Dukes—in her mouth to asphyxiate her. A half gasp, half cry escaped through the stuffing, and Joely covered her mouth. Alec tossed back his head and laughed. Laughed! Ridiculous tears beaded in Joely's eyes. She couldn't hear words, but Heidi clearly cajoled him, switching from stroking his muscle to wrapping it with those fingers and tugging him toward Ina's door. For one second Joely held out hope as Alec put up one hand in protest. But it was short-lived. He laughed again, and followed her skimpy-shorted, cowboy-booted figure toward the door.

She had no reason to be upset. None. She'd told Alec to go take a hike.

But, please, Lord, not with Heidi Bisset.

"Your mouth is open and your eyes are shining. You must know the woman with your gentleman friend across the way. I'm guessing you might even be unhappy about it."

Joely turned toward the voice that rumbled deep and quietly almost in her ear, refined, slightly accented. Mayberry, now without his coat or hat but with the same brown, cuffed trousers and the addition of a blue, Mr. Rogers-style zip-front cardigan, stood beneath the park sign. She could see the gray ponytail fully now, surprisingly thick with a slight wave. It hung to the base of his neck, a peculiar contrast to the stodgy sweater.

"Mr. Mayberry!"

"Miss Crockett, I apologize for intruding, but you seem upset."

She had no idea how to respond. She didn't know this man from a potential serial killer, and it dawned on her that she'd never followed up with her grandmother on the contents of his note. How could she have forgotten? Yet his eyes were kindly and his concern sincere.

"I'm fine. It's been a long day, and I'm trying to decide if I want to brave the foot traffic with my bulky chair."

"And you're seeing things that upset you." He lifted his head toward the ice cream shop across the street, where Alec's broad shoulders and tapered waistline were just disappearing through the door.

"Really, I don't think it's—"

"Any of my business. You're quite right. But you were with him the last time we met as I recall. I thought perhaps, this is a tryst that shouldn't have been for public consumption."

She wanted to laugh at the man's proper speech and cry at his observation. He was more than an enigma and certainly far less than an appropriate confidant, but the urge to unload about the vague cruelties of the male gender was strong. She definitely wished she hadn't publicly consumed the…tryst. Those seconds of happy relief just before she'd seen Alec and Heidi were already a faded memory.

"Alec and I are just new acquaintances," she said and was surprised by the stab of sadness the admission caused.

"Really?" He smiled.

"I met him at my sisters' wedding less than three weeks ago. So yes, really."

"Sometimes, things happen very quickly."

"Well, not in this case, so I think you've read the situation wrong."

He bent slightly forward and rested one wrinkled hand on the back handle of her chair. "Good people are usually very bad liars."

"Mr. Mayberry, you don't know me. I think this is slightly…inappropriate."

"No need for the 'mister.' It's just Mayberry."

"But no real name?"

"Didn't Sadie tell you?"

"No. She hasn't offered anything from your…correspondence."

"Ah. A woman of discretion. Well, Joely, everybody and everything has a real name. It's just whether they choose to share it. I'm not sure the real name of the thing you saw across the street is what you think it is."

She was too intrigued by the man's existential rambling to be offended. His pop-spiritualism fit with his ponytail better than his clothing did.

"What do I think it is?"

"A man interested in a woman."

"Every man is interested in that woman." She laughed drily. "Men like perfect things. I know. I used to be fairly perfect."

"And you aren't any longer?"

She laughed for real.

"You know," he said, "most things look one way and are nothing as they seem. Like you. Your inside does not match your outsides, but don't people jump to conclusions about who you are? It's always up to you to set aside the conclusions you jump to and find out what's really going on. What the true name of something is."

"Are you some sort of Indian guru? A shaman? A spiritual leader?"

"Hardly. I just learned early on that we can't take anything for granted and very little at face value. Sometimes even people and places, solid ground that we've depended and stood on our entire lives are not what they seem."

She got the clear impression he was not talking about Alec and Heidi any longer.

"All right…"

"If I were you, I'd go at least tell that couple in there *your* real name. Some people learn early on how to take advantage of a hand they're dealt. But some of us take a little longer."

The man was not dangerous. But he was definitely certifiable. "You sound like a wise man," she said, hoping maybe he'd take it as a nice little wrap-up to their conversation.

"Not wise. I am a little bit crazy, however." He smiled as if the admission should reassure her. "But this time, I know what I'm talking about. You greet your grandmama for me, hear? Tell her Trampas said hello again."

In the literal blink of her astonished eye, Mayberry disappeared. She swung her gaze around and saw him behind her, already twenty-five feet away. How did the elderly man move that quickly?

Trampas? Of the Mantervilles her grandmother had told her about? How was that possible? She couldn't fathom why he'd be here all these years after the time Grandma Sadie had described. And living as a homeless man spouting wisdom in the form of weird riddles? She pinched herself to make sure she wasn't dreaming. Maybe she wasn't really divorced from Tim, and she was pinching herself in her bed at home.

But the breeze danced through her hair, and people continued filing past her on the busy street, their boots, shoes, and flip-flops percussing the air. Linden blooms from the park behind her filled out the scene with sweet fragrance. Her dreams were never that full of sensual detail.

Go tell them my real name.

What did that even mean? Everything has a name, he'd said. She supposed that applied to situations as well as things and people, but what was the name of this situation? Anger? Jealousy? Misunderstanding?

It hit her like a splash of ice water to the face. The name of this situation was Screwed Up, as in, she'd screwed up. In a huge way. She didn't want Alec out of her life. Not yet. Not before she figured out why every time she thought about him her emotions and her body took her on a roller coaster of feelings. He could make her tingle—he could make her feel like her body was on fire, actually, all from a kiss. He could make her angry and resentful. He could make her feel safe. How could she deny herself the chance to find out what it all meant?

But he was in the restaurant with Heidi. That hadn't taken him long—two days? What did that mean about his feelings? Clearly there hadn't been much of a fire for him. What did she really need to find out?

"It's up to you to set aside the conclusions you jump to and find out what's really going on." That's what Mayberry had said. It seemed like universally good advice.

Finding the courage to investigate, though—that was a skill she wasn't sure she had.

She closed her eyes. First she pictured Tim and the shock on his face over her assertiveness. Then she pictured Alec, laughing intimately with gorgeous, full-bodied—in more ways than one—Heidi. Were they laughing about her over ice cream or pie?

Mortification sprouted and she nearly blew off Mayberry/Trampas and rolled straight for home. She didn't need this aggravation. Fortunately, her brain was stronger than her yellow spine. She was ridiculous—why would they waste time talking about her? It was pure arrogance to think she'd have that kind of power over someone else's date.

She'd just proven to Tim and to herself she was not a door mat, and she didn't have to let herself be bullied. If she wanted Alec Morrissey, she had to go fight for him.

The idea was so far out of her comfort zone she might as well have been contemplating a naked pole dance in front of her grandmother. Nonetheless, she pushed herself away from the park entrance and stopped analyzing the choice. She didn't let herself think about what would happen inside the shop. The only plan she had was surprise. It was a stupid plan, but she could work with stupid. She'd had some practice lately.

She almost gave up when she faced the crosswalk. She had her wheelchair. How was that going to play? The shop was small. She'd get in the door, but she had no idea if she could navigate the angles around the tables. A moment of angry bravado could turn into a comedy of the klutzy. She'd see even more laughter from Heidi and Alec. No way.

But something wouldn't let her turn around. For long moments she sat in an unobtrusive spot next to a wooden bench in front of Wanda's gift shop trying to figure out why she was acting on the word of an odd old man she didn't even know.

Alec.

She imagined in one quick flash having him in her life. No delusions of forever, simply happy anticipation of what they could explore together—maybe including that hot cowboy body of his. At the very least more amazing kisses. And the comfort and safety, thought-provoking though it was, Alec brought to her entire being just by being around.

That was why she wanted to heed Mayberry's words. However crazy he might be—or she might be for acting on his words—he'd galvanized her feelings. Shoving away her doubts, she wheeled her chair to Ina's door.

She didn't see Alec or Heidi when she rolled past the main picture window. She'd decided to stay in her chair and not be too proud to ask for help, but at the last moment she changed her mind. She set her wheels' brakes beside the building and stood, balancing on her good leg, taking a little weight on the bad. She folded the chair, let it rest against the building, and then using the wall and door for stability, she entered the ice cream shop slowly but under her own power. One step, two, three, four…she assessed the distance to the counter. More than four steps remained.

"Joely!" Bonnie McAllister came around the counter and met her. With a huge hug, she gave Joely an excuse to stand still for a moment and steady her balance.

"Hi, Bonnie. It's great to see you again."

"You come for the usual?" Bonnie winked.

"Wolf Paw Chunk." She smiled. Despite the bismark she'd eaten with Tim, if she had to order something as a cover, a small dish of Ina's signature concoction, half dark chocolate and half milk chocolate ice cream with dark and milk chocolate chunks in it, would be small sacrifice. "Maybe in a few minutes."

She caught sight of them over Bonnie's shoulder. They sat in an end booth, their profiles to her. It was no surprise to see Heidi's jaw moving a mile a minute. What was a surprise was the look of forced pleasantry on Alec's face. Joely's heart gave a little leap. She might not know him perfectly, but she knew what excitement looked like on him, and this wasn't it. The surge in her pulse gave her confidence just enough boost to refine her plan. Surprise—plus great acting ala Alec Morrissey.

"I was surprised to see them come in together." Bonnie followed Joely's gaze. "Weren't you seeing him?"

"Nothing exclusive," she replied, adding a faked breeziness to her voice. "But, in fact, I did come in to meet them."

"Ahhh! For some reason I feel better about that." Bonnie winked again. "Go get him, my friend."

It was far too soon to let words like that ramp up her hopes, but they did. She gave Bonnie another squeeze and turned toward Alec and Heidi's booth. They didn't notice her making her way slowly from table to table. She concentrated on each step, hoping the exertion of trying to make the walk look smooth didn't show. Halfway across the room a muscle spasm knifing through her back halted her progress. She held in a gasp, bent slightly, and prayed for it to go away. When it released, she went on. She was less than six feet away when Alec saw her. His immediate transformation made every twinge and knot in her back worth it.

"Joely?" He shot to his feet and reached for her hand. "What are you doing here?"

Heidi didn't smile. "Yes, what are you doing? Look at you, making your way without a chair. That's so brave."

Joely ignored the barb and concentrated on putting every ounce of annoyance into a worthy performance, prefaced with a wink at Alec.

"Did you forget?" she asked. "We were going to meet here at eight thirty to discuss those lessons." His face went so blank she could have molded his features into any emotion she wished. She laughed. "It's all right. We made the plans so last minute."

His eyebrows shot high, disappearing into his bangs, and laughter filled his eyes. "Oh, that's right. Jeez, Joely, I did forget. I am so, so sorry. Heidi had some ideas about the rodeo, and I was giving her some names of people who might help her, since I'm not available."

"He's a stubborn man." Heidi finally allowed a smile to slip onto her lips—a pouty, teasing look aimed straight at Alec. "I would love him to be the spokesman for Bisset Furniture and the face for our sponsored riders. He's steadfastly refused despite all my best offers."

Joely could just bet what those offers included.

"I don't do 'be the face.'" He smiled. "I think she understands and will forgive me."

"Oh, what's to forgive?" Heidi practically purred the question. "Just take me to dinner, and we'll call it good."

He turned wide eyes on Joely and she almost laughed at the reined-in despair. She wasn't too late to pull this off.

"Alec doesn't hold grudges, Heidi." She didn't look at the woman in the booth. To Alec, she raised her brow in a question she hoped he understood. *Forgive me?* "You'll have to check his schedule about the dinner, though. I've got him booked for a while."

He rubbed his jaw, working hard to cover a grin. "That's right. When do you want to start those driving lessons?"

"Driving?" She gave him her most astounded look—she hoped—and her legs shook a little as she plunged all the way in. "Oh, no, not those! I meant when we talked about getting me back in the saddle and you showing me your strategies. You agreed to be my new riding instructor."

She gave him a moment for it to sink in before she leaned toward him, inhaling the scent of his soap, his skin, his chocolate-sweet breath, and whispered, "Close your mouth, you big goof, or she won't believe this. You want me to rescue you or not?"

Chapter Sixteen

"RIDING INSTRUCTOR?" HEIDI flew from the booth at that and placed her hand urgently on Alec's shoulder. "You told me you weren't riding anymore."

"Since when do riding instructors have to be mounted in order to give a lesson?" Joely asked. "Alec was a world-class rider, and now he knows what it's like to have an injury that affects control of the horse. He's the best person I know to give me some pointers."

Her performance pleased her. She sounded for all the world like she couldn't wait to get on a horse, when in truth the thought terrified her more than driving. Alec's broad grin as he settled into his role in this ruse, however, calmed her. She knew from experience she would now have to mount up at some point—he'd settle for nothing less—but she'd grin and bear it just to pay back fate for this moment. Her second show of doing what she wanted, consequences be damned, of the day.

"I don't ride broncs anymore." Alec smiled indulgently at Heidi. "But I have been on a horse once or twice. I can help Joely get her confidence back. I understand she's still got a few records that stand, so she's one of the greats, too."

"Yes. It's so sad when tragedy strikes a superstar." Heidi's words, almost mumbled more than spoken, nonetheless hid none of her sarcasm. She dropped her hand from Alec's arm and returned his smile. Hers didn't carry to her eyes.

"I can see that our lovely time here has come to an end. It was divine running into you, and I hope we can do it again soon."

"It's a small place. I'm sure we'll see each other again."

"Thank you for the ice cream. And the contacts."

"Sorry I couldn't be of more help."

"Well…" For a moment Heidi's familiar flirtatiousness returned. "You know you certainly could be with one little word. 'Yes' is easy to say."

"It's nice of you to offer, but yes is not a smart thing to say if you can't deliver."

"Oh, Alec Morrissey." Her hand returned to its favorite spot on his upper arm, and she stroked slowly down the bicep. "You would definitely deliver. That is not the question."

She stepped back and placed the same hand she'd just petted Alec with on Joely's upper back. "So good to see you, Joely. You take care of yourself, hear? I hope you continue to get better."

For the first time, Joely had to grit her teeth and force her smile to stay in place. "Why, thank you," she managed. "*So* nice of you to care. Alec's here to see that I definitely do."

Heidi left with a toss of her platinum ponytail and a sway of her scantily clad hips. Once she was out the door, Joely buried her face in her hands.

"Oh, good Lord," she said. "I feel like I just went a round in middle school."

Deep and hearty, Alec's laugh filled the air, and he grasped her upper arms, swinging her slowly around to face him. He released her arms to take her hands and pull them away from her face.

"Hi," he said.

"Hi." Her heart thrummed in happy excitement. His eyes shone a smoky amber, with that color rimmed with a hot, molten bronze.

"Before we even begin to touch on why you're here, I need you to know that you were, both an answer to a prayer and completely brilliant," he said.

"Yeah, that's not like me," she said with a self-deprecating laugh.

"It's completely like you. Now tell me how I got so lucky that you decided to come."

She fought for only a moment with the truth. It would be easy to say something flippant—that's what they always did when the emotions started to flow. Instead she pushed back her fears yet again. "I saw you walk in here with Heidi, and I didn't like it."

His grin spread even wider. "You didn't?"

She shook her head. "I really didn't. I was jealous, a little. Okay, a lot. It hit me over the head that I wasn't finished deciding whether I liked you or not. I'm—"

His lips pressed down on hers in a hot, frenzied crush. With quick hands he ran his fingers through her hair and held her head, tightly, desperately, giving his kiss a solid place to roam hungrily. She wrapped her arms around his waist, snaked them up to his mid back, and clung there, kneading in time to her thrusting tongue. Liquid sluiced to a hot spot between her thighs, and she pushed her hips into his, a moan that she felt more than heard escaping into his opened mouth.

He twisted and tasted, sent shockwave after wave into her pulsing feminine core, and held her firmly upright when she wanted to buckle in sweet desire. No way was she giving as good as she got, but she tried anyway—dancing with his tongue, moving in time with his sensuous mouth, craving more of the searing breakers of pleasure rolling through her.

"Ahem. This is a family establishment. Shall I call the Roadhouse down the street or would you prefer the newer Marriott Courtyard out on the highway?"

Bonnie stood before them, hands on hips, a droll smile lifting her lips. Joely turned from the kiss with burning cheeks but smiled back. Alec's lips remained on her temple.

"Sorry. Told you I was looking for him."

"If I'd have known what for, I would have stopped you." Bonnie's teasing finally broke them fully apart. She waved her hand from one to the other. "But I told you I like this better than the other and I meant it. Your sisters are married off and boring now—time for a little new romantic blood."

"Whoa." Joely laughed. "It's just a kiss."

"Uh-huh. Can I get you two non-love birds anything?"

Alec questioned her with his eyes, and she shook her head. "I'll just pay my bill, and we'll get out of your hair."

"Hey," Bonnie said, "I only broke it up because those two came in. You know how teenagers like to spread stuff around."

Two young teen girls stood at the counter looking over the case of ice cream selections. They weren't paying any attention to the adults, but they would have soon enough.

"Thanks." Joely laughed. "I guess you really don't need a reputation as the make-out spot."

"Happens enough anyhow. There's something about ice cream."

It felt entirely familiar to fall into step and let him support her weak side as they left the shop. She hadn't paid much attention to her back in the past ten minutes, but once outside she could feel the muscles along her spine start to tighten as if there were fists top and bottom twisting them like steel ropes. She leaned harder into his side without meaning to.

"You okay there, sexy?" He grinned.

She nodded and flexed her shoulders, hoping to ward off the growing pain. This happened sometimes. It's why she didn't walk on her own.

"Hey, wait, you're hurting." The amber in his eyes flared to green and gold with concern.

"Muscle spasms. They don't last once I rest a little. There's my chair."

"Oh no. No chair for you, sweetheart. Your chariot with its three hundred and eighty-five horses is right around the corner."

"You know what? I'll take you and your chariot up on that kind offer."

"Whoa, now *that's* new," he said.

"Don't you tease me," she warned. "That was hard. I got myself here; I should be able to get myself back."

"Hey." He placed his forehead against hers. "I wasn't teasing. And I know all about your independent streak. But this is you learning how to channel it efficiently, and it's a good thing. Makes your life easier and mine more fun, because I get to drive you home."

It felt wonderful to climb into the familiar seat and let her backbone curve into the comfortable bucket. Almost immediately the ropes of her muscles began to untwist, and she closed her eyes. The shivers began anew the instant Alec took her hand. They only intensified when he started stroking her palm with his thumb. By the time they reached her apartment, he'd almost succeeded in heating her up to restaurant status without a single further kiss. How had she ever thought it made sense to send him away?

Still, Sunday's big scene was the night's elephant in the room—and they couldn't pretend it hadn't happened.

Although, in front of her door, they did try.

"Come in," she said when he stood beside her. "We should talk."

She made to turn for the doorknob, but he turned her back to him and lowered his mouth just as hungrily as he had at Ina's. The difference this time was their total lack of audience and a pressure deep inside that had already been built up once. It took no time for the surge of power to rise again. Lips, tongue, teeth, nibbles, bites, suction, and deep, stroking dance moves—everything played together and harmonized into an erotic build-up that left them both murmuring and panting.

"You taste like sugar and wine," he said. "Like potent alcohol I should be careful about drinking. And you smell like a forest of minty oranges. Is that me going crazy?"

"Oil," she whispered. "Mandarin and peppermint. It's supposed to give me confidence."

"Does it?"

"Confidence enough to kiss you." She smiled against his lips. He took her top one between his and licked it slowly with the tip of his tongue. A cascade of sparks sizzled across her shoulders.

He pushed her back against the wall beside her door and locked her there with his body. His mouth opened, letting her lip go but making way for a deeper assault. She reached as far around his hips as she could, grabbed the hard muscles of his seat and yanked him to her without finesse, arching her pelvis to meet his, causing heat to explode through her limbs. He rocked into her hard to soft and she whimpered into his mouth.

"Open the door." His voice came out raspy and quick.

"Is that a good idea?"

"Probably not."

"Okay."

He pulled away enough for her to turn. Before she did, she pulled her key from her pocket and giggled, running its tip playfully down his nose, between his pecs, and just past his navel.

"Hello," he said.

"There are lots of kinds of doors." She ignored the flare of embarrassment at her boldness and in response it faded almost immediately. If somebody had hinted earlier that she'd be standing here tonight making sexual come-ons to Alec Morrissey, she'd have called them all kinds of delusional. Now she felt drunk on the crazy events of the past hour.

"I only care about one of them," he replied. "Open it."

They nearly fell into the living room, groaning and laughing. She lost track of details as he kicked the door shut and lifted her into his arms. Her good leg wrapped around his hips, the other leg, tighter tonight and less flexible, only reached as high as the back of his thigh. He carried her smoothly, so quickly, to her sofa, turned and sank with her on his lap into the deep leather cushions.

"Are you okay?" he asked.

"Better than. But I'm thinking about you. How do you stay so strong with me hanging on your neck, throwing your leg off balance?"

"I think about every move I make, although I do it in the back of my mind most of the time. Believe me, walking is not distracting me at the moment."

"The extra weight on your leg doesn't hurt?"

"It doesn't matter in the least."

She started to protest that he was in pain, but he slid her hips forward on his lap and locked her against the firm length of his arousal. Sparks fired off for all the hidden parts of her body. "Any discomfort has very little to do with my leg," he said and kissed her again, making her forget she'd wanted to say anything.

She melted into him, meshing at the spot that quickly became the focus of every nerve in her body. A sweet groan escaped her lips, and he pressed gently upward—fanning the sparks hotter. She reached for his kiss and he gave it, lipping her, kissing, open-mouthed and playful. She studied what he liked, what made him twitch beneath her, or what made him groan in pleasure. The frantic first discoveries that had driven them into the house melted into sensual exploration.

He lifted into her again, causing *her* to whimper in pleasure.

"Soft," he whispered. "Girls are so much softer than guys. Sexy. Sweet."

"Soft wouldn't matter without hard," she replied. "We need that from you."

"Man alive, the things you say."

Deliberate. Unhurried. They kissed and touched, building the passion, learning to synchronize. One strong-fingered hand slid under her shirt, journeyed up her side and burrowed beneath her bra. After pushing it out of his way, he cupped her breast and grazed his thumb over the tip, plying the nipple with gentle strokes until it rose into his touch.

"I guess there's a little hardness to be found on even the softest of girls." He transferred his lips to the side of her neck and goose bumps poured down her body and into her belly. Some pooled there, the rest raced for her toes.

Digging and scrabbling at the hem, she found her own path to the skin beneath his polo shirt and ran the pads of her fingers up his stomach, pulling back enough to give herself room. She reached his chest, splayed her fingers over the flat plane of his breast, and sighed when she buried her touch in a soft thatch of hair.

"You have hair on your chest. Marry me tomorrow."

"That's your criteria?" He squeezed her breast softly, regenerating the gooseflesh all over her body.

"Not a deal breaker, but it is icing on the cake." She shivered deliciously. "What you're doing there? With that hand? That's the clincher."

"Okay then. I have to leave now, though, so I can get the ring."

"Don't need a ring."

"You have no concept of getting what you want, do you?" He chuckled, rocked against her, pulled back and scraped her T-shirt all the way up her body until he exposed her breast. Bending forward, bracing her spine with a strong hold, he closed his lips over her skin and let his tongue take over what his fingers had so expertly accomplished until then.

Warm, wet, and slippery, his mouth brought her closer to a stunning cliff edge she really didn't think she should look over. Because if she did, she'd want to fly off it with him.

"Alec," she murmured. "That is..."

"Beautiful," he said against her. "You're beautiful, Joely."

Beautiful? In that moment, fighting tears of wonder, she almost believed him. All at once, she could imagine them entwined, wholly joined, rocketing toward that cliff—and she wanted it.

He kissed her one last time, took the aroused nipple between his teeth, and wriggled his jaw.

Her breath left in a rush.

He lifted his head, pulled down her bra, and straightened her shirt. "Yeah," he said. "Oh yeah."

"Why are you stopping?" she asked, setting her forehead against his lips and circling her hand through his chest hair. She understood exactly why they had to quit.

"Because you didn't show up at Ina's shop for this," he said.

"Oh, what do you know?"

She laid her head on his shoulder and withdrew her hand from under his shirt. He took it and clasped it to his chest.

"I need to be honest with you," he said somberly. "I can't marry you tomorrow."

"Well, dang."

She straightened then and grimaced as she rolled off his lap to settle beside him. "My legs aren't used to that."

"Then how do you expect to ride?"

"Yeah, about that..."

"You aren't getting out of it, so don't try."

"I know. I know. I did that to myself." She sat quietly and let her body calm, get used to the idea that it wasn't going to follow the exquisite sensations she and Alec had just shared to their natural conclusion. Finally she let out a long, regret-filled sigh.

"I didn't get a chance to say I'm sorry for last Sunday."

He hugged her into the crook of his arm and chuckled softly. "Yeah. You broke up with me, and we weren't even going steady."

"I did. And everything would be much easier if we just blew that day off, but we both said some harsh things."

"We were both upset."

"I know, but there was truth behind some of the words. For both of us."

"You were right. It's none of my business to tell you what to do about Tim. Dickwad," he added under his breath.

"True, but it's done so it doesn't matter anymore."

"It…what's done?"

"Papers are signed. He's gone."

He turned a little and put both arms around her. "Oh, Joely, that's…a huge blow. Should I say I'm sorry? Or I'm happy for you? More than happy?"

"Definitely happy, not sorry. But Tim isn't the issue. Just because I like you—a lot I'm starting to realize— doesn't mean our pasts suddenly went away or we've changed. I do things that tick you off. You're overbearing and bossy. Those are the issues."

He released his bear hug and relaxed again. She cuddled back against him and placed an arm across his chest. "I said one thing that remains true," he said. "I'm not looking for a deep commitment. What I want is time with you. You're good for me—you draw me out of my reclusive shell. I'm good for you—I make you rethink what you know about yourself. And if you didn't notice, you turn me on—fast and hard. How can all that be anything but great?"

"Are you suggesting friends with benefits? How awful and clichéd is that?"

"It's kind of exactly what I'm suggesting. And why is it awful?"

"I don't need a friend who's out to save me. Neither do you. I just want to see where this goes."

He didn't respond. He sat so quietly for such a long time that she finally pulled away and peered into his eyes. They were focused somewhere in the distance until he turned back to her. He cupped her cheek.

"Maybe I can help you get through some things in your life because I've been where you are. I will sound like I'm trying to boss you around sometimes because I'm a dumbass guy. But don't ever think I'm out to save you. I'm the last person you'd ever want in that position, Joely."

"Hey, come on. What's that mean?"

"I've tried saving people. I'm not good at it." Two heartbeats after the words were out cheerful Alec returned. "Here's how we put last weekend behind us. I was obviously wrong when I said you were afraid because I kissed you—that's been proven without question over the past fifteen minutes. So let's go from here. We won't talk about vet school. We won't talk about rodeo. Maybe we'll get to those topics in time; maybe we won't. But we have so much we can do. So much more we have in common."

"Easy peasy lemon squeezie," she thought. It's what she and her sisters had always said when a solution seemed more than obvious. Alec's cut-and-dried plan was flawless on the surface, but beneath it ran something scared at best and cowardly at worst. To ignore problems was the worst way to start a relationship.

And yet. What could she say about it? Her family was fantastic at ignoring relationship issues. She and every one of her five sisters—six girls—had left home so they wouldn't have to face the problems each had had with their father. If that wasn't burying one's head in the sand, nothing was. Maybe a handful of them had come back—but not to face the difficulties or feelings that had been brushed under the rugs of time.

"I don't have a better plan," she said. "I'll take it."

"It's not a plan," he said. "It's just a step forward."

She hoped he was right. The funny thing was, although he'd adamantly insisted he was the last person to count on when it came to saving someone, her heart had never felt safer than it did while she was cuddled into the curve of Alec Morrissey's body.

Chapter Seventeen

ALEC FACED THE center of the sixty-foot-round pen, his back against the fence, the boot heel on his prosthetic foot propped on the bottom fence rail, and his arms draped backward over the top. A smile rode permanently on his face, and his heart doubled up on beats of happiness, partly because the evening sun shone hot and pretty across western Wyoming, and partly because he was enjoying every awkward moment of the scene unfolding in front of him.

"Trust your balance, honey," he called. "If that left leg slips back too far, don't try to force fix it—straighten up and ride from your seat bones. The strength will come."

It was a good thing he was in such a jolly mood, because his girl on the horse was as cranky as she could be without crossing the line that would make him pull her off for the day. So far she was infinitely kind to the horse and a shrill harpy only to him, and he loved every minute of her feisty, fighting side. Plus, she was doing a great job—she just wouldn't admit it.

"If you tell me 'the strength will come' one more time, I'll jump off this horse and deck you."

"I'm up for that. If you can do it, you graduate."

"Horrid man."

It was lesson number three that week, and Joely had mastered the walk and trot and was moving on to the lope. The challenge to its execution was in the cue for the horse: a shift of one leg to give a slight nudge behind the cinch so the horse would lift off into the three-beat gait. At the same time, the opposite leg remained long and strong to keep the horse straight. That was a lot to coordinate for someone whose joints didn't move as quickly or subtly as she wanted them to. Joely's physical therapy had given her decent range of motion, but she had poor core strength.

"You haven't had enough evil taskmasters in your life," he said. "I am the best thing that's ever happened to you."

She didn't reply, and he studied her closely, certain he was imagining the ghost of a smile playing on her lips. His heart swelled again.

"Don't get cocky, you arrogant cowboy." Lines of intense concentration creased her forehead, and she popped the handsome liver chestnut quarter horse she rode into a right lead lope.

"Fantastic! Seriously now, forget your leg and relax your backbone. Rock your hips. That's all you have to think about—the rest is instinct for someone like you."

A reining or pleasure class show judge would penalize her for her left leg, which trailed slightly behind the cinch, but for the first time that day Joely's sweet little butt and her gorgeous long spine rolled like an exotic dancer's in time with the horse's movements. Lord, he thought, his heart pounding anew, she was a beautiful woman. A talented woman.

A woman he wanted more with each day that passed.

She halted the gelding in front of him. "I'm calling that good. It was forty-five minutes. Don't want to push it."

"You feeling okay?"

"My back is sore, but not as bad as yesterday."

"Good. Improvement. It all counts. You can tell me when you want to go again, tomorrow or Thursday."

"Easy for you to say, you sadist. I don't see you up here getting sore."

"I ain't no ordinary dummy."

She blew out an exasperated breath and pulled her right foot out of the stirrup. Very carefully she swung that leg over the saddle while her weak leg held her weight. With a little adjustment she leaned across the saddle's seat, pulled her other foot free, and dropped to the ground. She hopped like a gymnast trying to stick a landing, but she stayed upright.

"Woo hoo! Most elegant dismount yet." Alec kept his hands in his pockets to keep compliant with her rule of no helping. He wasn't allowed to touch her until she had both feet on the ground—even if that meant she had to pick herself up off of it first. Letting her fall was excruciating, but he was learning. And the juxtaposition was humorous—she whined like a five-year-old at the hard work, but by gosh and golly she was going to do it herself.

When she stood by the horse's head she handed Alec her reins, and he finally got to gather her into his arms. Slender, warm, and horsey-smelling from riding, she filled his senses with things he was starting to crave when they weren't there. The thought of falling in love and being responsible for another human being's well-being and happiness still gave him panic attacks, but despite how hard he was trying to keep things casual, Alec was worryingly hooked.

"Still mad at me?" he asked, and slipped a kiss onto her lips, which were salty with perspiration and plump as juicy cherries.

She reached into the kiss, stroking his tongue with hers, lingering as if truly reluctant to part.

"I'm pretty much always mad at you," she said.

He lifted her chin. "But not really, right?"

She touched his lip quizzically with her forefinger. "You are such goofball."

"I'm paranoid. You'll take the six lessons we agreed on and get so good you'll leave and find a real cowgirl job. I'll lose you."

"I like that fairy tale, cowboy. It might become my favorite bedtime story."

"I should be lucky enough to hear bedtime stories from you." His imagination went far beyond bedtime stories.

She rose up and kissed him again—catching his bottom lip first and running her tongue lightly over it until she leaned in and sealed the kiss in sweet abandon.

She was the sexiest kisser he'd ever known. Joely's hot, sweet mouth and her long-legged, feminine softness induced fantasies of so much more than lips meeting lips—like heated nights tangled in cool sheets, and long hours when he didn't have to leave her but could stay wrapped, like he was now, in her embrace. But even though he waited for those fantasies to come true with the impatience of a horny schoolboy, he also dreaded the moment they would happen.

He fully believed he'd come to grips with his injury. He accepted what his leg looked like now, what its limitations were, and how to deal with his mobility issues. He also believed Joely understood the injury. Most women said they did. The reality of an amputated limb, however, was something totally different from intellectual acceptance. And making love to a man with a residual stump was a step into the unknown or even weird for somebody who'd never experienced a partial limb. Joely might be fine. She might not look twice. Or she might find it too uncomfortable or too creepy to come across a mutilated leg in the middle of sex.

Both had happened to him.

So he didn't push. And as a reward, concentrating on mundane things gave him time to see how much he also craved her company. It only took a week to start rolling with the rhythm of her moods and silence-filling pleasure of her chatter. Cooking her dinner one night, helping her grocery shop another, watching her play with Rowan, at which she excelled—each activity only made him want to spend more evenings, and more days, with her.

Joely grumbled, she laughed, she tripped on things, she cried, but most of all she bubbled sunshine into his life. He hadn't realized what a hermit he'd become since his recuperation, despite leaving the house every day for work and knowing how to be perfectly sociable around people. Even in Texas, before he'd come to Wyoming, he'd kept his nose pretty steadily to routine. Not a lot of nights in the bars with buddies. Not a lot of accepted dinner invitations. Far, far fewer nights in bed with a pretty girl than in his rodeo heyday.

But here he stood, back in the dirt of an arena, with a horse, the smell of leather and summer air all around him, and Joely in his arms—earthy, simple, and yet his contentment swelled so quickly he didn't know how to describe the feeling. Love? Did he even know how to recognize it? He wasn't sure he'd ever known love—the real, lasting kind—with a woman. Was love wanting to stay with one person, with no end to the togetherness in sight, because you made each other whole inside? If so, maybe he already did love Joely Crockett.

What he did know was that standing on this simple, dusty spot with her, he felt as if he'd found his way home. He hadn't known where that was since he and Buzz had run rashly off to Iraq, but home had always been his best definition of love.

Joely unclasped her arms from around his neck and lowered her heels to the ground, smiling as she wrinkled her nose.

"You're lucky, cowboy," she said. "You get to have cranky old me as a student. Not everyone is so fortunate."

"Dang right."

"Honestly, I'm sorry I'm so awful when I'm up there."

"You're angry at your body. I get it."

She thought for a moment and surprise crawled across her face. "I am," she said. "I really am. But why?"

He shrugged. "Grief. Anger that your leg and your back and your face weren't strong enough to survive the blows they took when the rest of you didn't die. What's wrong with them anyway?"

Her eyes widened with the understanding. "It's all true. I've always thought I was just angry at the universe."

"Hey. Sometimes that, too."

For a moment he thought she might weep, but her eyes only softened in acceptance. "Do you ever get over it?"

He gathered the horse's reins into a loop and rubbed his knuckles down the bright white stripe on the gelding's face. "You get angry less and less often. Then one day you might watch a football game and see a player sprain his ankle and curl up in pain, and you want to punch him. Or you watch the Boston Marathon and think, I could do that but I'd beat my stump to a pulp, and you want to kick and punch someone or something else."

"Or you see a rodeo?" she asked gently.

A flash of resentment burned through his chest. They'd promised not to bring up that subject. But he fought the irritation and, to his surprise, it disappeared.

"I expect it might be the same." he murmured against her temple. "Most of the time you'll truly be fine. Just accept the anger when it comes, but then let it go. Letting it go is the secret. And you can do it, because you know it's okay if it comes back. It's not like you have to suppress it."

"You really did learn your lessons well."

"Still learning. C'mon, let's get Muddy here back to the barn."

She scowled. "Who names a horse Muddy Waters anyway?"

"A big blues fan. Here, want 'im?" He tried to hand her the reins.

"I'll let you." She grasped his arm. "Can I just use you as my crutch again? The leg's pretty rubbery."

His heart sank. This was the one area where she consistently reverted to her old, helpless self. She rode the horse, she groomed the horse for riding and turnout, but she barely touched him otherwise.

"You're starting to gel with him, I think." He tried the subject in a roundabout way. "He's got your number, too. For a five-year-old he's so well trained that I think he knows how to meet you right where you're at—he's not difficult, but he needs your guidance."

"He's a good lesson horse."

"Harper found you a good boy."

"He'll make a great cow horse," she agreed.

No emotion. No feeling. This was not normal for a former rodeo queen, however long ago her reign had been. Those women, he knew firsthand, worshipped their horses—more than any man who might come along.

"I thought Muddy was yours. Harper found him months ago as a surprise," she said.

"It was very nice of her, but it's hard to pick out a horse for someone else."

Her voice remained sweet and calm; she didn't snap at him for talking about the horse, but she didn't engage in any meaningful way. Alec sighed.

"C'mon," she said. "Let's get him back to his friends and go eat. Mia and Gabe are home again as of this morning, and I heard rumors there was going to be a chili feed—it's Gabe's favorite."

"I remember that," Alec said. "He used to go nuts for the gross canned stuff when we had it in the mess. Nobody wanted to sit next to him because he'd beg their leftovers. But your family has been feeding me a lot recently. Am I overstaying my welcome?"

"Hardly. You're their new favorite. They want you to start bringing Rowan along so they can adopt this dog they hear me go on and on about, too."

"Just what they need. Another horse."

Muddy Waters let out a long snort and bobbed his head behind them as if he understood. In fact he simply knew he was headed back to the pasture, and with an eye full of mischievous light, he thrust his muzzle forward and nudged Joely's shoulder, pushing her forward. Alec laughed but it died in his throat when Joely turned and scowled.

"Knock it off, you dumb horse. You have space and four feet of your own. You don't need mine."

He didn't know who he felt worse for, the horse or the girl.

THEY ENTERED ROSECROFT via the big back deck, and Joely relaxed once the fragrance of her mother's abundant flowers enveloped her. Roses, morning glories, gladiolas, Indian paint brush, daisies, and beautiful Asian lilies were just some of the blooms coming into their own now that June was half gone. It was a relief to be away from the barn, away from the horse, and away from Alec's well-meaning hints that she should bond more closely with Muddy Waters. She had no desire to bond. She loved being up on his back. Riding, as frustrated as it made her—and she was going to have to work on that—was still a glorious activity, but all the overhead that surrounded the moments on horseback only made her anxious.

Alec didn't push, however, and so she didn't argue or explain. He didn't understand about Penny. That was fine. She wasn't going to talk about her horse out loud. She could barely handle the gruesome memories—or the ones she imagined since she'd never seen Penny's body.

The mental pictures melted away when she and Alec made their way into the kitchen, redolent with the scent of chili spices and baking corn bread.

"This is why I've started eating here." Alec sent a longing look toward the large pot on the stove. "I don't create scents like this in my kitchen."

"I get riding lessons. You should take cooking—"

Eager, excited voices from the living room cut her off.

"Why this is wonderful. Sadie why didn't you tell us?"

Joely caught Alec's questioning look and shrugged. She led the way out of the kitchen and saw the knot of family members in the front foyer.

"I wasn't certain he would come," Sadie said. "It took several notes and some severe arm twisting. Family, I'd like you to meet an ancient old friend of mine, Trampas Manterville."

Mayberry—Trampas—appeared in the middle of the small crowd and started shaking hands as he addressed Sadie. "How do you do? Pleased to meet you. And, madam, I am not that ancient and hardly ancient and old together."

"Don't make me sorry I invited you into polite company," she retorted and gave his coat sleeve an admonishing flick of her hand.

"Whoa, Grandma!" Joely whispered to Alec and bit back her laughter. "Is she *flirting* with him?"

"Hope so. I think maybe she's just happy to have someone her own age in the house."

Trampas was ushered all the way in and ensconced in the biggest armchair. Grandma took her usual spot across the floor in the gliding rocker beside her knitting basket. Trampas greeted Joely warmly. "I see that all went well the other evening."

She flushed and nodded. "It did. You gave me good advice."

"Advice?" Alec asked.

"Mr. Manterville gets credit for telling me to follow you into Ina's the other night."

"Is that right?" Alec grinned like a cat that had a parakeet by its tail. "In that case I owe you a handshake at the very least. I was so glad to find her there."

"Excuse me, I wasn't a lost dog," Joely said, indignant.

"You were not." Alec gave her a kiss, soft and quick, on the lips, in front of everyone there. "You were a lost piece of my heart."

"Awwwww." Mia clapped and nudged their mother. "Even if he's just kidding, and I'm not sure he is, that was class-A romantic."

A hundred comments that would make light of Alec's shameless kiss rushed to Joely's lips. *You're so strange. What a dork. Isn't he weird?*

Suddenly, however, she didn't need to excuse it. He'd kissed her, and she was kind of blown away. Despite her limp, despite her mercurial moods, despite her scars and all the things she lacked—like skills or a job—he'd kissed her in front of her mother and her sister and her grandmother. In an old-fashioned, unliberated sense he'd staked his claim and told the world he wasn't embarrassed to do it.

The fantasy was over-the-top. But she wrapped herself in it anyway.

"I'm sorry, I'm sorry! I'm late!" Harper trotted into the room, feet clad in brightly striped socks, black ponytail slightly frayed, and an aqua tank top splattered with dark, round stains. "I got roped into helping Bjorn fix one of the four-wheelers, and I shouldn't be allowed around oil cans. I'm going to run and change and then dinner will be on in ten minutes."

"Harpo, it's fine; don't fuss." Mia stood. "You're not late. Gram's dinner guest just arrived, so no worries. I'll set the table."

"Gram's guest?" Harper squinted at their quiet grandmother, sitting placidly in her chair, and let her eyes stray to Trampas. She headed across the floor, extending her hand to him. "Hi. I'm Harper Wainwright, Sadie's granddaughter."

Joely smiled. Hearing her sister's married name still caused a ripple of surprise.

"Harper. I'm delighted to meet you. I'm Trampas Manterville. I know who you are, of course. Your Community Arts Guild and all the programs you run out here are much talked about in town. You're doing a wonderful thing for this area."

Harper grinned from ear to ear. The Double Diamond Arts Center she'd founded, on Paradise land that had once been owned by Cole's family, was her pet project. "I'm so flattered, thank you, Mr. Manterville. I've been hearing rumors that you were back in the area."

"Everybody, please call me Trampas."

Harper turned to their grandmother. "I like him already, Grams."

"Well, you don't know him." Grandma Sadie flashed a beatific smile across the room as if daring him to tease back.

"I don't know," Joely whispered to Alec again. "I have no precedent for this. How do you handle a flirting nonagenarian?"

"You don't use that fifty-cent word for starters," he said and kissed her on the cheek.

"I could define it if you didn't understand."

"Later. I'll take you home, and you can define whatever you like."

"Be careful what you wish for."

Once all the men were back from work, dinner passed in gales of laughter and endless stories. If his parents hadn't kept him from monopolizing the conversation, Rory would have told Disney adventure tales the entire time. Gabe declared the Disney roller coasters top notch but the spinning teacups an alien plot to eradicate the human race. The storyteller of the night, however, was Trampas. His adventures since leaving Wyoming seventy years before were innumerable.

He'd become an itinerant farm worker and traveled around the country for six years. At twenty-one he made his way across the ocean by working on a freight ship and lived in England where he met his wife.

"Once I married my Nina, I knew I had to stop wandering and become respectable. I loved the open skies and traveling, but I went to school, became a teacher, fell in love with Shakespeare, and managed to work at everything from teaching to trash collecting when the need arose. We moved to the United States after fifteen years to finish raising our two children. I got a professorship in a tiny college in Kansas teaching English Literature and Shakespeare."

"That's why you have a slight accent," Harper said. "From living abroad."

"I spoke like a country hick when I arrived in London. I learned proper speech at school there, and I guess a little of the pronunciation became permanent."

"So what brought you back here?" Joely asked.

"I never earned tenure at my college, and when budget cuts inevitably occurred, I was forced to retire at age seventy-one. Nina and I lived in our home for eleven years before she passed away five years ago. I decided that before I died I was going to go back to the traveling life I loved. I receive a small social security check each month," he said cheerfully. "It's enough for food and shelter and other necessities. I have a tent. I can stay in a hotel when it's cold. I have used shelters and spent time working at them when I do. When I save enough, I can travel to a warmer or cooler location. It's a good life."

"It's an amazingly brave life," Harper said. "What do your children think of this?"

"They don't like it, of course. Their homeless father. But I've lived with each of them, and we have better relationships the way things are. I'm no braver than a hardworking rancher. Yours is not a life for sissies."

"Did you come back here to visit? To see what it was like?" Mia asked.

He and Grandma Sadie exchanged a meaningful look—this one not the least bit flirtatious.

"And so we come to the reason I decided to accept Sadie's invitation," Trampas said. "I have a story about Paradise Ranch I thought you'd all like to hear."

Chapter Eighteen

"THERE YOU ARE."

Alec found Joely sitting on a garden bench far beyond the house, in the clearing that overlooked the Tetons. This time of night there were no mountains visible, only pinpricks of stars and the waning crescent moon in the vast western sky.

"I just needed to breathe a little. Everyone else is wrapped up in conversation. I didn't think they'd miss me for a few minutes."

"I missed you." He set his hands on her shoulders. "It's been nearly forty-five minutes. Thought I'd better check."

"Has it? Oh, then I am sorry."

"No. I'm just making sure you're okay. Did that story about your great-grandfather bother you?"

For a moment she didn't speak. He rubbed her shoulders, and she shrugged into his touch. Tilting her head back, she pointed into the starry sky. "The Big Dipper.

There's Draco the Dragon curving around Polaris." She made sure he saw what she was showing him although he didn't know how it followed his question. "Gemini, Leo, Cassiopeia."

"Cool," he said.

"I'm sure there are lots of places in the world to see the stars, but none of them are like this. Even when electricity came into use and it reached here, my grandfathers made sure no artificial light from the ranch yard or the house obscured the sky—how much foresight did that take? Every generation has tried its best to stick with traditions that allow humans and the land to sustain each other. Now Harper and Cole have the wind turbines out along the highway in an area that doesn't obstruct the views or dig up the land. They're talking with the triplets about raising some organic cattle for the girls' restaurant in Denver. Those are the stories of Paradise I know and love."

"Ahhh," he said. This *was* about the old story their visitor had told.

"No matter how crappy things were in my life, even during the worst in the hospital, I knew Paradise was here—flawless, almost pristine, built and sustained by honest, hard-working, iron-willed men like my father. All because they inherited it from the first Crockett, who worked his young ass off to make it great. Now they're trying to tell me that it's a lie?"

"Oh, honey, it's not a lie. Even if it's true that Eli won the land in a card game, he started with just a small part of what Paradise has become."

"It was the kernel. The start of everything. My great-grandfather was basically a cheat and a liar and one step from a murderer."

"Oh, now, I didn't get that from Trampas's story."

"Eli Crockett forced Simon Manterville to play poker for the land by holding a knife to his throat while he dealt the cards. That's exactly what I heard."

"Doesn't sound like Simon was a guy worth feeling sorry for."

"That doesn't give someone the right to threaten his life because he wants the property."

"They don't know why the game was played."

"The point is, Eli didn't work for the land like I've always been told. My legacy is based on a gambler's lucky night. And even then he forced his luck. Simon wasn't a real poker player but Eli was a card sharp. That sounds like fixed odds to me."

"Eli was a twenty-four-year-old kid who was brilliant."

Alec moved to squat in front of her and grasp her hands. "This is ancient history. It should be a fantastic story that's all. Like the Australians who now search ancestries to see if they have some original colony prisoners in their lineage. It's a matter of pride."

"An entire family was forced to move. We're living on what had been their dream."

"Joely, come on. You heard the same story I did, not just from Trampas but from Sadie, too. The Mantervilles were defaulting on payments. They'd lost their cattle. They probably abused their kids. I'm not saying we know everything, but Eli only hastened something that would have happened anyway."

"You don't understand the matter of pride."

"I do." He understood *that* she was angry but not why.

"And now there's the great-nephew. He seems to think the land was stolen from his family. What if this Tyrone guy does have proof the deed was never signed over?"

"But that was the point—Tyrone Whatever-his-name-is has given up the claim and gone back to his home in North Carolina. He has a family now. Trampas just wanted us to know the history between your family and his."

"Maybe the land actually does belong to his family."

"Oh, good grief. Joely, honey, are you just looking for a reason to be worried?"

"Yes," she said irritably. "Because I love worry and misery. Haven't you figured that out about me?"

"That's not what I'm saying. I'm trying to figure out why you won't look at this as a great family story. What's really bothering you?"

"I don't know. It just got to me."

"Would a hug help?"

She offered him her first wisp of a smile. "It sure couldn't hurt."

"Scoot over." He sat and put both arms around her, pulling her close. "Okay?"

"Mmm." A minute later her sigh went through him like a shiver. "Okay, I do know what's wrong."

"Good."

"I feel like I'm losing ground. My savings are almost gone. I need a job. I have no skills. I have no car to go get any skills. And all that's okay—they're things to be dealt with. They tick me off, but when they need to get done I'll find a way. But now there's this whole big Fourth of July thing at the rodeo that Harper got us involved with. I'm supposed to go and be some honorary past queen ambassador, and trust me the idea isn't all that appealing. Then here comes Trampas Manterville and suddenly big, wonderful Paradise Ranch, whose owners brag about all the things we do to help the town, is not that great a role model."

"Well, that's just ridiculous," he said. "What happened nearly a hundred years ago has nothing to do with today, but I think you'll see that better in the morning when you aren't so tired. Tell me instead about this queen ambassador thing."

A sense of relief flowed through him now that she'd brought that subject up. He'd known about it ever since Vince had told him, but Joely had never mentioned it so he'd kept his mouth shut.

"I've been afraid to tell you. Why would I want you to know I was participating in the rodeo?"

"My gosh, Joely, I don't care if *you* go to the rodeo. I'm happy for you!"

"Great. Terrific. Thanks. But you wouldn't be there to cheer me on, right? Not for a million dollars."

"Well, for a million…" He tried to joke, but she pulled away.

"You'll kiss me in front of my whole family. Which I liked, by the way. You like being with me as long as I don't step foot in a rodeo ring. Then I'm on my own. Do I have it about right?"

He couldn't answer. She *was* right. If she wanted to go to the rodeo and make good on an invitation, he had no problem with it. He'd hoped she'd understand that it was the one thing he'd chosen never to do again. Then again, how could she know it was about more than a decision? It was about his vow. He'd never told anybody about that."

"You're the one who doesn't understand now."

"And God forbid I should be able to ask you to help me understand. I'm terrified to bring up the subject. Simple Rules for Alec and Joely to Live by Number One, as I recall."

"I don't go because I promised I wouldn't." The words came out stiffly, but she deserved to hear them.

"Promised who?"

"My cousin."

"Your dead cousin?"

He stood up. "Yeah. My dead cousin. Who can never be there again either. It's that simple."

"I'm sorry. I didn't mean to be so insensitive, and I was. But, Alec, you can't make promises to people who don't care. Your cousin wouldn't want this."

"That's the cliché thing to say and why I don't tell anyone about it. It's my decision. My promise. That's all there is to it."

"Okay."

"Really?"

"Look," she said, laying a hand on his forearm. "I do get it. And I'm sorry this ranch thing hit me wrong and I took it out on you. You're probably right that it'll all seem funny in the morning and everything will be fine. In fact, I've been thinking that I'd like to stay here tonight. Would that be okay?"

He had no say on where she slept. It stung because it was a shutout—no long good-byes on her front stoop— but of course it was okay.

"If that's what you want to do. Do you still want to ride tomorrow?"

"Why wouldn't I?" Her surprise at his question was genuine.

That made him feel marginally better. "Okay, then I'll be here. Three thirty after work?"

She nodded and stood to meet him. "Alec, I am sorry. Tomorrow will be a better day. Promise."

Before she turned, he placed a hand on the back of her head and pulled her in for the kiss he'd miss on her doorstep.

"People argue," he said. "This wasn't a big deal. I love your emotions—you're just figuring them out after everything that's happened."

"You don't always have to be so nice, you know. I wasn't today."

"You know plenty well enough I'm not always nice either. I'll be right in."

She smiled and headed back to the house. He sank back onto the bench.

Moments later, a hand dropped onto his shoulder in the dark. For some reason it didn't even startle him, but he was surprised she was there.

"I wasn't spying," Sadie said. "Trampas headed back to town, and I saw Joely come in alone. I'm sorry she was upset."

"She's a wonder," Alec said. "Underneath her pain, she's one of the most empathetic people I've ever met. This all boils down to her feeling sorry for Simon Manterville, believe it or not. I think that's incredible, even though it makes her feel sorry for herself, too."

"Can I ask a personal question?"

"Yes. Sure."

"Why, exactly, do you avoid the rodeo?"

He frowned into the darkness. "I can't ride broncs anymore."

"That's why you don't go to the rodeo to compete. Why do you avoid it altogether? You were once the equivalent of a rock star. I would think the whole atmosphere would be in your blood."

"I appreciate that you care." Alec kept his tone even. "But I have my reasons, and they even have to do with Joely. I want to be as perfect for her as I can be, so I can hold her up when she needs it. I've failed at that for so many people, so many times in my life that falling for her scares me to death. So, I refuse to be a person who hangs on to the old. Those days weren't good for me. Rodeo had its turn in my life."

"Do you plan to marry her?"

"What? I've known her a month. No, I'm barely learning to deserve her."

"Do you want to make love to her?"

"Now, Sadie!" He spun on the bench and stared at the quiet old woman who didn't look the least concerned at her breach in privacy. "That's a little personal don't you think?"

She only smiled. "There are a lot of meanings for the phrase making love. The one thing every meaning has in common, however, is trust. And believe me, Alec. When it comes to trust, a woman doesn't need you to be perfect or even strong. But she does need you to be whole."

"And that's exactly what I'm talking about," Alec said.

"You have done a better job than most making yourself whole on the outside. But you're forgetting about the inside. I don't believe you'll be whole until you make peace with the rodeo. If you do that, then you can decide you never want to go again. Until then you aren't ruling your decision, it's ruling you."

"Sadie. I don't know…"

"That's all right. My lecture is done. So is my prying." She patted his shoulders with her slightly gnarled fingers. "But I won't apologize. Anyone who's after one of my girls better be ready to prove himself worthy."

Sadie left him, slipping back into the shadows until all he could hear were her footsteps and cane on the deck steps returning to the house. He laughed almost in defeat. Prove himself worthy? He'd believed he wasn't worthy from the moment he'd met Joely Crockett.

Now he knew for sure.

Ten minutes later he let himself into the house and headed to the living room. He came upon the group there, and he stopped for a moment, struck by the tableau. Harper, Cole, Mia, Gabe, Joely, Bella, and Sadie sat in a square made from chairs they'd shoved close together. Close as they were, they still leaned in toward each other. He vaguely heard references to somebody calling the triplets.

They were quite a family.

Family.

Understanding slapped him in the face. They were family, and they pulled together. No matter how angry they'd once been at each other or how annoyed they got now—they bent their heads and came up with a plan.

That's what he no longer had—what he hadn't been able to save. When he'd failed to rescue Buzz; when his aunt and uncle had blamed him for coming back alive without the real son; when he'd lost his cousin, who'd been more like a brother, the person he'd really loved most—he'd been truly alone. No bent heads. No roots. No connection.

Suddenly he got it. Why Joely wanted him at the damn rodeo so bad. She didn't care about the rodeo itself. She didn't want him there necessarily to see her participate. She was hoping to find her old self somewhere, and she was clinging to her family with all her might. She was trying to add him to it.

He didn't know if he could do that for her—become her family. He was only as sure as he'd ever been that he was able to mess up any family unlucky enough to take him in.

Chapter Nineteen

HE HADN'T HAD the dream in a long time. It was one of the indicators that his two years of therapy had been helpful— the nightmares had stopped. Tonight, however, he could see the surface of sleep through a field of fire and destruction, just out of reach, as if he had to swim through the pictures to reach wakefulness. He didn't want to get anywhere near the fiery images, and he tried to stay under, to push further down, but the currents dragged him upward.

"Alec, man, I'm sorry. I'm sorry we missed him. You okay?"

"Yeah, sure, of course."

"You want me to drive?"

Tell him yes. Yes. Switch places with him goddammit.

"Nope. No, it's good, gives me something to concentrate on. Thanks."

Buzz was dead. Gone. No body, no hope. They'd missed him by a week. The insurgents had arrived the damn day he'd landed in the country. It had taken five precious days to start his job, contact his old unit, tell them what he knew. They'd taken him with them, against all regulations—a civilian embedded.

"Alec you sure you okay, buddy?"

He wasn't fucking okay. But he needed to drive. He needed to hit every hateful pothole and…

Screams tore into his ears before the shrapnel slammed his body. Light seared his eyes, took away all sight. How ironic was that? Darkness out of light. The world rotated way too quickly so many times he lost count at two. Or three. His head. His neck. God, his leg.

"Pritch? Sandman? Morse?"

Nothing.

Petroleum. In his nose. In his mouth. And copper—an ugly vomit-inducing taste. He finally caught sight of an opening in the smoke. He tried to move. It worked. He wriggled free of his seatbelt. He noticed in passing that the steering wheel was gone. Huh. Convenient.

"Morse? Pritch? Sandman?"

He cleared the smoke field.

He knew for sure he was dreaming. He could see the surface of his dream much closer now, and it made no sense to try to go back into deep sleep even though he knew what was coming.

But the dream took a turn.

Hands reached through the burning Humvee, like a ghost beckoning for him. Not the disembodied hands of Frank Pritchett and Harry Sands, but real, solid, living hands. Grabbing for him.

He reached back, indescribably relieved for the help. Up and up he went until he woke above the chaos. Safe in his bedroom. Safe in front of Aunt Chris and Uncle Rick. "Thank heavens you were there," he said. "Thank you. It's so good to see you."

"How could you fail us?" Aunt Chris asked. "You promised you'd bring him back."

"You brought back the wrong son," Uncle Rick said, sobbing violently into a tissue.

Alec swiveled his head to take in his surroundings. It looked like his bedroom. What were they doing here?

"I couldn't bring him back." He tried to touch his uncle's shoulder, but he kept moving just out of reach. "They took his body and they..."

To this day he had no idea what the insurgents had done with the bodies of those they'd killed.

"You promised," Uncle Rick said. "You promised. You promised. You prom—"

Alec awoke fully with a jolt that lifted his torso what felt like ten inches off the bed. He landed back into the mattress with an audible grunt and stared wildly around the room. His aunt and uncle were gone. He lay back, exhausted, and concentrated on yoga breathing. It was the only yoga he did or ever planned to do, but his therapist had insisted he learn three different techniques. They worked.

It wasn't hard to figure out this dream's trigger.

Your dead cousin? Joely had blurted earlier that night.

He'd realized at her words that he never referred to his cousin as dead. He was Buzz. Past tense, yeah, but always as if he might, nonetheless, walk through the door any moment. But Buzz *was* dead, and even though Alec had given up rodeo in penance because it was his fault Buzz had lost it forever, too, he was very fuzzy at the moment as to what purpose a promise to a dead man served.

Slowly the purpose solidified—it always solidified at some point—as the sleep cleared from his brain. The purpose was to pay his uncle back the only way he could. He'd only cried twice since Buzz's death. Once at the funeral. The second time when he'd first faced his uncle after returning from Iraq and heard his fateful words.

"You brought back the wrong son."

He'd cried because he'd agreed. At the very least, Alec should have turned over control of the Humvee to one of the others and been one of the passengers killed. He'd had no business driving as distracted as he'd been. Hell, maybe he'd have seen the damn IED if—

He stopped the downward spiral of thoughts and climbed out of bed. This would not be his third time to cry. It also wasn't a time to curl up and analyze the dream or face his fears as he'd been taught to do. He knew what he wanted, what he needed to do. He'd lost his family, but he had a chance to help Joely keep hers. If he loved her, he could help her reach her dreams. He could get her back to *her* rodeo.

At six o'clock in the morning it was too early to call anyone to make plans, but he could start on his own. He dug out a map Gabe had given him of Paradise Ranch—a simplified drawing Harper had worked up for guests and students of her art classes and retreats who might want to take excursions deeper into the ranch. Minutes later he was engrossed in scoping out the geographical and physical features of the Crocketts' land.

"I'LL BE BACK at two!" Harper waved from her car and left Joely on the sidewalk in front of her apartment building.

One nice thing about her sisters: now that Joely had her apartment set up, the other girls offered to help all the time but backed away if Joely claimed it wasn't needed. She said she could walk with her crutches just fine to her front door, and Harper believed her. Other overprotective people, she thought with a little dart of desire through the stomach, weren't so easy to get rid of.

Alec.

Not that wanted to get rid of him.

In fact, she wished there was a way to get closer and break down the few but substantial walls he still lived behind. She didn't know if he'd ever let them crack much less crumble, but she wasn't ready to give up on him. And to be fair, she had her own walls. They were slightly more transparent than his, but solid nonetheless.

She looked into the robin's egg sky and squinted at the sugar-white clouds dotting it. Perfect kids' clouds, she thought. The kind that made shapes. There was an elephant—it made her think of Rowan. She picked out an ice cream cone—that made her think of kissing Alec. One cloud looked like a…oh, for crying out loud, something that made her think about way more than kissing.

She dropped her gaze quickly and turned for her house. She didn't even want to think about making love with Alec. Well, that wasn't exactly true. What she actually didn't want to think about was him making love to her. Oh, crap. That wasn't precisely true either.

She reached her door and dug her key out of her purse. What she didn't want to think about was him *looking* at her while they made love. She knew what he'd see—an underweight woman with anemic curves, breasts that were adequate but so far from her Miss Wyoming days it hurt to think about, one leg that had been flattened atop the thigh and crushed in the calf and was now striped with three, yard-long scars to match the meandering white and pink line on her face.

Romance novels always fixed scars by having the man kiss them tenderly, thereby rendering them beautiful. That was the very last thing Joely wanted. In fact, she feared that reaction from Alec more than she did revulsion. She imagined herself nauseated at the first touch of his lips to any spot of twisted, shiny skin.

But maybe he wouldn't. He hadn't done it yet. In all their amazing time together, he'd never once kissed or licked or otherwise paid attention to the scar on her cheek. Most of her wanted desperately to give him the chance not to notice them on the rest of her body, but the part of her that never wanted him to see her leg without pants was a tough, strong, fearful little part, and it had the rest of her cowed.

Of course, there was also the possibility that, after yesterday, Alec wouldn't want to see any part of her at all. In the words of her father's favorite clichéd phrase, she'd been a piece of work all day.

She seemed to have no control over her moods. She'd done better in full-time rehab and assisted living. Everything had run on a schedule. No thought. No stress. No crankiness.

There had been depression—strong, deep, unclimbable cliff faces of depression. To her credit she'd never once considered ending her life, but she'd definitely considered moving to a monastery in Tibet and refusing all visitors.

She pushed into her apartment and basked in the sweet surprise of familiarity. Hers. Her pictures on the wall. Her chosen pillows on the old sofa. Her table. Her bed.

Bed again.

Alec.

Stop it!

She laughed out loud at herself, but then it dawned on her that thinking about Alec and sex was depression-free fun. It was not anxiety-free, but it was *definitely* on the fun end of the emotional spectrum.

And today was a better day, just as Alec had predicted. The whole thought of Eli Crockett's unethical acquisition of his first piece of land still pained, but the sun was out and she had a long morning planned. There was no time to dwell on Paradise Ranch's past.

Instead she concentrated on repairing the damage from her huge, embarrassing whine fest the night before. If she wanted to stop whining, stop worrying about her future, stop having to rely on rides everywhere, she needed further independence. Independence required her own vehicle. To ever get one of those, she needed a job.

She'd spent the morning finding five possibilities in the tiny *Wolf Paw Pass Pioneer* want ads, all within walking distance of her apartment. The most desirable was a receptionist and administrative assistant's position in the local real estate office that would pay sixteen dollars an hour. She'd known the two owners for years, and she felt confident she could handle the position. Another job was at the yarn shop, one at the small grocery store on the far end of Mountain Street, a fourth at a storefront women's gym, and finally, a last resort right above her in the thrift shop.

She had her route planned so she could use her crutches and not her wheelchair, which she figured would make for less dramatic entrances. She dressed in a pair of dark purple dress slacks that hung on her hips now, a white silk blouse with a modest open collar, and a patterned, pink-purple-and-red, short-waist jacket she'd always loved. She camouflaged her scar and highlighted her lipstick, and by the time she left, optimism practically oozed from her pores. Today she would finally accomplish something worthwhile.

Two hours and three very friendly interviews later, her pores produced nothing but frustration and sweat in the form of rivulets down her spine. The admin position had been filled. The grocer took one look at her and sorrowfully explained that the job required long periods of standing, some lifting, and ladder climbing, and could she handle the physicality? She'd asked question after question, but in the end, it simply wasn't a practical job for her. Two other positions had also already been taken—the receptionists at both the gym and the yarn shop, Have You Any Wool? To her sorrow, there'd been a second job opening there for a knitting instructor. Her grandmother would cluck at her lack of qualifications for that one. Sadie had been trying to teach all her granddaughters to love knitting their entire lives. Five of the six could make a passable garment or blanket, and Grace had inherited Grandma Sadie's exquisite talent. Joely was the last-place sister in that lineup. Her basic garter stitch scarves were warped disasters, and it was sad. Who couldn't knit a row, purl a row?

All that had been left was the thrift store option. Kitty Carlson had tearily and with great hopefulness offered her the job on the spot. Kitty, a heavyset woman of great, sincere feeling, was lovely, but Joely wasn't certain after talking with her that she could handle the emotional coziness. She'd told her she had several more interviews and would get back to her.

Traversing the length of Mountain Street had led her to a bench just outside Dr. Ackerman's veterinary clinic. The little storefront window was charming, with a series of animal silhouettes marching across the bottom of the picture window and friendly but professional lettering spelling out Wolf PAWS Pass Veterinary Clinic. Subtitling below it read Hooves, Claws, Feathers, and Scales Also Welcome.

Joely smiled. The neat brick matching so many other buildings in town, the picture on the door of a welcome sign hung around the neck of a whinnying foal, and the door handle, shaped like a gecko, all made the little business friendly and enticing. Anyone would want to bring a beloved pet here.

The door opened and Sheila Ackerman stepped through. To Joely's surprise she waved and beckoned. "I saw you sitting here, and you look hot and thirsty. Come on in, I've got iced teas or waters in the refrigerator."

"Hey, thanks, Sheila. That's awfully nice of you."

After she had a cold bottle of iced tea in hand, Joely sat in one of the comfy purple armchairs in the narrow lobby. Sheila, a tall woman with black-rimmed glasses and a mop of pretty strawberry blonde curls, was maybe ten years Joely's senior. She'd started her practice fresh out of vet school and had been a favorite in the area from day one. An all-around practitioner, she really could treat anything from a hamster to a llama.

"I've wanted to call you and check up on that little guy you delivered last week. When I spoke to his owner last, the foal was doing well?"

To her embarrassment, Joely found she had no idea. She'd seen the colt a few times in the pasture with Pan, but she'd never given him more than a passing glance. She hedged her answer.

"He looks good. I think he'll make it." She had nothing on which to base that opinion, but she shrugged.

"What are you up to today that brings you to my end of town?"

Joely hesitated briefly and then shrugged. "I was job hunting, truth be told. But I had no luck at five stops."

Sheila wasn't listening to the details. "Wait. You're looking for a job?" She looked to the sky and clasped her hands. "Heaven above, I swear an angel sent you. Come and work here."

Joely frowned and swiveled her head to search the office. "Am I being punk'd?"

"Lord, no. I'm dead serious."

"What kind of help are you dead seriously looking for?" Joely still didn't truly believe it wasn't a joke. The way Alec went on about her animal skills, he could easily have set this up.

"I'm looking for a genie, that's what kind of help. The lady who cleaned for me just had to give notice, and my tech found a better-paying job in Jackson where she lives. Techs are notoriously difficult to find out here, but I'm looking. Meanwhile, I desperately need a maid, a nanny, a person to ride along with me on big calls, and an answering machine. Pick any of those jobs and it's yours. In fact, pick any three and I won't pay you more, but I will love you with dog-like loyalty forever."

Joely laughed at the genuine hint of begging in the doctor's voice. "I can't say I'm not excited," she said. "Working for you would be a dream."

"It would actually be gross sometimes. But I like the phrase 'a dream.' We'll go with that."

"You know I have limited mobility. I'm afraid I wouldn't be able to do all you'd require."

"Are you kidding? I heard that you moved around the foal last week just fine. If you have the strength to help straighten a dystocia and deliver it safely, you can handle anything a dog or cat can dish out. I admit to you, I don't pay well—thirteen dollars an hour. But I have all the free drinks, sometimes even alcoholic, that you wish; mostly flexible hours; and I really like sweet foods around here on Fridays."

"How many hours a week?"

"How many do you want?"

"I was hoping for fifteen to twenty."

"Sold."

Joely laughed out loud. "You really are serious?"

"Like I said, deadly so. As of next Monday I am down to two dog-walking volunteers, a board-certified small animal surgeon who comes in Tuesdays and Thursdays to help, and my mother who files for me once in a while. I would love to hire another veterinarian, but I couldn't staff for him or her. Oh, and a side benefit? You see ninety percent of the strays that ever show up. It's an all-you-can-cat buffet for choosing as many pets as you want."

"Oh no. That's all I need. Look, don't you need references? My resumé? Don't I need experience?"

"No to the references. You're a Crockett—best animal husbandry experts around. No to the resumé. You've been around animals longer than some of my recent techs. And as for the experience. What I just said."

"Can I watch you do surgery once in a while?"

"Any time you're here."

Joely stuck out her hand. "If I find out I'm being punk'd I'll cry. When do I start?"

THREE HOURS LATER, Joely could barely contain her excitement as she rode behind Cole on the four-wheeler to the barn. It was just after three, and Alec had agreed to meet her at three thirty. She hoped he wasn't upset about last night, but even if he was, she had an elaborate apology planned.

"There he is," Cole said. "Lord, that is one enormous dog."

She peered over Cole's shoulder in surprise. She'd hoped for a few minutes to surprise Alec by getting Muddy ready without help, but Cole was right, there Alec stood, looking like a model for a Hot Cowboys calendar—leaning on the round pen fence, arms folded, black cowboy hat pulled low across his brow, and stubble shadowing his cheeks. Rowan sat like a queenly guard dog at his side, and Muddy, along with one other horse, was tied to the rail behind him.

Joely's stomach filled with butterflies, and a hungry pulse throbbed in her throat, making it hard to swallow. Forget guilt. Forget anxiety. He looked good enough to eat.

"Hey, Bronc Buster," Cole said when he'd idled the four-wheeler just short of the horses. "That your next ride?" He nodded at Rowan.

Joely held her breath. She never would have dared call him by that nickname, but Alec only lifted a corner of his mouth in a lazy greeting. "No. Too placid."

"She's an amazing animal," Cole said. "Never seen one in real life, just pictures. Is she friendly?"

"Dangerously friendly." He nudged Rowan on the shoulder, and she looked up at him adoringly. "Look who's here, big dog. Can you find Joely?"

Rowan woofed and stood, her head turning and eyes scanning. When they locked with Joely's, she gave a howl of delight and bounded for the vehicle, stopping beside it and whining, her entire body wiggling.

"Hullo, beautiful," Joely cooed and reached for her head. "You finally got to come. I'm so happy to see you!"

Cole got in a good pat and received a free hand washing from a long gray-and-pink tongue. "Okay," he said when Joely had dismounted the four-wheeler. "Have a great trip!"

"Trip?" She shot a questioning frown at Alec.

"It's like this," he said. "I figured if you're going to be a proper alumni rodeo queen, you need a proper entrance. That would be on a horse. And if you're going to ride a horse in a rodeo arena in just a couple of weeks, you need a crash course in getting into shape and riding in a big space."

"What are you plotting?"

"Nothing you can't get out of with a simple refusal. But, if you're ready for an adventure—a real one—and you brought the things Harper told you to bring..."

"Oh my gosh, she was in on this?" Joely held up a small backpack filled with a rain slicker and her favorite thick hoodie. "She lied. She said she didn't know what it was for except you wanted them for some kind of riding exercise."

"That wasn't a lie. This is a very big riding exercise. We're heading out to check two of the old trail cabins for Cole. Numbers five and six. Nobody's really been out to any of the eight for about two years according to Bjorn."

"That's almost thirty miles one way!"

"We have four days. Longer if you want to take it slower. I took more personal days from that company that loves me so much."

She shook her head, unable to hide her excitement any longer. "No, I have to be back by Sunday. I got a job with Sheila Ackerman today."

"Joely, you did?"

The laconic, sexy cowboy morphed into a jubilant, grinning cowboy. He grabbed her around the waist and lifted her high, planting a kiss on her lips as she returned to the ground. "I'm so proud of you."

"Don't be," she said and laughed at his brief confusion. "I'll tell you all about it. But even though I think the job could be pretty fun, I had very little to do with landing it."

"I can't wait to hear. But, have I landed you, my little fish? If you say yes, we can leave within fifteen minutes. Everything's locked up at home?"

"Well, that further explains what all Harper's fuss at my apartment was all about." Joely flicked his upper arm lightly with her finger. "Are the windows closed? Is the stove off? Make sure the toilet's not running, nothing's leaking. I was ready to brain her."

"Sorry," he said. "I got your sisters on board early this morning. We've been planning all day. Horses are ready. Harper raided the few clothes you have in your old room and rolled you a saddle pack with blankets, your sleeping bag, extra underclothes, and some supplies. Saddlebags are packed with food."

"Pretty sure I'd say yes, weren't you?"

"I wasn't at all sure. We had a rough time last night. There was every chance you'd be angry enough that you wouldn't want to spend four days with me."

"Mr. Morrissey, I would love to spend four days with you, although this is the craziest idea I've ever heard."

"I'm sorry I didn't let you help with the packing. This plan is only about eight hours old. To keep with the spirit of crazy—I took a chance."

"I need my hat."

"Hanging on the saddle horn. And, just so you don't think I'll be taking care of Muddy this whole trip, I'll tell you now. This was a one-time thing. You don't have to love him, you just have to deal with him."

Contrition filtered through her, and she nodded. "Not a problem."

"Then," he said, "the last question is whether you can spend four days without those." He pointed at the crutches on the ground beside the fence.

"With you along?" She winked. "I don't need anything else."

Chapter Twenty

JOELY LAID ANOTHER piece of wood on the fire and hopped backward two steps to where she could sink back onto her sleeping bag. Instead of reaching it, however, she landed in Alec's embrace when he caught her and tucked her tightly against him. She giggled. This was positively decadent. Rowan slept, secured to a nearby tree and dead to the world after a slow but long day on the trail. The horses chewed contentedly, tethered twenty feet away, and the campfire's flames danced crazily in a mounting breeze. All of it led to time. Plenty of luxurious, unscheduled, kiss-all-night time. If Joely's legs and spine hadn't ached like she'd run back-to-back marathons from her day and a half in the saddle, the night would have been perfect.

Fortunately, Alec was in the same boat.

"We're a pair, aren't we?" she asked, rubbing her thighs. "What were you thinking?"

"More like hoping. That by the time we get back, we'll magically be in shape."

"Oh boy, I sure hope you're right."

The night before, they'd made it to the first of the two cabins they were checking. All together eight of the one-room shelters were scattered across Paradise's nearly eighty square miles. In the past they'd been used during cattle round-ups and hunting expeditions. Now they were more curiosities than anything, but they still made good shelter for crews mending fences or for trips like this. It had been fun straightening up and sweeping out animal droppings, leaves, and dust from the tiny house. They'd talked of nothing important, kissed a lot, played cribbage with a travel set Alec had tucked into his packs, and slept curled next to each other.

Rather, Alec had slept. His deep, even breathing had lulled Joely into catnaps, but her insides had quivered all night from being so near to him with his arm flung across her torso, his belly snugged up against her back, and his right leg draped over hers. Every body part that had touched her radiated heat and had sent shards of pleasure at wildly unexpected moments in directions she couldn't predict. Deep sleep had been permanently out of the question.

At the same time, there'd been relief. She hadn't had to face baring her disfigurements to his eyes, or his touch, and she hadn't had to deal with his shock, or for that matter, his sympathy. She wanted his touch. She wanted to trust this man she feared she was falling in love with— but she wasn't sure how to trust herself with him.

There was also the message he sent by leaving his prosthetic attached. She'd never seen him remove the limb, but she'd also never spent a full night with him before. The assumption that he'd have to rest his own leg at some point seemed to be false, and it confused her. She didn't know very much about prosthetics, but she did know that even the best could quickly and suddenly turn painful without proper care. Leaving it on seemed an effective way of keeping distance between them. She didn't know how to broach the subject without having to talk about her own physical issues, but as the anticipation of another wonderful but frustrating, sleepless night grew within her, Alec's leg—and hers—were nothing less in her mind than two elephants in their midst.

"Warm enough?" he asked. "Your back's okay?"

"I'm plenty warm. And my back aches. It'll be fine in the morning."

"Shouldn't we try to make it fine now? What would make it better?"

"Hiring Sven the masseur?"

He chuckled. "Role playing, huh? Your version of the cabana boy fantasy? Fine, I can do Sven." He made an extremely poor imitation of Leif's Norwegian accent.

"Oh, this oughta be good."

She was joking; he was not. "Come on. Stretch out on your stomach."

She started to turn and changed her mind. "What about you? How are you?"

"I'm fantastic. I have a beautiful woman about to let me touch her wherever I want to."

"Wait, I never said that."

She wrapped her arms around his neck and kissed him, long and deep, taking the lead, pushing him onto his back instead of following his directive to lie down. When he groaned and pulled her to lie on top of him, she broke the kiss. She'd done it now, and her nerves almost got the better of her. Instead she closed her eyes and took a brave breath.

"Your leg has to be killing you," she said. "I'm worried about it. I have no idea how to ask you about it because you never say anything, so I'm just blurting it out."

"My leg is okay," he said.

"You haven't taken off the prosthetic in two days."

"I have. Didn't you ever wonder what the heck took a guy so long in the woods at night?" He took his turn kissing her and she reveled, not just in his kiss but in the breadth of him beneath her. And in the swift, undeniable swell that proved what power her mouth had over him. More thrills pooled low in her pelvis.

The next words hung in her throat for a long time. If she said them, she'd have to be willing to offer the same should he ask it. Her greatest fear rose in front of her.

"You don't have to leave it on." She whispered the words almost fearfully against his mouth. "I want to know all of you. I want you to…trust me."

"I haven't wanted to weird you out."

The words were light, slightly jokey, and still she clearly heard the underlying tension. With a start she recognized her own fears in the sound, and deep inside a little of the anxiety she'd battled so long started to disintegrate.

"That's just dumb, Alec. Weird? It's not weird. It's you."

Did she mean it? Of course she did. Then how could she do anything but open herself up in return? She couldn't have his body without sharing hers no matter how much it scared her.

"You've never made love to a one-legged guy."

The fear flared hot just before her grin broke loose. "Am I about to?"

He pulled her back down against him and ran his hands over her seat, pulling her tight to groin and rolling his hips. "I think it might be too soon."

She pushed up and away again, resting one elbow beside his ear and brushing his hair back with the other hand, drinking in the texture with her fingertips. "I'm afraid to let you see, too."

"See what?" A light, perhaps one of hopefulness, brightened his eyes.

"I have more scars than the one you've seen on my face. My own arsenal to use in weirding you out." She stopped combing through his hair. The breath she took this time was shakier than any so far. "I'd show you mine if you show me yours. Let's be weirded out together." The words were silly, and her heart skittered around her ribcage—a scared bird that had trapped itself.

He didn't speak. Carefully, he rolled her off of him and placed one hand on her stomach. With gentle fingers he unsnapped her jeans and slowly rasped down the zipper. Then he sat up, and reached for her boots. One at a time he tugged them off.

Next came his. It took him a minute to work the left one off and expose the shapeless foot with its intricate mechanical joint. She sat up, nervousness evaporating steadily.

"Show me how it moves."

He did.

"Amazing," she said.

Making him lean back on his elbows, she undid his snap and opened his zipper. He closed his eyes, and a long, hard "ahhhh," escaped when she brushed the bulge of his erection.

"Naughty man," she whispered. "All I cared about was seeing the leg. Take your jeans off and behave yourself."

He laughed softly with a hint of disbelief in its tenor. "I can control the leg. I can't control other things as well. Besides, it's your fault."

He got to his feet and pulled down his jeans. The socket that cradled Alec's real leg was colorful, and it delighted her in a fascinated kind of way. The swirling rainbow decorated the top of the prosthetic and the covering that tapered along its carbon fiber shaft. He stood before her in his boxers, his right leg as beautiful and muscled as an athlete's, his left thigh muscled and strong, the knee half covered with a silicone sleeve that flexed when he moved. The limb itself was anticlimactic—dark and powerful-looking, but attached so securely that it was just him. The bionic man. And at the moment he was hers.

And he had body parts that were much more interesting than the artificial leg.

"You're pretty gorgeous," she said. He caught her staring at the tented boxers, and he burst out laughing until it rolled over them both.

He sat on the sleeping bag and silently, deftly, removed the artificial limb. "You're amazing," he said when he'd set it aside.

His stump did divert her attention from the part of him she really wanted to explore. The first thing she noticed was the smoothness of the skin and then the redness along the front and sides.

"Oh, Alec, it looks rubbed. I'm sorry you couldn't take it off before."

"It gets sore, but not painful. And having it off now makes everything fine."

"Honest?"

"Honest. Now lie back and let me take care of you for a minute."

She closed her eyes and, suddenly, her bravery threatened to flee again as he shimmied off her jeans. Inch by inch he got closer to revealing her twisted leg, and she bit her lip to keep from crying out to stop him. And then the denim was gone, the jeans tossed aside.

"Look at you." The prayer-like whisper brought tears to her eyes.

"I'd like it better if you didn't." All she wanted was to pull him down, roll over and mesh with him, make herself invisible and stop the shivers coursing through her body.

"No, don't say that. You had a terrible accident. Now that you're part of me, of my life, I hate that it left you feeling ugly. But you aren't. The scars aren't. They're here because you are, and thank God."

Tears spilled down her temples, hot and healing. He'd never seen her scarless, and he didn't care. He didn't compare her to anything, least of all who she'd been before. She had a clean slate with him. The knowledge slammed through her.

"Don't cry," he said. "Don't. It's okay."

"It's more than okay."

"I want you, Joely. I thought it was because you're beautiful, and I'm just a guy with a typical one-track brain, but that's not it. I want you because you're you, and you make me feel like the only man on Earth who matters. Because I think I'm falling in love with you."

In love?

"I thought you weren't in this for serious." She held his cheeks between her hands, searching for the truth in his words.

"Helluva thing. I'm still trying to reconcile it."

Joely sat up and scrambled, with only a little awkwardness, into his lap. Heat against heat, she pressed to his hard length until they both groaned in desire. Without taking time for finesse, he pushed her torso away so he could yank her T-shirt over her head with eager hands. A fluid movement of his fingers at her back flicked apart her bra, and she fell forward to kiss him, tunneling beneath his shirt and hitching it up between them.

For the shortest moment she could manage, she broke their kiss so she could shuck his shirt off, then she spread her hands across his pecs in exploration. His bare chest, with its perfect dusting of sexy hair, thrilled her.

They lay back, he beneath her first and then vice versa. Multiple times they changed their positions to explore each other, and when every item of clothing had been shed and their bodies touched skin to skin for the first time, Joely felt like she'd climbed Wolf Paw Peak to reach the beautiful top. What she'd thought was going to be a painful journey had been spiritual.

They rolled to their sides and Alec ducked his head to catch first one breast and then the other in a delicious kiss. His strong hand pressed sensually against her lower belly and sought the spot between her thighs that controlled every sensation in her body.

"How's that?" He circled his finger gently, and his words went straight into her core.

Within seconds she couldn't stop the swift pressure within every muscle and nerve fiber. Higher and higher he pushed her until she looked right over the top of the mountain and prepared to explode over the edge.

And he stopped.

She cried out. "You can't!"

"Ssh. Trust me."

She opened her eyes. The tension in his face surprised her. Pleased her. He pulled away and grabbed a foil packet from above their heads. "Where did you get…?" she asked, breathless, craving his touch back.

"A magician never reveals his tricks."

"Let me put it on."

"I'm not sure that would be a good idea." He laughed, but it was choppy and harsh with desire.

She let him do it just so she could get him back into her arms sooner. When his fingers picked up where they'd left off, he brought her straight back to that brink of explosion. One last time he left her teetering, just long enough to shift and glide into her with a long, hot, silken stroke. Her explosion detonated, and she kept only enough wits about her to grab hold of him and make sure he was caught in the blast with her. Time—how long the fireworks lasted or how long she hovered with Alec in pure ecstasy—ceased to matter. When they finally floated back to reality, a fresh well of tears overflowed. This time, however, she laughed through them and wrapped her arms and legs, which now felt more whole and healthy than at any time in her life, as thoroughly as she could around his spent body. She wanted him this close forever—as if they'd truly shared the same body, flesh, and soul for those moments, and she'd lose him if she let go.

"You okay?" His question rolled into a deep, chuckle.

"More than." Her heart swelled with joy. With freedom. "Thank you."

"Aw, Joely, don't thank me. That was us. Together."

"Then thank you for allowing me to say I'm falling in love with you, too. I haven't wanted to scare you off."

"Don't kid yourself. It scares me plenty."

"Try not to let it."

"Okay. If trying this again in a few minutes is part of the fear management therapy." He nuzzled the hollow between her neck and shoulder.

"It would be my first choice of treatment."

"I feel better already." He gnawed the tender skin below her ear, tickling it and eliciting a happy shriek. "But at the moment, you're cold. I can feel it. Let's clean up and get in where it's warm."

"If you're talking about the goose bumps, they are not from the cold."

"I see. Well, nevertheless, let's try making more of them under the covers."

The "covers" were their two sleeping bags, zipped together to make one down-filled cocoon. They tucked themselves in, and Alec enveloped her, making her safe, turning her goose bumps into warm contentment.

"Wake me when you're ready." She grinned dopily and drifted into sweet oblivion with her head pillowed on his arm and his kiss pressed to the top of her head.

THE WORLD EXPLODED for real, tearing into the middle of Alec's very hot dream that had, exquisitely and erotically, nothing to do with Humvees or Iraq. A screech and the convulsive jolt of Joely's warm, naked body in his arms punctuated the enormous crash of thunder that had scared them both awake. She buried her head in his arms.

"Jeez," she said. "That was close."

"It was." He kissed her, his mind racing between detailed images from the interrupted dream he now desperately wanted to turn into reality, and the actual reality of what encroaching thunder meant. "Come on. I know what I promised, but I think finding shelter before the rain hits has to come first."

They scrambled reluctantly into clothes. He put his leg back on, safely holding close the memory of his unbelievable Joely and the way she'd turned his moment of greatest concern into a moment that connected her to him forever. The wind picked up swiftly, and Alec threw dirt on their mostly dead fire until the embers were suffocated. Rain would extinguish it, but he didn't want to take any chances with coals in the wind.

Joely rolled everything quickly into their saddle packs and cleared their campsite. "Of course it has to do this the only night we're not going to be in a cabin."

"I think we made the thunder gods jealous with our own storm." He took a moment to capture her and brand another kiss across her lips. She melted against him.

"That was unbelievably corny," she said. "But I say, let them try and best us."

He wanted to keep going. His undisciplined body was only reacting harder, literally, to her touch, her scent, her lips, but they needed the leeward hillside and the rock overhang they'd scouted before making camp under the trees. Trees were a godsend in normal weather. They could be lethal in a thunderstorm.

More thunder roared and rolled toward them. It was pitch dark except for the constant show from lightning. He pulled their flashlights from his saddlebags and handed one to her.

"Put the saddles deep under the pine trees and put the saddle blankets over them. They'll be okay. Let's grab the horses first…" And that's when he realized what was wrong. "Shit. Where's Rowan?"

"She was tied up under the tree."

"But she's not there. She must have gotten scared and snapped that little leash. It's what it's meant to do if she got tangled or in trouble, but she should have come to us."

That started frantic calling, desperate listening, and a panic he couldn't control roiling in Alec's gut. He didn't realize how frenzied he'd grown until Joely stopped him and pressed to him in a tight hug. She breathed deeply for him. Calmed him with a steady, certain voice.

"It's okay, Alec. We'll find her. I promise."

It took five long, precious minutes before they heard the high-pitched whine.

"Rowan! Here girl, come on, don't be afraid," he called to his dog.

The whining came again along with a thunder crack and a gust of straight-line wind that nearly toppled them both.

"Crap and a half," Joely said. "This is not funny."

Finally Rowan let out her low, unmistakable woof. They found her beneath a cottonwood tree pinned by a five-inch-thick branch taken down by the storm. Joely let out a cry. Alec knelt, his panic surging again. The big dog raised her head and licked his hand.

"The branch is caught and looks like it smashed into her knee," Joely said, holding the flashlight steady on

Rowan's leg. We can get it off her, but I think she might be in tough shape. I can't tell if it crushed her sides, too."

"Oh, God." He moaned. "Rowan, I'm so sorry. We'll get you out."

It took only seconds to move the long, heavy limb. Alec prayed for his dog to jump up, happy to have her prison opened. But she didn't move. She thumped her tail and lifted her head to look at him with confused eyes, then lay back down.

"Oh, God," he said again.

"Let me look." Joely knelt behind the dog's back. "Dogs get hurt all the time on a ranch. Hold my flashlight."

She ran her hands slowly over Rowan's belly, ribs, and back. The dog didn't make a peep.

"I don't think anything's out of place here," she said. "It's all her leg. But I can feel a bone out of place. And there's a gash right above the joint. I don't think she lost a lot of blood, but it's hard to tell."

She stood and left him so she could hop and shuffle to the saddle rolls. Quickly she extracted a white tank top from her pack. She returned and in moments had ripped a makeshift bandage out of the shirt. Carefully she wrapped it tightly enough around Rowan's leg to stop the bleeding.

"We have to figure out a way to get her home," she said.

"I'll ride out."

"No."

The forcefulness behind her single word made him stare, too numb with worry to start an argument. "No?"

"We have to wait until the rain passes, and then I'm the one who should go. It won't be light for hours yet, but I know this area like I know my name. I can get close enough to the highway to maybe get a cell phone signal. If not that, I'll get home faster, and Cole can get the truck and trailer close."

"We'll discuss it after the storm."

The rain started five minutes later. Between the two of them they hefted Rowan to the shelter spot and led the horses out of the worst of the wind. Joely's bravery in forcing use of her injured leg humbled and astounded Alec. By the time they sat mostly out of the rain all five of them were soaked. Rowan slept, and Alec held her big head in his lap, stroking and talking. Joely held him, rubbing shoulders and convincing him everything would be fine.

The student who had been learning how to find her strength had definitely become the master.

She left the instant the rain slowed and the thunder faded into the east. It ate at him like acid that she was headed out by herself, but she never wavered. Rowan would be more relaxed with him, she said. She would have someone back before suppertime. If she rode quickly it would only be a few hours.

As she headed off, all Alec could think was how little fast riding she'd done and how her legs had to be like rubber. He convinced himself she was undertaking an inevitable suicide mission and created a long list of possible disastrous outcomes. When he went to work on a list of successful ones, the only item was "miracle." Rowan whimpered in her sleep, distracting him, and he tried to wake her. She opened one eye and thumped her tail, but then slept again almost before the thump ended.

Finally exhaustion hit him, and his eyes closed, too. He fought to stay awake, to keep prayers heading heavenward for his dog, and for his girl. It had only been a few hours since her lovemaking had made him feel like king of the world.

What was it Sadie had said? Every form of lovemaking involved trust? He brought back the memory of how hard it had been to drop his jeans. He'd bared every ounce of vulnerability he still kept hidden, but her reaction had defined the word trust.

She had defined the word love. He'd said he loved her, and now as he had no choice but to wait in half panic, he knew he'd meant the word in every way.

Chapter Twenty-One

THE WILDEST PART of the storm might have passed, but rain still drove like fine needles into Joely's skin. The gamble she took by leaving before it cleared was that she'd had to guess this was the end of the system and the rain would end soon. Fifteen minutes into her trip, Joely wondered what had possessed her to be so bold.

She'd never been afraid of the dark, so the night didn't bother her. She'd always known that nocturnal animals prowled the darkness—cougars and coyotes among the most dangerous—but she and her sisters had learned as children how to beware of and avoid the creatures who were the true residents of this land. She wasn't even afraid of storms, although she knew the idiocy of getting caught without shelter in a Wyoming plains tempest.

What she feared was falling off the horse. If she did she wouldn't be able to get back on without Alec's help. If she'd had Penny, she'd have believed she could ford head high rivers and never fall. But Muddy was an unknown. An interloper. A horse she'd had no part in choosing and, therefore, a horse she hadn't wanted. Unfortunately, their lives now more or less depended on each other.

"Don't be melodramatic," she said out loud, and let the darkness swallow the sound. Muddy Waters swiveled his ears back, listening for more of her voice. "You aren't depending on me for anything are you?" she asked him and knew the question was stupid on its face. Any horse united with a human by virtue of a saddle and bridle had to trust every minute its rider wouldn't put him in harm's way. Muddy needed her as much as she needed him.

She wasn't sure she had any ability to promise this horse he could trust her. Her legs had been strong for the first five minutes. Now they felt like noodles tied to the stirrups with licorice.

Alec had argued that she should be the one to stay with Rowan. From a strictly physical standpoint he'd been right. He had five times her stamina and strength. But Rowan had started to whine and whimper in her sleep. It took a great deal of pain to make a dog complain out loud. She had a long, deep laceration on her leg, and although it didn't look like it had punctured the joint capsule, Joely couldn't be sure in the dark. Joint infection was a possibility and that could be life threatening. At the very least the wound needed stitching, and the longer they waited to get help, the less likely it would be that Rowan survived. If Alec were to get lost, a highly likely scenario, nobody would come looking for them for two more days.

The musings helped her pass another five minutes. She knew exactly where she was, and it didn't comfort her much. She hadn't made much progress over the soggy ground. She might as well have been plodding along pulling an old milk wagon. A solid thirty miles remained to the ranch and she'd be able to access certain cell coverage once she was within a couple of miles. The section of highway traversing the ranch was slightly closer. She might find cell coverage sooner, but the coverage was spotty at best and she could wander miles out of her way to find a clear signal.

For the moment she told herself she was doing her best. It wasn't as if they could gallop through the root-studded trails. Muddy, for his part, didn't seem bothered by the uneven ground. He missed the roots efficiently and moved willingly at whatever pace she allowed. In fact, she thought, he'd been like this the entire ride. He didn't lag; he didn't jig or forge ahead. He waited for instructions and carried them out.

Good boy.

She patted his neck absently. It wasn't his fault they were making slow time. But she couldn't go any faster.

Why?

She hated voices in her head, especially when they weren't hers. This one belonged to Alec. He'd been in her head pretty much constantly since she'd met the man, and the thing that made his voice so aggravating was not that he was wrong or even right. It was that she'd grown to appreciate it. She'd started to trust it when she didn't even trust herself. The fact that she wanted to listen to this man, who had plenty of his own issues, irritated her inner self—the one who wanted help from nobody.

Why?

That voice was hers. Why should she trust him?

Because it was his doing that she wasn't sitting in her tiny apartment insisting she couldn't go out into the world. Because he'd arranged this long ride, this arduous task for her weak body, just so she could ride in the rodeo—something that was an obstacle in his own life.

Because he'd said he loved her.

Loved her! Heaven help her, she loved him right back. And if she loved him she must trust him, and if she trusted him she had to believe him.

Hadn't Alec said she could do anything she put her mind to doing?

She and Muddy broke out of the woods, and the long, sloping eastern meadowlands stretched before her. The choice had to be made here: go for the highway or head for home?

If she got back to the ranch, she wouldn't have to wander her way home from the highway. She could bed down the horse, connect with Dr. Ackerman and, more importantly, she could return to Alec and Rowan with the rescue crew and help with Alec's horse while he dealt with the dog.

Right. You're going to deal with the horse. You can't even ride this one.

Suddenly, she didn't much like her own voice anymore.

"Let's go home, Muddy," she said. "But we have to go a little faster than we've been doing. I can do it if you'll keep your lope nice and easy on me. Okay?"

It took almost more mental energy than she had left to urge Muddy from a jog into a gentle lope. She had managed the gait in the confines of the round pen, but she didn't know Muddy or what he'd do given the chance to run on open ground. She should trust her riding skills, but that ship had sailed months before. All she could do was hope Muddy would forgive her awkwardness and not take off.

He lifted into a gentlemanly lope, his ears flicking back as he listened for further instruction. For a long minute she struggled with coordination. Her seat slipped and her thighs burned until she ended up pinching improperly with her knees to stay tight in the saddle. Her body fought against everything she knew was correct. Where the heck was her muscle memory? Riding was counterintuitive to the neophyte: sit up to stay in closer contact with the saddle, don't squeeze your legs to stay on, and don't pull back to slow down, use your seat and back. Nothing felt right—until it did.

Muddy's long, swooping lope was much swingier and level than Penny's had been. It rode like a BMW rather than a sporty little Audi. Comfortable and easy—yet filled with unleashed power. Joely sat up straighter and forced her weak leg back from where it had slipped out in front of the cinch. Immediately Muddy dropped his ear back as if to say "okay," gave a quick snort, and dropped into a trot.

Joely let out a low whistle of appreciation for his training, but it was cut short when Muddy's next step took him into a slight depression. He hitched to compensate,

Joely's left leg flopped away from the saddle leather and threw her off balance. In a split second she was sliding off the left side of the saddle smoothly and inevitably. She landed hard on her left hip and butt cheek with a splat. Instantly the storm's aftermath had her soaked but she was grateful the waterlogged prairie grasses had saved her from serious injury.

It still hurt.

And it sent her into helpless panic. Her nightmare had come true.

Every ounce of strength drained away, and hopelessness enveloped her the way it had the day the mustang foal had been born, and Joely lay on her back with sharp cold rain pricking at her skin and hot fat tears pouring down her temples. She didn't know where Muddy had gone and she didn't open her eyes to find out if he'd run off. She didn't care. She couldn't even go for damn help anymore because she was the one who constantly needed it herself.

Failure.

It blew in rapid fire bursts through her life and had ever since she'd won the Miss Wyoming pageant and allowed two men who saw her as pretty and delicate tell her what to do with her pageant winnings. She'd given it all away, along with her self-esteem.

The losses played through her mind for the millionth time. Her father, her husband and their marriage, the baby whose near weightlessness still weighed her arms down, and the horse. Now the dog—most likely. It was the same overwrought sadness—the same grief that seemed destined to control her emotions no matter how many steps she took to climb back out of her hole. At least this time Alec wasn't here to witness the weakness. She could remember his arms around her during that last breakdown and feel the mortification as he'd rocked her and said nothing—the one time she'd needed the man who'd given her unsolicited advice on everything to really fix something.

Nothing.

But he hadn't needed to; he'd *been* there. Been there with her and for her but not trying to fix things he couldn't and shouldn't fix. That was Alec Morrissey's great strength—he jumped in when he knew what he was talking about. He supported her silently when the battle had to be hers. Whether she liked it or not.

And he was still back there. Waiting for her. Trusting that she would do what she had the expertise to do. Her head swam. She wanted his arms around her again. Now. Now she understood how his silence could fix everything.

But it was her turn to buck up. She was the only one who could fix this, and the only thing holding her back was the little voice she'd allowed to make a home in her head that kept saying she couldn't.

A primitive cry full of frustration and pure anger burst from her lungs. She slammed her fist into the wet ground and pushed up onto her elbows. Something warm and dank-smelling nudged her cheek, startling her until she turned to the wet horse and started to laugh. Muddy snuffled curiously around her ear and snorted, adding horse sneeze to the rain still falling. She laughed harder and grasped the sides of the halter she'd put on under his bridle so she never had to tie him by the reins.

"Pull me up, big guy," she said.

He didn't really obey, of course, but he snorted and backed away. Amazed, she used his weight as leverage and got to her feet. The instant she was fully upright, she threw her arms around Muddy's neck, burying her face in his wet coat, and letting his animal heat infuse her with strength and hope. He allowed the tight hold, bobbing his head and shaking it once to clear the rain from his face.

He wasn't Penny. But then, Alec wasn't Tim, and nothing else about her life was the same. Fine. She'd fallen off the horse. Figuratively and literally. They said you weren't a real rider until you came off at least once. Well then, she must be a damn good rider.

"Thank you," she whispered. "Now all you have to do is let me lean on you until we find a hillock I can use as a mounting block. That or you'll have to drag me all the way back to the barn."

They found a perfect rise where she mounted from the wrong side. Muddy stood statue still, making her question her belief that he didn't really understand.

They galloped two long stretches on the way home. Once she decided she wasn't afraid to fall off again, the rest of her fear disappeared. She had the strength in her hips, after walking with crutches so much, to curve her thighs and calves around Muddy's broad sides, and she'd developed enough flexibility in her back to rock down into the saddle. Her left ankle and foot were less flexible, but she worked out how to compensate for not having them as shock absorbers—the same way Alec couldn't feel his prosthetic foot yet managed fine.

At last, within two miles of Rosecroft, Joely finally got service enough to call Harper. By the time she and Muddy made it to the barn, pain circulated through her body as if her blood were made of it and the breeze after the rain had chilled to her marrow. But the truck and trailer were ready to go, and a plan was in place. Her mother took Muddy, handed Joely a dry sweatshirt and pair of jeans, and despite what had to be her hideous, bedraggled sight, not a single person argued when Joely said she was going back with Cole and Gabe to pick up Alec and the dog.

That alone made the wild ride triumphant.

THE FOLLOWING SATURDAY Alec rose from beside the giant dog bed and smiled at his oaf of a pet. She was the perfect convalescent. A lazy girl perfectly happy to be waited on hand and paw. Sadly, he was only too willing to give her anything she wanted. She'd be incorrigible if he didn't stop bringing her treats every five minutes.

He was just so grateful. One week ago, twelve stitches and a bandage on a badly bruised knee had been the result of her accident. She'd be restricted for another week, but she'd be fine. He looked out the window, knowing their savior would be there any second for lunch. She'd started her new job at the beginning of the week, and she was happier than he'd ever known her.

Unless it was when they were together in that physical and nearly spiritual bond they were perfecting at night...but he needed to stop thinking about that so much.

Or not.

He didn't hear her arrival in the car she was borrowing from Mia—to see if she was ready for her own. Since her ride to the rescue the past weekend, she finally seemed to believe she could do whatever she put her mind to. She'd taken to driving by herself like she'd never been fearful of the task, and each time she tried something new at work, her confidence took bigger leaps.

"Time for lunch!" she called, surprising both Alec and his dog, who jumped to her feet as Joely entered, wearing a backpack Alec suspected was loaded with goodies.

He grabbed Rowan's collar and forced her to sit. She wiggled like a two-year-old confined to a stroller.

"Hello, baby," Joely cooed at the dog. "How's my girl?"

She stroked and kissed the dog until Alec cleared his throat. She looked up laughing. "Oh hi, you're here, too."

He grabbed her into a kiss, and she dropped her crutches on the couch so she could wrap her arms around his neck.

"I like this," he said when they parted. "So domestic."

"And you who says he doesn't do commitment."

"I don't rescue people and dogs either. That's your department."

"And don't you forget it. All right, since it's Saturday and I'm sorry I said I'd work, I brought some stuff to make giant chef salads tonight. Ice cream for dessert. You know, to make up for healthy."

"You are really handy to have around."

"Don't forget that either."

She put away her groceries and called on him to carry sandwiches she'd brought for lunch to the living room, but she tugged on his hand before he could pass them out. "Come and sit for a sec. In the interest of a hundred percent honesty in this relationship, I have something I have to tell you. You may not be happy with me."

"That won't happen."

She grinned with the barest hint of uncertainly behind the light in her eyes. "Then I'll just spit it out. I contacted your aunt and uncle, and they called me back this morning."

He went dizzy, blown away with the complete unexpectedness of her announcement. "You did what?"

She planted a solid kiss on his lips. "I know you told me about them in the name of getting to understand each other, but I couldn't make myself believe they were really angry. Or that you were really angry with them."

"I'm *not* angry. But I know they don't want to be reminded of the son I lost for them. I've never blamed them, Joely; they blamed me."

"But you miss them. You say Rowan is your only family, but I can see in your eyes that's not true."

She held his gaze unapologetically, which, for a woman who only days ago might have apologized for breathing wrong, would have been miraculous had this been any other subject. Alec took long minutes fighting his frustration. He'd fallen for this woman, to the point of being ready to take a chance on long term, but this was an area she had no business mucking with. When he'd calmed enough to keep his reply civil, he took her hands.

"I wish you hadn't done that."

"I know."

"Then why? I haven't talked to them in a year. Don't think for a second you can compare my family to yours. Hell, we were dysfunctional before I went to Iraq. Before Buzz and I ran off to join the rodeo. My aunt and uncle don't have anything to say to me now."

"I'm pretty sure you'll find out that's not true."

"You didn't have the right." His voice tightened defensively.

"Look." She set her jaw in the way he found cute when she was mad at him. "I expected you to be annoyed, but I don't expect you to be stupid about this. Maybe your aunt and uncle won't contact you at all. If not you're no worse off. If they do? Well, you're a big boy. You can handle a phone call."

As if answering a summons, Alec's cell phone rang from the coffee table where he'd left it. He stared at it until Joely picked it up.

"Richard Waverly," she read off the screen. "Your uncle. Take it."

His gut lurched, and he shook his head. "This is not a conversation I can have without warning."

"For crying out loud. Don't be an ass."

"Don't you dare answer it, me."

The phone quit. Joely set it down and glared at him. "What the crap, Alec?"

"You don't understand. This isn't something you can fix because you suddenly have a sunny outlook on life. Save that for us."

"Us? Really? Tell me, what is 'us'?"

"It's beginning to be the most important thing in my life. You've become a part of me—that's what's important. Leave the past in the past."

"I feel like I'm part of you, too, Alec. I don't take what we started last weekend lightly or for granted. And I don't make love to you to prove anything. I do it because I have this corny belief we have two of those clichéd souls that were meant to find each other. Because I love you."

"I love you, too."

"So don't be afraid."

"I'm not afraid. You've made me the opposite of afraid, Joely."

"It might not be me you're afraid of, but you are. You're afraid of your aunt and uncle. Of the rodeo. You're afraid of your cousin's ghost, Alec."

Something hot and fierce flashed within him. He wanted to call it anger but he couldn't honestly give it that name. It was resentment. It was defensiveness. It was standing there being accused of abusing Buzz's memory—a memory he'd felt so self-righteous about honoring. It was the start of fear. Not of the things she'd listed, but that she might have a point.

No.

She was wrong. She *didn't* understand how things were between him and his aunt and uncle. She couldn't understand how much Buzz had loved the rodeo in a way completely different than Alec had. To Alec riding broncs had been a goal, a challenge, almost a cheater's way of making a living because it had been so much fun, but to

Buzz it had been a love affair—a reason to breathe and to fight for. If Buzz couldn't have his love, neither would he. So Alec had made his decision.

"Don't talk to me about my cousin's ghost. You don't get to bring him into this—you have no idea what ghosts I face."

"Then tell me. Tell me what you see in your dreams at night and why you won't even step foot on the hallowed ground your cousin loved. Tell me why you don't trust me enough to help you after all you've done for me."

"There's nothing more to tell. I made a promise, and I won't go back on it."

"Then there's not much of a future for 'us,' is there?"

"I don't see what this has to do with us."

"Come on. You just went to enormous effort to get me on that long-distance ride to build up my strength. You nearly lost your dog convincing me I was strong enough to face my fears, get over being an idiot, and ride in the stupid Fourth of July rodeo. But you won't come to support what you've helped create. It's mean." Her gaze fell, and she hesitated long seconds as if deciding to say more. Finally she bit her lip and drove the knife of guilt deeper into his heart. "And it hurts."

He'd never experienced bitterness mixed so thoroughly with crushing sadness. "Hurting you is the last thing I want."

"Then come."

"Why is it okay that you don't respect a decision *I* made to help me live with what I was dealt?"

"Because you're not living. You're ignoring."

"Right. It's hard to ignore something you think about every damn day."

For another long, tense moment she remained silent, staring at the floor again, her face as drawn as a funeral mourner's. Even as he watched, tears filled her eyes.

"I can't do this."

"Do what?"

"I can't live with this. I can't live with the double standard. You have one set of rules for me and another for you."

"That's ridiculous."

"Is it? You've made me clean out every closet, open every wound and cleanse it, and then start fresh. You get to bury a ticking time bomb by pretending it's all in the name of love. You get to be self-righteous and call this all a decision you've made. Well, maybe I've made decisions, too. If I can't have all of you—all your trust, all your secrets, all the skeletons in your closet—I don't want any of it. In order to be whole again, I need all or nothing."

The words slammed into him like the hot shrapnel from the fiery Humvee. She couldn't be serious. She couldn't really believe his personal decision was something selfish that meant he didn't trust her.

She shook her head when he tried to take her in his arms. "I need to go back to work, Alec."

"You'll leave in the middle of this?"

"It's not the middle. It's the end."

"Not for me. We'll work this out at dinner."

"We probably could. But I think I'm too selfish. All or nothing—I'm not interested in a compromise."

"You have it all. Damn it. You have it *all*."

She rose on tip toes and kissed him. Tears had welled over and spilled down her cheeks.

"All but the power to bring you out of the past or help you slay your demons," she said. "I don't expect any more from you than you do of me, Alec. Someone I thought was a wise man once said to me, 'don't say you can't, say you can.' Now he's the one saying he can't. I won't go back there."

She pulled away, but he grasped her hand. "This is ridiculous."

"You thinking so is one of the reasons I'm leaving." She picked up her jacket and purse, walked to where Rowan lay, tail thumping like a pedal on a bass drum, and knelt to wrap her arms tightly around the dog's neck. "I love you, gorgeous. Be a good girl and heal fast."

She passed Alec on her way to the door without touching him, and then turned back with her hand on the knob. "Do me one last favor. Stop your self-pity long enough to call your aunt and uncle back. Leave the past in the past, but don't keep them there. They don't deserve that."

"They're the ones who shut me out."

"I know. Do it anyway."

She left, taking the fragile new meaning he'd found in his world with her. Stunned, he looked around his empty house unable to comprehend what had just happened. How did a person eff-up his life in the course of twenty minutes, just because he didn't want to go the damn rodeo?

Chapter Twenty-Two

It took him two hours to realize he couldn't answer his own question. It took him five more to get over being angry over Joely's demand that he call his aunt and uncle.

It took him an entire awful, sleepless night to understand that he couldn't let Joely end their fledgling relationship. In two short months she'd woven her way permanently into his heart, and if he didn't fix something, everything he believed about his inability to love and save the people he loved would be true.

Sunday morning he sat bleary-eyed at his table, praying for the caffeine from his coffee to kick in. His world was still off its axis, but in his long night he had come up with only one concrete piece of knowledge. The first thing to fix was the thing he bucked hardest against. The thing that would do the least good. Nonetheless, he let the coffee work its magic, then he picked up his phone and hit the redial.

His aunt answered on the first ring. "Alec?"

He recognized her hopeful desperation even though he hadn't spoken to her in so very long. She'd clearly been waiting for this call. Guilt stung quick and deep. When had he stopped being the bigger man?

"It's me, Aunt Chris. How are you?"

He got no reply. All he heard was a small choked sob before his uncle picked up the phone.

"Alec? Son? I'm sorry. Chris will be right back. Believe it or not she's so happy to hear your voice I think it plain overwhelmed her. Are you all right?"

"I'm okay, Uncle Rick. I was away when you called. I...I'm sorry."

Finally he *was* sorry. Truly angry-at-himself sorry that it had taken him so long to call even just to hear their voices. Whatever words had been said, whatever the future held, these were his only living relatives. No matter what they needed, he needed them.

"Alec the last thing on God's little green earth is for you to be sorry. I'm really kinda glad your aunt is too choked up to talk. I have some things I've needed to say for a long time and I haven't known how to begin."

"Rick, no. We don't need to go into the past."

"Oh, yes, we do. In a big way."

Alec had expected a cordial call. An obligatory conversation. He'd been willing to accept that, and once he'd heard Rick's voice, he'd even welcomed it. Honest, open feelings, however, were not something for which he had prepared or developed armor. He tightened his voice and tried to brush the looming deep emotions aside. Keep controlled. Tell them all was forgiven. Everything was past and everything was good. That was how he'd get through the call.

"I don't know why," Alec said. "It's just great to hear your voice."

"I should have called you long ago."

"That could be my line just as well."

Perfunctory. Expected. Good; Alec could work with this. He swallowed and started the next platitude, but his uncle plunged them straight into the fire.

"I can't ever take them back." For the first time Rick choked up, and Alec's throat closed over a thick, painful lump. "The ugly words, Alec, you'll never unhear them. And I will never truly be able to live with myself for saying them."

"Don't—"

"Let me finish. Please, son. Then I'll let you talk to your aunt. People say that words blurted in the heat of emotion reflect honest feelings you would normally hold back. I don't think it's true. I believe I would have said something just as awful if Buzz had come back without you. I can't prove that—but I was so damn angry at the war, the military, at Buzz, at you. At myself for not stopping either of you."

"I know, Uncle Rick. I do know this." Alec wanted him to stop. He needed time to breathe, and to halt the reopening of wounds that had finally, after three painful years, scabbed over.

"Grief is an ugly thing, Alec. I handled mine about as poorly as a man could by leaving it to fester for so long.

It's not enough, but I'm sorry. I didn't ever mean what came out of my mouth."

It was just an apology. Alec didn't want it to matter or be enough, because if it was, then everything his wall of strength had been built on was gone. He had nothing to brace against, nothing to hold himself accountable for, and no reason to hold onto the stubborn resolve that convinced him he was strong. If he forgave his uncle as simply as this, it would mean Joely was right—he'd been holding part of himself back, and he'd never really healed.

"I love you, Alec. I miss you."

He felt it. The crumbling of the wall built from isolation and heartache. The hole it left was big but no longer painful.

"Alec?" His aunt came on the line.

"Chris. Is he all right?"

"Darling, he's a big, stubborn mess, but he's smiling. And I love him as much as I love you."

"I want to talk to him again."

"Okay. But me first."

"Wait. I have to ask you, why? Why finally after all this time?"

"That wonderful girlfriend of yours. She's a special lady, Alec. She said she learned about us from you, and she believed you were ready to hear from us."

"She shouldn't have called." He fought lamely for the last shred of indignation, but it was useless. The hole in his life was filling rapidly with something warm and grateful and belonging entirely to Joely Crockett.

"You're wrong, Alexander. She got through to your uncle in a way I've never been able to. Convinced him that saying what he's wanted to say for so long wouldn't be useless. Don't ever be angry at her for coming to us."

"I love you, Aunt Chris," he said.

"We love you. With all our hearts. We despaired of ever telling you again."

"I know. I'm sorry. I really am sorry. I should have understood your grief better. Rick's grief better. Please, let me tell him that."

"He's still composing himself. First we need to talk about your cousin."

"Oh, I don't think—"

"No interruptions," she said, the warmth in her smile as audible as her words. "We're going to talk about Buzz and this crazy idea you have that you need to avoid the rodeo because of him. And if you're going to argue with me, then settle back into a comfy chair, because I'm going to keep you on the phone until we come to an agreement."

In the space of one old-fashioned lecture, his aunt made him laugh. He didn't know why; he was pissed as hell at the new topic and her threat. At the same time, it was hard to stay angry when he'd gotten back a mother, a father, and a woman he loved all in the span of five minutes. He could argue with Aunt Christine until he was blue in the face, but in the end, she was going to talk him into something they both wanted.

"HAT IN HAND, literally I see." Vince opened his back door to Alec two days later, wearing a shit-eating grin

Alec would have wiped off his face with a smack upside the head earlier in the week. Instead he simply stared at his friend, who thought Alec had simply come to have a couple of pictures taken, and work out an extravagant introduction for Ghost Pepper's return on the Fourth of July.

"This is going to be pure gold," Vince added. "Glad you came to your senses."

"No. I've lost my senses," Alec said.

"C'mon, man." Vince led him through the kitchen and into the same dining room where Joely had met him weeks before, and where Alec had been such an asshat. "This'll be great for rodeo, fantastic for your fans, and it won't hurt you either."

"Well, now? I'm not so sure about that." Alec half-smiled for the first time. "Truth. I'm not here for a damn picture. You bragged once you could teach a one-legged cowboy to ride a saddle bronc. I'm asking you to make good on that claim."

Vince's ugly, bearded mug twisted into such utter shock that it made this asinine plan of Alec's almost worth the soul-searching he'd done in order to get here.

"What the hell? Is this the apocalypse? You got inside information about Armageddon?"

"Yeah. I got it from my aunt."

"Christine!"

"Tough as ever in that way that always made us feel good about being told what buttholes we were. Remember?"

"One of a kind, your aunt."

"I need to ride that horse. Evidently Buzz is up there raising some kind of holy hell because I'm disrespecting his memory. Don't ask me, please. Chris is also just a little bit of a nut job when it comes to heaven."

"I remember that, too. And if Buzz is causing holy hell, it's gonna get him kicked the wrong way back through those pearly gates. I'd best get you riding, son."

Alec patted his cheek firmly with the flat of his hand. "Wipe that smirk off your face or I'm outta here, even if my cousin's eternal fate might suffer."

"Fine. When do you want to start?"

"You've got a mechanical bucker. Take me out there."

Vince truly looked as if he'd just matched his lottery ticket to the winning numbers. "Let's go. First you're going to show me every little inch of that peg leg of yours and we're gonna figure out what it can do. Then, by God, we're gonna turn you back into 'Morr-i-SEE!'"

Alec hadn't thought about that in a very long time. The name chant the crowd had always bestowed on him before and after a ride.

"I'm not him anymore," he said as he followed Vince back toward the door. "I'm not looking for or expecting crowd approval. Just get me three seconds on GP and I'll name my first born after you."

"Shit, what'll you give me if I get you eight?" Vince led him out into the yard.

"I'll kiss you in public."

Vince sputtered. "Three it is. By the way, where's your girl?"

"That's the other thing." Alec stopped and grasped him by the arm. "She doesn't know a thing about this, and you're not going to say a word. Not to her and not to anybody. Nobody knows until the announcer tells the crowd in two weeks. That's nonnegotiable."

"You sure?"

"More than. What's not sure is whether or not I'll actually go through with this insanity. Hell, I might not survive today."

"Tell you what. You die, I'll kiss you in public before they close the casket."

"Freak."

"C'mon, cowboy. Let's go buck you off a fake horsie."

Chapter Twenty-Three

ALEC'S SAFETY VEST and heavy fringed chaps felt like a lead straitjacket and shackles to his quivering body. He'd been donning them daily for two weeks, but today they might as well have been foreign shackles he'd never seen in his life. He brushed his hand over the PRCA logo on his breast, and the sponsorship badges, some of which were obsolete now but brought back memories so strong they nearly obliterated his real thoughts.

To his right, looking like he, too, was gathering strength from old memories, Ghost Pepper waited to be loaded into the chute. Vince came around the horse's rump and slapped Alec on the shoulder.

"Son of a bitch, I didn't think you'd really do it. Damn, I am the happiest man alive."

"I hate you." Alec gave his annoying friend a weak smile. "You didn't tell her, right? She doesn't know?"

"Relax, Morrissey. This is the best-kept secret this side of the key to Fort Knox. She'll faint dead away, I promise."

"She'd better not."

"Well, she's about to have her two minutes in the spotlight, and then you'll find out. You ready?"

"Hell and a half, no."

"You worked hard. I'm impressed. I truly am."

The truth was, Alec wasn't scared of the idiotic ride he was about to make. Vince and one of the best sports medicine guys Gabe had been able to find him had definitely worked hard to teach him how to make the spurring motion required, and how to fall safely with his leg. What he was scared of was that Joely would hate him for it. For not telling her his plans. Again. For not letting her in on the reconciliation with his aunt and uncle who were, in truth, the ones who'd begged him to do this. For making her live with the thought that he was still angry about her interference.

His life had spun one hundred and eighty degrees. He could still hear his uncle's words once he'd come back on the line. "My greatest regret is that I made you believe your ability to protect the people you love was flawed. But look at you—you love Buzz so deeply that you've put a knife through your own heart to protect his memory. You've stripped yourself of something that you love, and there's no need. Go. Show that girl of yours who you are, and give me back my son."

Well, here he was for one last three-second ride. Rick said show her? He'd show her.

"Put the horse in," Vince said to the handlers.

Maybe he was a little nervous. Alec lost his ability to swallow and his stomach lurched. Good, he told himself. Nerves were good.

JOELY SAT ASTRIDE Muddy Waters, her heart rate strangely calm considering it had been a runaway train all day. Now that the lights were about to go out in preparation for her ride, there wasn't any more she could do to prepare. Harper had schooled her all week, letting her practice her gallop even after she'd fallen once and scared the pants off of everyone watching. That had been ten rides ago. Tonight she'd either triumph or fall on her ass. It hardly mattered.

She scanned what she could see of the crowd, wondering why she tortured herself. He wasn't here. But she'd heard the most bizarre rumor. From Heidi Bisset. She'd found Joely earlier and sauntered up in her spangled finest.

"I heard Alec was back."

There'd been nothing to say except no, Heidi was mistaken. Joely knew for a fact. Heidi hadn't pushed it, and she'd walked away leaving Joely with another insight— she didn't feel the least bit of jealousy. In its place was a weird sense of compassion. Heidi looked like what she was—a thirty-year-old buckle bunny. Joely didn't miss it at all. She might have lost her man—despite the flowers that had been delivered every day since she'd walked out on him—but she'd gained something more substantial than anything Heidi had—total self-respect. She hoped one day Heidi would find the same pot of gold.

She thought about Alec's roses. One a day until she'd received a full dozen in twelve different colors—a rose rainbow. She had no idea what they meant, but they made her miss him. Made her know she needed to not give up on him—the way he'd never given up on her.

"Ready, Jo-Jo?" Mia and Harper stood on either side of Muddy and patted Joely's legs.

She pushed Alec to the back of her heart and nodded. The lights went off and the arena was bathed in grays and blacks. Her heart started pounding again.

"Ladies and Gentlemen," the announcer said. "We have a treat for you. You all know her, one of Jackson Hole's most beloved queens. We almost lost her last year to a terrible accident, but our girl has fought back and is here tonight to celebrate our nation's birthday and a very, very special night at the rodeo. Put your hands together for Jackson, Wyoming's own sweetheart, Miss Joely Crockett!"

"Ride 'im, cowgirl!" Harper cried.

She pressed her heels into Muddy's sides and urged him forward with her hips and seat. He shot into the arena just as they'd practiced, and the spotlight hit her like a beam from the heavens. She flew, her legs steady from hours of practice, her seat secure because now she knew her horse. The crowd buoyed her, and she knew who she raced for—the man who'd gotten her to this moment. She wouldn't give up on him. Stubborn, bossy, arrogant Alec Morrissey was the man she loved.

ALEC LET HIS breath out once Joely flew out of the gate and his chest swelled with pride. Damn, she'd been beautiful. The ride had been perfection. He wiped tears of relief from his eyes and listened to the crowd cheer.

"Okay. Get your ass up there, Morrissey."

He shook his head clear and nodded at Vince. He had a bet to win. And a score to settle—with himself. Then, maybe, he could be the man Joely Crockett deserved.

He took the deepest breath he ever remembered taking and looked up to the heavens. "I'd like a sign if you don't mind," he said. "An easy one. If you'll give me five seconds on this sucker, I'll ask that girl to marry me." He climbed, and looked down at his horse's saddle. "Okay, GP. Let's dance."

JOELY HANDED MUDDY off to Bjorn and turned, exhilarated, back to the gate. It was time for Ghost Pepper's big return. From what she understood, they'd given him three test rides in the past week, and he'd dumped every cowboy just as effortlessly as he ever had. Chance Smith, who'd drawn him tonight, was in for a great, probably short ride.

Mia and Harper stepped up beside her. Her mother crowded in as well. "You had an awesome ride, sweetheart," she said. "I'm so proud of you."

She was proud, too, and desperate to tell Alec how it had gone, but first she had to watch his horse. He'd have to hear about this whether he wanted to or not. She smiled. The irritating man.

"And now, ladies and gentlemen, the moment you've all been waiting for. The moment we've been promising you all summer long. The return of the most popular saddle bronc ever to buck his way through Jackson Hole."

The crowd roared.

"But we have a bonus surprise for you, folks. We've got you a cowboy who had to buy an extra room in his house for all his championship belts. A man who fought for our country and then came back stronger than ever. A man who went to help a fellow soldier and came back wounded himself."

Joely's mind followed slowly along with the announcer's introduction, and as the words took hold in her mind, her heart felt as if it stalled in her chest. Her hands shook as she gripped the bars of the gate.

"What the heck?" Harper asked.

"This man has been away from rodeo for four years, but he has a bone to pick with this here horse. He might have lost a leg, but he hasn't lost his will. Folks, whatever happens tonight, you're witnessing the best on the best. Give him eight seconds of your love. Ladies and gentlemen, Alec Morrissey and the only horse ever to beat him…Ghost Pepper!"

It started with a wild blur. The gate swung open, and Ghost Pepper seemed to shoot out in two directions. Atop him, Alec's right arm went straight up and a bright white Stetson went flying. Joely set aside her disbelief and counted. One second. Two seconds. Three seconds. His longest ride on this horse was five. Alec spurred perfectly, both legs reaching straight up Ghost Pepper's neck and raking down his shoulder. Four seconds. Five seconds. Tears rolled down Joely's face. The man was crazy. The horse nearly flipped sideways and then instantly dropped his head between his legs. Alec came fifteen inches off the saddle. Six seconds. Seven.

The horn sounded and the crowd went insane.

Morr-is-SEE! Morr-is-SEE! The old, traditional chant filled the stands.

Alec threw himself off the horse and landed flat on his back. Joely screeched his name when he stayed down. She wasn't supposed to enter the arena, but she didn't care. She made sure Ghost Pepper had been caught, and she threw the gate open. Without thinking, she ran for the first time since her accident, nearly tripping herself with the one crutch she carried with her. She reached him, expecting to find him unconscious and bleeding.

"Alec. Oh, please, Alec…"

He was grinning and weeping, his fist clenched. "Hey, you," he said. "Surprise."

She helped him up, and he dusted himself off then raised his arm for the crowd. The decibel level rose higher yet.

"Are you insane? Are you trying to kill yourself?" She threw her arms around his neck and kissed him so hard he started to laugh.

"No." He kissed her back. "I knocked the leg out of alignment a little, though. Let me lean on you."

"Anytime," she replied.

They walked slowly over to his hat, picked it up, dusted it off, and waved it to the crowd.

Her eyes opened wide in surprise. "This is Buzz's hat."

"Yeah. Gave it one last ride. Now it's time to let it go. C'mon."

He pointed to where a man and woman entered the arena. Joely knew immediately who they were.

Alec met them as the crowd cheered and handed the hat to his aunt. She sobbed as she hugged him. Then his uncle embraced him. They hugged Joely. They hugged Alec again, and he gave a final wave. The significance of the hat was lost on the crowd, but its meaning was crystal clear to Joely as Alec limped slightly out of the arena, his arm around Joely's shoulders for support.

"Eight seconds," she said. "That's like a fairy tale."

"Yup."

"Do you have any more shockers? I'm tired of these surprises."

"Actually." He stopped right outside the gate and faced her with her family and his watching. "I do. Joely Crockett, will you marry me?"

Epilogue

Valentine's Night

"LOOK AT YOU, Miss Joely. I tol' you, you would be the
most beautiful bride of all."

Mary, borrowed for the day from the VA's nursing
staff, stood behind her in the master bathroom off of
her mother's room, and wound two side curls around
her fingers while they both looked in the mirror. She
let them go and they sprang loosely back around Joely's
face, joining the other tendrils tumbling from her simple
chignon.

"Perfect." Mary's soft, rolled R whispered into her
ear as her former nurse and now her friend made final
pats to her hair and makeup, and then kissed her on the
cheek. "You are ready to go and marry your handsome
cowboy."

Her pulse fluttered at the words. Married.

Joely Morrissey. It had taken her a little time to get used to the ending alliteration, but now it rolled off her tongue as prettily as Mary's Rs.

"Are you ready?" Mary asked. "Shall we go and show them?"

Joely took one last look at her reflection. If she squinted, she could see another image right beside her—a five-year-old girl with a sunny smile and a halo of wheaty-yellow curls. If she squinted a little harder, the child moved her lips. "Mirror, mirror on the wall. Who's the fairest Crockett of all?"

She laughed.

"What?" Mary asked.

"Memories. Come on. My sisters are mad enough that only Grandma and Mom have seen the dress. Sisters are supposed to help with that, I've been told. But then again, nothing about this ceremony has been done the normal way."

It was true. This was a Tuesday, and the ceremony would start in half an hour at seven thirty in the evening. The weeknight wedding had to be because it was Valentine's Day, and one of the sisters had to do something clichéd like get married on the holiday of love. Joely loved that Alec had wanted this sentimental date even more than she did.

The other concession to the holiday were the flowers—red roses and pink stargazer lilies. But her dress was not white—it was her five bridesmaids who wore creamy ivory crepe. She wore no veil and had chosen the dress with only her grandmother's help. It was not

a bright sunny afternoon, but still the wedding was out-
doors. She smiled and swept the hem of her gown out
the door of the bathroom and into the bedroom where
the magpie chatter of her sisters ceased as if a switch had
turned them all off at the same moment.

"Oh, Joely." Grace was the first to utter a sound. "I've
never seen anything like it."

The dress was strapless and trainless, but it needed
no train. Sparkling crystals of bright silver covered the
dress bodice to her waist where silver began to blend with
a dark blue until, at the dress bottom, there were only
spangles of silver shot through the deep, rich midnight
hue. The skirt swirled wide and flowing like a sea of star-
capped waves.

"I told you it was different," Joely said.

They smothered any further words, engulfing her
with hugs and squeals that lasted until her mother and
grandmother had to come and break them up because it
was time to go.

"Have you checked the sky?" Joely asked.

The weather was the only thing she'd bridezilla-ed
about all week, as if ranting would control anything
about Mother Nature. But February in Wyoming was iffy
at best when it came to weather. The mountains created
their own weather patterns, and even her beloved Paradise Ranch was not immune to those frivolous changes.

She just so badly wanted there to be stars.

"It's cloudy, Jo-Jo," her mother said. "But it's lovely
and so warm for this early. It's beautiful."

Her heart fell. It was stupid. It didn't matter.

They reached the living room, and her grandmother handed her a cane. She'd graduated to the simple walking aid months before, and she smiled in secret satisfaction. Her guests, even her family had no idea how different this was going to be from the wedding where a bridesmaid had been pushed down the aisle in a wheelchair.

And then the waiting was over. The garden was ready. Her man was there.

But as she stepped onto the porch, Cole appeared, a piece of paper in his hand.

"Hold up there, you, bride," he said. Then he took a second out to whistle. "Joely, darlin', you take my breath away."

She flushed but peered nervously at his hand. "Thank you. What's wrong?"

"Nothing at all. Special late delivery." He handed her an envelope.

"What on earth?"

He shrugged. "Your bronc rider said I had to give it to you and see that you opened it."

The envelope was addressed to her, the postmark seven days old. When she saw the return address her hand flew to her mouth. *Colorado State University, College of Veterinary Medicine and Biomedical Sciences.*

She stared wildly at Mia, who took the letter in concern but then grinned. "Your application!"

"You open it." Joely's voice, hands, and pulse all vibrated like they did whenever she thought of Alec. She couldn't make herself wonder, yet, how he'd gotten this.

Mia tore the flap neatly and withdrew the folded letter. Joely nodded.

Mia opened it, read for two seconds, and lifted her eyes. With unhidden excitement she extended the letter to Joely. "From one doctor to another—prepare to work your little buns off, sweetie."

Joely took the paper in disbelief and read it for herself. "I got in," she said in wonder.

Her mother was right. The status of the sky no longer mattered in the least.

Kelly ran the letter into the house. Raquel adjusted the flowers in Joely's hair. The next thing she knew she was at the head of the short, glitter-strewn aisle beside her mother's garden—pretty and neat even in prespring. Fairy lights strung across the space with abandon created plenty of starlight. And he was there.

Alec.

With a grin that even from across the lawn spelled impish trouble, he held up a small sign edged in blue and silver for everyone to see.

Come and marry me, Doc.

Wait. How could he know? She'd just opened the letter…

In the wonder and confusion of the moment, she nearly forgot the surprise she had for him. As the music started, however, she squatted in place and laid the cane on the ground. Rising again, she adjusted and took her first step, then her second, and her third. She wasn't perfect yet but she had enough steps to reach him. And when she did, there were tears in his eyes.

"Hello, my love," he whispered.

"How did you know?"

"I called them. Told them this was how I wanted to give you the news if it was good. The admissions lady now thinks I'm romantic and sexy."

"Are you ever going to stop butting into my life without telling me?"

"Sure, when you quit telling me what to do with mine—which I hope, judging by our track record, is never."

"I love you," she said.

"I love you back."

And then, because nothing about this wedding was like it was supposed to be, he kissed the bride before the ceremony had even begun.

THE END

Did you miss Mia and Gabe's story?
Keep reading for an excerpt from the
second breathtaking book in Lizbeth Selvig's
Seven Brides for Seven Cowboys series,

THE BRIDE WORE RED BOOTS

Dr. Amelia Crockett's life was going exactly the way she had always planned—until one day it wasn't.

When Mia's career plans are shattered, the always-in-control surgeon has no choice but to head home to Paradise Ranch and her five younger sisters, cowboy boots in tow, to figure out how to get her life back on track. The appearance of a frustrating, but oh-so-sexy, former soldier, however, turns into exactly the kind of distraction she can't afford.

Even though Mia can't stand the sight of him, Gabriel Harrison has never returned the sentiment. He can't seem to resist teasing the gorgeous doctor who pushes all of his buttons. And the searing hot kisses they share are turning him inside out.

As she begins to work with Gabe, helping former vets recover from severe PTSD with the aid of some wild mustangs, Mia finds herself becoming more like the person she used to be. She never expected to alter her life plans, and definitely never expected to fall for anyone, least of all the handsome Gabe. But fate and some lucky red boots have a way of changing things. As their lives become more complicated, will Mia and Gabe's love be enough to smooth the way to a happily ever after?

Now Available from Avon Impulse!

An Excerpt from

THE BRIDE WORE RED BOOTS

DR. AMELIA CROCKETT adored the kids. She just hated clowns. Standing resignedly beside Bitsy Blueberry, Amelia scanned the group of twenty or so young patients gathered for a Halloween party in the pediatric playroom at NYC General Hospital. She didn't see the one child she was looking for, however.

Some children wore super-hero-themed hospital gowns and colorful robes that served as costumes. Others dressed up more traditionally—including three fairies, two princesses, a Harry Potter, and a Darth Vader. Gauze bandage helmets had been decorated like everything from a baseball to a mummy's head. More than one bald scalp was adorned with alien-green paint or a yellow smiley face. Mixed in with casts, wheelchairs, and IV poles on castors, there were also miles of smiles. The kids didn't hate the clown.

Amelia adjusted the stethoscope around her neck, more a prop than a necessary item at this event, and glared—her sisters would call it the hairy eyeball—at Bitsy Blueberry's wild blue wig. Bitsy thrust one hand forward, aimed one of those obnoxious, old-fashioned, bicycle horns with a bulb that were as requisite to clowning as giant shoes and red noses at Amelia's face and honked at her rudely. Three times.

Amelia smiled and whispered at Bitsy through gritted teeth. "I detest impertinent clowns, you know. I can have you fired."

She wasn't *afraid* of clowns. She simply found them unnecessary and a waste of talent, and Bitsy Blueberry was a perfect example. Beneath the white grease paint, red nose, hideous blue wig, and pinafore-and-pantaloons costume that looked like Raggedy Ann on psychedelic drugs was one of the smartest, most dedicated pediatric nurses in the world—Amelia's best friend, Brooke Squires.

"Look who's here, boys and girls." Bitsy grabbed her by the elbow and pulled her unceremoniously to the front of the room, honking in time with Amelia's steps all the way. "It's Dr. Mia Crockett!"

She might as well have said Justin Bieber or One Direction for the cheer that went up from the kids. It was the effect Bitsy's squeaky falsetto voice had on them. Then again, they'd cheer a stinky skunk wrangler if it meant forgetting, for even a short time, the real reasons they were in the hospital. That understanding was all that kept Amelia from cuffing her friend upside the head to knock some sense into it. She waved—a tiny rocking motion of her wrist—at the assemblage of sick children.

"Dr. Mia doesn't look very party ready, do you think?" Bitsy/Brooke asked. "Isn't that sad?"

"Not funny," Amelia said through the side of her mouth, her smile plastered in place.

Bitsy pulled a black balloon from her pinafore pocket and blew it into a long tube. Great. Balloon animals.

"I know a secret about Dr. Mia," Bitsy said. "Would you like to know what it is?"

Unsurprisingly, a chorus of yesses filled the room.

"She…" Bitsy dragged the word out suggestively, "is related to Davy Crockett. Do you know who Davy Crockett was?"

The relationship was true thanks to a backwoods ninth cousin somewhere in the 1800s, but Mia rolled her eyes again while a cacophony of shouts followed the question. As Bitsy explained about Davy and hunting and the Alamo, she tied off the black balloon and blew up a brown one. She twisted them intricately until she had a braided circle with a tail.

"You're kidding me," Mia said when she saw the finished product.

"That's pretty cool about Davy Crockett, right?" Bitsy asked. "But what isn't cool is that Dr. Mia has no costume. So I made her something. What did I tell you Davy Crockett wore?"

"Coonskin cap!" One little boy shouted the answer from his seat on the floor at the front of the group.

Mia smiled at him, one of a handful of nonsurgical patients she knew from her rounds here on the pediatric floor. Most of her time these days was spent in surgery and following up on those patients. Her work toward fulfilling the requirements needed to take her pediatric surgical boards left little time for meeting all the patients on the floor, but a few kids you only had to meet once, and they wormed their ways into your heart. She looked around again for Rory.

"That's right," Bitsy was saying. "And this is a bal*loon* skin cap!"

She set it on Mia's head, where it perched like a bird on a treetop. The children clapped and squealed. Bitsy did a chicken flap and waggled one foot in the air before bowing to her audience.

"I want a boon-skin cap!"

A tiny girl, perhaps four, shuffled forward with the aid of the smallest walker possibly in existence. She managed it deftly for one so little, even though her knees knocked together, her feet turned inward, and the patch over one eye obscured half her vision. She wore a hot-pink tutu over frosting-pink footie pajamas, and a tiara atop her black curls. To her own surprise, Mia's throat tightened.

"But, Megan, you have a beautiful crown already," Bitsy said gently.

Megan pulled the little tiara off her head and held it out. "I can twade."

Mia lost it, and she never lost it. She squatted and pulled the balloon cap off her head then held it out, her eyes hot. "I would love to trade with you," she said.

Megan beamed. Mia placed the crazy black-and-brown balloon concoction on the child, where it slipped over her hair and settled to her eyebrows.

"Here," Megan said, pronouncing it "hee-oh." "I put it on you."

She reached over the top of her walker and pressed on Mia's nose to tilt her face downward. She placed the tiara in Mia's hair and patted her head gently. It might as well have been a coronation by the Archduke of Canterbury. Megan had spina bifida and had come through surgery just four days earlier. No child this happy and tender and tough should have such a poor prognosis and uncertain future.

"You can be Davy Cwockett's pincess." Megan smiled, clearly pleased with herself.

"I think you gave me the best costume ever," Mia replied. "Could I have a hug?"

Megan opened her arms wide and squeezed Mia's neck with all her might. She smelled of chocolate bars, apple-cinnamon, and a whiff of the strawberry body lotion they used in this department. A delicious little waif.

She let the child go and stood. A young woman with the same black hair as Megan arrived at her side. It could only be Megan's mom. She bent and whispered something in her daughter's ear. The child nodded enthusiastically. "Thank you, Doc-toh Mia."

"You're welcome. And thank you."

The young mother's eyes met Mia's, gratitude shining in their depths. "Thanks from me, too. This is a wonderful party. So much effort by the whole staff."

"I wish I'd had more to do with it."

"You just did a great deal."

Megan had already started on her way back to the audience. Mia watched her slow progress, forgetting about the crowd until a powerful shove against her upper arm nearly knocked her off her feet. She turned to Bitsy and saw Brooke—grinning through the white makeup.

"What the heck? Clown attack. Go away you maniac."

A few kids in the front row twittered. *Bitsy* honked at her, but it was *Brooke* who leaned close to her ear. "That was awesome, Crockett," she whispered. "It's the kind of thing they need to see you do more of around here."

"They" referred to the medical staff. It was true she didn't have the most warm-hearted reputation—but that was by design. She grabbed Bitsy's ugly horn.

"*They* can kiss my—" *Honk. Honk.*

All the kids heard and saw was Davy Cwockett's Pincess stealing a clown's horn. Bitsy capitalized, placing her hands on her knees and exaggerating an enormous laugh.

"Hey! I think I have a new apprentice clown. What do you all say?"

Bitsy pulled off her red nose and popped it on Mia's. The kids screeched their approval.

"I'm going to murder you." Mia's tone belied her pleasant smile.

"Our newest clown needs a name. Any ideas?"

Princess! Clowny! Clown Doctor! Sillypants! Stefoscope!

Names flew from the young mouths like hailstones, pelting Mia with ridiculousness.

"Stethoscope the Clown, I like it." Bitsy laughed. "How about Mercy?"

"Princess Goodheart." That came quietly from Megan's mother, standing against the side wall, certainty in her demeanor.

"Oh, don't you dare." Mia practically hissed the words at her friend the clown.

"Perfect!" Bitsy called, her falsetto ringing through the room. "Now, how about we get Princess Goodheart to help with a magic trick?"

Mia's sentimentality of moments before dissipated fully. This was why she couldn't afford such soppy silliness, even over children. If she was going to turn to syrup at the first sign of a child with a walker and a patched eye, perhaps pediatrics wasn't the place for her.

On the other hand, Megan represented the very reason Mia wanted to move from general to pediatric surgery. She had skill—a special gift according to teachers and some colleagues—and she could use it to help patients like Megan. They needed her.

"Pick a card, Princess Goodheart." Bitsy nudged her arm.

Mia sighed. She'd have thought a party featuring simple games, fine motor skill-building, and prizes would have been more worthwhile. The mindlessness of magicians and the potential for scaring children with clowns seemed riskier. Indeed there were a few uncomplicated, arcade-type games at little stations around the room, but the magic and clown aficionados had prevailed. Mia grunted and picked a six of clubs.

"Don't show me," said Bitsy.

"I wouldn't dream of it."

"Now, put the card back in the deck. Who wants to wave their hand over the deck and say the magic words?" Bitsy asked.

"Oh, God, help! Oh, help, help please. Something's happening to him!"

Bitsy dropped the card deck. In the back of the room, next to a table full of food and treats, a woman stood over the crumpled body of a boy, twitching and flailing his arms. Mia heard his gasps for breath, ripped the ridiculous nose off her face, and pressed into the crowd of kids.

"Keep them all back," she ordered Brooke, right beside her and already shushing children in a calm Bitsy voice.

The fact that she continued acting like a clown in the face of an emergency made Mia angry, but there was no time now to call her out for unprofessionalism. In the minute it took Mia to reach the child on the floor, five nurses had surrounded him, and the woman who'd called for help stood by, her face ashen.

"Are you the boy's mother?" Mia asked.

"No. I was just standing here when he started choking."

"Out of the way, please." Mia shouldered her way between two nurses, spreading her arms to clear space. They'd turned the child on his side. "Is he actually choking?"

"He's not. It looks like he's reacting to something he ate," a male nurse replied.

She knelt, rolled the child to his back, and froze. "Rory?"

"A patient of yours?" the nurse asked.

"The son of a friend." Mia hadn't seen him arrive. She forced back her shock and set a mental wall around her sudden emotions. "Is there anything on his chart?"

She'd known Rory Beltane and his mother for three years and didn't remember ever hearing about an allergy this life-threatening.

"I don't believe there were any allergies listed," the nurse said. "We're checking his information now. He's a foster kid."

"Yes, I know," she replied with defensive sharpness. "His mother is incapacitated and temporarily can't care for him. Is the foster mother here?"

"No. At work." The nurse said. "Poor kid. He was just starting to feel better after having his appendix out. This isn't fair."

She had no time to tell him exactly how unfair Rory Beltane's life had been recently. "I need a blood pressure cuff stat. Get him on IV epinephrine, methylpred and Benadryl, plus IV fluids wide open."

"Right away, Doctor." Nurses scattered.

The male nurse calmly read from a chart, and Mia's temper flared.

"Excuse me, nurse, are you getting me that cuff?"

"It's on the way," he said and smiled. "Just checking his chart for you. No notations about allergies. I'll go get the gurney."

Mia blew out her breath. She couldn't fault him for being cool under pressure. Another nurse, this one an older woman with a tone as curt as Mia's, knelt on Rory's far side holding his wrist. "Heart rate is one-forty."

Mia held her stethoscope to the boy's chest. His lips looked slightly swollen. His breathing labored from his tiny chest.

"Here, Dr. Crockett. They're bringing a gurney and the electronic monitor, but this was at the nurse's station if you'd like to start with it."

Mia grabbed the pediatric-sized cuff, its bulb pump reminding her of Brooke's obnoxious horn. With efficient speed, she wrapped the gray cuff around Rory's arm, placed her stethoscope beneath it, and took the reading.

She'd always been struck by what a stunning child he was. His mother was black and his father white, and his skin was the perfect blend, like the color of a beautiful sand beach after a rain. A thick shock of dark curly hair adorned his head, and when they were open, his eyes were a laughing, precocious liquid brown.

"Seventy-five over fifty. Don't like that," she said.

The male nurse appeared with a gurney bed. "I can lift him if you're ready. We have the IV catheter and epinephrine ready."

"Go," Mia ordered.

Moments later Rory had been placed gently on the gurney, and three nurses, like choreographed dancers, had the IV in place, all the meds Mia had ordered running, and were rolling him to his private room.

"We've called Dr. Wilson, the pediatric hospitalist on duty this week who's seen Rory a couple of times. He'll be here in a few minutes," said the male nurse, who'd just begun to be her favorite.

She frowned. "It wasn't necessary to bring him in yet. I think we have this well in hand. We need fewer bodies, not more."

"I'll let him know."

The epinephrine began to work slowly but surely, and most of the staff, at Mia's instruction, returned to the party to help the remaining kids. The older nurse and the male nurse remained.

Ten minutes after he'd first passed out, Rory opened his eyes, gasping as the adrenaline coursed through him and staring wild-eyed as if he didn't believe air was reaching his lungs.

"Slow breaths, Rory." Mia placed her hand on his. "Don't be afraid. You have plenty of air now, I promise. Lots of medicine is helping it get better and better. Breathe out, nice and slow. I'm going to listen to your heart again, okay?"

Mia listened and found his heart rate slowing. A new automatic blood pressure cuff buzzed, and Rory winced as the cuff squeezed. Tears beaded in his eyes. Mia stared at the monitor, while the nurse calmed the boy again.

"That's a little better," Mia said. "But, I think we need to keep you away from the party for a while. That was scary, huh?"

"Dr. Mia?" He finally recognized her.

"Hi," she said. "This is a surprise, isn't it?"

"You saved me," he whispered in a thick, hoarse rasp. "Nobody ever saves me."

For the first time Mia truly looked at the two nurses who stood with her. Their eyes reflected the stunned surprise she felt.

"Of course I saved you," she said. "Anybody would save you, Rory. You probably haven't needed saving very often, that's all."

"Once. I ate some peanut butter when my mom wasn't at home. I couldn't breathe, but Mrs. Anderson next door didn't believe me." His voice strengthened as he spoke. "I can't eat peanut butter."

"What did you eat today? Do you remember? Right before you couldn't breathe?"

He shook his head vehemently. "A cupcake. A chocolate one. I can eat chocolate."

"Anything else?"

"I had one little Three Musketeer. Bitsy gave it to me. She said the nurses said it was okay to have one because my stomach feels better."

Bitsy again. Rory looked solely at Mia and avoided the nurses' eyes, as if he feared they'd contradict his story.

"And you don't remember any other food?" Mia asked.

"I didn't eat nothing else. I swear."

"It's all right. It really is. All I care about is finding what made you sick. Look, I'm going to go out and talk to some more nurses—"

"No! Stay here." He stretched out his arm, his fingers spread beseechingly.

"All right." She let him grab her hand and looked at him quizzically. "But you're fine now."

"No."

He was so certain of his answer. Mia couldn't bear to ignore his wishes, although it made no logical sense. At that moment a white-coated man with a Lincoln-esque figure appeared in the doorway.

"My, my, what's going on here? Is that you Rory?"

Rory clung to Mia's hand and didn't answer. Mia looked over the newcomer, not recognizing him, although his badge identified him as Frederick Wilson, MD.

His eyes brushed over Mia, and he dismissed her with a quick "Good afternoon." No questions, no request for an update from her, the medical expert already on the case. She bristled but stayed quietly beside Rory, squeezing his hand.

"How's our man?" Dr. Wilson asked. "You doing okay, Champ?" He oozed the schmoozy bedside manner she found obsequious, and the child who'd been talkative up to now merely stared at the ceiling.

Dr. Wilson chuckled. "That's our Rory. Not great talk show material, but he plays a mean game of chess from what I hear. A silent, brilliant kind of man. I'm Fred Wilson." He held out a hand. "You must be one of the techs or NAs?"

She stared at him in disbelief. A nursing assistant? Who was this idiot? She looked down and remembered her badge was in her pocket. She fished it out and shoved it at him. "I'm *Dr.* Amelia Crockett, and I've been handling Rory's case since the incident about fifteen minutes ago."

"Crockett. Crockett." He stared off as if accessing information in space somewhere. "The young general surgeon who's working now toward a second certification in pediatric surgery. Sorry, I've been here two weeks and have tried to brush up on all the staff resumes. I'm the new chief of staff here in peds. Up from Johns Hopkins."

She had heard his name and that he was a mover and shaker.

"Dr. Wilson," she acknowledged.

"So, since you're a surgeon and not familiar with Rory's whole case, maybe I'll trouble you to get me up to speed on the anaphylaxis, and then I'll take over so you can get back to what I'm sure is a busy schedule." Dr. Wilson crossed his arms and smiled.

She glared at him again. He may as well have called her *just* a surgeon. And to presume she hadn't familiarized herself with Rory's case before prescribing any course of action . . .

"I'm sorry, Dr. Wilson," she said. "But with all due respect, I happen to know this child, and I'm also well aware of the details of his case. I, too, can read a patient history. I believe I can follow up on this episode and make the report in his chart for you, his regular pediatrician, and the other docs on staff who will treat him."

"It really isn't necessary," he replied, and his smile left his eyes.

Unprofessional as it was, she disliked him on the spot, as if she'd met him somewhere else and hadn't liked him then either.

"I was here to help with the Halloween party," she said. "My afternoon is free and clear."

"That explains much. So that isn't your normal, everyday head ornamentation?"

For a moment she met his gaze, perplexed. *Oh, crap.* Her hand flew to her head, and in mortification she pulled off the tiara still stuck there with its little side combs.

"I didn't mean you needed to take it off. It was fetching," Dr. Wilson said. He winked with a condescending kind of flirtatiousness—as if he were testing her.

She flicked an unobtrusive glance at his left hand. No band, but a bulky gold ring with a sizeable onyx set in the middle. She got the impression he was old school all the way, a little annoyed with female practitioners, and extremely cocky about his own abilities.

"Rory is improving rapidly since the administration of Benadryl and epinephrine. We are uncertain of the allergen. From what he's told us he has a suspected sensitivity to peanut butter, but as far as we know he hasn't eaten any nuts."

Dr. Wilson nodded, patting Rory periodically on the shoulder. Rory continued his silence.

"Rory, do you mind if I do a little exam on your tummy?" Dr. Wilson asked.

"Dr. Mia already did it." He turned his head just enough to look at her.

Again he smiled, ignoring Mia. "I'm sure she did, but I'm a different kind of doctor, and I'd like to help her make sure you're okay. Maybe if everyone left the room except you and me and Miss Arlene, it won't be so embarrassing if I check you out? Dr. Crockett and Darren can go and make sure there's nothing out at the party that will hurt you again."

Arlene and Darren, she noted absently. She hadn't taken the time to look at their nametags.

Rory shook his head and squeezed Mia's hand again.

"As you can see," she said, curtly, "the child is still fearful and a little traumatized. Perhaps in this case you and I could switch roles? I'll stay with my patient, and you'll make a better sleuth with Darren?"

Dr. Wilson's mouth tightened, and he drew his shoulders back as if prepping for a confrontation. In that instant, the sense of recognition—the confrontation if not the chauvinism—she'd had earlier flashed into unexpected clarity.

Gabriel Harrison.

Her stomach flipped crazily. Fiftyish Dr. Fred Wilson didn't look a bit like the arrogant, self-important, patient advocate she'd met six weeks before at the VA medical center in her old home city of Jackson, Wyoming. In truth, nobody who wasn't making seven figures as a big-screen heartthrob looked like Gabriel Harrison. The trouble was, just as Dr. Wilson knew he was good, Lieutenant—retired Lieutenant—Harrison knew he was gorgeous. Both men believed they had the only handle on expertise and information.

She'd met Harrison after a car accident in the middle of September had left her mother and one of her sisters seriously injured, and he'd been assigned as a liaison between them, their families, and the hospital. He'd made himself charming—like a medicine show snake oil salesman—and her sisters, all five of them, now adored him. Her mother considered him her personal guardian angel. However, he'd treated Mia like she'd gotten her degree from a Cracker Jack box, and he continued doing so in all their correspondence—which was frequent considering how he loved ignoring her requests for information.

Mia was glad that at her planned trip home for Christmas, her mother and sister would be home and Gabriel Harrison, patient advocate, would be long gone from their lives. Unfortunately, it wouldn't work quite so easily with Fred Wilson. She was stuck more or less permanently with him.

"I want Dr. Mia to stay."

Rory's fingers tightened on her hand, and the last vestiges of memories from Wyoming slipped away.

"That settles it in my opinion," she said. "At my patient's request, I'll stay with him. Darren, would you be willing to accompany Dr. Wilson to the lounge and ask some questions about the food? Arlene, would you please get Mr. Beltane here a glass of juice and maybe some ice?"

"Yes," Darren said. "Sure."

"Of course," Arlene replied, with the first smile Mia had seen from her.

Fred Wilson, on the other hand, looked as if he might need the Heimlich maneuver. "If I might have a word with you outside, Dr. Crockett."

She met his gaze coolly. "Rory, I need to help Dr. Wilson with some things, but I'll be right back. I promise."

"No."

"I promise, honey." She smoothed the child's hair back and he nodded, his eyes shining.

Dr. Wilson patted Rory on the shoulder a final time. "I'll see you tomorrow, young man. You may even get to go home. Bet you'd like that."

Rory gave an anemic shrug.

She slipped out of the room with Fred Wilson behind her, took several steps away from the door, and spun to face him.

"Would you care to explain what this is about?" she demanded.

"Dr. Crockett, I have heard your reputation as the wonder child of this medical community," Wilson said. "But in this department you have no seniority, and a fast track to the top is not impressive. No matter how good you are technically, nothing can take the place of years of experience. And just because you wear a stethoscope and have been in this physical location longer than I have, doesn't mean you possess anywhere near the experience I do. You were insubordinate in front of the patient and my staff. I won't have that."

She didn't blink or raise her voice. She put her hands in her lab coat pockets to keep from showing her flexing fingers. "In point of fact, Dr. Wilson, you treated *me* like a first-year intern in there, even though I am the lead medical staff member in this matter. I also have the trust of the patient, and you ignored that along with his wishes. I treated you with the respect you commanded. It's not my style to kiss up to anyone or brown nose a superior to make my way. Good medicine is all I care about. You or one of your hospital staff docs will handle his care in regard to his recent appendectomy, but at the moment, because he is still in a little bit of shock, that is secondary to aftercare from the anaphylaxis. I didn't appreciate you not bowing to my expertise or asking me to debrief you—even if I didn't just come from Johns Hopkins."

"You take a pretty surly tone."

"I apologize."

For a long moment he assessed her, and finally he shook his head. "I don't like your style, Doctor. But the staff thinks highly of your skill. We'll let this slide because the child did request your presence."

"I don't love your style either." She smiled. "But I've heard the staff thinks highly of your bedside manner. I hope we can grow to understand each other better as we are required to work together."

"I hope that's so." He nodded curtly and left.

Why were older doctors so prejudiced when it came to believing surgeons knew their stuff? Mia was tired of dealing with the game playing and politics of staff. What was wrong with just being a damn-good physician?

She let herself back into Rory's room, and he smiled with relief. "How are you, kiddo?" she asked. "Do your stitches or anything inside your tummy hurt?"

"No."

"You didn't want Dr. Wilson to stay and examine you. Do you not like him?"

"He's nice."

That stymied her. "Then why--?"

"He didn't have nothin' to do with making me better," Rory interrupted. "Only you and Dr. Thomas who took out my appendix. And…you…" His huge, dark eyes brimmed with tears that clung to his lashes like diamonds but didn't spill.

"I what, Rory?"

"You saved me. And I want you to save Jack."

"Jack?" A slice of new panic dove through her stomach. She knew Jack. "Your cat?"

"Yeah."

"Why does Jack need saving?"

"Buster has him," he said. "But Mrs. Murray, the foster lady, she said I couldn't bring him with me 'cause she's allergic to cats. And Buster said he'd keep him for a while, but he can't keep him forever because mostly the shelters won't let him have a cat neither."

A slight dizziness started her head spinning. "Who's Buster?"

"I lived with him awhile after my mama got taken away."

"Where does Buster live?"

"Everywhere," he said and Mia's stomach slowly started to sink. "He's my best friend. Sometimes he goes to the shelter by the church in Brownsville. Sometimes he lives under the bridge by the East River. Sometimes he stays in the camp with his friends."

"Rory? Is Buster a homeless man?"

"Buster says he doesn't want a normal house. He says he owns the whole city of New York, and he should 'cause he fought for it. But Jack does need a house 'cause it's going to snow pretty soon, and he'll freeze. So . . . will you save him like you saved me?"

"Oh, I don't know if . . . "

She thought about all the animals she'd had growing up on one of the biggest cattle ranches in Wyoming. Until leaving for college she'd never imagined that some kids might not have pets. No dogs, no cats, no horses.

"Please? Jack's the only one left who really loves me."

"That's so not true, Rory. I know it's not true." She sighed and sat next to him on the mattress. "I love you. I'm your friend, right? And your mom loves you so much."

"Mrs. Murray, the foster lady, said Mom was too sick to be a good mother. 'Cause she's in the hospital, too."

"Again?" Mia stared at him, heartbroken. "Rory, since when? What happened?"

"I don't know when. Before I came here. I tried to call her to tell her I was sick, but she wasn't at the jail."

For the past three months, Monique Beltane had resided in a women's prison in upstate New York where she was serving one year for theft and illegal possession of a narcotic. She was also living through treatment for breast cancer.

"That's not true, Rory. Your mom will never be too sick to love you. And she's a good mom, too. She's just been sick for such a long time."

Mia knew Monique's story well. She'd become addicted to prescription opioids after botched shoulder surgery. One year after that operation, Mia had been the one to operate again and managed to relieve some of Monique's permanent pain. During the three years that had followed, she'd kept in touch with Monique and her son, Rory. She liked the woman, plain and simple. Monique wanted to get well. She was just weak when it came to pain. Still, she'd gotten herself clean, and Mia believed she might have made a success of it. Then, six months ago, she'd been diagnosed with the cancer.

She'd managed the chemo, but the mastectomy and the oxycodone to which she was so highly addicted had pushed her back over the edge. Three months ago, she'd purchased oxycodone from an undercover agent, and that had been the end.

But she was back in the hospital. Mia didn't know what was wrong, but her intuition left her worried. At this stage in her recovery, no illness boded well. She made a mental note to track down Monique's physician.

And now here was Rory.

You couldn't make crap like this up.

"But even if Mom gets better, she's in jail for a long time. All I got is Jack."

"But if Jack can't stay with you at the Murrays, where would he go if we find him?"

He shrugged, and his eyes filled with water. Mia sighed. This was so *not* in her job description. How did one even begin to try looking for a homeless cat in New York City?

"Please, Dr. Mia."

She smoothed his thick curls. She'd never find one cat in a city that must have a billion. "All right, listen to me, okay? I will see what I can find out, but you're practically a young man and you're smart. You know I might not have any luck. You promise you won't be angry with me if I don't find him?"

He smiled a watery-but-genuine true, toothy, ten-year-old's grin. "You will."

About the Author

LIZBETH SELVIG lives in Minnesota with her best friend (aka her husband) and a gray Arabian gelding named Jedi. After working as a newspaper journalist and magazine editor, and raising an equine veterinarian daughter and a talented musician son, Lizbeth won RWA's prestigious Golden Heart Contest® in 2010 with her contemporary romance, *The Rancher and the Rock Star*, and was a 2014 nominee for RWA's RITA® Award with her second published novel, *Rescued by a Stranger*. In her spare time, she loves to hike, quilt, read, horseback ride, and spend time with her new granddaughter. She also has many four-legged grandchildren—more than twenty—including a wallaby, two alpacas, a donkey, a pig, a sugar glider, and many dogs, cats, and horses (pics of all appear on her website www.lizbethselvig.com). She loves connecting with readers—contact her any time!

Discover great authors, exclusive offers, and more at hc.com.

Give in to your Impulses . . .
Continue reading for excerpts from
our newest Avon Impulse books.
Available now wherever ebooks are sold.

EVERYTHING SHE WANTED
BOOK FIVE: THE HUNTED SERIES
by Jennifer Ryan

WHEN WE KISS
RIBBON RIDGE BOOK FIVE
by Darcy Burke

An Excerpt from

EVERYTHING SHE WANTED
Book Five: The Hunted Series
By Jennifer Ryan

Ben Knight has spent his life protecting those
in need and helping abused women escape their
terrible circumstances. He'll stop at nothing
to save the lives of his clients, especially the
hauntingly beautiful Kate Morrison, a woman
threatened by a man whose wealth allows him to
get away with everything—including murder.

Ben pulled in behind several police cars nearly thirty minutes later, their red and blue lights flashing. He turned off the car's engine and sat staring up at the massive house. Morgan's prediction played in his mind. This late at night, the woman meant for him had to be in that house. He hoped she wasn't the dead woman Detective Raynott called him about.

Evan Faraday hit Ben's radar when Detective Raynott caught the case of a man found beaten to death in an alley after gambling with some guys in the bar, including Evan. That man was the son of one of his Haven House clients. Ben stepped in as a legal advocate for the family. The guy was only trying to scrape together extra money for his mother and sister. Evan played cards with the guy, but Raynott couldn't link him to the murder. Not with any actual evidence, but the circumstantial kind added up to Evan drunk and pissed off about losing to the guy. Evan killed him; they just couldn't prove it.

More recently, Evan got into another bar fight. Donald Faraday paid off the guy with a heavy heart. He knew what and who his son was, but that didn't stop him from getting Evan out of trouble. Again.

Detective Raynott caught that case too. Ben asked the detective to call him if Evan got in trouble again. Ben wanted to take the selfish, smart-mouthed prick down. Then came the DUI arrest. Now he'd killed again.

Ben got out of the car, tucked in his shirt, and straightened his tie.

"What am I doing?" He was at a murder scene, not meeting a date for drinks and dinner.

But she was in there. He knew it. Anticipated it. And hoped he wasn't a fool for believing in Morgan.

The anticipation and hope swamping his system surprised him more than a little. He hadn't realized how much he wanted a woman in his life. Not just any woman, but the right woman.

"I'm sorry, sir, this is an active crime scene. Law enforcement only," the officer guarding the police line said. Ben noted the neighbors' interest. They lined the street, whispering to each other and staring at him. Some in their bathrobes, others in lounge clothes. This late at night the sirens got most of them up out of their beds. In this neighborhood, a murder was the last thing they expected.

"My name is Ben Knight. Detective Raynott called and asked me to come."

The officer held the tape up for him to pass. "He's in the living room. Give your name to the officer at the door."

Ben did and stepped into the elegant home and surveyed the officers and crime scene techs working the scene at the back of the house and what looked like the entrance to the kitchen. He spotted Detective Raynott standing over a woman with long brown wavy hair, a baby sleeping in a car seat at her feet. With her back to him, he couldn't see her face, but something about her seemed familiar. A strange tug pulled him toward her.

"Ben, you made it. Thanks for coming," Detective Raynott said, waving him forward.

"Anything to nail Evan Faraday and see him behind bars."

The woman turned and raised her face to look up at him. He stopped midstride and stared into her beautiful blue eyes. Like a deep lake, the soft outer color darkened toward the center. "Kate?"

He never expected her. Morgan had been right though—they'd shared a moment at a wedding reception for a mutual friend and colleague. That had been more than a year ago now. They sat at the same table and talked, mostly about work and how out of place they felt at the event, made even more uncomfortable when they realized they were seated at a table full of singles and the bride had arranged them as couples, playing matchmaker. They shared some laughs and danced, deciding to make the awkward situation fun. They fell under the spell—the music, champagne, the celebration of love—and Ben enjoyed himself more that night than any other date. He kissed her right there on the dance floor during a particularly slow, sweet song. He remembered it perfectly. The way she stared up at him with those blue eyes. The way her mouth parted slightly as she exhaled and he leaned in. The softness of her lips against his. The way she gave in to the kiss with a soft sigh. The tremble that rocked his body and hers when the sparks flew and sizzled through his system.

The startled look on her face when he pulled back just enough to see the desire flaming in her eyes. A split second later she bolted for the door.

He went after her, but didn't find her. She didn't answer his calls over the next two days. He still didn't know if he'd overstepped, done something wrong, or simply scared her.

"Ben." Her soft voice, filled with surprise, startled him out of his thoughts. "What are you doing here?" Her sad eyes narrowed on him.

An Excerpt from

WHEN WE KISS
Ribbon Ridge Book Five
By Darcy Burke

In the fifth novel in the Ribbon Ridge series, thrill-seeker Liam Archer will try anything once—except falling in love—but what happens when the one woman whose kiss is better than any adrenaline high puts an end to their no-strings fling?

Aubrey Tallinger finished drying her hands and set the towel down. Lifting her head, she caught her reflection in the mirror. Her hazel eyes stared back at her and seemed to ask what she was doing dawdling in the bathroom when a perfectly lovely wedding reception was going on.

Isn't it obvious? I'm avoiding Liam.

She was proud of herself tonight. She'd done a good job of ignoring the one person who always seemed to command her attention: Liam Archer. It helped to have a date along. A date she should get back to.

She took a deep breath and opened the door. Liam stood on the other side of the threshold.

He grabbed her hand and dragged her to the left through a doorway. He let go of her to close the door then stood in front of it, his blue-gray eyes narrowed. "Who's the loser?"

Aubrey registered that they were in a sitting room attached to his parents' bedroom. She wanted to turn and look at the sun setting over the garden through the back windows, but couldn't tear her eyes from Liam. Dressed in a crisp black suit with a natty, striped tie, he was the sexiest best man she'd ever seen. His dark wavy hair was perfectly styled and, as usual, she had an almost irrepressible urge to mess it up.

She tensed as she forced herself to present a cool demeanor. "I introduced you to him at the church."

"Yes, Stuart the Accountant. But why did you bring him in the first place?"

She cocked her head and gave him a sarcastic stare. "Was I supposed to wait for you to ask me? You don't take me on *dates*, Liam. You never have." The dinner he'd surprised her with at her house when he'd been home for the long Thanksgiving weekend didn't count. Dates were *public*.

He frowned, and she was shocked when he didn't fire a snappy comeback. "I might've, actually."

Ha! She'd believe that when she saw it. "Too late. I told you at New Year's that our little . . . *thing* was done."

"It wasn't a *thing*."

"No, I think you're right. It was a series of convenient hook-ups, and they are no longer convenient to me."

She called them hook-ups, but they'd been more than that. Every time they were together, she'd felt as though they'd connected on some sort of intimate level that went beyond just sex. But that was stupid. While she'd come to know him at least a little bit, they hadn't spent enough day-to-day time together to allow anything meaningful to spark. Except for Labor Day weekend. They'd spent the better part of four days in each other's company, and it had been bliss. They'd laughed, they'd danced, they'd talked. And yes, they'd had a lot of sex. The physical aspect of their connection was so far the most powerful.

He prowled toward her, like a jungle cat on the hunt. She had no intention of being his prey. Nor did she want to run. She stiffened her spine and crossed her arms over her chest.

Meager protection when she knew just how dangerous his weapons of mass seduction could be.

"Come on, they were a little more than hook-ups. We *planned* to hang out over Labor Day."

That was true, but they'd both been going to the Dave Matthews Band concerts up in central Washington anyway. It wasn't like they'd formulated and executed the trip together.

He stopped in front of her, his lips curving up. "And you have to admit it was pretty great."

Incredible. Right up to the point when she'd suggested they see each other again soon. He'd said, "Sure, I always call you up when I'm in town."

Like she was a convenience. And there was that word again. She didn't want to be anyone's hook-up girl. She'd quashed her burgeoning feelings, but it had maybe been too late. She'd already been crazy infatuated with him. So much so that when she'd seen him at Thanksgiving, she'd allowed herself to be the convenience she didn't want to be.

But no more.

She gave him an arch look. "So it was a great weekend. You still can't argue it was more than a hook-up. I walked away from that without knowing when—or if—I'd see you again."

He frowned at her. "That's absurd. You're our attorney. Of course you'd see me again."

Was he being purposely obnoxious?

He put his hands on his hips. "I suppose you're going to tell me Thanksgiving was just a hook-up, too? I brought you dinner."

After they'd flirted all day at a winery event they'd just happened to meet at. She'd accepted his sister Tori's invitation to attend without realizing Liam would be there. Wait, had he known? "Did you know I would be at the winery that day?"

He arched a brow. "Who do you think suggested we invite you?"

Damn it. She didn't want to know that. "Now you tell me," she muttered.

He flashed her a grin. "Am I wearing you down?"